High Praise for Lizzie Page

When I Was Yours

"This, at times, brought tears to my eyes and
equally a warm glow to my heart."
—Stardust Book Reviews

"Brilliantly blends fact and fiction."
—Jill Mansell, bestselling
author of *It Started with a Secret*

"Lizzie Page has gone and done it again with this
beautiful, poignant, and immensely emotional story."
—Chicks Rogues and Scandals

"A delightfully intertwined story...it has the
heartbreak of war and a gorgeous love story."
—Short Book and Scribes

"You'll find yourself engrossed till the last page."
—My Pert Opinions

"The story is heartbreaking...This is an all-round
excellent read, without a doubt 5 stars from me."
—Booking Good Read

"This book was hard to put down...One of the best
historical fiction books I've read in a very long time."
—Shelly's Book Nook

Daughters
of War

OTHER BOOKS BY LIZZIE PAGE

When I Was Yours

Daughters
of War

FOREVER

New York Boston

Copyright © 2018 by Lizzie Page
Reading group guide copyright © 2021 by Hachette Book Group, Inc.

Cover design by Debbie Clement. Cover photography © Alamy; Shutterstock. Cover copyright © 2021 by Hachette Book Group, Inc.

Forever
Hachette Book Group
1290 Avenue of the Americas, New York, NY 10104
read-forever.com
twitter.com/readforeverpub

Originally published in the United Kingdom by Bookouture, an imprint of Storyfire Ltd., in 2018
First North American edition: December 2021

Forever is an imprint of Grand Central Publishing. The Forever name and logo are trademarks of Hachette Book Group, Inc.

The publisher is not responsible for websites (or their content) that are not owned by the publisher.

Library of Congress Control Number: 2021937838

ISBN: 978-1-5387-5454-2 (trade paperback)

Printed in the United States of America

LSC-C

Printing 1, 2021

To my lovely mum, Patricia Lya Lierens

"I am a woman. My life is a long, strong, twisted rope, made up of a number of human relationships, nothing more."

—Mary Borden

Daughters
of War

<u>Things to consider</u>

Try not to have too many naps. Every other day is perfectly adequate.

Is it time for new apples? Ribston Pippin or Blenheim Orange? Ask Mrs. Crawford what she thinks.

Go to Morleys for more writing paper, consider lined as well. Lines are NOT a sign of failure.

CHAPTER ONE

That term, when the girls were away at school, I was scared I would lose my mind. I had always been prone to melancholy, but by spring of 1914, it was worse than ever. I dreamt of escaping. If I could have run away to do high kicks at the Moulin Rouge or even become a lady librarian, I would have, but both required an energy that had completely deserted me. I wanted only to lie in bed all day long. Was that so wrong? After all—as my mother frequently liked to write in her poisonous letters—I had made my bed and now I had to lie in it.

My life was so far from how I had imagined "London life" that the slightest unexpected thing—a bee in the bathroom, a snag in my stocking—could reduce me to fat tears. As for bigger, expected things—my marriage, for example—I felt trapped and utterly useless.

It was Mrs. Crawford, the housekeeper, who called Doctor Grange, and it was Doctor Grange who said I must avoid reading the newspapers. It was true that the news did sometimes send me into a downward spiral: the sinking of the *Titanic* had. So many people had died, yet here I was: the unfairness of that was enormous. I wished I could have swapped places with any of them. At least then my existence might have had a purpose. It wasn't just the people I mourned either; it was the ship itself. *Unsinkable*, they had said. And then it had sunk, just like that.

It just showed you.

And yet, I felt bad to be so distressed by it. "Were you affected personally?" Doctor Grange asked kindly. When I explained, "Not personally, no, but..." he gave me a severe look. "Stop reading. You have too many books," he advised, looking around my room, "and you don't take enough activity." He snapped his case shut.

George wasn't interested in helping me. To be fair, I wasn't interested in being helped by George. His attentions were firmly elsewhere. How did I know this? Not just because of the petticoat I discovered in the outhouse—*who did it belong to?*—or the sudden fascination he had for oiling his mustache (and the strange scents it gave off); it was his jaunty demeanor. George did not usually do jaunty. He was up to something and there was nothing I could do about that either.

Mrs. Crawford refused to bring up the newspapers. Just five minutes in attendance with Doctor Grange and her loyalties had been transferred. This wasn't a great problem though. As soon as George had done with them (he merely glanced at the horse-racing), I slipped to the dining room and stole them back to my room, where I could peruse in peace. I had always been a reader and I wouldn't stop. There was a whole world out there, a world I was never going to see or experience, but I *would* be a witness. It was my duty. It might make me damn miserable, but in another way, it kept me going.

I also wrote poems—oh, nothing serious, just whimsical snippets about my London life. The silver birch by the front door. The lines in the lawn after Mrs. Crawford's son, James, had mowed. Misery wasn't good for much but it was good for poetry.

I did take on board one of Doctor Grange's recommendations: I started taking a daily constitutional around Tooting Common. When I first came to England I hadn't known what a common was. Now I understood it was shared parkland, owned by no one, loved by everyone. Well, not *everyone*, obviously.

Within two days I had discovered a short-cut that involved covering only half the distance but allowed me to cross "walk" off my list of things I ought to do. One morning, slyly taking my short-cut, I noticed several women of mixed ages moving en masse toward some bramble-covered iron gates. The women didn't have the shiny look of churchgoers, nor the focused demeanor of suffragettes: *what could they be up to?* Curiosity piqued, I followed only to discover a sign for a bathing lake. Interesting. I used to like a swim: for my height (small), I have large feet. George used to say I was an L-shaped woman and while these flippers were not much use on dry land, they were a bonus in water.

Women were allowed to swim on Thursday mornings from March to October. It was Thursday and it was March. This was a small window of opportunity but nevertheless it *was* a window I could realistically fit through. So, the next Thursday, I went. Even though I liked swimming, it remained a challenge to get myself up and my bag packed, but I did it. I didn't *want* to be sad all the time. That's what people didn't understand. Mrs. Crawford waved me away overexcitedly, prematurely imagining I was cured, no doubt.

I arrived before the gates had opened, and we all waited outside. The queuing women were enjoying themselves and it was infectious. There was a great deal of laughing anticipation about how shriveled up we were all going to get.

"First time?" someone asked me. I nodded wordlessly—I never like to look the novice—but she patted my arm. "Don't be nervous, duckie, we're not going to eat you."

I had been anxious about many things, but this was one fate that had not occurred to me.

Once the gates were swung open, everyone did elbows out and fast (but not to the point of rudeness) walking to the chocolate-box-sized cubicles on the edge of the pool. I changed, came out gingerly, afraid I was wearing the wrong kind of suit, then was relieved to find I was perfectly in keeping.

It was a long shimmering rectangle of blue.

I got in.

Feet to knees, knees to thighs, thighs to belly, belly to rib . . . then the hardest bit of all, the shoulders. *Aieee!* Within a moment, I could tell it was doing me the world of good. It was cold, yes, but invigorating. My body felt free and unencumbered. The sun made dapples in the surface and on my face. I became light-headed with delight at my surroundings and myself. I found myself saying "hello," "good morning" and "isn't it marvelous?" to the other floating women.

I had been bobbing around for a good ten minutes or so when I saw feet—ghostly white feet, pointing skywards, feet where they shouldn't be. Others may have been avoiding them, but I didn't hesitate at the sight of those feet. I swam over with my fiercest strokes: *ten, twelve, fourteen*, until I was there, and I yanked at the heels, hard. The feet kicked, a body maneuvered itself around. Whatever it was, it was still living. Helpfully, I hauled up the body, finding it belonged to a woman. Her hair was covered by a bizarre flowery swim-hat and her face scrunched up. She spluttered. I was about to slap her in a kindly manner when she hissed:

"What *is* the matter with you?"

I realized, belatedly, she wasn't pleased.

"I'm…" I swallowed. I was still breathless myself. It had been years since I had swum with such commitment. "Aren't you drowning?"

"No, I'm not." It seemed I had given her quite the fright. "I'm trying to do a handstand. Obviously!"

I stared at her. "Why?"

She scowled. "Kindly give me some space, please."

I did back off then, apologizing. We trod water, both of us, panting at each other, droplets streaming down our faces. A handstand hadn't occurred to me. What an appalling person I was.

I met her eyes and she suddenly laughed. The sound was loud and playful and rippled across the pool.

"Where are you from?" she asked.

"London," I said, deliberately misunderstanding her.

"Before that?"

I told her, reluctantly, but fortunately, she didn't ask all the usual boring questions but instead gave me a wide smile. This time we both laughed. What a relief! Her teeth were tiny and neat. She was pale-skinned, not as brilliant white as her feet were, but not far off. "You must come back to mine for tea."

Although this level of social interaction was what I had been yearning for, oh, for at least the last twelve years, I found myself shaking my head. *I couldn't. I shouldn't. I wouldn't.* Spontaneity was beyond me now. I was underprepared, underdressed, under-everything.

"Oh no, it's too much bother."

I almost wanted to cry. I wanted nothing more than to make a friend, but my mouth was refusing.

Fortunately, Miss Pale-foot wouldn't take no for an answer. I saw she was the kind of person for whom no was simply a minor inconvenience, not to be taken seriously.

"I insist." She winked at me, drawing attention to her barely-there eyelashes. "After all, you saved my life."

Her name was Elizabeth and she drove a motorcar when very few women did. What's more, she was utterly blasé about it. It did judder under her control and she did curse the other drivers (when I believe it may have been her that was in the wrong), but I was impressed. Her hair was bright red-gold and, now braided, it dripped onto the steering wheel. Mine, in an untidy bun, dampened my blouse. To be out in public with wet hair was a thing my mother abhorred: I felt quite cheered.

Elizabeth looked so different without the arrangement of cap and bathing suit that I almost hadn't recognized her at the gate, where we had arranged to meet. Her striped dress would have drowned me—pardon the pun—but it made her look like a very graceful deckchair.

Elizabeth explained that although she lived with her mother, her mother wouldn't be at home. Her mother was *never* at home in the mornings. She was an active committee member. Elizabeth was too.

You wouldn't believe the number of groups there were in London then: committees, leagues, reformers, branches, meetings about everything and nothing. From Elizabeth's description, I gathered her mother was wealthy, but the liberal, open-minded type of wealthy, not like the churchgoing conservatives who populated my and George's families. Elizabeth added that her mother was a widow and she herself a spinster. There was no shame attached to the word "spinster" the way there was when George said it. Elizabeth made it sound like a prize.

Elizabeth clearly didn't feel her motorcar needed to be on intimate terms with the sidewalk either, for she came to a sudden halt right in the middle of the road.

"Here we are then!"

We were outside a tall, handsome, white-brick townhouse. Elizabeth bounded out the car and I followed, a mix of nerves, curiosity and discomfort from the damp. Inside, there were cats, cats and more cats. At first I thought there must be ten, at least, but Elizabeth, laughing, explained there were only three—they just managed to get about a bit. She introduced me to each of them seriously, holding up their paws in turn: this was Tiggy and this was Winkle—like the hedgehog in Beatrix Potter (Elizabeth's mother was a big fan)—and the third was Delia. (Elizabeth didn't say how she acquired her name.) Tiggy climbed onto my lap, purred and let me stroke her. Winkle leapt onto the back of my chair. Delia leapt to the windowsill, then sulkily left the room.

"She doesn't like guests." Elizabeth shrugged.

"I'm sorry," I said.

"No, she just doesn't like anyone," Elizabeth explained, matter-of-factly.

It was a man-free zone. A child-free zone. The room smelled of perfume, candles and something sweet. What a change it made from my dusty home, packed to the rafters with George's gloomy family heirlooms, so cold to the touch. *Everything* here, including the cats, was elegant. I wondered what Elizabeth and her mother did with anything that wasn't.

It was the most enjoyable morning I had passed for a long time. Drinking tea, then strong coffee and crunching macaroons in this graceful room with its pretty cats transported me from my ennui. The cookies outdid Mrs. Crawford's (and she was no slacker in that department). I imagined shopkeepers went out of their way to serve Elizabeth's mother the best of everything.

Elizabeth wasted no time in finding out about me.

"How did you meet your husband, May? You *are* married, aren't you? I can always tell."

"It's a long story." I sighed, hoping to be enigmatic. Actually, it was a short story, short and brutal. George fell down the steps outside my church in Chicago. I can still remember the sound he made and the upturned-beetle look of him as he landed. Everyone else walked on—no doubt suspecting the part alcohol had played in his downfall—but I stopped. My Grandma Leonora was a nurse in the Civil War. She knew Walt Whitman (just to say hello to) and I suppose I had fancies of being a nurse too. I was sixteen and in a rush to help everybody. I let George use my knees for a pillow, my cardigan for a blanket. I tended to that gash on his head. I told him, "It's the shock, that's all," which is what Grandma Leonora used to say to me. It always made me feel less of a baby.

He called me "Angel." "Thank you, Angel" and "Sorry, Angel." I had read the great English books—Shakespeare, Chaucer, Dickens—but I had never met a real-life Englishman before so I didn't realize that "sorry" and "thank you" is almost the national sport. He was handsome and, more importantly, he seemed captivated by me. By the time the ambulance crawled toward us, we were practically engaged.

George was in pier insurance, and it was thrilling to have a grown-up talk to me about their work. I nodded eagerly as he talked about

the beautiful Victorian structures that he couldn't wait to show me:
"Don't be fooled though, May, they're riddled with woodworm." He
also told me he liked women, but rather than hearing it as the warning
it probably was, I was flattered—I thought, *I'm a woman now!*

We married quickly, perhaps before either of us dared change our
minds, and we took the ship to England.

"What shall I do in London?" I asked, drinking my first champagne as we waved goodbye to the Statue of Liberty.

"Do?"

"Yes." I had developed a tinkly little laugh that George seemed to
like. I did it then. *Tee hee.* "What will I do with myself?"

"Have a good time, I expect," he said and we kissed and I laughed
in that tinkling way again. Later, I recognized this was like one of
those questions that one needs to ask *before* the exam, and not during.

I didn't have a good time. The pier insurance industry was more
demanding than I could have imagined. George worked away a lot,
so it was just me in the house with Mrs. Crawford clattering saucepans
downstairs. I felt isolated and foolish and that sense of foolishness
made me isolate myself further. Around the same time that I realized
I had made a mistake, I found out that I was pregnant. I was well
and truly stuck. Bed made.

"You'll swim next week?" Elizabeth asked. Once I agreed, she
added. "And come back for tea?" I nodded gratefully. Things were
on the turn.

I had known Elizabeth only four or five Thursdays when I confided
in her about how unhappy my marriage to George had become.
This was a short amount of time by anyone's standards—particularly
English people's standards. Most wait a lifetime before disclosing
anything beyond a shameful preference for peas over carrots, but I
really was *desperately* unhappy. And Elizabeth was the first person I'd
ever met who didn't think much of the institution of marriage. She

said, "Why would I want a husband, when I've got Tiggy, Winkle and Delia?" She did astonish me. Tiggy and Winkle were darling, though. I wasn't especially fond of Delia but our antipathy was mutual.

So, I threw caution to the wind and exposed the reality of George and me: we may have begun as an "international love affair" or "Atlantic romantics" as I had once, pompously, considered us, but recently I wasn't sure if I even *liked* him, let alone—here, I stuttered slightly, for these were virgin words—*loved* him anymore. Elizabeth didn't squeal or gasp but just shrugged and said, "Mm, I see..."

She was so unperturbed that I went on, saying that I suspected, but could not prove, that George had affairs "by the dozen." I was going to say, "the baker's dozen"—the charming phrase I had learned from Mrs. Crawford that very morning—but I thought it might be inappropriate.

"Why would you need to prove it?" Elizabeth said, poking her finger into her teacup. Delia trotted over, licked the fingertip, then glared at me.

"I don't know."

I couldn't help but feel Elizabeth thought I was weak, but then, I knew I was. I didn't know why I wanted to know, but I did. I *had* to know for sure. I remembered the cabin from our Atlantic crossing, with its perfectly round portholes. What an adventure it was. How excited I had felt! I had adored George once and I would have liked to feel that again.

When I told Elizabeth that he used to flirt, chronically, with Bella, a timid housemaid with poor references who had recently done a bunk in the night and thus had become the chief repository of my suspicions, she murmured, "It *is* hard to employ good staff."

It was nice to have a friend, and it was very nice to have a friend who didn't judge—for who doesn't fear that?—but a little more emotion either way might have been helpful.

<u>Things to do</u>

Swim.

Take nice present to Elizabeth's—Ribston Pippins?

Read the newspaper every morning—it clearly has no discernible effect on my mood.

Circumnavigate Tooting Common—NO SHORT-CUTS.

Get more paper from Morleys. Plain IS better for the self-esteem.

Eat less dessert. Resist the macaroons. They only make you miserable in the long run.

CHAPTER TWO

I must have walked past the notice in the post office a dozen times before, one sunny morning, it caught my eye. I don't know whether it was the cold-water swimming or my friendship with Elizabeth, probably a mixture of both, but I was feeling quite buoyed up.

I thought Doctor Grange should have Elizabeth on prescription! I would have told her this, only I knew she would have laughed. She found the unlikeliest things to laugh at. She would say, "This is the twentieth century, May, and I'm a normal girl leading a normal life," but she wasn't. She wanted to teach me to do handstands. She was much better at them in her living room than in the lake. She could hold herself the wrong way up for a good twenty seconds. But while she enjoyed gymnastics, swimming was her first love. One afternoon, she showed me a newspaper cutting of a handsome man with a twirling mustache (the kind that would make George green with envy), a barrel-shaped athletic man in very few clothes, showing off his muscles.

"Is this your boyfriend?" I said, reading the line, "*Captain Matthew Webb was stung by countless jellyfish.*"

This made her fold over in laughter. "Don't be daft, May! He was the first man to swim the Channel."

"And?"

"And I plan to be the first woman."

I looked hard into her face to see if this was another of her jokes.

"The Channel?" I thought it was the sea between England and France, but maybe I was wrong.

"Dover to Calais, that's it, all twenty-one miles. There is no reason I couldn't do it," she added firmly.

"I don't doubt it," I agreed. In my mind, Elizabeth could and would do anything she wanted. I had never met a woman as ambitious as she.

Although not quite restored to my premarital self, I was now able to get up most mornings and passed most days without tears running down my cheeks. This was progress. Indeed, Mrs. Crawford had stopped staring at me with that intense look of sympathy and disdain she had. The newspapers were allowed back in my bedroom and only rarely did they set me off.

The notice in the post office was for an assistant to an artist. *Friday Afternoons Only. Pleasant Young Woman.* I had never met an artist before. George hated artists, but this only served as further incentive for me to apply. George certainly wasn't reining himself in on my account, so why would I for him? I wasn't sure I was young any more—I was two years shy of thirty—but Mrs. Crawford had said I could pass for twenty-one—(not about this—I didn't tell her about this. I didn't think she would approve). As for pleasant, I felt I could act pleasant—at least for such a short duration as this.

The artist's name was Percy Milhouse and he asked outright if I had heard of him before. I hadn't. He chuckled. It was unclear whether he minded or not and I considered it best not to pursue it. He had an apartment—he called it a "studio"—in a converted old house only about fifty yards down the road from me, another point in favor of the visit. The studio was about fifty yards skywards. It felt like the stairs were never-ending: the six flights to the third floor meant I always arrived slightly and shamefully out of breath. (*I* would not be swimming the Channel any time soon.) It was a massive room with large windows overlooking the common, three easels set at curious angles and canvases resting on them and against the walls. There was also a chaise longue, a small square table with spindly legs and a couple of battered brown leather armchairs, but other than that, there was not much furniture for a room that size. It was nothing compared to Elizabeth's beautiful house, but I liked its mismatched artiness.

When Percy learned in that interview that George and I lived in a whole house to ourselves, he made digs. "Ooh, you wealthy people!" "Oh, an entire building, my, how do you stand to be with the riff-raff?" His jealousy surprised me. Percy referred to himself as a bohemian and I didn't know bohemians cared about such trivial things.

Percy's artwork was popular with London's fashionable set. When he told me the prices he asked for his pictures, I had to stop myself from looking astonished and make my expression suggest, *quite right too*. (Being pleasant is harder than it looks.)

"For just the one?!"

"You've got enough walls in your house to hang them all, haven't you?"

Percy was always on the precipice of a new style, a new school or a new wave. (I always forgot which was the right word.)

I confess I had hoped his work would be more old-fashioned. For me, the best artists were the Pre-Raphaelites. Dreamy women with luscious hair, who looked like they had the world at their feet. But Percy dealt with blocks of color, sharp-ended squares or elongated triangles; humans rarely featured except in rectangular form. Or in profile with only one eye. I did grow to like the pictures eventually—familiarity will do that to you—but secretly, I couldn't help but feel that poor Percy was wasting his talents.

The next Thursday as we undressed in adjacent changing cubicles by Tooting Bathing Lake, I excitedly told Elizabeth about my Friday working for Percy. I hoped to impress her for once. Elizabeth loved art, she loved adventure. I had already prepared an anecdote about Percy's paintings that involved a six-year-old being able to do them. (It may have been unoriginal, but it was true.)

"You went to an artist's studio, an artist you don't know?" repeated Elizabeth.

"I did."

Her tone was a surprise. It was like talking to George or Mrs. Crawford. I had rather thought Elizabeth would encourage me. This was a woman who hoped to swim across the English Channel one day! Whose motto was "Cats first, marriage last, swimming in between!"

"So, how did you assist?"

"Well, I didn't do much of anything, to be honest..." I began.

"Well," Elizabeth said haughtily, "how peculiar."

Actually, Percy had said, "I like to have someone here when I'm painting," but I didn't think Elizabeth would find that acceptable. I felt strangely protective of the softly spoken, kind man who just wanted company.

"It was perfectly safe, Elizabeth," I trilled. "You needn't worry."

"But what if he makes a pass at you?" She flicked a green insect away from a leaf.

"He wouldn't!"

"But if he did?"

She removed her swim-hat: it made no difference to her how wet her hair got.

I liked Percy, but I didn't find him attractive. To tell the truth, I didn't find *any* man attractive. Constant suspicion that your husband is philandering can do that to a girl.

I explained all this, adding daringly, "I would put him in his place."

Elizabeth smiled then. Those teeth, like shiny bathroom tiles, twinkled at me. Her slicked-back hair made her look like a silent movie star. "Coming back for tea?"

*

The day the poor Archduke and his wife were splattered over the newspapers, Percy *did* make a pass at me. *The Times* were giving the terrible murder the front-page treatment. The gun, the unlikely detour, the young assassin, Gavrilo Princip, his sandwich, the riot—this was the kind of news that really *was* news and I was fully immersed in the story when I realized Percy was looming over me.

"Put down the paper, May."

Percy wasn't holding his brushes, which was unusual (usually they were an extension of his hands). I stopped reading but I didn't put the paper down. Percy had a habit of covering the floor with old newspapers, so his paint didn't destroy the carpet. It always felt odd to be walking over "New Ambassador to London" or "Seven dead in coach accident" and I didn't want to walk over the Archduke and his wife before I'd had a chance to read about them.

"Darling May, would you consider a dalliance?"

"A dalliance?" I pretended I didn't understand the word. I pointed at the newspaper: "Isn't this awful?"

Percy repeated, "A dalliance, May, what do you say?"

"How do you mean?"

Grim-faced, Percy went on: "Could we have intimate relations, do you suppose, May?" (I think *anyone* would agree that, put that way, it did not sound very inviting.) "You're an attractive young woman."

"I'm twenty-eight," I said.

"Well then."

I looked at him. Percy had an unremarkable face. As he lacked distinction in his features, he tried to make up for it in his clothes. Today he was wearing a long cream smock, the kind that you would imagine an artist to wear. He always took a great deal of care to look like he did not take a great deal of care.

"I'm flattered, Percy, but I will have to decline your kind offer. You see, I take my marriage vows seriously."

This was what Elizabeth had advised me to say in such a situation. She had decided that pretending that, if it were not for my being married, I would have jumped at the chance would soften the blow. Just as she had predicted, Percy took this reasoning very well. I may even have detected a little relief around the gills. I was glad that we had got it out the way because ever since Elizabeth had put it in my mind, it had been haunting my Friday afternoons. There was no need for me to leave his employment, Percy insisted. Company was company, and he liked me very much, whether I dallied or not.

I felt pleased for Elizabeth: I knew she would be triumphant that she had read the situation right. When the next Thursday I related the incident to her, as we changed side by side in the changing rooms, she said that I had managed it brilliantly and that made me happy too.

CHAPTER THREE

The morning the girls finished school for summer vacation, and we were due to go to collect them, George announced that he wasn't feeling himself.

"Oh, that's a shame, George," I said, wondering who he was feeling now and how I could catch them at it.

He came on the trips up to Leamington less and less nowadays. The last time he had joined me was last Christmas, but he hadn't taken the girls to or from school in the Easter nor the summer term. We were at breakfast. On the rare occasions I could face going down, George would usually say something like, "Oh, you're joining us today? To what do we owe the pleasure?" but he hadn't this morning. Mrs. Crawford gave me her nervy smile and poured more coffee. Mrs. Crawford did an excellent job, but as a household we disappointed her. She would have been happy with a whirl of activity, child-rearing, cake-making. Instead, she was lumbered with a master with gout, a melancholic mistress who struggled to get dressed of a morning and children who were never at home. We didn't have parties, we didn't have a social circle—we didn't even have a social dot.

George tugged at his starchy collar as though it were strangling him, then smoothed both his cheeks downwards. George's cheeks were often puffy, but to my mind that morning, they were no puffier than usual. He was faking, I was sure of it.

"Isn't it stifling today, May? I'm unbearably hot."

"It's not particularly warm," I murmured. "There's a lot of cloud cover," I went on as though I were the expert on such things. In fact, my blinds had remained resolutely closed since I had woken at four. "You must be coming down with something."

I tapped my egg with renewed vigor and watched the shell crack.

"Will you manage the journey by yourself, May?"

"If I have to," I said mildly. "Perhaps you will feel better with some food inside you, George?"

"Doubt it."

George dabbed his forehead with his handkerchief as though it were streaming with sweat. He was such a ham.

He spread an itty-bitty spoonful of marmalade on his toast, then leveled it to his mouth. His chewing seemed to go on forever. I peeled my eggshell, trying to appear nonchalant when in fact I was on tenterhooks, waiting for the verdict. *Please let George stay home, please.* I had got used to taking the journey myself. There was little worse than sitting side by side with George on a train, pretending we were a normal, happy couple.

Finally, George made his announcement. I had my wish. He couldn't take his head any longer: he would *have* to return to his bed.

Without its shell, my egg appeared a most brilliant white. I couldn't help but admire its pale, imperfect beauty.

"Poor soldier," I called after George's retreating figure. "I will tell the girls how disappointed you are."

I should have liked to have done a celebratory jig right then and there on Mrs. Crawford's expertly ironed tablecloth.

In my excitement, I got to Paddington too early and had to wait a full forty-five minutes before my train pulled in.

What a pleasure it was to watch the world go by without George grumbling by my side about ladies' fashion failings. A group of elderly day-trippers were obediently following a man with a canary-yellow umbrella. They moved each time he moved, even if it were just to scratch his ankle or put his paper down: it was funny, like watching a cat and several mice. They were going to Shakespeare country to see "The Scottish play," which meant they were going to Stratford-upon-Avon to see *Macbeth*. I enjoyed listening to their amused chatter. I wished Elizabeth were here; she would have had the best witty observations. She and her mother were spending most of the summer in Northumberland. Elizabeth wasn't looking forward to it—her lip had trembled when we said goodbye—but we had made plans to see each other in the middle of August, if not before. We also made plenty of promises to write. Percy had been less understanding about my commitment to my girls. "I won't see you for a whole six weeks! Is that absolutely necessary?" I knew he would manage fine though.

With time stretching ahead of me, I took a stool at the kiosk, where I treated myself to a creamy coffee and a delicious fly biscuit. The coffee was gritty, but so delighted was I about imminently being with my girls that I swallowed it down with gusto and ordered a second.

It was going to be a good day.

Back in America, you have to travel a long way to see a change in the scenery. When my parents were busy, Grandma Leonora and I would cross the country and I would be allowed to meet her friends in restaurants with high ceilings and shiny chandeliers. They would usually have a candy in their pocket or a pinch for my cheek. I loved whiling away the hours on a steam train, my head on Grandma's shoulder, my nose in a book. Occasionally, she would point out something for me to remark upon: a stretch of water here, a copse of trees there—and dutifully, I would comment, but mostly I liked just dreaming with her arm around me.

In England, the outlook altered every few hundred yards or so. You had flatlands, you had hills, you had slopes, you had fields. And there was a myriad of colors too: you had greens, then yellows, then browns, oranges, then green again. Sometimes, a train whooshed past on the other line and I might catch a glimpse of a woman at a window, traveling in the opposite direction. It felt strangely like a mirror was being held up to me: I would wonder where she was going, who she was going to see, or, simply, how was life working out for her?

I remembered the night before George and I got married: I still have the diary entry. *I must be the most fortunate girl in the world. A handsome groom, money, travel, who could want for more?*

Turns out that I could.

Two men in my carriage were discussing the assassination in the Balkans. The younger man, with a ridiculously tall hat, was what George would call a "gloom and doom merchant." The government were ineffective. "It's like the country is a horse without a rider," he said scathingly. I felt horrified—a runaway horse has always been one of my worst fears—but the older man disagreed. He'd seen this sort of thing umpteen times before and it would blow over. As if to prove the point, he blew on his pipe several times.

I readied my contribution to the debate. Although I was probably the younger man's age, I inclined toward the older man's perspective. I would also remind them about something I felt had been neglected—that the assassination was not just an international crisis but a tragedy on a personal scale. Franz Ferdinand and Sophia were *parents*. How terrible all this was for their children. Sadly, but perhaps unsurprisingly, the men didn't invite me to share my riveting opinions, so I resolved to save them for my diary (which was always far more receptive). I peeled and sliced an apple (Mrs. Crawford had told me it was an Orange Pippin, but disappointingly, I could hardly tell the difference), then offered it around. Tall hat accepted, but the older man declined.

Fine. I didn't intend to force my apples on anyone.

At Leamington, I was delighted that automated cabs were available as well as the usual horse-drawn carriages. The driver, while a chatterbox, wasn't interested in speculating about political developments. I wondered if the prospect of war was just a London obsession, like peacock feathers and shiny bead earrings. The driver and I discussed at length how it was, indeed, very warm.

There was a lake, tennis courts, a hockey field and an outdoor stage but it was the cool white columns at the very front of the girls' school building that had sold the place to me. It had an air of Ancient Rome, or was it Ancient Greece? Wherever it was, I could imagine everyone floating around in togas, carting grapes and scrolls. (The pillars were, of course, artificial. I hadn't known that when I first visited, I had thought everything in England was antique.)

I hadn't wanted the girls to go to boarding school—it was something I had agreed to before Joy was born. But if there was one thing George was good at, it was being a stickler for someone else's promise. But I was sixteen when I agreed—boarding school sounded fine to me. George was insistent: if our girls were to become companions to the right men, they would need the right education. I think he was afraid my American ideas would rub off on them. Joy was eight and Leona only seven when we sent them.

If my girls ever gave any signs of not liking school then I would have swept them away as fast as you could say "Leamington Young Ladies College," but the heartbreaking thing was, from that moment two years ago when they set their patent boots on that marble floor, they adored it.

Here they were, coming out those ostentatious doors, making their way between the faux-antiquated pillars toward me. My daughters. My girls. How I adored them! They were the best of me and George. Joy saw me first, Leona was too busy chatting with her friends. Joy ran over. Her dark hair was conservatively clipped back. My eldest child: slender, long-limbed, serious-faced, arms crossed in front, her usual pose.

"I thought you were coming at two," she said accusingly, sounding more like my mother than a ten-year-old girl.

"I thought you'd be pleased." In fact, little pleased my inaptly named daughter.

Leona, however, was delighted. Miss lightness and breeze, with curls and baby-soft hair still on her forehead, Leona was always easy-going. She saw me, waved, trotted down and then gripped me round the waist, burrowing her face in my skirt like she used to when she was tiny. "Mummy, you're so early!"

Nine years old last April, she was tanned and lightly freckled: they never stopped them from going out in the sun here. I examined her face and kissed her. If we were in Chicago, people in the streets would have stopped us to say she was a shoo-in for a beauty queen.

On the train back to London, the girls reeled off the events of the term: picnics forbidden, parties suspended. *The Song of Hiawatha* recited, nobody expelled, Christina moved away, Hester *run* away (recovered that same night), hockey practice canceled due to waterlogged pitches. They wolfed down the bars of chocolate I had brought for them. Leona told us some excruciatingly bad jokes. An older lady leaned over. I thought she would scold us for noise, but she said: "Lovely to see such exuberance."

I sometimes had to remind myself that not *everyone* was as miserable as George. I should not be so quick to judge.

"Our maths teacher said there might be a war, Mummy," Joy said, looking closely at me.

I didn't like this serious turn. Wanting to make it better for her, I put my hand over hers. "He should try concentrating on Pythagoras' Theorem and not political theories."

Joy's expression remained anxious. It was the older lady who helped. "If it happens, it happens. Worrying won't change a thing."

*

Back home, the girls chased in and out of the rooms like puppies. I tried to tell myself their exuberance was lovely, but if George really did have a bad head it might make it worse—and if not, well, he wouldn't like the noise anyway. However, when I dared to go up to his room I discovered he wasn't there. Instead, there was a bowl of discarded nutshells on the floor next to his bed.

The girls were waiting for me when I came down.

"Can we go to the tennis club?"

My daughters loved the Balham and Tooting North Tennis Club more than anywhere else on God's earth. Unfortunately for me, it was open for most of the year (I found this blisteringly unfair, given how rarely the bathing lake was open to Elizabeth and me).

"Please, Mummy, please!"

I have always loathed tennis. My mother used to play.

"If we absolutely must," I said. "If there is simply nothing else that you can contemplate doing—"

They ran straight up to their rooms to change.

If the patrons of the Balham and Tooting North Tennis Club were concerned about the possibility of war, I didn't catch wind of it. The women there talked about staff who cut corners, dressmakers who were never fast enough and untrustworthy chaperones. There was much discussion about a party at the weekend. It seemed everyone was anticipating a most excellent disaster.

I wasn't invited. I had never received an invitation from the ladies at the tennis club, not once. I once heard said that English women didn't like American women coming over here and stealing their men. I don't know if that was the problem they had with me, but I wasn't sure what else it could be. How I longed for the friendliness of the Tooting Bathing Lake on a Thursday morning, where you couldn't move for women calling: "You'll get used to the cold," or "What a day for it!"

One time a rogue tennis ball flew out of nowhere, whacking me in the stomach. I looked up, feeling, if not quite hearing, everyone laughing. I pretended it didn't hurt; I smiled, hoping my tears wouldn't be noticed. No one brought me tea or offered me a gin. No one said, "*It's a shock, that's all.*"

Around the third week of the holidays (and after approximately twenty-one days at tennis club), the girls were invited to visit their school friends in Suffolk. The Pilkingtons had a rambling house with rambling grounds, hidden tree houses, babbling brooks and paddling streams. The Pilkingtons were the friends everybody wants. The Pilkingtons had not met George or me and, consequently, our correspondence was always warm and friendly. My heart said: *do you have to go away*? But I had to let them go, of course. Once again, the vast gaping abyss of nothingness lay ahead of me.

As I grew quiet at the prospect of being without them again, Leona placed herself on my knee, twirled my hair around her finger and inquired politely, "Won't you be glad to get on with your own things, Mother?"

"How do you mean?"

Joy was brushing her hair. Electricity made it fly. She stopped mid-motion and gazed at us as though about to say something important.

"That's what the other mothers say," continued Leona.

"Well, I'm not like other mothers," I said tautly.

Joy looked over with a peculiar expression on her face. I guessed that she wished I was. Well, I wished I was too.

CHAPTER FOUR

Joy and Leona returned from paradise at the Pilkingtons' browner than ever, with bigger, bolder stories. Leona had been stung by a wasp the size of a bee, *no, Mummy, the size of a butterfly!* It had got her under the chin. Grandmother Pilkington thought she was having a heart attack, but Doctor Price said it was just constipation. The Pilkington brothers were so funny. And awfully good at cricket. Two kittens were living in the tree house; no one knew who they belonged to.

The girls had only been home an hour before they clamored to go to the tennis club again, and we had only been at the tennis club for two and a half matches when Mr. Mason came running in with a newspaper: he was trying to read as he ran, if you can imagine such a thing. Once he checked he had his audience, he yelled, "This is it, everyone!"

Everyone peered down at his outstretched newspaper as though it were a crystal ball. Pretending to be uninterested was not an option. I climbed out of my chair and smoothed down my skirt. My laces had a habit of becoming undone and although they weren't undone at precisely that moment, I bent to fix them. Self-consciously, I walked over to the crowd.

"What has happened exactly?" I asked.

"Germany has invaded Belgium!" shouted Mr. Mason, whose previous effort at conversations with me had extended no further than "Is this chair taken?"

"That'll put the cat among the pigeons," Mr. Frampton, the father of one of Leona's friends, said hotly into my ear. He pressed his hand on my shoulder and squeezed. I leaned away from him.

"Does this mean war, do you think?" someone else asked, gripping the pearls at her throat.

"Certainly," Mr. Mason, self-appointed expert on international relations, said confidently. "We can't weasel out of this."

Cats. Pigeons. Weasels.

"Where *is* Belgium anyway?" I whispered to Mrs. Frampton, not because she was someone I would, under normal circumstances, interact with, but because she was now standing next to me. She pulled her pale cardigan tightly over her chest even though it wasn't cold and let out a sigh. "I *am* American," I reminded her defensively.

"Frankly, we are *all* aware of that," she said huffily. "Belgium is not far away. Just across the Channel and then..." Here, her geography seemed to have failed her. "Up a bit."

I squinted at her, the way George did when he wanted to intimidate me. I thought of Elizabeth and her swimming plans. I hadn't realized how ambitious they were. I couldn't wait for her to come back from her trip.

"How would one normally cross the Channel?"

She looked at me coolly, then fanned her jowls ineffectively. "By boat, my dear. Presumably you have heard of one of those?"

The children realized that something was going on. Some parents told them, "Go back to your games." Others squeezed their children's shoulders. "Nothing to worry about."

The *thunk, thunk, thunk* of balls flying across nets continued. Leona tucked her sweaty paw into mine.

"What does it mean, Mummy?" asked Joy. She was torn, as we all were, between excitement and anxiety but unlike the rest of us, she lacked the experience to cover up the excitement.

"I'm not sure," I admitted.

Mr. Mason looked at me, as though noticing me for the first time: "Mark my words, this is war."

"Go play," I said lightly, and both Joy and Leona obediently skipped away.

I don't know if it's a characteristic of all children, but *my* children were remarkably good at putting bad thoughts to the backs of their minds.

George was drunk; he could barely walk in a straight line. I sent the girls up to their rooms: they shouldn't have to see him like this. I hadn't seen him so discombobulated since the police insisted that fire at Weston-super-Mare pier wasn't arson. Even though I no longer liked him, I still regarded my husband as an oracle of news from the outside world. That's how it had been with us from the beginning on the cold sidewalk in Chicago, and it was a hard habit to break.

At the dinner table, listlessly spooning parsnip soup, I wondered what was happening in Elizabeth's apartment right now, or in Percy's. I would have given my hind teeth to be discussing political developments with either of them instead of my drunken husband.

George was as adamant that there wasn't going to be a war as Mr. Martin had been that there was.

"But we have an agreement with Belgium. The British government promised them neutrality," I said in a voice quite unlike my own.

"What's that?"

Although I wasn't *quite* sure of the details, I plowed on regardless. "An agreement, I understand, that they are to remain free. We can't allow the Germans to trample all over this. The Belgians have a right to our protection."

"It's just a scrap of paper," he said, as indeed the German generals were already maintaining. "Who cares about that anymore?"

But then only four days later the church bells were making a deafening peal, quite unlike anything I had ever heard in England before. Shouts rang out in the street, and I hastened to the window, adrenaline coursing through me. The newspaper chap was surrounded by people talking animatedly. People didn't usually talk to strangers here, but they did now. Everything was different today: Britain was at war.

For once, I could hardly wait for George to get home.

"What *is* going to happen?" I asked him at the front door. My heart was racing. This was it. Finally, change. I had been waiting for change and here it was.

George hung up his hat and his coat, he took off his shoes, before turning to me with his big crooked face. "Whatever it is, it won't affect people like us, May."

CHAPTER FIVE

Despite the war, the girls were told they were to return to school after summer vacation just as usual. They squealed with delight at the news. "We didn't want to miss school, Mummy!" Leona explained, while Joy smirked into her suitcase.

"I know, darlings," I said, whipping an unconcerned smile onto my face. "And that's good."

I was surprised George came up on the train to the school with us, but once we had dropped off the girls, he sprang it on me that he had business to attend to in Coventry. I remembered that Bella, our runaway maid, had family from Coventry and I was not impressed.

It was hot and dry that August. Two days after my girls left, I went back to working at Percy's: he was pleased to see me. From his front window, you could see new recruits walking across Battersea Common. Lines and lines of men were snaking their way to the recruitment offices. They didn't look much older than my girls.

"Not tempted to join them, Percy?"

It was snide because I knew that, like George, Percy didn't have plans to join up. I just wanted to hear what convoluted excuse he would come up with. Unlike George, Percy was not too old.

Percy rested his hand on the small of my back. He was often handling me recently—I hoped he didn't have paint on his fingers.

"Maybe." I turned in surprise and he added quickly: "I would need to know more."

"I wish I could contribute somehow," I mused.

"But you're a woman!" He gazed at me as though it had never occurred to him that I might have feelings on the subject. Frustration with one's lot was clearly a quality that belonged exclusively to men.

"I still have dreams, Percy! I still want to make a difference."

He nodded slowly. "Every day is an education with you, May!"

How delightful it was to be reunited with Elizabeth in her lovely house. She told me she had missed her dear little American friend terribly. I blushed.

"We must not leave it so long," she insisted, and I agreed, although when I counted the days on my fingers, it had only been five weeks.

Our conversation swiftly turned to the outbreak of war.

"What does it all mean?" I grabbed a restorative macaroon. "What's going to happen? I'm so worried about my girls."

"I do understand, May," said Elizabeth sympathetically. "I'm the same—awfully worried about the cats."

I sighed. "How is Winkle?"

"If you mean Tiggy, she's recovered from her fall, thank you."

All the committees, leagues, reformers and branches were now working toward the war effort. Similarly, when she was not doing cartwheels, or swimming, Elizabeth was now knitting for soldiers. I was too but I was not so adept at it as her, probably because I tried to read at the same time and whenever I turned a page, it went awry.

Elizabeth said, "The good thing is that with the men going away we should be able to swim more."

This felt sacrilegious to me. I think she caught that because she added defensively: "I must practice—I still propose to be the first woman to swim the Channel, May."

"Of course, but what about the war?"

"It would boost the morale, don't you think? Imagine the headlines: 'Englishwoman succeeds where all others fail!' Can you think of anything more patriotic?"

Patriotic wasn't the word I was thinking.

"Anyway, the war will be over soon. We'll win, we always do." She lit another cigarette.

"Do we?" I asked. Recently I had been wondering whether I was included in the "we" or not.

"We may be small, but we are a very mighty nation," Elizabeth said so stirringly that Winkle jumped. "It will be over in no time, you'll see."

I realized suddenly that I didn't know Elizabeth as well as I had thought.

How to contribute to the war effort

Knit faster.

Walk more—soldiers have to walk a great deal.

Eat less—not nice to eat loads when our soldiers are suffering. "An army marches on its stomach," said Napoleon. I am NOT an army.

Applaud soldiers when one sees them, if appropriate, of course.

Keep reading the newspapers.

Send letters of condolence to families who lose boys.

Support George, Percy and Elizabeth in all their endeavors. Maybe this is my destiny—to be a cheerleader of others?

Hmm...what else?!?!?!

CHAPTER SIX

Elizabeth, like George, was wrong about the war being over quickly, although Elizabeth, like George, would never admit she was wrong about anything. Our troops were ill-prepared against the Germans. We had taken bayonets and swords, knives for hand-to-hand combat, but instead we faced industrial war, war on a huge scale. We had to catch up, improve, wake up, and fast. There were many losses in the early days; even the proud newspaper editorials couldn't cover up the lists of the fallen soldiers. They were longer than your arm.

I didn't know that many people in England but still I scanned the names assiduously: it felt important to honor the dead or at least to acknowledge their contribution. But other than that, my life had not changed. I saw Percy every Friday afternoon. I met with Elizabeth regularly. I wrote my diary and I tried to write poems. I also, ridiculously, humiliatingly, tried to get George to notice me again but his heart could not have been further away. I went to the hair salon, where all the talk was of husbands, sons and brothers leaving for the front, and for the first time, I experienced that hollow feeling of shame when someone asked what *my* husband was doing for the war effort.

Back home with the latest look, I asked George coyly, "Do I look different?"

"Do you?" George looked me up and down as though checking for structural faults. "I'm off, pier business tonight." He put on his coat, then squashed his hat onto his ungainly head.

"Do you have to go out?" I said under my eyelashes, in a way some might call flirtatious and others—Elizabeth—might call desperate.

"I do."

"It's no life for me here, alone, day and night…" I began. But I think George realized I was about to launch into a tirade because he dismissed me.

"Go and read a book or something, May," he said, striding to the door.

And read a book was all I *could* do, because in every other way, I was a bystander. I was bored and I was ashamed of being bored, especially *at a time like this*. I realized I was useless, a pointless, meaningless person. The sort of person who plumped herself merrily into a life-raft and waved up at the people on the sinking *Titanic*.

History was passing me by.

At the end of August, when we had been at war for just over three weeks, I was sitting in Percy's studio, half-heartedly knitting, wholeheartedly despairing at the newspapers. On this occasion, however, instead of painting, Percy was whipping around like a fellow possessed piling paints to one side, rearranging easels and canvases; I had never seen anything like it.

"Am *I* tidy enough for you?" I joked.

"Good-good," he said absently. I raised my ankles as he swept underneath my feet and then emptied the dustpan out the window. "A friend is coming."

"Oh?"

Percy had smoothed down his mustache and pushed back the rebel lock of hair that dangled over his pale forehead. He had put on a colorful cravat. A peacock would have been subtler.

"Should I head off?"

"Oh n-no," he said, but his cheeks had gone pinketty-pink and not from the exertion of dusting. He should have tried painting the sky this shade of mortification, so dramatic it was.

"You'll l-l…like her…"

"Her?" I echoed. Percy's friend was a "she"? This *was* interesting. How had I never noticed Percy's stutter before?

"Will I?" I looked at him. I didn't feel jealous. I felt a faint pity for him, I suppose. I felt intrigued. "Are you courting this *friend*?"

"I wish," he said brightly, then laughed.

At three o'clock, Percy's friend whirled in like a dervish. I heard the downstairs door slam, then someone swept up the flights of stairs with more verve and energy than all those men marching across Battersea Common put together. This someone was wearing a great overcoat, quite masculine in style, with large shiny buttons, but underneath that was a beautiful green dress. Her boots were faded black and their tips were muddy. She gave me a broad, uncensored smile. Her eyebrows were dark and determined and I was instantly charmed. She was one of those real English eccentrics. It seemed to me that no other country produced women like this—self-assured, capable, but beautiful too. She seemed perfectly at home here in Percy's studio, although she said she had never visited before. *She would seem at home anywhere*, I thought. She stalked around the apartment, taking in Percy's pictures. I noticed that he didn't ask her what she thought, and she didn't offer an opinion but rather stared at each with a slightly mocking expression on her face. I got the feeling that, like me, she thought Percy could do better. I hoped she didn't think Percy could do better *than me*, though.

Percy was all at sea. "Have I introduced you?" he said. He couldn't remember his right hand from his left.

"I am," she said, shaking my hand vigorously, "Elsie Knocker."

We talked about the weather. She said there was far too much of it; it was abominable. Percy roared even louder at her jokes than he did mine.

"And what do *you* do, May?"

I cringed at the dreaded question. Here I was, pointlessly hanging around a studio—a geisha in a tea-house for a tormented male artist. "Not much at present," I said as though my malaise was a temporary thing and not the situation I had been in for the last twelve years.

"And what did you do before 'not much'?"

I smiled at her, shaking my head. "I have two daughters," I said, as though they were (a) very young and (b) took up *all* my time.

"May was a child bride, weren't you?" Percy was trying to be helpful.

"I married young, yes."

Elsie Knocker said that she had recently joined Doctor Hector Munro's flying ambulances. She seemed to think everyone must have heard of them, so I pretended *Oh, yes, of course.* Fortunately, Percy was more honest about his ignorance than I was, so she explained it to him: they were a group of doctors, nurses and volunteers who would drive to the front to pick up injured British or Belgian soldiers and either treat them or transport them to the nearest hospitals.

She would be away to the continent by the weekend.

"Tomorrow?" I asked breathlessly. Already I admired her greatly. Percy's taste in women had come as a pleasant surprise.

"To Harwich, yes, then onwards."

How wonderful to speed off on an adventure! Men and women racing to do their bit, not like me, mooching around the tennis club with a bunch of people who hated the very deckchairs I sat on.

I could feel myself becoming tearful again.

"Why don't you volunteer, May? We are desperate for nurses," Elsie suggested, in the same easy way others might say, "Why not have a slice of Dundee cake?"

I thought of sitting on Grandma Leonora's knee as she told me her stories about bandaging men in a field hospital—*Broken men, desperate for a kind word.*

The dreams I had. The dreams I had lost sight of a long time ago . . .

My heart was beating faster when I said, "Unfortunately, I don't know the first thing about nursing."

Elsie shrugged. "You brought up two girls."

"Hardly," I admitted. "I had plenty of help."

Elsie had a throaty, sexy laugh. I could see why Percy adored her.

"Nor can I…" I listed on my fingers, "drive—I've never even been on a motorcycle…as for horses, they petrify me." I was going to go on about their pounding and unpredictable hooves, but I stopped. Few people seemed to feel about horses as I did: my rants usually succeeded only in making them dislike me further.

I looked up smiling, as though proud of my non-accomplishments. "I'd be more of a hindrance than a help."

"All those things can be overcome," Elsie said lightly.

"I don't think I could learn anything now." I did my tinkly little laugh. "I'm useless."

"'Course you could." She eyed me suspiciously. "You're younger than I am. Plus, there are more important qualities."

"Like what?"

"Are you kind?" She answered herself: "Clearly you are, otherwise you wouldn't be hanging around this odd specimen." She poked Percy in the chest and he dissolved into helpless giggles. "Are you cooperative? I'll wager yes. Are you willing? Are you able? That's what we need. We desperately need women like you on the continent, May."

This "we" again. She clearly didn't know the half of it. Half of me.

"I really don't think they do…Most people don't like me." I choked back an entirely inappropriate tear. "I'm not a very pleasant person," I couldn't help adding, "I have dark thoughts sometimes."

"*I* like you," she said. A warmth spread over me. *This remarkable woman liked me.* I couldn't be *all* bad.

"Why don't you join us in Belgium, May? You'll never be bored again."

"I'm not bored," I lied. "My life is fulfilling."

She looked around at the tubes of oils and the stained cloths. Piles of colorful testers squeezed onto boards. A collapsed easel against a paint-splattered wall. This was Percy's world, not mine.

Leaning toward me, Elsie whispered, "This isn't the answer, you know."

She squeezed my fingers. I was going to make a joke: "*It suits me*," but deep down I knew she was right. Percy wasn't the answer; even Elizabeth wasn't the answer . . . swimming wasn't the answer, constitutional walks weren't the answer, not to all *my* questions anyway.

Percy stayed upstairs while Elsie showed me her shiny motorbike in the street. I couldn't believe it was all hers. Elizabeth was enough of a rarity with her car; I had never even heard of female motorcyclists. There was a sidecar with a broken door and Elsie asked if I wanted to go for a spin. Wordlessly, I got in. I was petrified but I didn't want her to know it.

She looked at me. "You're shaking like a leaf."

"Just go," I muttered, and we did. A clatter of noise and then a tug and we were away, and I was laughing like a lunatic in my vibrating tin box.

Hadn't I wanted to pep up my life a bit?

"How about a go on the back instead?" Elsie shouted.

"M-Me?" Funny how I had acquired a stutter too.

"Get on," she said, patting the seat behind her.

I clambered up, gripped her tightly and with a vroom and a whoosh, we were off. It was as alien to me as flying on a broom. Elsie was considerate; we didn't go too fast—in fact, someone on a penny farthing zipped past us—but gradually we built up some speed. It was wonderful: if I hadn't stopped believing when Grandma Leonora died, I would have thought we were being propelled along by the hand of God.

I was still trembling when we stopped outside Percy's place. I didn't want it to end though.

"So that's one down, two to go."

"What?"

"Those things you said you can't do—you can almost ride now. If I had an afternoon with you, I'd see to it you could drive and ride horses too."

I could only laugh.

Back in the studio, while I drank a measure of gin to steady myself, Elsie put an arm around Percy's shoulders. She was the same height as him.

"Won't you release this poor woman?"

Looking embarrassed, Percy squeaked: "Release her? May is free to do as she wishes!"

"My husband wouldn't want me to go," I said, flushing red. Elsie didn't blanch though; she just said, "Hmm, then maybe he's not the right husband for you..."

At the door she said, "You're your own woman, May, don't ever forget that."

I couldn't bring myself to speak. It was something I had longed to hear all my life. It turned out to be one of the few things that got me through until Christmas.

CHAPTER SEVEN

The autumn term of 1914 was not half so bad as the autumn term the year before had been, nor the one before that, yet I was at constant battle with myself. It was as though I had had a taste of freedom, only to have it snatched from my jaws.

Elizabeth had found herself a swimming coach and most of our conversations were now peppered with what this Mr. Albert thought on the perennial questions such as: France to England or England to France? And spring, summer or autumn? There were up and downsides to all, apparently. At first, I thought Elizabeth might fall in love with Mr. Albert, but she protested robustly, "Heavens! Mr. Albert is expedient, that's all." Elizabeth scrupulously followed Mr. Albert's exercise program, which consisted of diagrams of little stick people. And when she wasn't exercising, she was teaching English at the Belgian refugee center. About half a million Belgian refugees had rolled up to Britain and about thirty of those were learning English phrases with Elizabeth. "How do you do?" "It's a nice day for it." I had no doubt that soon they would be wrestling with the issues of summer/winter France/England as well.

When she wasn't doing any of those things, Elizabeth spent time with me. We knitted for our soldiers together. Imagining the delight on a soldier's face when he unwrapped my socks helped keep me focussed. I also played with Tiggy and Winkle, who would have dearly loved to get their paws into our handiwork (one time, Delia somehow did).

Hypothermia was the swimmer's great enemy, so in order for Elizabeth to acclimatize to the cold of the Channel, Mr. Albert insisted that she did not wear a coat or cardigans any more. She should only have a single sheet at night and lighting the drawing room fire was strictly forbidden. My visits were less comfortable than before, but I was allowed to pull a blanket across my knees and there were still plenty of cakes. Every so often Elizabeth would rise, stretch her legs and touch her toes, which I supposed was to warm herself up.

George was out of the house more than usual, which was a good thing. He was snappy when he saw me and asked for information only about the running of the house. He never looked at me—it felt as though he looked through me. In another last-ditch attempt at affection, I wrote him a sweet poem called "husband of mine," but if he read it he never said and it disappeared from the bedside table where I had positioned it. By contrast, Percy continued to be more touchy-feely than ever, and although I could talk about most anything with Elizabeth, I couldn't confide this. She thought she had solved the Percy problem, while I was realizing we had merely postponed it. She already thought he was a shirker and a loafer. (I did think of saying, *Well, what about your Mr. Albert?* But I didn't.)

I didn't like to admit it, even to myself, but the fact that Percy found me desirable *did* warm me, especially in the light of George's lack of interest. I felt guilty about it though. Not only because I was married, but because I was taking from Percy and offering very little in return. I told myself that, until the issue came to a head, Percy would prefer that I continued my visits to his studio, which after all were a highlight of my week too.

As for the war, well, that was defying all predictions—it had taken on a whole life of its own. Or perhaps the reverse of that—it was as if the Grim Reaper was walking among us. My mother wrote that it was godlessness that allowed the war to happen; we had opened the door to the Devil and invited him in. She didn't say it was *my* godlessness, but I knew that was what she meant.

*

In mid-December George had "pier business" in Hull, so I traveled up to get the girls alone. My favorite tea boy from the train station had joined up—I wouldn't have thought he was old enough—and was replaced by a grumpy elderly man who spilled almost as much tea on the counter as he put in the cup. There were fewer people in the station. I thought back to July when the platform had been teeming with life. There were no tourists, nor tour guides, now. There were still plays in Stratford but only in the side theater. Most of the young players were fighting in Flanders or the Dardanelles, apparently.

Some soldiers got into my carriage, overwhelming it immediately with their size and smell. They hauled their battered packs onto the shelves and trod grime into the floor. Low gruff voices. They passed their cigarettes around, murmuring about the Bosch: "you could smell his sauerkraut from one hundred miles away," etc., etc. I gathered they were stationed in Belgium. I couldn't help but think wistfully of Elsie Knocker and wonder about the difference she was making out there.

I hoped they couldn't smell the contents of the lunchbox that Mrs. Crawford had diligently put together. Opening it, I asked them if they wanted anything from it. It turned out they were ravenous.

"Is it *very* hard out there?" I asked, as they munched through Mrs. Crawford's ham and cress sandwiches and chewed on her painstakingly sliced carrots.

"It's bad," one of them said. Alarmingly, another man's eyes filled with tears. I had never seen a grown man cry in public before. I felt stricken. "Terrible. Horrendous."

"Thank you for asking," the first said, handing his friend a handkerchief. "No one asks."

"I should do more to help," I mumbled. "Another carrot?"

Leona had borrowed *The Wind in the Willows* from the school library. She wanted us to act it out on the train home. As Leona rarely stayed still long enough to read anything, I had to encourage it. She was Mole and Joy was told to be Ratty. I was surprised Joy didn't kick up. We didn't know who I should play but Joy insisted, "Daddy is absolutely Mr. Toad! You can't be him!," which condemned me to being Badger (a dear fellow but nothing like me). I read most of the other parts anyway. Leona said I made an excellent train driver and washerwoman, so it wasn't like I was a complete good-for-nothing.

Once home, my girls mooched uselessly around the house. Unforgivably, the tennis club was closed for the Christmas vacation. I know Joy wrote at least one letter to Frances Pilkington, begging her for an invitation.

The newspaper's lists of the dead grew like children gaining inches. One December morning, at the breakfast table, Joy paled: a girl from school's older brother had been shot in the head in Belgium. He had been kind to her on Open Day. Joy burst into floods of hot tears, knocking over her boiled egg. George had the cheek to say: "Only one? Is that the first you know who has died? Oh, why the face, May? I would have thought there would have been more by now, that's all."

I wrote a letter to the family to express my commiserations. I took my time over the words. It was a distressing task, but I didn't make a pig's ear of it.

Percy went down to spend Christmas in St. Ives to absorb the light there. His friends were joining up, or, as he put it, "dropping like flies." He didn't know what to do with himself.

Before he left, he gave me a present. Actually, he didn't give it to me, he just nodded casually over to the window seat: "There's something for you there." He shrugged as though he himself had played no part in it. I had bought him a wallet, an impersonal gift, but it was slightly better than what I had originally thought of getting him, which was nothing. The whole idea of us exchanging gifts made me nervous, and when I saw what Percy's was, I became very nervous indeed. It was a charcoal portrait of me. In it, I was reading the newspaper, and I looked composed, or even serene. A little melancholy maybe, like someone who had married the wrong man and perhaps, in the artist's mind, was pining for another. Percy was watching me intently, so I kept my eyes on the paper. *Oh dear*, I thought. I couldn't share *this* with Elizabeth.

"What do you think?" he asked in a low voice. He got a washcloth and wiped his hands.

"It's very beautiful," I whispered. It was far more lovely than anything of his I had seen before.

"*You're* very beautiful!" He was facing away from me, so I couldn't see his expression. I laughed like he'd cracked an enormous joke.

So, I was quite relieved he was going away for a few weeks.

I was probably more disappointed than the girls that there was no snow on either Christmas Eve or Christmas Day. Charles Dickens had led me to believe that snow was a certainty in London. Still, the sky was a beautiful blue and the trees without their leaves looked strangely romantic as we walked home across the common after church. You could smell Christmas in the air. I imagined that anyone watching us might have thought we looked the very definition of the happy family. Leona and Joy were wrapped up in their winter best, their hands locked in mine. Leona was reciting the stream of jokes she said she had been saving for us.

"Knock, knock."

"Who's there?"

"Anna Partridge."

"Anna Partridge who?"

"Anna Partridge in a pear tree, of course."

I didn't dare meet Joy's eyes.

George—whose head had hurt too much to go to church—and I exchanged presents in front of the fireplace, in front of the girls—for the sake of the girls—quietly and without affection. The fire danced and I thought of Elizabeth shivering in her room at home. She wouldn't cheat, she told me, even if it was Christmas.

George had got me a bracelet. It was so pretty, I found it hard to take in. George had got this for *me*? Perhaps he *did* still love me. Then I saw the tiny "B" hanging from one of the links: B is for Bella. It was like being punched in the stomach. I knew immediately that it was intended for her. The ex-housemaid. The Coventry resident. It just was him all over. He used to buy me gifts with "M" on them. Had he done this on purpose?

He seemed utterly oblivious to his faux pas.

Joy wasn't, though. Examining it like a curator at a museum, she asked: "Why is the letter 'B' on it, Daddy?"

George blustered before coming up with: " 'B' because Mummy is the bee's knees."

Later, he leaned toward me: "Forgive me, May, I got my parcels mixed up. There is an 'M' upstairs on my bed. *This* one was meant for my Great-Aunt Beatrice in Ireland."

One of my presents to George was a scarf. While my early knitting attempts had wound lopsidedly, mismatching blacks and grays, this was a treat, smooth and straight—with any luck it might strangle him.

"Thank you, I think," George said.

I had also got him a first edition of *Treasure Island*, a pair of winter gloves and a silver hip flask from the girls, which I had even had engraved. Now I wished I hadn't plumped for *Joy and Leona*, but rather chosen more relevant words: *Alcoholic, Philanderer* or why not *Adulterer*? Imagine the look on the engraver's face had I requested that!

George unwrapped it. "Are you trying to say that I drink a lot?"

I thought, *we hardly need presents to say that.*

"Don't you like it?" Leona asked placidly.

"It's fine!" he declared.

There were just the four of us for dinner, and although four was vastly preferable to two, of course, I couldn't help thinking: *What kind of family life is this? What example am I setting my girls?*

I don't know how Mrs. Crawford did it: she deserved twice the salary we paid. And yet although the Christmas spread was delicious, nothing could disguise the bitterness in my mouth. This was such a sham, all of it. George didn't love me. He didn't even care about me. Why was I allowing myself to be treated in this way?

Joy picked at the turkey—she was studying domestic science this year and thought she knew everything.

"Are you sure it's cooked?" she asked as Mrs. Crawford proudly sliced.

"Of course," I whispered, annoyed that she would offend my main ally in the house.

Leona ate it all, declared it yummy and, strange child, could she please have some more Brussels sprouts?

Meanwhile, George was pouring himself drink after drink. Each glassful made him more slurry than the last.

"Nice leg." He brandished the turkey on his fork. "You used to have nice legs, didn't you, May?" Ignoring him seemed only to agitate him further. "And breasts," he said, thickly. "Remember those schoolgirl blouses you used to wear?"

"Can't we play a game?" Leona asked loudly.

"Charades?" I said.

"I Spy?" said Joy heroically. I knew she didn't want to. She hated games and jokes, but she understood when a distraction was needed.

But before we could do anything, George roused himself. "Well, needs must. I have an appointment."

I spy a man who can't wait to weasel out of his family life.

"Not today, surely?"

He tugged awkwardly at his cravat. (Not his new scarf.) "I'll take my hip flask."

Like that made up for it.

"Right." Leona didn't even bother to look up.

"Wish I was at school," muttered Joy.

I wished we were *all* at school. I wished we were anywhere but here.

Once he had gone, the girls and I played a desolate I Spy for a few rounds. "Sill" was Joy's "S." Leona thought "black crow" was a "B" and one word. Mine was "L" for Leona, which infuriated Joy, so I did "J" for Joy, but this just annoyed them both.

Our fire was nearly out but I didn't like to call Mrs. Crawford, not today. She was aching to get back to her boy, James, who was home on leave.

"Why don't we go for a walk?"

"We already walked to church and back," said Joy flatly.

A noise from downstairs made me go over to the window. The girls followed me, and there I saw her—"B." George went over to her, reached for her and embraced her. They stayed conjoined like that for one, maybe two minutes. All this in front of my house. In front of my girls. There was my proof.

I realized suddenly what Elizabeth had meant when she said it changes nothing.

Two days later, an envelope arrived, postmarked Belgium. I couldn't think who was writing to me from the continent, so opened it disinterestedly. Inside was a card, a late Christmas card. On the front was a sketch of a robin redbreast on a snowy branch, a sweet, endearing image. Somehow, it was a surprise to find it was from Percy's friend, Elsie Knocker.

Sweet May, I have moved to a cellar . . .

"A cellar?" I said aloud.

The letter went on: *I know! I had to get nearer to the wounded: the long journeys were killing them. I have founded an emergency clinic only fifty yards from the Western Front. The faster we treat them, the better: the men are coming on a treat. Don't worry, I am not alone. I am with a wonderful wee lassie named Mairi—she and I may be crazy fools, but if you were here, and you saw what we see, I know you would understand.*

I wasn't sure that was true.

I bet you are wondering why I sent you this robin? It's a reminder— you can fly...

At the bottom was an address: *If you are still "bored," get in touch with these people. You do not need experience with them. I repeat, you do NOT need experience. Tell them I sent you. Oh, but May, whatever you do, don't tell them you're married.*

<u>Things to do!!!</u>

Pack!

Sort out the girls.

Inquire after Mrs. Crawford's boy, James.

Will Mrs. Crawford want to stay? Emphasize that it is her decision. She is HER OWN WOMAN.

Cheerio to Percy!

Farewell to Elizabeth.

Tell George!!!

CHAPTER EIGHT

Joy asked if she could see in the New Year with the adorable Pilking-tons. Apologetically, I told her she couldn't, not this year, *this* year was going to be different...

She didn't speak to me for the entire evening.

Everything felt as though it was happening for the last time. Even the most mundane things were suddenly meaningful and huge. The French Red Cross had called me in for an interview. Two older women asked questions in heavily accented English. I didn't have to lie outright about anything, for they didn't ask *directly* if I had a husband and daughters. I skirted around the question of commitments but told them that I absolutely must be home for the summer. They agreed that I would be entitled to two weeks' leave. What's more, with a bit of prior notice I could return to England any time I requested ("Oh good heavens, yes, it's a hospital not a prison"). The only thing that had confuddled them was that I was American, but funnily enough, it was on this topic that I could speak with the greatest fluency: "For me, it's not about patriotism, it's not about nationalism, I simply want to help those most in need."

I like to think it was my polemics that swung it, but most prob-ably it was a testament to their desperation. I would be joining a Voluntary Aid Detachment. "Not quite nursing," the older of the two women said vaguely, "but with some nursing duties."

Later, I realized something else. The interview had mostly con-sisted of questions about my finances. Would I be self-supporting? Yes. Was I sure? Er, yes, quite sure. Would I be able to afford the uniform? "Certainly," I said before I discovered that it consisted of three dresses, sixteen aprons, a cap, sleeves, a stiff white collar, black stockings and black shoes (rubber soles only).

"Sixteen aprons," I repeated, wondering if there was not some mistake with the numbers. "So many!"

They gave each other a look, and I feared the look said "work-shy."

"I'm not afraid to get my aprons dirty!" I said quickly. "Sixteen it is. Perfect!"

I was given a date, a chit I could exchange for a ticket to France, a further list of items I'd need and an address, and that was it: "toodlepip," as Leona liked to say.

Mrs. Crawford had been shocked when I told her my plans, but once she got over her surprise, she said warmly, "I never expected this of you!" and "Mrs. Turner, you're doing us proud—I can't wait to tell my James!"

"Thank you," I said. It was such a rare thing to be praised I hardly knew what to do with it.

"To think, last year, you barely got out of bed and now you're going to be helping our boys in their hospital beds."

"Exactly so," I grimaced. This memory was hurtful but I don't think Mrs. Crawford intended to be. "And very kind you were to me then too."

Mrs. Crawford was adamant she would help with my girls, especially if there was a hold-up or whatnot in France. I knew she would, too. She had always been there for us; she was the first person I knew in London—but it was still reassuring to hear her commitment. "I'll even take them to their tennis if I must," she said, wincing slightly. I had ranted about that club often enough. "It won't be necessary," I assured her. "I'll always be back for the girls."

January fourth was the girls' last night at home. They still bathed together, and that night they laughed, fought and sprayed water over each other like they usually did. Then, when they came tumbling out, I wrapped them up in towels and cuddled them down. Leona liked me to brush her hair but Joy said I was "too pully" and even "Ow, you did that on purpose!" Leona liked to borrow my clothes and walk around the room in my grown-up shoes. (Joy did too, but she would never admit it.)

I taught my daughters a game that Grandma Leonora and I used to play: I set out some objects on a tray, which they could look at for no more than five seconds. I took it away, then returned with the tray but with one item missing that they had to guess.

"Is it Daddy's old spectacles?"

"No, they're there."

"The thimble?"

"Try again!"

"Was it the magnifying glass?"

Leona got it first. "It's Mummy's locket…"

It was my most precious thing. A gift from my grandma when I was younger than Leona was now. I showed it to them both. A picture of each of them, one in each side. Two smiling sisters with wide eyes.

"I'll always wear it," I said, suddenly tearful. They looked at me nervously.

"Is it my turn?" asked Leona.

Packing the girls' trunks, I found the bits that had crept under their beds or were rolled up at the back of the drawers or, in the case of Leona's bear, Cardinal Wolsey, had found its way into the large china wash-jug. Leona hugged me and her bear again tightly.

"Daddy says you're rubbish at everything, but you're not. You're very good at finding the things that are missing," she said.

"Don't believe everything Daddy says," I said as lightly as I could.

"Don't believe *anything* Daddy says." Joy looked at me slyly, then whispered, "Sorry."

I had to tell them about my trip.

"I will pick you up first day of vacation. Don't ever think I won't be there."

Joy scowled. "Of course, Mummy, why wouldn't you?" She stopped mid-brush, waiting for my answer.

I said in my most casual voice, "Well, I'm going to live in France for a bit."

They both stared at me.

"I'm going to work in a hospital. It's about time Mummy did her bit for the war effort, don't you think?"

I had feared an upset, but they both took it in their stride. Joy nodded thoughtfully. "You'll be here in summer though, yes?"

"Yes." I would have promised anything; I was so relieved that she, especially, hadn't taken it badly. "Nothing could hold me back. And Joy, make sure you practice your backstroke as often as you can."

"Back *arm*, Mummy," she corrected me.

"And that one."

"I'll write," said Leona, hugging me again. She held my chin in her pretty paws. "You'll write to me?"

"All the time." I felt suddenly choked and relieved and confused all at once. *Was it fair? Was it right?*

Leona jumped up and snatched the hairbrush from Joy. "Mummy, Mummy, why should you never fall in love with a tennis player?"

It took me a moment to realize that this wasn't life advice, this was Leona telling one of her jokes. "I don't know. Why?"

"Because love means nothing to them. Do you get it, Mummy?"

"I *think* so," I said cautiously. "It's funny, yes."

I warned the girls we might have to stop *The Wind in the Willows* before its conclusion, but that evening I couldn't stop. We carried on through the weasels storming the hall. I had to see it out. Justice was restored. Toad was winning back his home. Leona was half-asleep, her little mouth open. Joy was pressed into me.

Why hadn't I done this more often? My mouth grew dry and I began to skip the extraneous words. I read on and on, until Joy was asleep too, and then I slipped out from between them.

In the end, I didn't have to tell George. The next day, while I was taking the girls back to school, he went through my room (something he liked to do occasionally) and, although my diary with all its unpleasant opinions was well hidden under my bedside table, he managed to find my notebook of lists. Fortunately, there was nothing too incriminating in there. Except for this one thing.

He wobbled at the top of the stairs, waving my notebook around. He was drunk.

"'Tell George' what?"

I considered lying—I still had two days to go—and I had planned the reveal to be at the last moment. All the better to stop any resistance. But a sudden bravado seized me. *I am my own woman*, I told myself. *What would Elsie Knocker do?*

"I'm going to France, George. I'm going to help the war effort."

He was silent at first. I don't know what he had expected. *Tell George we are out of pie*, probably. *Tell George the hat stand fell.*

He did not expect momentous things from me.

He just went downstairs. I could see he didn't know how to react. Finally, he must have settled for the old, *oh, May is a dunce, what does she know?*

I shouldn't have followed him, but I suppose I was looking for a row or a resolution of some kind. Human nature, isn't it? The walls smelled of alcohol; come to that, the whole house probably did. George laughed to himself as he knocked back the whisky. *Silly May, always in la-la land.*

"What can *you* do to help?" he said, sneeringly.

"I'll do whatever I have to do," I said steadily.

"You're not going."

"I don't see why not."

"For one, you're useless, you don't even know the price of a pint of milk."

I blushed. Early in our relationship, he had caught me out, once, and he had never let me forget it.

"You're as much use as a nun in a brothel...I forbid you."

"You can't."

"I can. You're my wife."

"I thought a promise was just a scrap of paper to you, George." I still hadn't forgiven him for his enthusiasm to abandon Belgium to the lions.

He snorted. "What about the girls?"

Nice of him to show an interest after all these years.

"They *board*, George. Anyway, it's all arranged. I'll be home for the school breaks, Mrs. Crawford is determined to help and the Pilkingtons are always pleased to have them."

George stared into his drink. When he next looked up, he had dramatically changed tack. I don't know how he managed it, but tears were rolling down his cheeks. It did nothing but harden my resolve.

George fumbled for my hand.

"Is this all about the...my...lady-friend? Don't go overreacting." Translation—*lie down and let me trample over you.* "It's nothing."

Here's the thing: George didn't even realize how much he had hurt me, and if anything, that made it worse. It's *nothing*? *If you're going to throw away your marriage, at least make it meaningful.*

"A hospital in France?" Percy, who had been hunched over *Morning Light in St. Ives*, stood bolt upright. This canvas was the size of a small child. An "abstract," he called it. In my head I called it a "distract." "I didn't know you spoke French!"

I had been home-tutored by a Madame Durand before she had been trampled on by a horse, then a Mademoiselle Martin. Twice a week from when I was eight until I left with George. "Mais, oui," I said playfully, but Percy wasn't in the mood to be amused.

He rubbed his paint-streaked elbow. "It isn't because of Elsie, is it? Because she's always like that, she does stuff first and then thinks about it later. Only…" He paused. "I don't think she thinks about it later at all."

"It's not because of her," I said, offended he didn't think I was capable of doing something by myself. "I want to serve."

"There are plenty of hospitals in London though."

"Yes," I admitted. "But I'm itching to get in the thick of it—I think I can make a contribution."

I thought of Grandma Leonora. She had always said I took after her. So, if she was strong, so was I. She always made me feel capable. Unlike my mother, who was all doom and gloom.

Percy paused. "I've never doubted you've got hidden talents."

"Well, what's the point of having a talent that is hidden?"

Percy sighed. "What does old Georgie say about it?"

For a brief, crazy moment, I wished George would turn himself around, fall in love with me again, give up the booze, give up the women, give me some freedom and I could stay in this warm studio forever with Percy: *what was so bad about my life now that I had to dismantle every single piece of it?*

But the brief crazy moment passed. Europe was at war. I was more determined than ever.

I didn't want to go back to blackness any more. The melancholy had left me the instant I had signed on the dotted line: I was a woman on a mission.

"He doesn't have much choice," I said firmly.

"He's not a violent man, is he?"

I laughed. "Oh no, George is harmless."

"Are you sure?" Percy looked relieved.

I thought of George falling over, dropping glasses, ripping curtains, smashing plates. "He is the very definition of a buffoon."

My heart contracted unexpectedly. I *had* loved him once, I told myself, *don't be so cruel.*

Percy wanted me to look "properly" at *Morning Light in St. Ives.* It felt like I was taking a test that I hadn't studied for.

The painting had been blue, brown and gray but then, last-minute, Percy had elected to cast a great red smear down the middle. He mumbled that he had been influenced by the outbreak of war. He had started out with an image of something simple and pretty, yet it had ended up like this.

"It's not like anything I've seen before," I said truthfully.

He continued painting, while I read and knitted for a while. Neither of us was much in the mood for talking. I saw that I ought to be home. One more day and then I was off.

Percy cleaned his brushes thoroughly. The water swirled around, red. I thought of spilt blood. I thought how delighted everyone in France would be to see me. *A volunteer all the way from America!*

"Is this goodbye then?"

"I suppose…"

Although I knew Percy was very fond of me, I was still surprised that he was this downhearted. I supposed that at heart he was a lazy fellow, and he was probably wondering how he would find a new "friend" without having to go to the effort of leaving his studio.

"When will I see you again?"

"When the war's over? Or this summer? Whichever is soonest."

Percy walked me all the way down the many stairs, which he never usually did. The musty hall was full of old newspapers and letters to people who had long since moved on.

"This is absolutely what you want?"

I said that it was. I said I could think of very little else since I had decided. My melancholy had become a mere blot on the far horizon and, for the first time recently, I felt I might not be swept back toward it at any moment.

Percy nodded slowly. He had a little swoosh of black paint just under one ear and I leaned over to brush it off. He caught my hand and pressed it to his lips.

"Stay safe, May, you are..." He hesitated, searching for the right thing to say. "Very precious to me."

<u>Things to pack</u>

Uniform (including sixteen aprons and rubber-soled shoes—
black!).

Summer clothes, nothing too heavy.

Swimming costume (perhaps ambitious, but you never
know. Even volunteers must have some time off).

Shoes with heels (just in case there are parties), beautifully
polished! Thank you, Mrs. Crawford.

French/English dictionary.

Matchbox.

Towels.

Scissors.

Forceps?!

Needle.

A tin cup, knife and fork.

Nice pens/notebooks from Morleys.

Chocolate for journey.

Ditto apples (any variety).

Walt Whitman Poetry Collection.

CHAPTER NINE

It was after eleven and I was in bed. The street was quiet, apart from the occasional bark of a worried dog. Some people said that when the wind was blowing a certain way, you could hear the guns going off in France.

My suitcase was by the door. It looked respectable. It said: Voluntary Aid Detachment reporting for service. I had tried on my uniform several times and was pleased at how responsible I looked. The dress material was harsh and starchy but it had smooth lines and was unfussy. Underneath, I would be wearing the new, softer-style corsets and the regulation black stockings.

I pictured my matron falling at my rubber-soled feet. (*My* matron—how I liked that!) "Thank goodness you're here. We're desperate for reinforcements."

George knocked on the bedroom door but before I could say "Go away," in he trotted. He was carrying a circular silver tray, the one we used for "best." Two glasses wobbled on it and a bottle of red wine. I suspect this was the second bottle, because he was already "tipsy," as he'd call it. Placing the tray on my bedside table, he plumped himself down like he was staying a while. My poor blankets sank under his weight. He was wearing his red silk kimono, the one that only just managed to belt up over his paunch. He used to say: "If I hadn't married you, I would have married a little Chinese."

He was still wearing his shoes—perhaps a hint that he wasn't *entirely* confident that things would go his way.

"May, let's make a baby."

I might have been tempted once. Then he kicked off his shoes, lay down on my covers and added, "We might get a boy this time."

"Oh, get out my room, George."

"But we make such beautiful children, May, you can't deny it!"

It was true, but I was no longer a compliant sixteen-year-old. I could see further than my nose.

"We don't *want* more children, George."

"Yes, we do."

"Well, *I* certainly don't. You're making a fool of yourself. Accept it, I'm leaving."

"You can't." He responded incredulously. "How will it look?"

Ah, there was the rub. George didn't care about me, or what I did or didn't do: I was showing him up. I was making him look like a man who couldn't control his own wife.

"You promised to obey your husband, remember?" He moved closer to me on the bedspread.

"You promised to be faithful, remember?" I quipped back.

He threw his glass, but instead of smashing dramatically, as I imagined he intended, it rolled onto my bedspread. That stain would be a bugger to clear up.

"Can't you do anything right?" I hissed. George stood glaring at me for a moment, like some giant who's just discovered his golden-egg-laying goose has gone. Then he turned, sloping away, his head banging the side of the doorframe as he left. With any luck, that was really going to smart in the morning.

George *wasn't* a tennis player, but love meant nothing to him.

<u>How to get to Field Hospital 19</u>
<u>in Bray-sur-Somme in six easy steps</u>

Taxi to station (or ask Elizabeth?!)

Train

Another train

Ferry

Train

Car

You can do this!

CHAPTER TEN

The journey to the hospital in France wasn't half as painful as I had anticipated. I had mostly been worried about crossing the Channel—there was talk of torpedoes—but it was smooth sailing that day. I loved the sensation of being at sea. I drank copious amounts of coffee and smiled at everyone. *Here she comes*, I told myself, biting my lip with pleasure, *May Turner. American VAD, Brave War Nurse.* My shoulders felt gloriously light. (I shouldn't have drunk so much coffee though, I kept needing the loo.)

Elizabeth had driven me, in her inimitable way, to the station. She was wearing just her blouse and skirt, no winter coat, but insisted she was just dandy. It was all part of the process. We were quiet to begin with; it was as though everything that had to be said, had been said. (Actually, we had hardly spoken of it at all.)

The Tooting Bathing Lake would open soon, and Elizabeth had high hopes of other places she could swim, ones that were open for longer hours: Hampstead Ponds, Clapham Municipal Pool. The bad news was that expedient Mr. Albert had only gone and been conscripted, but Elizabeth had got over it quickly. She had devised herself a new training program, bizarrely involving more handstands and more somersaults for "strengthening." She was also trying to eat more to bulk herself up.

I told Elizabeth about my parting with George. As I retold the story, I realized I didn't feel sad about leaving, I just felt sad about how little affection we had for each other now. How could this have happened?

"You could have separated without going to France," she offered quietly, echoing Percy.

A funeral cortège was blocking our way. Elizabeth clumsily put her car in reverse and I felt my heart in my stomach as, at high speed, we sped backward down the high road. Once we reached the bottom of the street, the procession could pass. The horses went by horribly close to us and I found myself holding my breath to make myself smaller.

Behind it, a group of children were irreverently running with buckets, ready to pick up the manure. When they saw us they shouted, "Ladies, lady-driver!" I waved at them regally. (Sometimes, I did surprise myself.)

"I know," I continued, more cheerful now the horses had gone, "but this is more final. And I so want to do my bit. This is"—I used one of Mrs. Crawford's wonderful phrases—"killing two birds with one stone."

Elizabeth sighed, crunched into forward and careened ahead, narrowly missing a small boy. I prayed no one else would run out in front of her. Once she had driven over a man's foot and had the audacity to shout at *him* for it.

"I wish things were different."

"Me too," I said, nodding vehemently.

"For us, I mean."

I wasn't sure what she meant. I watched her profile as she drove. Elizabeth was such a fine-looking woman, with her striking red hair, and I was reminded that she had been a great friend to me. I felt a surge of gratitude to her for putting me together when I was so lonely. If it wasn't for her, I would probably still be crying in my gilded cage. I owed her, I knew that. And I knew, from bitter experience, that it is much harder to be the one left behind than the one leaving.

Even with my untrained eye, I could tell which regiments were going out for the first time and which were the regiments *returning* out. How could you tell? You just could. It wasn't that the men were older, but that they looked older somehow, more ragged, more gnarly, less keen...I touched the bun I had cajoled my hair into. Was I suddenly going to look older too?

The driver dropped off two engineers and then I was alone with him, as he took me onwards to Bray-sur-Somme (or Goodness-knows-where, as I had christened it). What would the matriarchs at the tennis club say to this? *"May Turner, alone in a car, with a man who wasn't her husband?"* But the driver had no qualms, or at least showed no signs of any. He explained that mine was a smaller field hospital along a long mud track. There was a bigger military hospital only one mile away and if necessary, we'd house their overflow. I liked the way he referred to the hospital as "yours."

He was trying to reassure me: "Yours is quiet."

As he drove, he pointed out other buildings and half-erected buildings and troops marching and men with spades and buckets.

"That's the Canadians," he said, then squinted. "The New Zealanders are somewhere here too," he said vaguely.

"Quite the world effort," I observed happily.

"Chinese laborers. There's Indians too, down that way."

"Indians!" I exclaimed. "Heavens! In London, they think it's just English people out here," I added, although by "London" and "they," I was thinking mostly of George. George sang "Rule, Britannia" as he shaved in the oval mirror that made his face look so much larger than it really was.

As soon as we arrived, it became apparent that the word "hospital" too was something of an exaggeration. The main building was a glorified shed. It wasn't that glorified either. I later found out that it used to house cattle. Outside, there was a selection of white tents. I thought of the Native American villages we'd learned about at school.

"What a noise," I said as I awkwardly got out the car.

"Not too bad," he said. "Between here and the front line there are twenty, thirty hospitals. It's a good starting point, not much going on in this part of the Somme."

"Oh?"

"Bit of a deadlock."

We walked on. "Mind the—" I nearly tripped. "Ropes."

Ropes, ropes everywhere. I gingerly made my way through. "You'll get used to it." He was in a hurry now. "Big push..."

"What's that?" I asked, thinking of Joy pushing over Leona in a squabble over Mrs. Crawford's teacakes.

"It's a decisive attack," he explained. "Everyone involved..."

"Here?" I asked, alarmed. It was so quiet; it didn't look like they were ready for supper, never mind a decisive attack.

"Over in Belgium." He smiled weakly. "Poor chaps. I'll leave you to it, Nurse Turner."

Nurse Turner, I thought. He was the first person to call me that. I could get used to it.

The person I was sharing a tent with had barely left a mark or a footprint. Both camp beds were beautifully made. In between them stood a small table and on that was a Bible and a small vase of posies. How thoughtful of someone to have got those for me. I hung my bathing costume on a hook on a pole. The heeled shoes for the weekend I slipped under my bed. The just-in-case party dress disappeared amid the sixteen aprons in one of two painfully slim wardrobes. I wouldn't mind if my roommate wanted to borrow any of it occasionally. I wasn't as spoiled as to imagine everyone had as nice clothes as I had. I made sure I was as tidy as I could be—Mrs. Crawford would have been impressed.

Unpacking didn't take long and I went out to look for someone to report to. There were fewer people around than I'd imagined there would be, until, some tents further along, I heard voices in what sounded like a meeting. I stood outside, swinging between nerves and excitement. The wind whipped up the tents, making a flapping noise. In the far distance, muffled explosions—and was that gunfire?

The people inside the tent were discussing a gramophone, oblivious to me. When there was a break in the conversation, I took a deep breath, ready to duck in and introduce myself, but I was beaten to it by someone saying: "Have you met the new VAD?"

"Not yet…"

"She's got a strong accent."

"So have you…" Someone else laughed. I smiled to myself. This was true. Although I wasn't great with English accents, I guessed this one was from the East End of London.

"It's foreign. American, I think."

"God help us," said an older woman's voice. I stopped smiling. My heart dropped. "I'm sharing with her."

"Matron, you should have put her in with the other volunteers," said a man.

"We can't have three in a tent, it's ridiculous. No, she'll be absolutely fine in with me."

There was a silence, which I couldn't help but feel was everyone disagreeing with her.

"She's attractive," said the younger voice. "In a posh kind of way."

Posh?

"She won't be for long…"

They took bets. They actually bet on how long I would say. No money changed hands, but still. The man gave me one month, which I thought was mean-spirited until the woman with the strong London accent chimed in with two weeks, then the older woman declared: "I don't give her one day. She'll have a bad night's sleep, complain about the mattresses, then disappear before dawn."

I made a mental note never, ever to complain about mattresses.

"I've seen it before. The volunteers like to be called Nurse"—I flushed—"but they won't stoop, they're not used to hard work."

There was more laughter. I couldn't hear what the man said.

"I bet she's brought a bathing costume with her," someone said and sniggered.

Oh God, I thought. My cheeks flamed, and I resolved to secretly dispose of my swimsuit before anyone saw it.

At the next lull in the conversation, I decided to interrupt. I didn't want to hear any more of their terrible assumptions, however accurate they might be. Chirpily, I called out "Knock, knock," and pushed through without waiting for a reply. I was just in time to see two younger women look at each other guiltily. Maybe they guessed I had heard. The man didn't even glance up; he was fiddling with the gramophone. The older woman stared me up and down. I felt like a fish about to be descaled. She had a severe expression that matched her voice.

She was Matron, so also my roommate. At thirty-eight, she was only ten years older than I was, I found out later, but on first impressions she seemed ancient. Physically, she was a little like Mrs. Crawford, with a shelf-like bosom and a stout behind. Her hair was swept back severely and streaked with gray on top. I thought she was one of those fierce types, slow to smile but when she did it was worth it. However, she didn't smile.

When I asked her name, she shook her head at me. I shook mine back. I was beginning to feel like I did at the tennis club, about to get whacked in the stomach by a stray ball.

"Why do you ask?" Her head was tilted to one side.

"I . . . since, we're sharing a room, I mean, tent—"

"You will call me Matron at all times."

"Of course, Matron." It was tempting to curtsy. Out of the corner of my eye, I noticed the man had stopped his forensic examination of the gramophone and was smirking at the girls. He winked at me.

Matron walked me back to our tent, which was a shame because I would have liked to get to know the others. I followed her meekly, doing a good job of avoiding the ropes.

"There is a line here." She pointed down the middle of the tent, from one end to the other. I looked, I squinted, I prevaricated, then finally I said, "I can't see anything, Matron."

She rolled her eyes. "It's an invisible line, but WE.DO.NOT. CROSS.THE.LINE."

"We do not cross the line," I repeated.

"Think of it like the equator," said Kitty helpfully, grinning, in the canteen later when I told her what had happened. I had a feeling I would like Kitty. It wasn't just her name; she *was* catlike. She was small, fair, with dark eyes and dark eyelashes. She was slow to speak, careful, as if she didn't want to say the wrong words.

"I think she might be mad."

She giggled, spooning broth into a bowl. "DO NOT CROSS MATRON."

I sat down with my tray opposite the other girl, Bonnie. With her wide features and eyes set far apart, Bonnie reminded me of a whale. Leona, who used to collect pictures of deep-sea monsters, would have been delighted. Bonnie was tall—about a foot taller than me—and broader even than Elizabeth. She had long muscular legs and a healthy head of hair. Despite her stature, there was something charmingly childlike about her, and although I shouldn't have, I privately labeled Kitty the clever one and Bonnie the not so clever one. Kitty and Bonnie had trained from the moment war broke out and had been out here for three months.

"At first, the real nurses didn't like us volunteers—" Bonnie started.

"It's not that they didn't *like* us, they didn't trust us," corrected Kitty.

"I suppose three months' training sounded paltry compared to what they had."

"Exactly, so they used to keep us segregated, but we showed them we work as hard as anyone and they accepted us eventually."

"Not everyone…" Bonnie leaned forward to say. "It's all a bit topsy-turvy here."

"I like topsy-turvy," I said, thinking of Mrs. Crawford and how sometimes you might be forgiven for thinking she was the boss of the house.

"Yes," said Bonnie. "It's the way Gordon likes it too. He's not keen on divisions or hierarchies."

"Gordon?"

"Doctor Collins." She smiled. "He's a law unto himself."

Cases at Field Hospital 19, Bray-sur-Somme

Heartbreak/Homesickness
Trench foot
Pneumonia
Typhoid
Sepsis
Bullet wounds
Shrapnel injury

CHAPTER ELEVEN

On my very first morning in France, I had to give a man a bed-bath. *What an initiation*, I wrote to Elizabeth, knowing this was the kind of story that delighted her. In my VAD guidebook, it had advised "avoid the front area," but there was no avoiding it. My victim didn't seem too embarrassed once I got going with the sponge, so I wasn't either. I had told myself to think of Grandma Leonora to get me through any awkwardness, but I found I didn't need to. He was in some pain—he had some minor shrapnel injuries in his arm and back—but he didn't cry out. I admired his dignity and told him so.

He said, "After the things I've seen, preserving my dignity is way down the list of my priorities."

Matron, who had been overseeing the process from the other side of the room, said, "Do the others now, please," so I assumed it met with her satisfaction too.

It was mostly cleaning, making beds. Sheets needed wringing, needed working in the mangle, not just plonked into hot water, thank you, Nurse Turner. Preparing patients for surgery or looking after them when they came out. Bringing bedpans, removing bedpans and writing letters home for them. Jugs of water bedside. Checking temperatures, looking out for fevers, infections, oozing wounds. If there was anything too heavy, I could call the French orderlies, who were mostly elderly former soldiers who didn't speak English, or the English orderlies and stretcher-bearers, who were mostly volunteers from England. If there was anything more onerous, I was instructed to fetch a real nurse. It was hard to tell who was who at first. There were some cleaners but not enough, as I later found out, and there were cooks, kitchen and administrative staff too. Some seemed experienced, others less so. Everyone seemed to muck in.

We were divided into two teams, and we each worked long days: 7 a.m. to 10 p.m. (with a break around 2 p.m. for three hours) or the night shift from 10 p.m. to 7 a.m. I enjoyed the stillness of the night shift but I struggled to sleep the next day if the tent was bleached with sunlight. Katherine, Lucille, Sybil and Beryl were the nurses and volunteers on the other shifts. Occasionally, my team would whine about them: who had forgotten to put the blankets in the right place or who had left the poor fella in bed three without water. I'm sure they complained about us too, but it was understood that we were never to make a thing of it, and most transitions were smooth. They were all sympathetic, hard-working women, and occasionally, when our matron was being particularly heartless, I wished I was on their team instead. Their matron was a perpetually concerned-looking woman whose motto seemed to be "Happy nurse equals a happy patient," whereas our matron's motto might have been "A nurse's job is never finished."

We didn't talk about our patients at mealtimes. It was another of those unspoken rules, meant, I supposed, to protect us. Instead, we talked about light, irrelevant things: revues we had seen, places we had visited or wanted to see. There was a farm not far from us belonging to a lovely man, Farmer Norest, who, unlike many, was staying put. His chickens laid only occasionally. We spent hours discussing this. I thought the noise of the guns must put them off, but Gordon loved to expand on his theory that they were pacifist chickens. Conscientious-objector hens.

"Conchies?" said Matron, disgusted. "Then they should be shot."

She had a mean streak the size of France.

*

Kitty didn't write soldiers' letters; she preferred bedpans or carting off soiled dressings! That was fine by me—I loved writing. Sometimes, if we had time and if the patients were so inclined, I would steer them toward romance. When I admitted this to Doctor Collins, or Gordon as he let us call him off-shift, he burst into laughter.

"Think about it, May. One day our poor lady gets a letter saying, *I miss you and the flowers in your hair*, the next day Bonnie writes, and she gets *the tea is flavorless and the porridge is even worse*. She won't know where she is."

I laughed but it didn't stop me from pushing the men to a sweeter style. After all, it was what I would have liked to receive.

Gordon admitted himself that he should not have fraternized with us lowly female volunteers but he said wearily, "I was at all-boys school for years and years—I've had enough of all that…"

I had only been in France for approximately two and a half weeks when I was called into the canteen for a meeting before my seven o'clock shift. It had been another bad night, with lots of noises of explosions, whistling shells and screeching vehicles. The air that morning was thick with dust. There were lots of people in there who I recognized and many I didn't. Some looked like they had dressed in a hurry. I could tell something bad was happening by the hushed whispers. I joined Kitty and Bonnie on a bench and waited—it felt like we were in church.

Gordon spoke quickly: "I'm afraid I have something disturbing to report. A young VAD was shelled in her tent last night, not one mile far from here."

He told us her name was Elle Harcourt, she was nineteen and she had only been out here a few weeks herself. We might have come out on the same transport. The short length of her service shouldn't have made the news worse, but somehow it did. She hadn't even had her chance to make her contribution. Her family wouldn't even have the satisfaction of knowing that she had done her bit.

Gordon continued. I could tell he didn't like what he was having to say.

"It's very sad news," he said, "but it also spells out to us how vulnerable we are here. We are in a dangerous position and these are dangerous times. We do our utmost to keep you all secure, but don't ever be deluded into thinking we are safe, so anyone who wants to go, please let me know today. I don't mean to go home necessarily, I mean we can look for a new placement for you—a hospital further back along the line maybe, where there is less chance of shelling."

"Will you be staying here, Doctor Collins?" Bonnie called out, and someone from the other team said, "And you, Matron?"

Those in charge looked at each other.

"Yes, the hospital will be staying here…" He paused. "But please think about it."

Bonnie, Kitty and all us VADs and nurses nodded at each other. Sybil defiantly put out her hand and we all shook it. "We're none of us skivers here," she called out. "We're staying." Gordon looked pained but said that he was glad.

I swallowed hard. I had known in my head it was dangerous but now my heart felt it too. As I lined up with the others to leave the tent, Gordon put his hand on my shoulder and said, "You can change your mind any time, Nurse Turner," and I flushed that he had singled me out. Was it because I was new or did he think I was weak?

Later that day, Matron and Kitty left with daffodils pinned to their coats for the funeral of Elle Harcourt. RIP.

Other than work, and my free time spent in the canteen, it was the mail that gave shape to my days those first few months in France in 1915 (spring term, as I thought of it).

Elizabeth sent funny postcards with tales from committees.

"I am spending too much time with my mother," she wrote. "This is *never* a good idea."

She wrote about driving across the country to find somewhere that would admit women for her early-morning swims—she was up to a grueling one hundred lengths now. She wrote about her Belgian students. She was compassionate about their situation, although she became exasperated with some of the slower learners. "But don't worry, May, I am very tolerant to their faces." She wrote that she was growing sick of porridge and occasionally, she wrote about the exploits of Tiggy and Winkle. Delia, the black sheep/cat, featured only rarely.

From Percy I heard nothing, which was a relief—I had half-expected frantic love notes to arrive at camp—although maybe it was just a question of him not having my address.

Joy's letters came infrequently, as they had done in England—and each was a long, laborious account of the escapades of other girls. Joy positioned herself as the aloof, disapproving friend. I adored hearing from her and would read her letters over and over again, imagining her writing them. I slept with them under my pillow. Leona's letters, like her, were sunny and sweet and would often be accompanied by tiny gifts: A pressed flower. A chocolate thumbprint. A wavy golden hair. "Kisses for the best mother in the world," that sort of thing. George did not write, fortunately, but he did forward mail from America, even though I'd expressly asked him not to. It was always horrible to read my mother's methodical character assassinations of me. I shouldn't have read them, but I couldn't help myself.

Elsie wrote occasionally, but her cards were so infuriatingly slim they made Leona's missives look like *The Iliad*. I sometimes wondered if they were worth the stamp.

When it's busy you will long for tedium! or *Keep your head up, May. Better than mooching around Percy's apartment, waiting for life to happen.*

I wrote cheerful, upbeat letters to my girls, Elizabeth and Elsie. I didn't feel I had the right to grumble—complaints wouldn't be well received by anyone. It's not that I had many complaints as such (besides the concrete mattress), only small grumbles, which I saved for my diary. Or sometimes for Kitty.

"Who knew there'd be so much cleaning?"

"What on earth did you expect, May?"

"I don't know, I just imagined something a bit more..."

"Glamorous?" laughed Kitty, her hair scraped back, her nursing cap askew. Her apron ripped where she'd caught it on a scalpel. "I can't imagine anything *less* glamorous."

Soldiers' favorite songs

"Keep the Home Fires Burning"
"Pack Up Your Troubles in Your Old Kit Bag"
"If You Were the Only Girl in the World"
"It's a Long Way to Tipperary"

CHAPTER TWELVE

On days off, Kitty, Bonnie and I cadged a lift to one of the towns back from the front line: Pretty Cappy, Chuignolles, Suzanne, Proyart, or our nearest town of Bray-sur-Somme. It was quite the thrill to discover that, in France, shops were open on Sundays. On the other hand, we became quite blasé about the beautiful fountains. We would sit on their cool stone edges and after a while, we'd barely comment on the spitting cherubs or the lions pouring water from wide-open mouths that surrounded us.

Kitty and Bonnie missed their sandwiches and cups of tea, but I delighted in coffee and French pastries, with their tiny currants or surprising cream centers. I had never loved English tea. (The foodstuff I missed most was American doughnuts, which were something I hadn't eaten in years but now unexpectedly found myself craving.)

We had become firm friends. Bonnie and Kitty were closer—they had known each other a long time—but they never let me feel left out. I didn't tell them about George or the girls, which was fine at first. However, as time went on and I knew the ins and outs of Kitty's sister's appendix and Bonnie's father's failing business, I felt more acutely that I was hiding something from them and that made me feel both dishonest and guilty.

One time, a street seller called us over to show us his pretty little hand mirrors edged with seashells that he was selling out of a battered suitcase. I knew Leona and Joy would love them. The street seller delighted in practicing his English on us. He kept up a long stream of compliments: "She is pretty, she is charming, and you"—he said to me—"you are the beautiful one, hey?" He liked charming Bonnie best. Men usually did. "Shall we marry? You and I?"

We admired the mirrors and finally I succumbed, picking out two of them.

"Who are they for, May?" asked Kitty.

I looked up, suddenly remembering that no one knew about my family in England. I remembered Elsie's instructions, and the interviewing panel: *any commitments?*

"No, none whatsoever."

"My friend's daughters," I said, quickly. "Tiggy and..." I hesitated. This was ridiculous. "Delia."

"Tiggy?" echoed Bonnie.

"It's a nickname," I said quickly. "Her real name is...is..." I cast around for a clue and saw a street sign: Rue du Clemence.

"Clementine..."

"How on earth did that get shortened to Tiggy?" pondered Kitty.

It was one thing to pretend there was no George—it was *enjoyable* to pretend there was no George—but quite another to pretend there were no girls. It felt horrible, like I was tempting fate.

Doctor Collins—Gordon—shared his tent with Doctor Rafferty from the other team. They were rarely in the tent at the same time. Sometimes, after a long shift, Gordon would tell us we could unwind in his tent with him. I liked the word "unwind": it reminded me of Leona's musical box. Wind it up and the little ballerina would twirl to "Twinkle, Twinkle, Little Star." Wind it up, wind it down. *How I wonder what you are.*

Gordon's tent was very different from Matron's and mine. Not only was there the gramophone, but also rugs, throws, cushions and pictures from all over the world. Gordon had been a doctor in Africa and India. He would happily tell anyone that conditions here were worse than anywhere he'd been before. The doctors also shared a small desk, most of which was obscured by a large typewriter. I had watched Gordon type once and it was very labored, surprisingly for one so deft with a needle or tweezers. I would have liked a poke at those keys—the things I could write on that!

Gordon knew that I liked poetry. One evening, he told us a verse a patient had written for his sweetheart.

Roses are red,
Violets are blue,
War is stupid,
And so are the leaders.

"I like it," I said, laughing.

"It doesn't even rhyme," said Gordon, chuckling.

"I bet May could do better," Bonnie said unexpectedly. "You're always writing, aren't you, May?"

Kitty looked at me, then quickly looked away. I wondered if I'd upset her in some way.

"I only write lists and my diary…" I responded. They were all looking at me. "And yes, a little poetry sometimes, but it isn't very good."

"I bet it is," said Bonnie.

"You're very talented, May," said Kitty finally.

"I think so too," said Gordon.

They have no idea, I thought, but at the same time, I was delighted they'd formed such a high opinion of me and I resolved not to disappoint them.

Tasks of a nurse/volunteer

Bed-baths

Dressings

Bedpans

Take temperatures

Make beds

Write letters

Paint on a smile and cheer everybody up, whether it's with a song, a letter or a joke

CHAPTER THIRTEEN

For the first few weeks, I cried at the end of my shifts into my flaccid pillow (I had to be silent because Matron would have no sympathy). I wasn't habituated to seeing men injured, I wasn't accustomed to suffering. After a while, though, I stopped crying and instead went straight to sleep. I don't know how exactly this change came about, but it did. I was doing my best on shift, and I realized it did neither me nor the men nor my team any favors to dwell on the soldiers' tragedies. To be in the best state I could be was far more important than that I wept at their hardships.

In general, spirits were surprisingly high. We knew things were terrible in Belgium, particularly in Ypres, where Elsie was, and we knew there were other areas in France—not very far from here—that were getting hammered, but in our corner by the winding River Somme, strange to say, we were relatively quiet. Our hospital was running well. Maybe once or twice a week, we would receive a telegram from along the front line: In-coming two men: leg and abdominal injury, and we would make the appropriate preparations.

At each changeover we smiled at our counterparts, handed over our notes and wished them a good day or good night. I don't think I was imagining it: there *was* a sense that we were winning the war. I was sure I would be home long before the school vacation. Soldiers smiled shyly at us as they marched past us toward the front. We could see their different regiments. It seemed they were pouring in from all over the world. How could the Germans possibly compete? So many volunteers had responded to Kitchener's call that the Army had been overwhelmed by the numbers. I thought back to that moment in Percy's apartment as he said, *maybe... I would need to know more.*

It isn't so bad, Percy. I thought to myself. *You should try it.*

One day a new nurse arrived for the other team, replacing Sybil, who for all her bravado about staying the course had now gone back to Wiltshire to take care of her elderly father. I almost pitied the new arrival for catching only the tail end of the war. *She's missed all the action,* I thought. *She might as well turn around and go straight back home.*

I looked over and saw blonde bun, round spectacles. It was someone I recognized very slightly from the Tooting Bathing Lake. Elizabeth had once told her she was using her legs wrongly. (Elizabeth was a great one for correcting other people's legs.) I introduced myself. She jumped up so fast that her chair fell to the ground. She shook my hand vigorously, exclaiming, "It's you, isn't it, from the swimming club?!"

Everyone in the canteen was very pleased for us. Her name was Millicent Sumner and, like me, she was a volunteer. Afterward, I thought, *but I hardly know her at all*; all I knew was that she was a proficient diver and wore a disarmingly old-fashioned bathing suit— but it made me feel at home. It was lovely having someone from London here. In a way that was confusing, though. I had so yearned to escape my life in London, yet now I was away, I felt increasingly nostalgic about it too.

I heard rumors that Nurse Katherine, from the other team, had fallen in love with one of our patients. And then, at changeover one evening, I spied her mooning over the bug-eyed man with a nasty ankle injury in bed four.

"Saying goodbye is such sweet sorrow," she said, misquoting Shakespeare. Shaking her head sadly, she left the ward.

"You'll be back in tomorrow, won't you?" I said. She gave me a sharp look.

The fella was a charmer, with smooth dark skin and feminine eyebrows. Being prostrate in bed, in his unflattering hospital blues, hadn't daunted his confidence an iota. He had the charm of a snake-oil seller.

Although it was another of the unspoken or invisible rules, Matron strongly disapproved of romance on the wards, but she wasn't leading Sister Katherine's team so it wasn't her call. Millicent also seemed to disapprove. Whenever I saw her, she rolled her eyes so hard, she would nearly drop whatever it was she was holding.

Next day, Katherine cooed to me, "Love changes everything."

"I can imagine," I said.

She leaned over and kissed the fella on the forehead. He closed his eyes theatrically and then opened one eye, then the other, checking I'd seen.

"You should try it, May," she pursued.

I shook my head. Love was overrated. The last thing I needed was complications. I wondered if George missed me. I found I didn't care much if he did or didn't—I was dreading seeing him again.

"Telegram from Morlancourt," said Matron. She always recited the names of the towns. They were meaningless to me; I rarely knew if they were located near or far. "Two men, possible head injuries. Prepare beds, Nurse Turner."

You didn't have to ask Kitty for a thermometer or a bandage; she anticipated things. We were good at caring, all of us, in both teams, but our Kitty was exceptional. Gordon said, "If she were a man…" His voice trailed away guiltily. I knew what he was going to say: *If she were a man, she might have trained to be a doctor.* As it was, those doors were closed to her. She was a woman and not a wealthy one at that. While most VADs were self-supporting, Kitty and Bonnie's expenses were paid for by their local church group.

Matron had asked Kitty and me to dole out the medicine in convalescence, which was normal, but I was trapped with a poor patient trying and failing to pee into a bottle, so I told Kitty, "Go ahead, get started without me."

When I next looked up, I saw Kitty had stopped still.

"What's the matter?"

Kitty hesitated. It was as though she'd been frozen on the spot. She stared at the rectangular medicine packet, then turned it over and over. I wondered if it was one of the damp shipments we'd had to throw away the week before.

"I'll just get Bonnie."

"Leave Bonnie."

Bonnie had been looking pasty for the last few days and Matron had sent her for a rare lie-down. The last thing we needed was Bonnie giving everyone the flu. "Just give out the pills, Kitty."

"I can't make it out," Kitty said in a quiet voice.

"Is it in French?"

"No..."

Then what is the problem? "Oh, bring it here then..."

Kitty, usually so sprightly, didn't move a muscle, so I walked over and took the box from her. I peered at the writing. No, it definitely wasn't wet. The instructions were perfectly clear. In English. The font was none too small either.

I looked up at Kitty. She was looking at me pleadingly.

"Oh, no, Kitty," I said incredulously. "Really?"

Bonnie had been covering for Kitty all this time. Everything was so chaotic when they enlisted, and everyone had liked how hard she had worked, but now she was well and truly caught out. I don't know how they had ever thought they'd get away with it.

Kitty broke down in tears. I was too shocked to comfort her properly.

"It's fine," I said, but it was anything but. I couldn't bear to think of her returning home, defeated. I knew she didn't want to go back to east London either.

"Are you going to tell?"

I thought of the letters she refused to write, the prescriptions she refused to put in the notebook. I thought of the tiny name-bands each patient wore. Somehow I hadn't realized this before, but they had been written only by me or Bonnie. How the hell had Kitty managed until now?

"We'll sort something out," I said.

"Jesus Christ!" Gordon said. "Not Kitty!"

"Uh-huh," I said flatly. I had told Gordon not because he oversaw us—he didn't—but because it was better telling him than Matron. Matron would come down hard. He knew that too.

"What *are* we going to do?"

Gordon chewed his pipe pensively. Gordon would be easy to fall in love with, if one were able to fall in love. Which I was not.

"I've never seen anyone so sweet with the patients. You can't learn that. You can't teach that . . . She's got a wonderful bedside manner."

"But what about reading?"

"Keep her clear of medicines, obviously," Gordon continued.

"But reading, Gordon, *reading!*"

"Oh, I'll teach her." He shrugged as if all were simple. "She's *here* now, what would be the point of sending her back?"

"But what about Matron? She won't . . ." I paused. "Stand for it."

"Give us a month," he said. And I thought, *but we may be home in a month anyway*. "If she's making no progress by then, I'll tell Matron myself."

I nodded. I couldn't think of this place without darling Kitty.

"Let's face it, she's a clever little thing if she's got this far," he added.

From then on, Gordon and Kitty studied together most evenings. I lent them my Walt Whitman poetry collection and they got books sent over from England. Matron didn't like it—she liked to spend time with Gordon after a shift, wrapping up the details. I privately imagined he was relieved to get away from her and her contraventions.

As time went on, I teased Kitty about Gordon, but she wouldn't say a word, she just shrugged non-committal. I thought maybe Kitty was playing it cool so Bonnie didn't feel like a third wheel, which was reasonable. One time, though, I asked Bonnie what she thought about the two of them, and she said, "Be a waste if she did."

Eh? I thought. Gordon was the most handsome and, more importantly, the most emotionally intelligent man out here. *How could that be a waste?*

Usually, you could take one week's leave for three months' service, so to get two weeks, you'd have to have done at least six months. But although I was still one week short, Gordon said, "Take two weeks this summer, May. You've worked your socks off."

Although delighted, I was also wary. I didn't want to be singled out for special treatment. I didn't want to be different here. I had had a lifetime of being the odd one out and it had done me no favors.

There was something very leveling about being on the front. Yes, there was a strict hierarchy—however topsy-turvy we were at our hospital, we still knew our place—and yes, there were all the different nationalities. But when a man was presenting in front of you with a chest wound, you were all trying to assist, whether doctor or cleaner, man or woman, American or German, rich or poor, illiterate or not. We were all on the same side when it came to giving of our best to help. Whenever a telegram came, we all snapped into action: wind us up and we twirl to the music.

The sentiment of "The Rich Man at His Castle, the Poor Man at His Gate," George's favorite hymn, was shattering around us. Good rich men and women and good poor men and women were engaged in this outrageous war together.

"Is this a test, Gordon?" I asked. "Do you expect me not to come back?"

He laughed. "May! Don't be so paranoid. Aren't you desperate to get away from us?"

I wasn't, actually. Although I was desperate to see my girls, this was the first place I had been where I felt I truly belonged.

CHAPTER FOURTEEN

I arrived home feeling some trepidation, but Mrs. Crawford greeted me warmly with the news I hadn't dared hope for: George was away! Hallelujah! I'd known Mrs. Crawford ever since I'd been in London and had never hugged her, but I hugged her then and she hugged me back. She didn't know exactly where George was or how long he'd be away for, but who could care less? What a glorious start to the holidays!

Mrs. Crawford wanted to bring up some food to the dining room for me, but I asked to have it downstairs instead. She looked askance at this irregularity, but complied. In the kitchen, the fire was blazing, the kettle was on the stove and it made a far cozier place than upstairs, which, after all, was all done out to George's (questionable) taste.

After we had been chatting for some time, I screwed up my courage.

"Mrs. Crawford, I hope you don't mind me asking, but has there been a woman here?"

I don't know what I expected. Would we try again if he said he had been missing me all this time? I didn't think so.

She wiped her hands on her apron, giving herself time.

"A woman? No…" She looked at me shiftily, then in a lower voice said: "*Women*, more like."

"Overnight?" My voice was shaking a little. I shouldn't have been disappointed at this news, but I was.

"I don't do mornings any more, Mrs. Turner, I'm at the post office now—the war effort…"

"But?"

"But…"

We looked at each other. The kettle began to whistle on the stove.

"They stayed over?"

"I think so. The sheets, you see, and the glasses, and the breakfast plates, and the…I think he pays them."

"He'd *have* to pay them…"

"But not recently," she said suddenly, like that would make me feel better. "His gout has come back."

Strangely enough, that *did* make me feel better.

The next morning, I went up to Leamington. There were my darling girls, trotting down the marble steps. As soon as they saw me, they pulled up their long skirts and ran, throwing themselves around me. I was nearly toppled by the wonderful weight of them.

"You're back!"

"Why are you crying, Mummy?"

"Happy tears, darling."

On the train, Leona told me she was far too old for *The Wind in the Willows* now. Joy had started reading *Journey to the Center of the Earth*, but it was too much about boys so she had borrowed *Jane Eyre*, while Leona was attempting Mrs. Gaskell's *North and South*. They argued over whether that was too hard for her or not. Leona insisted she could manage, but Joy and I saw her skipping pages and winked at each other.

Once the girls were home, it was business as usual. Which unfortunately for me meant: tennis club.

My parasol wouldn't stay up. I fiddled with it for a while, then gave up; it seemed pointless. Three days ago I had been comforting a man who had lost a leg in a sniper attack, now I was worried about a little bit of sun. I couldn't have been further away from the field hospital in the Somme. It wasn't just the distance, somehow; it was everything. It suddenly felt unbelievable that I had ever been out there, as though my life with Matron, Kitty and Bonnie and the others might have been nothing more than a strange dream.

Members of the club were complaining about their staff as usual.

"Her fiancé died, which was sad, of course it was, but I had to let her go."

"I know, you can't have them sobbing instead of cleaning the windows."

"Exactly, how long are you supposed to give them to grieve? I have a household to run."

Joy was playing against a strong blonde girl who seemed all brute force. I was pleased to see my daughter holding her own. Leona and her group of friends were sat on the grass, drinking iced lemonade and telling jokes. I heard Leona suggest "I Spy" and one of the others sighed and said, "You always want to play that."

Listening to the thwack of the ball on the racquets and the shouts of the players, looking at the gleaming white of the shorts and dresses, made such a contrast to the sights and smells of the hospital that I found it overwhelming. I found myself closing my eyes, shutting them out and then, just as I was drifting off to sleep, a shadow fell over me. The Framptons' eldest son was standing square at my front; I don't know why but I thought he was going to pick an argument. I knew his parents weren't fond of me, and I had seen him shout at umpires plenty, but in fact he said quietly, "Mrs. Turner? So sorry to bother you. Father says you are working in a hospital in France."

"That's right."

"Might I ask, how is it out there?" he asked softly.

I explained to him that I was based in a quiet area, and that we didn't see much action, but what we did see could be difficult. We talked together for some time and I was grateful for his interest. The disconnect I had been feeling lessened. He was far politer than his parents and I thought what a shame it was that he and not they who was going off to fight and maybe (no, *probably*) to suffer.

I couldn't wait to meet Elizabeth at the Tooting Bathing Lake on Thursday morning. I didn't see her as I arrived, so I entered the lake in my usual slow, self-conscious way. This was as warm as the water would get, yet still it made my ribs tingle and took my breath away. I did my inelegant splashy head-out-of-water crawl, but I was enjoying myself. The pool was a fantastic blue, sparkling with little diamonds. And then, when I paused to catch my breath, I saw Elizabeth: she was dawdling at the side in such a way as to give the impression she was reluctant to get in, but then suddenly she dived in, smooth as anything, straight as a knitting needle. It reminded me of the unexpectedly tidy way Gordon could do surgery. Then she proceeded to do her breaststroke, which was both elegant and immensely powerful. Unlike me, a fish out of water, reluctant to wet my hair, Elizabeth always looked part of the scenery.

"Elizabeth," I shouted excitedly, "over here!"

She raised a hand at me, then continued across the pool. It was a chilly reception. You wouldn't know we corresponded with each other twice, sometimes three times a week, or even that we knew each other very well. I felt disappointed—I had so been looking forward to seeing her. It seemed it was not reciprocated. But finally, Elizabeth swam over to me and when she was closer, I could see she was smiling, really smiling, with her tiny teeth on show. Relief ran through me.

"Sorry," she said, "I *have* to do it, or I'll never do it."

This didn't make sense, but I was too delighted to pursue it.

"New swim-hat?"

She shook her head. "The flowers fell off."

"It suits you."

Her head smooth and egg-like, she looked athletic and serious.

"How is everything here?"

"Same."

This wasn't what I'd heard.

"What about the shortages of fuel and food?"

She nodded fiercely. "Playing havoc with my training. And of course, Tiggy and Winkle have suffered."

"How about Delia?"

She wrinkled up her nose, shrugged. "Delia still gets the best of everything."

The insects buzzed in the following silence. Then the whistle blew.

Even though no one was waiting, we had to get out because it was the end of the women's swim. (There was nothing topsy-turvy about the Tooting Bathing Lake.)

I wasn't sure whether I was invited back to tea, but as Elizabeth swept past me after changing, she called: "Why so slow, May?" and my spirits soared. I loved Elizabeth's house almost as much as I hated my own.

It was so exciting being with my friend on the streets of London that I didn't mind her driving half so much as I used to. It was nothing compared to traveling the crater-pitted roads in France anyway. Away from the bathing lake, Elizabeth was back to her usual self, ranting animatedly about the suffragettes' lack of action—*too delicate*—the government's incompetence, even the *pathetic* people at the refugee school. I grinned. It sounded like my brilliant Elizabeth was busy making enemies wherever she went.

Back in her living room, we sipped tea and I told her some of the things I had seen in the hospital. I was careful though; I didn't want to turn the poor boys into sob stories or even funny anecdotes. And I certainly didn't want her to think I was doing anything special, because I wasn't. I needn't have worried really, because Elizabeth was never that sympathetic about anything except the cats.

"And George?"

"George is George." I shrugged. She inhaled sharply.

"You're divorcing?" Now it was my turn to inhale.

"I imagine we will, it's just a matter of…" I didn't know what it was a matter of. I had never met a divorced person in my life although I had read about them in the newspapers and they all seemed somewhat of a type. A wealthy type, I supposed. I hated to think it would disadvantage the girls at school. How would the Pilkingtons—usually so kind and forgiving—react? It wasn't like I didn't already have a pretty hefty black mark against my name and a tag: *American*. Now it would be *American divorcée*. I knew exactly what people like the Framptons would think about that.

"A matter of what?" Elizabeth urged me on.

"Of paperwork," I finished, although I wasn't entirely sure it was. Anyway, Elizabeth nodded, satisfied with her interrogation. I asked for a cigarette, but she apologized—she had given up. Her new coach had decided they were a no-no.

"In that case," she asked, returning to the question of my relationships, "have you met anyone out in France?" She peered at me from under lowered lashes.

"Dear God!" I laughed. "Give me a chance!"

"A handsome doctor, *peut-être*?"

I thought of Gordon. He was handsome but the more I got to know him, the more I realized he was not my kind of handsome.

"I would have written you if I had, you *know* that," I said playfully.

"Would you?"

"I'm going to be a spinster like you anyway," I continued.

She gave a secretive smile to herself. "That's the ticket, Nurse Turner."

Elizabeth seemed happy with her lot, and still very focused on her Channel swim. "The first woman to do it," she repeated as though it were already accomplished. "What an accolade!" She did cartwheels across the room. The cats must have been used to it for they didn't move a muscle. I thought back to George's declaration that it wouldn't affect people like us. I supposed the war hadn't affected Elizabeth; she wouldn't let it.

I didn't visit Percy. His goodbye kiss on the back of my hand had felt too passionate. Meeting him might suggest that I had rethought the question of a dalliance or give him false hope. It was a shame because he had been there for me when I had felt so out of sorts and I *did* like his company. I hoped he didn't think too badly of me.

I had been home for just over a week when George came back. I saw his great shoes and his lightweight coat hanging in the hall, and fear congealed in the pit of my stomach. So much for my light-hearted discussion of divorce with Elizabeth. I dreaded the thought of bringing up any subject with him, let alone something as terrible as that. The girls were receiving group tennis coaching that morning from a dynamic young woman from Ireland, so they were out of the way. I stayed up in my room for some time. Opening the window, a fly buzzed in like it had been waiting a long time for the chance. I tried to read the newspapers, I tried to write a letter to Kitty—reading practice for her—but could not concentrate on anything. George was in the house. What would he do once he heard I was home too?

Providentially, that morning he left me unmolested. I found myself dreaming that our paths mightn't cross all week but when I went down for lunch, he was already at the table. He reminded me of a waxwork figure at Madame Tussauds. The kind of gray-suited, gray-skinned politician you can't place even after you have read their name-card. I took my place docilely at the other end of the table. A whole person could have fit top to toe between us. I imagined we would eat in excruciating silence, like we had done at so many mealtimes before, but he asked me how the weather had been, how my journey was. He even said I looked "well."

"And our soldiers?" George was asking my opinion on the war! This *was* a first.

He was still drinking heavily. I watched as he poured glass after glass of wine and his face grew waxier. He asked if I would take a stroll outside—he had some ideas for the garden but wanted to see what I thought. (Another first.)

I felt discombobulated; I was all fired up and nowhere to go. Our yard was small—a city garden—yet pretty. Now, though, I saw it hadn't been looked after. The grass came up to our knees, the ivy fairly muzzled the trees and the hedges had raggedy tops. Nevertheless, there was a watering can on the steps. Mrs. Crawford's, perhaps? She probably couldn't bear to see the garden getting too bad. It was a bright blue-sky day, and as we walked down the path, my spirits began to rise. George was a reasonable man. We *could* do this split amicably. We *would*. After all, we had the girls in common. We had to have their best interests at heart.

"The pier business is busy," George said, which was probably the most he had said about his employment since our courtship.

"How interesting," I said. "I had supposed it would be quieter."

I admired the rose bushes as George told me about his plans for the yard.

"We should grow vegetables here," he said when we were out of sight of the house, at the far-back fence.

"That sounds good. What were you thinking?"

"Potatoes, carrots, onions."

"I'm not sure the soil here is the best for growing—" I started.

George laughed bitterly. "You're an expert, now?"

I stiffened at some of the old George coming back. *I have to be careful*, I told myself. Some pears from the neighbor's tree had fallen onto our lawn, so I picked them up and put them in a stray basket—they were too maggoty to eat.

When I went back to his side, he snaked his arm around my shoulder.

"It's the gout. If it weren't for that, and my age of course, I'd probably have got the Victoria Cross by now. Everyone is fighting for the country. Even you are doing your bit!"

I tried to ignore the incredulous way he said, "even you."

He continued, "Yet here I am, like a cripple."

"You're doing your best, George."

"That's kind." He gripped my shoulder and turned me toward him so that we were only inches from each other's faces.

"I'm glad you're back, May."

He clutched me, burying my face in his chest. I froze. *He thought I was back for good!* How could this have happened? When had I given him the slightest indication that this is where we were? My mouth felt dry. *Oh God!* George leaned down, his face loomed over mine, then he proceeded to kiss me. I pulled my face back, but he had caught me. *Oof, his tobacco breath!* His tongue prodded at my lips.

"No, George."

"I've been an idiot, but you know me better than anyone, May. At heart, I'm a good man. And I love you more than…more than any of the others. We're made for each other."

The wind blew between the leaves. Over his shoulders, I could just about see the roses. I thought of the fancy women who passed through this house. Everyone knew about them, they probably laughed about them. This wasn't the life for me.

I said softly, "I'm going back to France, George."

"No."

"As long as the war is on I must continue doing my duty."

He backed off now. He kicked the watering can. It somersaulted across the lawn before clattering onto its side on the stones. It sounded like gunfire.

"If you go, May, you're never coming back here again."

"Don't be daft," I said coolly. "This is *my* house too." For good measure, I added with my arms outstretched, "*And* my garden."

"We'll see about that," he grunted, stalking off toward the street.

<u>Books for Kitty</u>

Peter Pan
War of the Worlds
Anne of Green Gables
A Midsummer Night's Dream
Wuthering Heights

CHAPTER FIFTEEN

I was just walking from my tent to take my first shift since my return from London when Katherine ran past me, sobbing loudly. I caught up with Millicent, who was dragging her feet along behind her.

I asked worriedly, "What on earth is the matter with Katherine?"

Millicent didn't look too troubled. She adjusted her spectacles. "It appears Katherine's sweetheart has a sweetheart...who is not Katherine."

"Oh dear."

She made a face. "In other news, we've lost a boy to pneumonia."

At tea, Matron dealt out some rock cakes that had been sent from England. "And that is another reason you should avoid romantic entanglements in service," she said. She examined her cake, then, with eyes closed, put it in her mouth. She struggled valiantly to chew it. Little crumbs spilled everywhere. "Not bad," she said, her cheeks purple with effort.

Kitty and I declined cake and smirked at each other. We managed to hold off laughing until Matron had left.

"Did you miss us?" asked Kitty, one eyebrow raised.

"Some of you," I said, smiling.

The worry never stopped. Even when I was tending to a man with trench foot, even when I was preparing for the arrival of "three from Mametz, head, neck and back injuries," my heart was also half at home. I was confident the girls were doing well at school but I missed them dreadfully. And I was concerned about George too, although in a very different way. Had I been right to leave him? *Other* people put up with husbands like him. Other people didn't mind the drink, the affairs. Was separating from him really the best answer?

I asked myself constantly, should I even be here? It wasn't like I had to do my service, not like the poor conscripted boys. And it wasn't like I had training and skills that made me indispensable, not like Gordon, Matron or even Kitty. Us volunteer nurses were two a penny, I knew that. But I liked it out here. I liked putting on my uniform, my apron, my cap, and being part of my team. I liked doing my best alongside the others. I liked that feeling that I had lightened the load or enhanced someone's day. How much better it was to be here, doing my utmost, rather than twiddling my thumbs back home. The war mightn't have finished this summer, but I was certain we would be done by Christmas 1915.

That autumn term, I was often in convalescence for nights. There had always been six beds in the tent, then one day, six more beds appeared. Bonnie and I got used to squeezing past one another. And now the beds were closer, the men could sometimes reach out to each other and light a cigarette, pour some water, or offer a kind word. If a patient died during the day, the orderlies would sort it out, but at night there was just Bonnie and me to deal with it. The second night after I got back from England, we lost one boy and it was terrible. He managed to say a few words near the end and I wrote them down. He said he was glad to have done his bit but he hadn't expected to die so young. "Not to worry," he said stoically.

Bonnie was always a remarkable cleaner, but one week in September she surpassed herself: she made everything in the ward spotless. The sheets, the pillows; she scrubbed the bed frames, she wrestled to clean the legs of the beds. She was a woman on a sterilizing mission.

"Scrape and scratch, scrabble and scrooge," I said to her, but Bonnie didn't get the *Wind in the Willows* reference. She stared at me bad-humoredly. Her hands had grown red-raw and gnarly. Still, I was surprised when she took to her tent right after dinner, apologizing that she needed a rest. That wasn't like Bonnie. The next day, she was still unwell and was lying prone when I popped in at break. I was wondering if she would have to go back to England. I didn't want that at all because she was a kind-hearted soul and she worked brilliantly with everyone.

After my shift ended, I went to Bonnie's tent with some dinner for her on a tray. It was tinned meat and crackers. Bonnie loved her tinned meat. Whereas some of us turned up our noses at the watery, fatty slop that was sent over from England, she insisted it was far superior to what she was used to eating.

"Don't come in!" she called, even though it was too late; I was in. "I'm not hungry."

She was kneeling on her bed, her head ducked down low. I thought maybe she was looking for something in the sheets. She clutched her pillow to her and groaned, very lightly, but for a long time.

"What is it, love?"

She didn't look feverish or jaundiced or any of the other ailments. I wondered if she was constipated.

"Get Kitty," she hissed. And this was unlike her too. Bonnie was usually scrupulously polite. And suddenly, I had a crazy, terrible inkling.

Kitty was busy with her lessons with Gordon in his tent, sitting among the cushions and incense. Kitty adored *Peter Pan* and when I told her I had read it to my girls, she had been full of questions: *Where is Mrs. Darling? Where did the Lost Boys live before?* They both looked up when I ran in, but before I could say anything more than a breathless, "Kitty, I think, if you wouldn't mind..." a screech came from the neighboring tent. They must have heard it in the men's hospital tent; they probably heard it in no-man's-land—they probably heard it over the other side. I pictured a German general demanding of his men, *wat iz zat?*

It was Matron who reacted first. Matron, usually so slow she made a tortoise look hasty, sped past us, her dumpy legs gathering pace toward Bonnie's tent, shouting.

"Towels, water and, dear God, find something to wrap it in."

Joy had been born in my bedroom at home. George had volunteered the services of his mother. Perhaps it was the prospect of that nasty woman sneering at my nether regions that got the baby out.

The doctor said I had had it easy because I was so young. It *wasn't* easy. I knew others had been cruel about me too, gossiping that I'd spent the full nine months of my pregnancy resting. I *had* spent a lot of time in bed, but that's because I was so miserable, I could hardly leave the room. Joy had eventually slipped out of me. When she was placed in my arms, I was sobbing so hard, I could barely look at her.

George wanted to call her Araminta after his aunt. *Over my dead body, George.*

What *had* I been thinking, having children with someone like George? He had been useless with the babies, of course. For him, having a baby meant wetting the poor soul's head. It meant more alcohol and cigars than you could shake a fist at. His church friends all came round, spending hours in the drawing room. (He still had friends then; he hadn't yet put them off with the scary amounts of liquor he would consume, and it was before the advances he made on their wives and daughters were public knowledge.)

He wanted to resume marital relations only three weeks after Joy was born (and only ten days after Leona). "I'm still bleeding, George."

"Quick wash will see to that," he insisted. "A man has needs."

He didn't understand why babies (and their mothers) cry.

"A thimble of whisky will help it sleep."

It, George?

"That's not a thimble, George, take the bottle away from her face…now!"

And when Leona crawled into his office once, dipping her finger into the ink and trailed it along the blotter, the desk, the bureau—"I'll get my cane."

"She's a baby!"

"Never did me any harm."

The jury's out on that one, George.

We got Bonnie up, we helped her lie down, but nothing was happening. Other than her pain, that is. The poor girl was obviously hurting everywhere.

"It feels like I'm being kicked from the inside out."

"You *are*, dear, that's the baby…"

Her back hurt—"Oh, how it aches!"—even down to her toes: "I've got pins and needles there now!"

Matron made the bed afresh, then told her to get on it.

"I don't want to lie down," she protested but Matron wasn't having any of it.

"You'll do as you're told, young lady."

"Let her sit upright," I tentatively suggested. "Gravity might help."

Matron glared at me. "And how many babies have you delivered?"

I couldn't reply. Noticing my distress, Kitty said soothingly, "We need whatever help we can get."

Gordon took us to the side. "How about morphine? The Germans use it in childbirth, they call it twilight sleep."

"Well, if the *Germans* use it…" sneered Matron.

It was Kitty who spoke against it. "How will we get the baby out if she's asleep?"

Bonnie moaned. I don't know if it was at the idea of the baby or the prospect of sleep.

"At least she won't be in more pain," I argued, watching as Kitty wiped Bonnie's forehead again. Poor Bonnie, I had never seen her in such a state. Was this what I had done? With Mrs. Crawford cringing by the door with a jug of cold water and washcloths? I could hardly remember.

"She'll have to cope with the pain," Matron decided firmly. "It's on its way."

Kitty was looking at me. "May, are you okay? May?"

I couldn't do it. Too many horrible memories were bubbling up. I ran out of Bonnie's tent, went over to the communal stove and, quite unfairly, made myself a three-teaspoon cup of coffee with a heap of sugar.

Fifteen minutes later, I heard Gordon calling: it was over. I approached nervously.

"What is it?" I sounded like I had something stuck in my throat.

"It's a baby!" he cried incredulously as though he didn't quite believe it himself.

"A baby!" I still couldn't believe it. *Bonnie had a baby!* "Is it a boy or a girl?"

"I forgot to look," he said sheepishly. I heard laughter from inside the tent, then Kitty's voice: "It's a boy, Doctor Collins!"

Bracing myself, I went in. Matron was gathering up the sheets, Kitty was sitting on the bed next to Bonnie and they were both clearly enamored with this tiny wee thing wrapped in a blanket. He was gorgeous, a proper heartbreaker.

"Meet Freddie," Kitty said with a big smile. Bonnie glanced up at me shyly, her eyes full of tears.

"What a beautiful name," I said.

"Is that after his pa?" Matron asked sharply.

Bonnie and Kitty looked at each other and laughed at some private joke.

Bonnie shrugged. "I just like the name."

Later, Bonnie fell asleep with her mouth open, her hair askew and her nightie disheveled. Even so, she still looked triumphant in that post-natal *I did it, I really did it* way. I remembered that euphoria, mixed with fear, the myriad of conflicting emotions.

The next day, with Bonnie's permission, I took the bundled-up Freddie into the convalescence tent and as soon as I did, Monty, a cheerful young lad from Hull, shouted out:

"Not more cleaning! Sister Turner..."

Walking carefully over to him, I held out the precious parcel. "No, look what I've got here!"

Monty couldn't believe his eyes. *A baby. Here in bloody France.* Tears came to his eyes and as I watched him, tears came to mine.

"Is it real?"

"Yes, he is very real."

"Is he yours?"

"Oh no, not mine, he's Bonnie—Nurse Matlock's."

"Well, I thought she was just fat!" he said. I blushed. There was an awful lot going on out here, but how we all hadn't noticed Bonnie's increasing girth was beyond me.

Freddie had gripped Monty's hand in that way babies do and wouldn't let go. His unfocused eyes peered around.

"I can't get my finger..." said Monty in a happy panic. "I've never seen anything so small. Or so lovely."

After that, everyone wanted a hold. James from Kent, with half his face blown off, was a natural: "I've got three at home," he explained as he got out of bed for the first time since his operation. He stood in the middle of the ward, rocking Freddie from side to side. He crooned to him, soft, sweet words, telling him where in the world he was and what day it was, and how the war would be over very soon so not to worry, little fella, for he would grow up in peace. I was on standby in case Freddie whimpered, but James calmed that little boy (and all of us watching) perfectly.

Lenny wanted a cuddle too. Lenny was eighteen, an angry young man from London. He didn't want to be here, didn't want to be anywhere. Skinny and dark, he couldn't get comfortable, wouldn't rest. He didn't like chatting; usually the only one of us he could be bothered to talk to was Kitty, but now he was happy to talk to me.

"Has he got a bottle? Let me give him the bottle."

"He's not on the bottle," I told him.

"Don't fight over him," Matron said protectively, but no one was fighting, everyone was happy to take turns. "You have a go," James offered.

And Lenny did. I knew Matron, like me, was itching to say *support his neck*, but we let him work it out and he did.

Lenny smiled broadly. "My girl's having a baby," he told us. "In spring. Can't wait."

Only Charles tried to resist Freddie's charms. No, he said firmly, he couldn't hold him. His right arm was all bust up and his left arm wasn't much better. But I knew he could do it. I got him comfortable with his pillow perfectly positioned behind him and heaved him upright, half-grumbling, half-eager to have a try. I pushed aside his doubts and placed darling Freddie in his arms.

"There, you've got him."

"I have, haven't I?" he said, his lip wobbling. "I've got him."

Bonnie slept, then slept some more. Kitty made sure she was by her side when she woke and unsurprisingly, a few more tears were shed. I was worried about Bonnie but Kitty was keeping an eye on her. I was also concerned about how they would find a replacement at this short notice. While we were by no means busy in Bray-sur-Somme, we needed a functioning team. And I loved my team just as we were;

I didn't want more changes. The next day, as we sat drinking coffee in Gordon's tent, Kitty told us her solution: Bonnie would take Freddie to England, then she'd return. She'd only be gone one week.

"How?"

"Her mother will take on the baby."

I thought of my own mother, far too busy extolling Christian virtues in churches across Chicago to take on a child.

"That's good of her."

"Why wouldn't she?" said Kitty, blowing into the coffee—force of habit, because the coffee was long chilled. "She's got ten of her own."

"Ten!"

"This one will hardly make a difference."

Freddie let out a cry, perhaps anticipating his large family.

Gordon picked him up. Freddie had wisps of black hair and surprisingly fierce eyebrows. He had pouty lips and a button nose. His cheeks were smooth and shiny. I suspected the father, whoever he was, must be quite the looker.

"Uncle Gordy's going to miss you, pipsqueak."

"We all will…"

I wrote a note to Elsie, smiling to myself:

When you told me to come out to the continent to nurse, never did I imagine I would find myself looking after a tiny baby!

Typical Elsie, she scribbled just three words back:

You lucky bugger!

I held little Freddie for one last time, choking back tears as Bonnie fetched her coat and trunk.

"Blimey!" she said, when she saw the shiny car that had come to collect her.

"Only the best for you and Freddie," said Gordon. "That's precious cargo, that is."

Kitty lent me her handkerchief to cry into. I was just wiping my eyes when Matron looked over at me.

"This is not an excuse to skive, Nurse Turner. Back to convalescence with you."

"I know, Matron." I responded sullenly. I was fed up with her scolding. The way she could suck happiness out of every occasion was quite a skill.

<u>Where to visit in Paris!!</u>

Eiffel Tower—Closed?

The Louvre—Closed?

Montmartre—Gordon's recommendation. Not sure.

Tuileries—Maybe closed?

The Seine—Oh yes!

Ooh la la!

CHAPTER SIXTEEN

Most people fled Paris when the Germans invaded the first time. Even after the Germans were repelled, many hadn't returned. Paris was a reduced, diminished city in 1915 but it was still Paris. You can't squash Paris—it's like one of the beastly cockroaches that Gordon chases around the tents with a broom, it will survive anything (only, of course, Paris is nothing like a cockroach at all).

Bonnie had just come back from leaving Freddie in England. She was resilient, but nevertheless, Kitty and I were determined to look after her and we had decided a day trip to Paris was the very thing to cheer her (and us) up.

We set off early in the morning, cadging a lift with a British ambulance crew going that way. Paris was approximately two hours south. The buildings were so magnificent, the bridges so beautiful, the fountains so spectacular, the sidewalks so wide ("The people are so small," marveled Bonnie). Some theaters were still open and ticket touts bunched around us, trying to sell us their shows. Lots of pharmacies and *vin et liquor* shops were open. Women in bonnets strolled around, trying to find special things to spend money on. There were more taxis here than in London. The Parisian taxis had famously transported men to the front line. Now some of the drivers shouted out to us, "Nurses, nurses *anglaises!*"

"How can they tell we're English?" asked Bonnie, mystified.

"They're not blind!" Kitty laughed. It was so jolly to be out, the three of us, on an adventure.

One time, I shouted back, "*Je suis Américaine.*" The man clapped his hands excitedly, then clasped his hands to his chest in excitement. "*Mon Dieu*, the Americans are here finally!"

He was being sarcastic. I decided to carry on letting them think I was English.

We took a boat trip down the River Seine. Admiring the curve into the islands, we didn't feel the wind blowing in from the north. We admired the white brickwork, the boulevards, the view of the bridges from underneath. The Métro stations with their beautiful squiggly writing. There was no escaping the great groups of soldiers: "*Bonjour*, English? English?" they'd shout when they heard us speak. Blue jackets, red caps and red trousers. Bonnie preferred the English uniforms, but Kitty and I were quite taken with the colorful French.

"The women here look so fresh," said Kitty, half-admiring, half-envious. We couldn't work out what it was, but their blouses seemed a more flattering fit and their fluted skirts were longer and altogether swishier somehow.

There were children in sailor outfits. I chuckled to myself—Joy and Leona would have had a field day. They had given up "child-ish" clothes as soon as they were allowed. And there were couples, smooching, far more openly than they did back in London, gazing into each other's eyes, stroking each other's faces.

"I wish I had someone to stroke my face," said Bonnie wistfully.

Kitty raised her eyebrows at me. "I'm saying nothing."

We found a sweet café with velvet curtains, where they were serving omelets and coffees. Inside were lots of French soldiers and their girlfriends (I don't know if they were proper girlfriends, because I heard one say, "What was your name again?"). Bonnie admitted that, on second thoughts, their uniforms were quite splendid, weren't they?

The owner said she had some fine cheese. I think Bonnie was expecting Cheddar or something, but when the owner proudly came back, her face fell. Of course, it was Brie.

"Smells like sailors' socks," Bonnie muttered, but she cleared her plate, and when the owner asked if she'd enjoyed it, Bonnie said it was like nothing she'd ever tasted before. The owner joyfully kissed us on both cheeks. Bonnie turned back to us, whispered, "Wha-at? Told her the truth, didn't I?"

There were many wounded soldiers in Montmartre, a reminder—as if we needed it—that it was not just in or around our hospital; the entire country was suffering terribly. It was hard to make your way through the wheelchairs and walking sticks but still, what a vibrant, colorful place it was. It felt like all forms of life were here. Someone struck up a tune on the accordion. Like a thousand artists, writers and poets before me, I couldn't resist thinking: *I am going to have to capture this.*

Bonnie wanted to have her portrait done, so we circled the artists, looking for one who appealed to her. She considered a few and then chose the elderly man whose pencil drawings were mostly of famous people. I didn't recognize many of them—most were French leaders, I think—but anyway, Bonnie decided she liked the work of this artist the best. They agreed a price and she sat down on his stool while he brought his paper to life.

Being among the artists in their colorful waistcoats and tilted berets made me think of Percy Milhouse. I had no idea what he was doing now. If it wasn't for him, I wouldn't have met Elsie Knocker, and if it wasn't for Elsie, I wouldn't be here, so I was grateful to him.

Kitty and I found a wrought-iron bench to perch on while we waited. Kitty sat still as though it was her posing for a picture. She was wearing very nice gloves that showed off her small hands. Women hung out wet clothes on the balconies above us. Two people were shouting about train times. Nearby, a soldier embraced a woman.

"I don't think I'm capable of love," I said suddenly, staring at the pair as they kissed. "All that has gone, emptied out." The thought of George stroking my face made me feel suddenly nauseous.

Kitty nodded sympathetically. She never said very much about herself. We got up and walked around the artists again.

"How about you?" I asked.

"How about me, what?" Kitty paused at a pencil drawing of a house wrapped in ivy. "This is pretty."

"Have you ever been in love?" This was my chance to get her to admit something about Gordon.

Just as Kitty was about to reveal all, Bonnie flew over to us, her cape flying, her grin broad. She unraveled her picture excitedly.

"What do you think?"

It looked nothing like her. Her moon-face had been slimmed down, her eyes placed closer together and her teeth had been straightened. At the bottom, there was a big scribble, the artist's name presumably, and the date: 29 October 1915.

I didn't know what to say. "Freddie will love it," I decided finally. Kitty joined in, without meeting my eye. "Oh, what a wonderful gift for Freddie!"

That evening, back at the camp, Bonnie couldn't wait to show everyone her portrait. She had no qualms: this was what the artist saw and that was that. In the canteen, amid the fug of vegetable stew, she untied her paper lovingly. She wouldn't let anyone else touch it. "Mind yer grubby mitts," she called as she held it in front of our noses.

"Who is that supposed to be?" Gordon asked before adding, "I'm joking, Bonnie, it's the very image of you!"

Matron sniffed. "How much did *that* set you back?"

*

It rained that night and the ground outside turned into mud. I listened to the raindrops pattering the cloth roof of our tent and the distant muffled sound of explosions. Matron, the woman I perhaps liked least in the whole of France, was snoring next to me. George used to snore, so I was used to it, but Matron's snores were more sporadic. That wasn't a good thing. Sometimes, when they stopped, I'd think she was dead. Then would come a cacophony of uneven breaths.

I thought about the poor men on our wards and on the streets of Paris: illness and sadness and injuries all over the place. And lice and lice bites and disinfectant. And the way they lived with fear. Then boredom. Then fear again. What a thing to ask of our fellow beings. I thought about my work: Bedpans. Dressings. Cleaning wounds. The taking and noting of temperatures. I knew I wasn't much more than a glorified housemaid. And I was constantly damp. Everything smelled damp. My boots were too tight. My socks never seemed to dry. And I was exhausted. We yawned from morning to night.

We now had our tea without sugar, without cream. Bread was rationed. Farmer Norest's chickens were still refusing to lay. We called the food "basic," but it was worse than that. And, even though the meals were diabolical, it still made me indignant to see that Matron seemed to get more than anyone else. And the mattresses: God help me, but they really were horrendous. Was there any point in them at all?

I spotted a cockroach hanging from the tent pole. It scuttled off, thank goodness—the last thing I wanted was that beast running over my face. As I lay there, damp, hungry, exhausted, I thought, *I have never been so content in my life.* I had escaped. I had escaped twice: my parents and now George. This was liberation, this was freedom. Out there was a repulsive war, yet there were beneficiaries and I was one of them.

Purpose, that's what it was: I was making a contribution, stamping my place. For the first time in my life, *I* mattered, I belonged. It was the best feeling in the world.

Best ways to begin a love letter for boys to send to their sweethearts back home

My darling

My dear

My sweetheart

My love

My wife

My beloved

CHAPTER SEVENTEEN

Two men were waiting at the entrance to my ward. Deep in conversation, they strode in, like they were attending a dinner party at an ambassador's house. They were talking in French although only one, the taller one, had a native French speaker's fluency. The other—short and tubby—I was almost certain was English.

"Have you met Elsie Knocker?" I overheard the one who was most likely English say to the other. "What a looker! My God, if only all the nurses looked like her, I'd make a blighty wound myself— He-llooo!" he said hastily as he noticed me.

"I'm sorry we can't provide more lookers for you, sir," I said brightly.

"He told me the nurses couldn't speak French!" he responded, grinning widely and pointing to his friend. He didn't seem at all embarrassed to be caught out.

"Some of us can," I snapped but at the same time, I smiled at him. It was hard not to. I turned to the tall friend. His uniform was crisp and smart and he smelled faintly of gasoline.

This one, the tall one, the one most probably a native French speaker, looked thoroughly awkward. His pale skin flushed from his collar upward. "I'm so sorry, we shouldn't have assumed," he said. The reddening of his cheeks did nothing to detract from his handsomeness. He had strong, symmetrical features and his eyes were intelligent and soft. "Please accept my apology." His English was perfect too, and I quickly realized he probably wasn't French or English but both. "And mine," said Short and Tubby quickly.

"We're here to take Sergeant Radcliffe to the ambulance train."

I was surprised. "Didn't they tell you? Our people will transport..."

But Tall and Slender raised his hand as though making a point in class. "We wanted to make sure he was comfortable." He looked at Short and Tubby. "It's the least we could do."

Sergeant Radcliffe was his driver. He had been shot and was now blinded.

"Three young daughters back home to support," murmured Tall and Slender quietly. He paused, searching for the right words. "A terrible shame."

As far as I was concerned, it was unusual for the higher orders to acknowledge not only the physical degradations their men were suffering but the financial indignities they were about to face too. I decided I liked this man—he wasn't *just* an extremely handsome face.

He introduced himself. He was Major Louis Spears and, like a fool, I thought to myself, *Louis, I've always liked the name Louis! That's a name fit for a king.*

"And I'm Winston Churchill," said Short and Tubby. "First Lord of the Admiralty."

"And I'm May Turner," I said. "I'm, er, a VAD nurse." It was fortunate I got it right, because in my head, ridiculously, I was trying out the sound of a brand-new name: *May Spears, May Antonia Spears.*

With great care, Major Spears—Louis—lifted the pillow and helped to raise poor Sergeant Radcliffe up. He'd been in for over a month and I had been moved by his positive attitude. Only one time, when he told me that he could only see darkness, did his voice crack. The rest of the time, he managed to smile, eat with great appetite and tease us nurses. "I keep going over in my head—which is worse, to lose a leg or an eye?" he once asked me.

"I don't know. Which is worse?"

"Both eyes."

Now they were all three laughing at something. I watched Louis and felt something I hadn't felt for a long time—since I was sixteen, maybe—that the world was full of possibilities. Then Gordon arrived and introduced himself and there was discussion and more laughter.

Gordon took them off to show them some of our new equipment. He was excited about the progress being made in blood transfusion and always keen to talk about it with anyone willing to listen. These men were the right audience. Winston was loudly asking questions; he was one of those curious souls, clearly hungry to find out everything. Louis was more measured. I saw him examine Gordon's box of tricks and then study his face. They all looked very serious suddenly, then Winston said something else and they all nodded in agreement. I could have watched them for a long time, but Matron returned and told me that we were nearly out of name-tags for the patients: "Run along, Nurse Turner," she scolded. "Make up some new ones, quickly."

I wanted to say something to Louis before he left. I felt—it sounds ridiculous—that we had what Gordon might call "a *connection*." Kitty might have said it was "a chemical reaction." She would go into the science, the biology or the hormones. Bonnie might say, "*Come off it, May, you just fancy him rotten.*"

I didn't dare to think what Matron would say.

We still had Sergeant Radcliffe to see to. I got the wheelchair and we lifted him into it, then rolled him out toward the road. Then Winston and Louis unceremoniously put him in the car. It was good to see their teamwork. Although Sergeant Radcliffe couldn't see a thing, he was still cracking jokes. "You always take me away from all the lovely girls..."

Louis and Winston thanked me, even though there was no need; I had done no more than my duty.

"Well," I said, like a star-struck fool, "you know where I am."

Winston laughed. "I try to avoid hospitals as much as I can."

"Except where the nurses look like Elsie Knocker?"

"Ah well…what's a rule without an exception?" He smiled at me, and I think if we had been in a different place—at a dinner party at an ambassador's house, perhaps—he might have pinched my cheek. "You're not so bad yourself, Nurse Turner."

Silly to be so flattered but I was.

"Anyway, it wasn't you I was talking to!" I grinned. He laughed—we both knew that.

Louis blushed, then, for some reason, saluted me. I found myself saluting back and then looking straight into his clear, bright eyes. He took my breath away.

"You're very close to the front line here," he said. "Doesn't it worry you?"

"It does worry me," I admitted. I thought of Nurse Elle Harcourt. "But I won't let it stop me."

He chewed his lip thoughtfully.

"You're braver than I."

Before I could deny it, he said, "I'm out to the Near East tonight. Eight weeks."

"Oh," I said regretfully. "Oh. Good luck."

"Thank you. Perhaps I might see you when I'm back?"

"Perhaps," I repeated, but because this sounded a little flat, I added, "definitely" and straight away regretted it because that sounded too keen.

I couldn't concentrate at all that afternoon. How ridiculous of me. What kind of catch was I, a separated woman with two children? I was as weighed down as any stretcher-bearer. I could not have looked more dowdy. And yet, those blue eyes alighting on mine transported me to a place of hope.

I started a wash of clothes that were already clean. Sterilizing scissors, knives and strange instruments. More name-tags. *You're braver than I,* he had said.

Kitty sidled over to me. "What *is* going on with you today, May? You're away with the fairies."

Eight weeks? I thought to myself. *Eight weeks is nothing!*

"Eggs for tea," I said. "Didn't you hear? Farmer Norest's chickens laid yesterday."

Kitty squinted at me playfully. "Hmmm...I'm watching you, May Turner."

CHAPTER EIGHTEEN

The war wasn't over by Christmas 1915. Instead, I had one week's leave. I had offered to accompany some patients back, but was told I wasn't needed, so from the moment I left our hospital I was free to dream without interruption about being reunited with my girls. I had scheduled every hour of the winter break; nothing had been left to chance. My action girls liked to be busy and, I suppose, I was afraid of what might come up if they weren't.

Gordon, Kitty and Matron were staying behind. Bonnie had already left to see her Freddie and to show her family her "Paris picture."

"No one can say I'm not sophisticated," she said proudly as she waved us goodbye, portrait in hand, in case anyone wanted a last admire.

"No one dare say it," laughed Gordon, patting her head affectionately.

Kitty hugged me goodbye, whispering: "We don't want another Somme baby, May!"

"That's the very last thing on my mind."

Kitty hugged me again.

"Shame Matron is staying," I ventured daringly. "She's determined to chaperone you and Gordon, isn't she?"

Kitty looked at me, her wide eyes wider than ever. "How do you mean?"

"Nothing!" I said. *Two could play at this game.*

*

On the boat was a young nurse who seemed to be struggling with her patients so, although I didn't know her, I went over to see if I could assist. She was in charge of six, I think, and some didn't look too healthy. Up close, she appeared even younger and her features were freckly and fresh. She briskly turned down my offers of assistance. One of her patients told me she worked in Belgium, and I was going to ask where exactly she was based, but she was so stony-faced that I didn't dare. I could only assume that, like so many people, she had recently had some bad news. And so I put her out of my mind. I would be with my daughters soon, I should concentrate on that.

There were fewer taxis at Waterloo than I had imagined there would be, another thing they were running out of in London, perhaps. Still, I had only to wait thirty minutes or so and it wasn't too cold for December. Changing into my civilian clothes had felt like shedding an old skin. I was looking forward to taking a bath—the showers at the hospital weren't too terrible but a bath in privacy would be a treat.

On the common, children were play-fighting the Bosch. It reminded me of how we used to pretend to be cowboys, back in Chicago. It seemed to me that children everywhere enjoyed a good battle with sticks. (If only they just used sticks on the Western Front...)

I was nearly home when I thought the day-to-day conversations I have with Kitty, Bonnie and Gordon would not be appropriate here. Back in civilization, I had to put on a veneer of decorum. It was not that our talk was crude; it was just that we were straightforward out of necessity. I suppose there was also a darkness in our conversations, a black humor that probably wouldn't go down too well in London, even if it was now nearly 1916. (How time had flown!)

By the time I reached the house, I was aching to see my daughters. The longing almost felt like a physical pain. Through the window the lights were golden and welcoming, but when I rang the doorbell, no one came. I rapped firmly. Finally, I heard unhurried footsteps in the hall: Mrs. Crawford was coming at last. I couldn't wait to sink into her arms, to tell her all my news. She had been proud of me, after all—but the door swung open and to my shock, I saw it wasn't Mrs. Crawford. It was a much older woman with white hair and tiny yellow teeth like corn on the cob. She looked even less pleased to see me than I was to see her.

"Much obliged," she said, trying to push the door shut. I had put my boot there though. She smelled of cleaning fluid. I thought longingly of the bath upstairs. Not long now.

"Who are you?"

This displeased her further.

"What's it to you?"

"I . . ." I thought I'd try a different tack. "Is Mrs. Crawford available?"

"Gone." I hadn't heard a word of this and I didn't see how it was possible—Mrs. Crawford was as much a fixture of the house as the Silver Birch or the hat stand was.

"Gone? Gone where?"

"Doing her bit, I 'spect," scowled the interloper, while trying to push the door shut again.

I told the woman who I was. Her mouth fell open; she wouldn't meet my eyes.

"Oh! No! But . . . you're . . . you're not allowed in, Mrs. Turner."

I was so bewildered, I almost burst out laughing. "What do you mean?"

"Mr. Turner says he don't want you here no more." She looked behind her, then leaned forward to whisper, "He says if you turn up, to call the police."

"Nonsense," I said firmly, but I was shocked. "This is my home." She shrugged.

"Where are my girls?" I asked quietly.

She hesitated. I fixed my eyes on her, squinting, until she answered. "Still at school. He's not getting them 'til tomorrow."

"But they finished *today*, they are supposed to be here now."

"He was too poorly to go. Under the circumstances, the head-mistress agreed to put them up for one extra night."

"Poorly? You mean he was drunk?"

She shook her head at me meaningfully.

"They'll definitely be here tomorrow? You see, I *wrote* George. He knows I'm coming."

She paused. "Not until tomorrow night."

"Why?"

"Master won't be up until after midday. He likes to sleep in." I sighed. *For goodness' sake.* "But you mustn't come, Mrs. Turner. He won't let you see them."

I needed to get to the school as quickly as I could, this much was clear. I had to get there before George. There were no motorized taxis available, so I had to swallow my fears and take a horse-drawn carriage back to the station. I hated every neigh and whinny that beast made, but I did it. Once at the station, though, I found my intrepidness had not paid off and luck was not on my side—there were no trains until late the following morning.

I had eighteen hours. I didn't know what to do. And then I knew. Elizabeth—of course. Oh, to be in Elizabeth's comfortable living room, with Tiggy, Winkle and even Delia. Oh, to sink my teeth into her sweet macaroons! This time I walked, or rather, galloped, to my favorite address in London, brimming with renewed hope: Elizabeth would sort this out. Nothing was beyond my brilliant friend.

It was about ten when I arrived, sweating despite the northerly wind. When the front door swung open and Elizabeth was stood before me, dazzled and beautiful, I could have hugged her. But my hopes were soon dashed. Elizabeth's pale skin reddened; her pupils were huge. She looked shocked, but worse than that, she seemed frightened.

"May! Why didn't you tell me you were coming back?"

"Aren't you pleased to see me?"

"I'm...I'm..." Finally, Elizabeth managed a smile. Those lovely, happy wrinkles stood in the corners of her eyes. "Always thrilled to see you, of course, but"—she lowered her voice—"it is *very* late."

I explained my problem in as few words as possible: "I need to get to Leamington before George does."

Elizabeth wrung her hands.

"I can't just drop everything for you, May. I have work, I have to train."

"In the middle of winter? Near Christmas?" I asked incredulously.

"Yes, I have a strict regime now."

"But it's my girls, Elizabeth. I don't know what to do." There were sounds of movement from upstairs. I slapped my hand over my mouth. "I'm so sorry, have I woken your mother?"

Elizabeth turned so pale that she looked ghostlier than ever. But I quickly realized it wasn't her mother coming down the stairs, it was a woman about our own age. She was wearing long white bloomers and a tight off-white corset. Her hair was loose, straight as a rod; it fell just to her fleshy shoulders. She was a plump woman, not fat, but rounded—the kind of shape George would make a big thing about. Her cheeks were pink and her lips were fashionably tulip-shaped.

She stood herself right next to Elizabeth—you couldn't have put a ruler between them—and held out her hand for me to shake. I thought I might recognize her from the bathing lake, but I wasn't sure.

"Evening, I'm Harriet Dobinson," she announced cheerfully. I didn't recall hearing the name before. "Don't worry, we weren't asleep, were we, Liz-bet?"

Liz-bet?

Elizabeth's lips were clamped tightly shut.

"Are you coming in?"

"No," said Elizabeth and I both at the same time. The awkwardness was mitigated by the arrival of Winkle and Tiggy, who scraped against my legs as though they were my biggest fans. Delia, of course, was nowhere to be seen.

When I looked up, Elizabeth and Harriet were mouthing words at each other.

"May, I'm sorry, Harriet's going to Barking tomorrow and I promised..."

Here, Elizabeth's voice trailed off.

"I'm on trams," Harriet continued for her. "It's not too terrible..." She paused, looking at us both searchingly. "We all need to pull our weight, don't we?"

I nodded. I couldn't have felt more bewildered if Captain Matthew Webb, deceased Channel swimmer, had come down the stairs wrapped in jellyfish. After an even longer pause, Elizabeth spoke again.

"You can take my car if you like."

"Me? No! Don't be ridiculous, Elizabeth. I can't drive."

But Elizabeth never took no for an answer. "You'll be fine, I'll show you. Harriet and I will take the train tomorrow. Just bring back the car when you're finished with it."

She made everything sound so easy. She looked over at Harriet, who shrugged and said, "I'm going back to bed."

"Clutch to change gears, brake to stop. Go the speed you like. Don't heed the other drivers, most of them are complete incompetents."

Elizabeth talked me through it. Once we'd got the vehicle started, which was an enormous task in itself, it wasn't as complicated as I'd feared. Or maybe I had grown in my confidence to tackle such things? I thought of meeting Elsie that time at Percy's and how she helped me to conquer my fears.

We took off down the street. Elizabeth made no mention of her guest, so I didn't either. I drove around the block, stopping and starting, ye gads, and all the way, she was repeating her instructions.

"Lights are here, of course. Wipers here. Fuel you've already seen . . . Ignore that man, he's a lunatic."

"I can't go all the way to Leam—"

"You can," she said firmly.

I must, I told myself. *Think of my girls.* If I were to see them this Christmas, then this is what I would do. I knew once George had them in his domain, he wouldn't give me an inch.

I did the same circuit four times, and by the fifth I felt quite capable. Elizabeth declared my driving was not significantly worse than that of anyone else on the road. I pulled up outside her house. I had thought I was sweaty before, but that was nothing compared to now—I was drenched. Trying to get some control over this humiliating situation, I found myself saying, "Your friend seems nice."

"You know everything you need to know," Elizabeth said. She tooted the horn loudly. I wasn't sure if I imagined it, but I thought the curtains flickered. Was Harriet up there, watching us?

"Good luck, May. I hope you get the girls back soon."

I had just left Elizabeth's street when I nearly crashed into a hedge. A fox frightened me, causing me to swerve away, squealing like a fool. It was a good lesson in concentration. I kept my foot on the accelerator and my eyes to the future. Clutch to change gear, all the other drivers are halfwits. My knuckles were white. At one point I wanted to stop the engine and just cry, but I was afraid I wouldn't be able to start the motor again, not in the pitch-black.

Then the night mail went by, and somehow, I felt my resolve harden. On that train were hundreds of letters to boys out in France, and if they could tolerate the trenches, I could surely tolerate this. *Clutch to change gear, brake to stop. Ignore that man, he's a lunatic.*

It was two twenty in the morning when I arrived. I parked near the school gates and tried to sleep, slung between driver's and passenger's seats. The gearbox jabbed my back. But it was far quieter than the Somme, the air was clear, there was no snoring Matron and I soon dropped off.

I woke at six, the same time as I usually did in France if I was on day shift. I was freezing. I flattened down my hair, which no doubt looked like some bird's nest, then rubbed my fingers together and wrote in my diary. I followed this with a ditty about cars and how you could get very far(s). The truth was, I was feeling quite proud of my driving, proud of myself.

"You're braver than I," Louis Spears had said and each time I remembered it, it made me smile. At seven, I made my way past the high wire fences and along to the entrance.

A maid answered and then someone else came, and then finally, the headmistress was stood in front of me, arms crossed.

"I thought Mr. Turner was coming this afternoon."

"Well, I'm *Mrs.* Turner and I've come this morning." I flicked my cape around me as though it gave me special powers. "And I'm just back from a field hospital in France."

CHAPTER NINETEEN

Out came my girls, dragging their suitcases behind them. The trunks caught in the gravel and made a terrific noise, but they were too heavy to carry. The gray wool coat Joy was wearing was not the coat she had left in and was far too big for her. She reluctantly planted a kiss on my cheek and when I whispered fearfully, "Is everything all right, sweetheart?" she responded that she hadn't been awake long and "Why wouldn't it be?" then, "Where's Father?"

Her hair was pulled back into a high ponytail and was as smooth and tidy as Leona's was messy. Leona, looking like she'd been dragged through a hurricane, smacked into my legs and squeezed me so tight that I had to laugh: "If I were a lemon, you'd have my pips flying." She was grinning broadly—where did those freckles come from? Even her teeth had grown!

What a pleasure it was to have them in my arms again. Were these not the best children that ever were? The most wonderful girls? The most radiant? I couldn't stop hugging them, although as usual Joy was less keen on physical contact than Leona and kept her cuddles to a minimum.

The headmistress came out to see us off. She said it was a very special thing to have a mother who was working overseas as a nurse: "Your mother is quite the career woman, girls!"

"Not quite," I stammered self-effacingly, while the girls nodded dutifully. The headmistress added that a friend of hers was a matron on the continent. When I asked where, she said, "Oh, somewhere out there," gesturing vaguely. "Modern gals get all over the place, not like my generation: we stayed put," and I agreed, although I wasn't sure what she was trying to say about either her friend or me.

The girls were thrilled to be in a motorcar and even more thrilled that I was driving it. Leona said she had never seen a woman drive a motorcar before. I joked that I still couldn't stop or reverse—I think she believed me for a minute!

Joy stared out the window, arms crossed. Her expression said, *don't talk to me*. I knew I'd have to work hard to win over my firstborn; I always did.

"There are fewer cars on the roads here than in France," I said brightly, which was exactly the wrong thing to say. I could see from her sour expression that Joy was thinking: *ooh, everything is better in France, now, is it?!*

"I hope you drive better than you style your hair," she snapped. She did not like me disheveled. I thought of something cutting I could say back, but then I reminded myself: Joy was hurting, of course she was. She wanted to punish me.

We drove through the lush Warwickshire countryside. I tried to get them to sing along with me, but Joy preferred to pretend to be asleep. Instead, Leona and I whispered I Spy. As usual, I could never guess hers.

When Joy next opened her eyes, she asked: "Is this your boy-friend's car?"

"What boyfriend?" I asked, mystified. She just looked out the window. I really wasn't sure what was going on with her, but I realized it wasn't good.

"It's Elizabeth's," I said. "Remember Elizabeth, my friend? The swimmer?"

Joy went back to sleep.

*

I didn't have much of a plan. Tentatively, I asked if they would prefer not to go back to school in January.

"What?" said Joy, even more horrified than I had anticipated she would be. "Leave school?!"

"Mother, you can't do that to us," responded Leona fiercely, her arms crossed in front of her.

"I just…if you ever change your minds…" I swallowed. "We could…" I didn't know what we could do. "Arrange something else."

"Never," they both said firmly. So that was one option out the way.

I knew I couldn't go back to the house, for when George found out what I had done he would be rabid with fury. I resolved we would stay in a hotel for a few nights and then I would take them back to the house in time for Christmas. I asked them how they felt about that, given that Mrs. Crawford was no longer there.

"If it's just for a few days…" Leona said mildly.

"We've been invited to the Pilkingtons' anyway," said Joy more brightly. "Straight after Christmas. You don't mind if we go?"

"No, darling," I said, relieved. "That sounds like a very good idea."

We used to go to the ice rink at Aldwych on a Saturday morning when the girls were little. In a world where George ruled with an iron fist, it was freedom on ice.

As the girls realized where we were heading, their excitement grew, but I felt increasingly apprehensive. On our approach, I saw cardboard boxes, bags and blankets outside in the street and the main door was adorned with padlocks. I had to tiptoe to see through the grimy windows and then I couldn't see the rink, only piles and piles of suitcases. A woman walking by took sympathy and explained that there was no skating any more: the rink was now home to hundreds of refugees from Belgium.

She told us there might be another place, only a fifteen-minute drive away, but she couldn't be certain. Suddenly, I felt like the whole success of my England visit, of my parenting, of my life, depended on this.

"Let's go," I said confidently, although my heart was in my boots. I could have done with Elizabeth by my side then.

For once, fortune favored the brave—there was a skate rink *and* it was open. Within minutes, my girls were out, twirling on the ice.

I let them drag me with them. At first, I could only stagger, clutching the sides. But I knew being bold was the answer, so soon I was pushing out with my feet, emulating the best of them. Not everyone could skate: in the middle, one girl with shaky legs like a baby deer was laughing and grabbing onto everyone.

Joy fell. For a moment, she wore the same expression as some of the men brought in injured: part bewildered, part appalled. I skated over to her, nearly stumbling in my haste. I tried to lever her up by the arm. She resisted.

"I'll do it myself…"

She pushed back ineffectually on her palms.

"Let me help, darling…"

"Stop fussing," she hissed.

I hovered over her, still desperate to assist. *You're my daughter*, I wanted to remind her. *I helped you walk, I dried your tears. There's no need to hide your vulnerability from me.* She shook her head before clambering onto her skates furiously.

"You're not hurt?"

"Do you *mind*? I skate far better than you!" she sneered as she spun away.

I was still reeling from the rejection when sweet Leona grabbed me. We skated smoothly together. I made sure to keep an eye on Joy as she went over to the side, her confidence knocked, but then she returned to her rightful place in the center of the rink: pirouetting and pirouetting, faster and faster, her mutinous face never more beautiful.

*

I sent a telegram to George explaining the situation: it was just for a few days and it wasn't my intention to worry him—I was just restoring justice. I was their mother, this was my right. How dare he try to deny it?

By late afternoon the girls were yawning, so we went to the hotel. It was the girls' first time in a hotel, and in the foyer they became quieter versions of themselves while I bizarrely came over all American with the staff—much to Joy's scowling disapproval.

Dinner was served in a room with paintings on the wall of shipwrecks and Napoleonic battles. How exciting the pictures made everything look: worlds of dashing red uniforms, flaming swords, battling flames and fearless horses rearing up and charging. I wondered what, in a hundred years, they would make of our gray war, with its endless flooded trenches, barbed wire plains and tented hospitals. Would they render the men flamboyant and eager, or would they show the dirty, muddy truth?

We ate pork chops and if they were fattier and smaller than pre-war chops, they still tasted good. I scraped off Leona's sauce—she still hated eating anything wet. She also loathed peas with a passion. They told me that the food at school was not half as good as Mrs. Crawford's offerings. And they told me about "the naughty girls." Naughty girls were a perennial favorite. Naughty girls hung out windows and passed notes. Naughty girls chewed mints in RE.

Joy couldn't seem to decide if she hated or admired them.

I wanted to tell them about my work, but they interrupted: *the new hockey mistress must be at least a hundred!* I would have told them about boys not much older than them who lived in that twilight zone between life and death, but they didn't even want to hear about Bonnie and the sweet baby, although Joy did ask what his name was and my answer of "Freddie" got their approval. There was something hurtful about their lack of curiosity, but, I reminded myself, these are *children*. It's natural they want their mother to be their mother and nothing else.

At least they didn't want to talk about George.

A band was playing dance tunes in the hotel ballroom. No one was dancing though and when you looked around, it was obvious why. There were no men of dancing age any more, they were in France or Belgium, Malta, Iraq or Turkey. The old men and their wives drank— they looked like they didn't give a damn what was happening in their names two hundred miles away—but I wondered if secretly they felt as guilty and useless as I used to.

Leona agreed to dance with me. Her back was soft and supple in my arms. She told me she had dance lessons at school. Her feet were always in the right place. She was quite the talent. And what a pleasure it was when an old man with a monocle and bow-tie called out "Lovely sisters."

Leona giggled. "He thinks we're sisters, Mumma!"

"He's as blind as a bat..."

He sent over a glass of wine for me and fizzy drinks for the girls.

"Will he be your boyfriend, Mummy?" Leona's eyes were on stalks.

I waved over to him, then leaned forward to whisper to her, "Darling, he's one hundred and three."

"Have you got someone in France?" Joy persisted. She had wrapped her long legs around each other and looked frightfully grown-up. In five more years, she would be the age I was when I met George.

Please, please, please, don't let her fall for a man like her father.

"How do you mean?"

"A boyfriend."

I thought of Major Louis Spears. We had met only once; for thirty minutes no longer. Two hundred words exchanged, if that. We would probably never see each other again. And anyway, he was probably bleeding to death in some desert in Egypt. Ridiculous that one's mind could play such tricks.

"No? Why?"

Four more weeks and he would be back. And I would still be married to George.

"Father says you have boyfriends."

"Loads of them," said Leona dreamily into her drink. "All of them."

"Father can be silly." I chose my words carefully. "I don't have *one* boyfriend, let alone several."

Leona fixed her beautiful eyes on mine. She fiddled with the clip in her hair, then whispered, "We met one of Father's girlfriends, Mummy."

"One of them?"

"She was *not* very bright," Joy said, intolerantly. Sometimes, she sounded more cynical than me. "She thought we were at war with France!"

I grinned but knew better than to say anything. Whenever I thought about it afterward, I thought, *Hmm, that's just George's type* and it was very satisfying.

Next morning in the hotel we had—according to the girls—"the best breakfast in human history." The food was all laid out on one big table under tablecloths that reached the floor, and the girls trotted back and forth and then back and forth some more. They were as at ease in this milieu as they were at the ice-skating rink, or in the park. That was the gift of their schooling: they felt entitled to be everywhere.

"They have bacon!" Joy shouted. "And porridge."

The next few days with my girls were perhaps my favorite ever. When we weren't admiring the sights of London, we kicked off our shoes and read together on the hotel beds. Clean sheets, warm baths, my girls waving out the window at a man on stilts. A Punch and Judy in the park, flags at half-mast at Buckingham Palace, hot sausage rolls, dancing in a smattering of snow that didn't settle. And then it was time to go.

I don't know why, an irrepressible optimism maybe, but I had expected George to be civil when we arrived back home. I expected him to have a sense of humor about our escapade.

Hadn't he once taken me from church class, taken me to a department store and bought me heels that were too high and a dress that was too adult for me?

As we pulled up in front of the house, there he was in the doorway, in full bloated fury. I didn't even have time to blot my lips raspberry, like I'd planned.

"Come in with us, Mummy," pleaded Leona.

"I'd better not," I said quickly. "I don't think Daddy wants to see me."

"Do you *have* to go back to France, Mummy?" Joy was unemotional again, the way she had been when I'd first picked her up. Foolish to be surprised by this, but I was.

"Oh, darling! I can't stay here, not with your father . . . and you've got so much going on at school and with your friends and your tennis."

I still hadn't realized it was too much to expect them to *like* me being away.

"The poor fellows out there have nothing," I added limply.

Trembling, I unloaded the girls' trunks. I told myself this was like skating away from the side: I had to act bold.

"Did you get my telegram?" I called out cheerily.

"How dare you go behind my back!" he bellowed back.

I smiled at him indulgently. *Treat him like a child*, I thought. *A petulant, badly behaved child.*

"Thought I'd save you the trip, George."

"This is never going to happen again."

I wasn't going to rise to it. He was stupid Mr. Toad, without a thought for anyone; nothing clever about that.

The girls wandered toward him. You wouldn't know they hadn't seen him for six months either. They lugged their twin trunks across the sidewalk and up the steps. He watched them without offering to help—that was George all over. He pulled the girls into the house without a hello or a welcome, then slammed the door on me. The house seemed to shake in sympathy. I could hear the reverberation, as if shells had gone off in the park. I knocked again, and he swung the door open.

"What?"

"George, can't we be adults?"

He glared at me, eyes bulging. I thought maybe "adult" wasn't the word I was looking for.

"We need to talk."

"What's there to say?"

"Well..." I was momentarily thrown. "Are we going to divorce or—"

"It's long overdue," he yelped. "I'll keep the house. You will get nothing, nothing, nothing." He had turned quite purple. "And I'm naming Percy Milhouse on the petition."

"Percy?" My voice was shrill. "What nonsense! As if—"

"If you deny it, I will drag you through the dirt...I know all about your dirty little afternoons."

"I have never been with Percy in that way, how dare you!" I hissed at him furiously. "What about all your women then, eh? I bet you don't even know half of their names!"

He shrugged. "Take it or leave it, May. Those are the terms I am offering."

I thought for a moment. I knew the law. I knew how crushingly hard it was for women to get a divorce. If George wanted to do it this way, then more fool him. What did I care? What did Percy care? Let us cut the ties as quickly and as cleanly as possible. What was it Gordon always told us about wounds? Clear it out, cut it off, because if that infection takes hold...

"Do it then, George, divorce me."

"Oh, I will," he said. "I will."

I turned on my heels.

"Merry Christmas then," I added coldly.

"Merry Christmas to you too," he snapped back.

Leona and Joy waved down from their old nursery window. I blew kisses at that old window until there was nothing to see anymore.

So, I was alone in London just two days before Christmas. I considered knocking at Percy's door—it might be fair to give him a tip-off about the divorce petition—but then resolved to write him about it instead. I wasn't sure how he would react. It would have been terrible news for a respectable man in society, but Percy never aspired to that. (Even if he was never as unconventional as I'd expected.) And it wasn't fair to ask to spend time with Percy, not when I didn't feel anything for him, and I didn't want to spend time with his pictures either. When I remembered the paintings, with their sharp lines and sinister reds, I shivered. At the time, I hadn't realized it, but he had caught the atmosphere of the war very well.

I thought about returning to the hotel, perhaps to dance again, but without my girls, I knew, it would be miserable. How would they spend Christmas? Would George even bother going through the motions for them? My darling girls: turkey and cranberry sauce against a backdrop of George's thunderous face. I had bought glass marbles for Leona and regretted it now. Might she think they were too childish? As for the notebook and pencils I had wrapped for Joy, would she think it was a hidden message about writing more often? (It wasn't.) At least they were going to stay with the Pilkingtons from the twenty-seventh. They would have a marvelous time there.

As I sat on the step, a pitiful fella sidled up and planted himself next to me. This was the last thing I needed. I didn't look up but stared into my hands. Hopefully he'd go away when he realized I wasn't interested in chatting.

"Here." He shoved his bread in my face. He thought *I* was hungry, he thought *I* was pitiful. "You look like you could do with a good meal."

I couldn't take food from the poor soul, but it was true, I *was* hungry—I hadn't eaten since I had dropped off the girls. He showed me where his arm had once been. I think he may have expected me to recoil but of course I was used to amputees—I had tended to enough of them.

"Belgium?"

He nodded. "Loos."

"I'm sorry."

"You should see the other guy," he joked.

We sat there for a few minutes. He told me about the things he had seen. He got money for his disability. Not much, but it should have been enough.

"I've got four kids. I give it all to the wife, she kicked me out."

"Oh," I said.

"She got with a fella who's only lost his foot."

I looked at him, wondering if he was joking. I decided he wasn't.

"That doesn't sound very nice," I said.

"No," he said after a pause. "It isn't."

I considered the wounded soldiers I could serve in France, I thought about my team and my place with them, and I didn't have to think for much longer. I drove the car back to Elizabeth's house and pushed the keys through the letterbox with a note of thanks. I didn't try to see if anyone was there: I didn't want to see her friend Harriet, and even if Elizabeth were alone, I wasn't sure I could face her either right now. Then I walked back toward the station.

I thought of Joy's question and my answer. Had I explained it well enough? Probably not. I was never good when put on the spot.

How could I convey to her how empty my life had been in London, and how full it was now? She would take it personally, I knew she would, when it wasn't personal at all. It was just who I was.

I was so sorry things had ended like this with George, so sour, so bitter. Hard to believe he was the same person who stood in front of our fireplace, cap in hand winning over my mother: *I will take care of May, I will devote my whole life to making her happy.* I bet Bella and his others got all those lines now.

George would come around soon enough, I knew that. And we were divorcing. It wasn't a nice thing but it was the best and only alternative available. And I was certain I would be back in England soon. The war had already been going on for over a year. It simply *couldn't* go on for much longer now. And if it did end up lasting another year—most people swore it wouldn't—I would be home for Easter and summer anyway. Perhaps I might buy myself a little apartment near the girls' school. Yes. We could spend every weekend together.

By the time I could see the station lights and smell the steam, I felt a renewed sense of purpose. I was on the move again. Back to my clearing hospital in France. Back home.

Things Grandma Leonora left me

A love of nursing.

A love of card games.

A love of reading, writing and poetry.

A Chinese fan (not sure if it's real).

An ornament of a Flamenco dancer
(this *is* real, unfortunately).

All her savings from her account.
(Take that, George! You can keep the damn house.)

CHAPTER TWENTY

I arrived back on the evening of 23 December. It was daft, but I really thought I might discover Kitty and Gordon together. For who else wasn't certain that the reading they did together was a ruse for secretive lovers to be alone?

Gordon was in his tent and—as I suspected—he was not alone. Classical music was playing and there was a pleasant hum of voices. I didn't want to make an indecent interruption, so I called out a few times from outside the tent. "Gordon, oh, Gordon!" I didn't have to wait long. He swept out toward me, pulling the cloth flap firmly shut behind him.

"What in God's name are you doing here, May? You're supposed to be in England!"

"What are *you* doing, Gordon?" I teased. I tugged at the tent walls, laughing. "Kitty, come out, come out, wherever you are. I won't tell anyone!"

Gordon did an excellent imitation of confused. He stared at me, his hands on his hips, a big triangular space behind which he was hiding my friend.

"I won't tell a soul..." I marched forward.

"No, May, no!" he yelped.

"KITTY! If you don't reveal yourself to me this instant, I'll—"

A small Indian man emerged, the tent door flapping uselessly behind him. "At your service..."

I found Kitty later, in the canteen, diligently spooning out peas so overcooked they resembled some deadly chemical paste. Lots of the kitchen staff had been granted leave over Christmas, so the remaining staff had their hands full. Kitty looked red-eyed but still managed to give me a welcoming smile.

"I was sure I'd caught you and Gordon out..."

"No, May!" Kitty was so startled that she jumped; her hat almost fell from her head. "How could you have thought that?"

I was still in shock. I said in a low voice that I didn't know which was worse: that Gordon was with *a man*, or that the man was an *Indian*! Kitty looked stricken. Her hand wobbled. The watery peas slipped off the spoon and back into the pan.

"Please don't tell anyone, for goodness' sake," she whimpered.

I gazed at her over the cutlery. I hadn't realized she was so upset. "Who would I tell?"

"Anyone. He'll be in terrible trouble if he's found out, you must know that, May."

When I next saw Gordon, I tried to be funny and friendly and knowing rolled into one.

"Ye gods, Gordon, of all the fellas to pick!"

"Of all the fellas to pick?!" he repeated incredulously. I noticed a vein tic in his forehead that I'd never seen before. I smiled nervously as he went on.

"Do you think I have a great deal of choice in romance, May?" he hissed.

"I don't know." I realized I had made a mistake with the conversation, but I wasn't sure how.

"If I chose the wrong guy, I'd get arrested."

"I didn't—"

"No, there's a lot you don't realize," he said enigmatically and stalked off.

*

I was on ward duty on Christmas Day. A young lad was brought in in the morning—shrapnel to the chest—and he didn't make it. We were subdued, patients and nurses alike. In the afternoon, we did some singing. Then Doctor Rafferty burst in, wearing a Santa hat and fake beard. Ho-ho-ho-ing, he gave out chocolates and cigars. We made a good fist of it, all things considered.

Many of our patients' thoughts turned to home, so that evening we wrote even more letters than usual. My wrist was aching by the time the shift ended but I was satisfied that there would be some happy families next week. After the shift, Kitty put her arm through mine and said we were invited to Gordon's. Given our most recent exchange, I felt uneasy, but didn't want to create a drama by not going.

There was mistletoe. Gordon and I kissed civilly on the cheek and it was as though we'd agreed to pretend we hadn't had an argument at all. We listened to his beloved classical music and dug into the Turkish delight he told us he'd been saving since he'd been on leave at Easter.

Gordon's Indian friend, introduced as Karim, arrived. He smoked a cigar. Now, in the lamplight, I saw that he was neatly built, probably around the same height as me and no broader. But his face—what a face he had! Heavy-lidded, sensual eyes, skin as smooth as satin. And he was clever too, talking about music and books and politics. I could see the appeal.

He didn't stay long though and after he had left, Kitty went to the wards to offer around the last of the Turkish delight so once again I was left alone with Gordon.

"I worry about you," I said tentatively.

"And I worry about you." He was tidying up the tent and not looking at me as he said: "We are the keepers of each other's secrets."

"How do you mean?"

"How are your children?"

I couldn't catch a breath.

"What children?"

He whispered. "I know, May."

He said he had worked it out way back, from my face when I waited for and then read my letters. My behavior when Bonnie gave birth. My "natural way" with Freddie. I felt collapsed from the inside out. That had done it.

"Will they send me back?"

"I shouldn't think so. It's frowned upon, but"—he smiled wryly— "so are a lot of things that go on. Anyway, so far as I know, it's not actually against any rules. You should tell your friends though—it might make life easier for you."

"Or they might send me home."

"I won't let them." He put his arm around me, squeezed. "Merry Christmas, May."

CHAPTER TWENTY-ONE

It was another six weeks before I felt I could tell Kitty or Bonnie about my girls, or George. It was bitterly cold. Sleep grew scarcer. The air was thick with dust, although the explosions had stopped shocking us; we'd just carry on as normal. Patients were more than plentiful. There were more painful losses to endure. Telegrams came more regularly and the numbers of injured were up. Six or seven men from Fricourt. They didn't say what injuries anymore because it could be anything. The times my team could sit around chatting were fewer now. I probably *could* have told them over a bedtime mug of oatmeal in the canteen or as we ate our crackers in the morning, but those rare times when we had the right moment, I could never seem to find the right words. And the longer I hadn't told them, the harder it seemed to find those words.

In the middle of February, Bonnie, Kitty and I sat at the corner table of Chez Tartine, our favorite café in the town of Bray-sur-Somme, not far from its ancient church. A man with one leg was playing the violin. After one particularly soaring piece, he said, "For the nurses," and we raised our glasses to him.

And that's when I told them the sorry tale of George and me. His fall outside my church. Our premature marriage. My dying hopes for an amicable split. And finally, I told them about my daughters.

"Tiggy and Delia?" asked Kitty. She hadn't said anything all the time I had been talking but had studied my face impassively.

"Actually, those are my friend's cats," I admitted, flushing redder still. "My girls' names are Joy and Leona."

"That's a relief." Kitty smiled.

"I quite liked the name Tiggy," said Bonnie.

I was worried they would be annoyed at me for lying but they were understanding. I should have known. They put their hands over mine.

"You must miss them," said Kitty.

"So much." I held back a sob. I thought of Leona pleading with me to come into the house, and how cold Joy was when she said hello or goodbye. Kitty's sympathy was making me feel worse. Could I have done more? Should I be with them now? Then Bonnie asked if Matron knew. I asked if they would tell her for me. Although I was keen to have everything out in the open now, I couldn't face telling her myself.

That same evening, Matron stalked over to me. I suppose because Kitty and Bonnie's reaction had been so positive, I assumed she too was going to say something heart-warming and that she might even admire me for my fortitude, but she had a cold glint in her eye, like a predator who'd found a weak spot.

"You have to go back to England, Nurse Turner."

"Wha-at? Why?"

"This is no place for mothers," she said.

"This is no place for *anyone*." I hissed back. "It's... it's not nice for sons, fathers, husbands, wives—anybody."

"It's against the rules."

"It's not. Doctor Collins said it's not."

She sniffed. I didn't wait for her to say any more; I extinguished my lantern quickly. I hadn't known I could dislike her any more than I already did.

I lay awake in the silence for longer than usual.

The younger men cried. It wasn't only the loss of their limbs, but the loss of a future, of work, of money, of love.

"I'm spoiled goods," they said, or "No one will ever want me." Kitty, Bonnie, even Matron did their best to put their minds at rest.

"You're a silly sausage," Bonnie might cajole them. Or, "With a face like yours, the girls will all come knocking..."

Sometimes, Bonnie would go too far. She would plonk herself on a poor fella's bed—she had to be told repeatedly to stop it, but she always forgot—and say "I'll be your beau."

Matron's words of comfort were: "Oh, there's plenty who've got it worse than you."

"In fact," Kitty would say, with her usual rationality, "after the war, there may be such a shortage of young eligible males that you may find you have quite the pick of the ladies."

I myself never knew what to say for the best. Perhaps they sensed that about me too, because they didn't seem to talk about it to me as much as to the others. If any of the boys did try talking about it with me, I would bring them some water, stroke their foreheads and try to make them as comfortable as I could. Sometimes I would read them the letters they had from their mothers—that seemed to work.

Eight weeks came and went in the blink of my very bloodshot and dusty eyes. Divorce papers were served and signed. Gordon was my witness. George had done what he said he would do and claimed that I'd had an adulterous relationship with Percy Milhouse. Occupation: Artist. (Unsurprisingly, Percy had not replied when I wrote of it to him.) The girls would continue at boarding school—George agreed he would pay.

"But you are losing so much," said Gordon. He feared I was being too hasty. Divorce in haste, repent at leisure. "Why would you admit to something you haven't done?"

"It's by far the easiest way. The law makes it near impossible for me to divorce George but easy for him to divorce me."

"Wait 'til the war is over," he advised. "Things will change. Women might have more rights."

But George and I couldn't wait. "Oh well, it's only a house," I said ruefully. "And my good name…"

Gordon raised his eyebrows at me.

"And what about the girls?"

"Oh, George wouldn't do a thing about them." I laughed. "He'd have to look after them himself!"

There was still no sign of Major Louis Spears.

Maybe that was a good thing. Who wanted that nonsense out here? It hadn't worked out for many of my colleagues: Katherine had been abandoned broken-hearted, Bonnie had been left with a baby and Lucille had a fiancé who was now a prisoner of war. And it hadn't exactly worked out for me before. What was one of Mrs. Crawford's strange sayings? Once bitten, twice shy? I was shy even before I was bitten.

I couldn't stop thinking about him. I found myself telling Gordon, who had already suspected, of course. "Just be patient, he'll come back."

But I no longer believed he would.

CHAPTER TWENTY-TWO

No one could escape Bonnie and her autograph book. She made everyone, staff and patients, leave their mark in it.

By hook or by crook I'll be first in your book, read the first one, and after that the pages filled up so quickly with lovely sweet messages that she had to write to her family in London to send more books. I loved flicking through them after our shifts. I wished I had thought of it first.

Sometimes there'd be a cheeky comment but mostly there would be gentle thank-yous, appreciative notes, riddles or reflective stories. I loved the drawings of butterflies, of deer or strings of love-hearts.

A patient, Private Stanley Jones, came in making a big hoo-ha about his ventriloquist's dummy. Even when he was groaning on the stretcher, he insisted that his wooden "boy" was carried upright. He even demanded it had a bed of its own. When we refused to comply, he begged for it to have its own chair, at least. To humor him, I got the dummy a blanket, then kindly wrapped a bandage around its gurning wooden head. I was quite pleased with myself.

"Better now!"

Stanley looked at me disdainfully. "It's Little Stan's foot that got hurt, not his bloody head, dear."

Something about Stanley reminded me of George. I tried to keep away from him, but he always needed a drink, a sit-up, a letter written to his ma or something. Noting my reluctance, Matron scolded me.

"You can't pick and choose patients, May," she said. "This isn't Selfridges."

Little Stan drew everyone's attention, as he sat on his chair next to his owner's bed. If you caught sight of him from the other end of the ward, you'd wonder what that schoolboy was doing here. That blank waxy face with the lines down its side and a playful yet sinister expression. He wore a paisley waistcoat and little patent shoes.

"Isn't he brilliant?" enthused Matron. She thought Little Stan was quite the thing; but then Matron was delighted with any wig or clown, and her all-time favorite form of entertainment was a man dressed as a woman.

Stanley was very glum. He had taken shots to the arm and leg and although a tourniquet had been put on fairly quickly, it had been left like that for a long time. The trenches were too narrow to stretcher him out and his best friend had been killed while trying to get help.

One day Stanley saw me looking at Little Stan. I made a show of dusting around him. He told me be careful, don't knock him off his chair. Irritably, I told him that I always was careful. I asked after his leg but Stanley insisted he wasn't bothered, it was the arm that worried him. The surgeons had worked hard through the night not to have to amputate it, but no one was sure how far the damage went.

"I was a ventriloquist in real life," he explained glumly. Only then did I begin to realize what a blow to his career the loss of his arm would be.

"In real life?" I said. I still didn't know what to make of him. "Isn't this real life?"

"This *isn't* real life, is it?" he said. "It's a bloody nightmare. Wake me up when it's over."

After that conversation, somehow Stanley and I got on much better.

One evening, Stanley said Little Stan wanted to entertain us, "to show his gratitude for your loving care." (I could never tell if he was being serious or not.) I was reluctant. Despite our best efforts, we had lost two men in two days (both from the same sniper attack—some German soldier must have been feeling very proud of himself). I didn't see the point of anything. But Matron was surprisingly keen, so when the other team were on duty, we moved some of the less poorly soldiers onto chairs and moved some of the beds around, so we could all crowd around him.

It turned out Stanley was a great raconteur. Through Little Stan, he told stories about David Lloyd George, Edward Grey, and the whole war cabinet. He did a good imitation of Queen Victoria—"We are not amused"—as well. (Any similarity to Matron, I guessed, was entirely intentional.) It did the belly good to laugh about those in power. I had forgotten that. It was as rewarding as a good meal and when we went back to our tents that night, we were still chuckling to ourselves.

CHAPTER TWENTY-THREE

Spring was coming. Small buds on the trees, green emerging underfoot. No need for our heavy overcoats and boots. I was making plans for my next trip home when Gordon pushed through the ward, gripping his stethoscope and mouthing exaggeratedly:

"He's here!"

"Who?"

"Your tall gentleman..."

My tall gentleman! I wished!

Major Louis Spears came in, stooping for the bowed ceiling. He was tall but the stooping was a little unnecessary. His face was every bit as lovely as I had thought the first time I saw him, but this time he was tanned and looked absolutely done in.

After we'd exchanged pleasantries, he held out his arm. "Would you be so kind as to look at my wrist?"

This was my first gulp of disappointment. Louis wasn't here as a suitor but as a patient.

"I don't have the authority..."

"Please," he said. His eyes really were very blue.

I looked. He could move it all right, and he could wriggle his fingers perfectly—and then it dawned on me that the wrist just might have been a ploy to come and see me. (A very poor one at that.)

"Will I be able to play the piano?" he asked.

"Of course."

"That's good. I never could before."

"That is terrible," I said.

"I have more." He smiled at me and it was as if we were old friends. "I can get Doctor Collins to have a look when he's finished his round," I said.

"I trust you," he said simply.

Stanley picked up Little Stan. He pulled the delicate strings and Little Stan said in that high-pitched, sing-song voice of his:

"Ooh, Nurse Turner, this one is sweet on you—"

"Sshhh," I hissed. "You're being silly, Little Stan!"

"Don't be embarrassed," Little Stan piped up. "He's a good 'un, I can tell."

I looked back at Louis. His face was flushed but he just shrugged. "Little Stan may be right."

"About which one?"

"Both..."

This admission made me bold. I pulled him away from our audience and whispered, "Are there no doctors between here and the Middle East?"

"Not a single one." He smiled.

I let go of his wrist, reluctantly. I had liked holding his arm.

"So, what *really* brings you here, Major Spears?"

"My friend told me I had to come, Nurse Turner."

He kept his eyes locked on mine. I felt transported from the hospital tent. His face was both familiar and exciting, his voice somehow thrilling yet soothing. He could make this sad, drab place come alive.

"And if your friend told you to stick your head in the oven, would you?" I teased.

He continued to gaze at me.

"Winston has many crazy ideas, but even he wouldn't go that far."

He wanted to take me out. I told him I was assigned seven days without a break. The disappointment on his face felt like a compliment.

"I *am* free later tonight, though..." My heart was thumping. *Was I really going to do this?*

"Eight?" He tugged at the sticky-out bit of hair just above his ear. "Nine."

"I'll pick you up in the car."

"What about that arm?" I called after him. "Are you sure you can drive?"

He looked at his wrist, shook it in a puzzled way, then winked at me. "It's a miracle!"

<u>Things to do</u>

Don't think about Major Spears
Louis. Louis. Louis.
Louis Spears
King Louis
The Sun King
Louis Spears
Asparagus Spears
Fighting Spears
May Spears

CHAPTER TWENTY-FOUR

I imagined we would drive to Paris. I pictured us hand in hand, gazing up at the Eiffel Tower. Or perhaps we would climb the steps to Montmartre, to sit among the tourists in the moonlight and have our portraits drawn. Our first night together captured in HB. Or we would sit in a candle-lit restaurant and stare mistily into each other's eyes over mussels and under-cooked steaks.

Louis drove fast. It wasn't long before I realized that we were traveling north, for goodness' sake, not south; we weren't heading to anywhere near Paris. Why, when Paris was the most obvious destination? I had a terrible sensation that we were driving toward the front line. Was the man mad? Was he trying to get us killed? Perhaps he realized I was suddenly afraid, because he turned his handsome face toward me and asked: "Have you guessed where we're heading yet?"

I had no idea.

"Belgium," he said.

Belgium?!

"There are still places in Belgium—" I stopped myself; I had been going to say, "where you can have fun?" but he knew what I meant anyway.

"There *are* still places in Belgium. Not many, but…"

He smiled at me. I grinned back, I couldn't help it.

"This was Winston's bloody idea, was it?"

"It's too crazy even for him." Louis was laughing to himself. "Don't you trust me?"

I didn't say anything, but I realized, almost in a happy panic, that yes, I did trust him. (And there had been a time I thought I would never trust anyone again.)

How nice to nestle in the passenger seat next to him. How nice to watch Louis' firm hand on the gear stick. Large, strong, indisputably male hands. His sleeve ran almost to his knuckles, but I didn't have to imagine: I had seen the arm underneath. I had seen the blond hairs coiled on his forearms, I had seen the knot of muscle there.

He talked a little about his driver, Sergeant Radcliffe—Johnny. It was clear how fond of him he was. I noticed his lower lip shook sometimes when he talked and that he had to pause to catch his breath. He told me that they had taken a detour that Johnny had cautioned against. There had been an argument. Johnny told Louis that it was a dangerous road, that there were snipers, it wasn't called the Road to Hell for nothing, but Louis was in a rush, and insisted.

He said that there was a flash, a white light, a terrible noise, then silence. Then he pushed Sergeant Radcliffe aside and drove himself.

"I blame myself," he said.

I thought of Sergeant Radcliffe and could say with some confidence, "*He* doesn't blame you though, does he?"

"No," he said reluctantly. "*He* doesn't." He made a kind of harrumphing sound. "Johnny is so reasonable, he doesn't even blame the sniper who pulled the trigger."

His knuckles were white on the wheel. I thought, after hearing that, *should I still trust him?*

I told him about Joy and Leona—I was determined to be honest from the start. If he was surprised that I was the mother of two nearly grown girls, he didn't show it. He dived in, asking me enthusiastically about them. I blathered on about their tennis, their reports, and then when I realized he was really listening, I told him about Leona's sweetness and her jokes, and how, deep down, Joy was very loving but didn't want anyone to know it, and that she studied hard, but didn't want anyone to know that either and...

"I'm going on," I said regretfully.

"Not at all." He took his hand off the steering wheel and reached for mine: I felt as though I went whizz-bang.

Later, he said, "When you talk about your daughters, your face lights up," which I thought was charming. No one had ever said anything like that to me before.

I told him to put his hand back on the wheel, he mockingly said, "Yes, ma'am," and I told him some more about my life in London. I talked about my favorite place, the Tooting Bathing Lake, and my favorite person, Elizabeth. I didn't tell him about my bouts of melancholy. It didn't seem the moment; besides, I told myself, it had been some time since I'd been troubled by all that. He need never know.

The sign, surrounded by small white lightbulbs, said, "La Poupée." It was in a narrow cobblestoned street, where houses and shops were closely packed together. We were parked right outside. The shops next to it were boarded up, some of them for the night, others, I think, abandoned ever since the Germans first invaded. (Not everyone had returned here when the Germans had been pushed back. You could smell explosives and alcohol mixed in the air.)

"The Doll?" I was mystified—I couldn't find much inviting about that. "What *is* this?"

It didn't look much from the outside and when two officers came out, drunk as lords, with their arms around each other, singing, "We're English, we're English...Ahhh!" I liked it even less. I sighed. *And the date had been going so well...*

Louis, however, was still grinning broadly. He tugged open the passenger door. I jumped out, trying not to look as disappointed as I felt.

"You'll enjoy this..."

*

The bar was noisy, full of people talking loudly. In the center, there was a girl throwing back her head with laughter, wearing a black dress. She couldn't have been much older than Joy. As we arrived, she sped over to welcome us. She was delighted to see Louis—she seemed to know him quite well.

"What's your name?" She spoke in heavily accented English.

"May Turner!" I yelled.

"Nurse May Turner and Major Louis Spears," she repeated. "Welcome!"

Louis said warmly to me, "This is Ginger, and this is the best club in Belgium!"

She leaned forward conspiratorially and whispered to me: "I think he means this is the *only* club in Belgium."

Before too long, I understood Ginger was not only witty, charming and beautiful, but she had a brilliant memory for names and faces: quite the perfect skill set for a club hostess.

In one corner, a soldier was playing a piano. He was thumping the keys and changing position on his stool—sometimes he was standing, sometimes sitting with his legs up in the air, other times sitting facing us, away from the keys. It was an amazing performance. I was spellbound.

Louis went to get some drinks and when he came back he said: "I've found someone who knows you!"

I was about to say "No one knows me here" when I saw that he was right: looking as magnificent as ever was the woman who inspired me, Elsie Knocker. I hugged and kissed her cheeks incredulously. What a small world it was! Elsie and her—boyfriend? I didn't know for sure who he was—had a table right by the bar, and I could see by the way everyone treated them that they were quite the favorites. His name was Harold and he was as good-looking as Louis, but a different type. He was as correct and accomplished as Louis was, and his manners were similarly impeccable, but he was confident too, assertive even, while Louis was more cautious. The two got on right away.

The men were talking logistics, so Elsie and I broke away and found a small table where we could talk privately.

How was the hospital? Who was I working with? Did I manage? Did I miss home? Elsie knew Gordon, "a brilliant mind," she said, and she had heard of Matron. She said, "Her bark is worse than her bite," so I decided not to launch into all my anecdotes about her miserableness.

She knew Louis "from Brussels"—whatever that meant—and she asked me if I had met his dear friend Winston Churchill? *("Of course, everyone knows Winston—he's going places.")* She didn't have much to tell me about Louis other than that he was doing well too. I said I wasn't sure what "doing well" meant. She said, "Oh, he's quite important in diplomacy, negotiations, decision-making, that kind of thing."

"Important?"

She sighed impatiently. "People are listening to him. Leaders, generals, et cetera."

She said it like Et Cetera was another person. I laughed. With my eyebrows arched, I whispered, "I like listening to him too," and joyfully, she held out her glass for me to clink. *"Santé."*

I tried to find out more about this Harold she was with. "Is it serious or not?" I asked. Percy had been clear that Elsie was not the type to settle; she was a free spirit. (I had always wondered if he was making a dig at me when he talked about free spirits.)

"Is what serious?" she asked. She reminded me a little of Kitty with her energetic deflections.

"You and Harold…"

"He's seriously my Man of the Moment," she laughed. She laughed a lot.

"Is that all?"

She raised her pretty eyebrows. They were dark and even, she didn't need a pencil.

"For now," she insisted. The crowd grew louder, and she leaned forward to be heard. Her words felt hot in my ear. "I'm superstitious," she said, laughing again. "If you get too attached, they die. Keep a rotation of them and the gods can't look down and shoot them."

Ginger collected our glasses. She was such a vision of loveliness; I couldn't imagine how it must have been for men to crawl out from the trenches to see her.

"So, Nurse Turner," she said, "you're Canadian?"

"American," I corrected her, "via London."

"An American war nurse?" She clapped her hands. "A rare species."

"Not at all." If it were anyone else I would have been irritated, but Ginger seemed so young and naive. "We are looking after our dear soldiers in America, Canada and all over Europe, and on the trains and the hospitals and..." I paused, both Ginger and Elsie were now looking at me sympathetically. "Many years ago, my grandma was one of the first war nurses. She served on the battlefields at Fredericksburg..."

I don't know why but I suddenly felt like crying.

Ginger pulled up a chair. She told us her eldest sister, Martha, was learning to nurse. Her father was there—she pointed behind the bar. She said I was her first American guest. She called to the pianist to play "Turkey in the Box" in my honor. I didn't have the heart to tell her I didn't know it but instead clapped and swayed all the way through.

"Can he play 'Gilbert the Filbert'?" asked Elsie. Ginger spoke to the pianist and he launched into a jolly tune. I didn't know that one either.

I was not used to drinking much. I suppose living with George had put me off but also if I drink alcohol, I can become even more morose and self-critical than usual. Not always, but tonight, after my third beer, I began to slur. The efforts I put in to straighten my words failed.

"It's thanks to you I'm here, Elsie. You made me believe in myself. I was so...so...unhappy back home."

I put my hands in my lap. It was too hard to say. If I told her that sense of waste and isolation I had experienced in London I would cry. How cruel everything in the world felt there.

"And how are you now?" Elsie asked.

"I feel even if I died tomorrow, I would know that I had done my best."

"Don't die tomorrow," she advised.

"I'll try not to."

"Oh God!" She sighed abruptly. "Harrowing, isn't it?"

I thought of the men we treated. The suffering we witnessed every day. The poignancy of the letters they dictated. The pathos of the growing cemetery out the back. The stream of warning telegrams we received: three injured coming from Friesland. Two from Herbécourt.

Louis was waving at me from the other side of the room and I thought of Johnny blinded and the guilt Louis carried. I waved back. There were several men at his table, talking earnestly, their drinks full, their beer mats drenched, but I only had eyes for Louis. What a man. I felt quite bowled over by him.

I tried to concentrate. "More harrowing than anything I could ever possibly have imagined."

"Hold tight because it's set to get worse."

I looked at Elsie, puzzled, but she forced her mouth into a smile, poured more whisky and quickly changed the subject. "So, in your place in France, do you have a special right-hand girl?"

I thought of Kitty, the favorite of all my colleagues, but she and Bonnie were the team, not she and I. Gordon *was* a favorite but we were separated by rank, by sex, by...just about every single thing that can come between two people. Then there was Matron. But Matron hated me almost as much as she hated the dreaded Hun. No, we weren't special to each other.

Back home, I had Elizabeth. Pale, sporty Elizabeth, training to cross the Channel. Elizabeth with her aspirations, her plans and her ability to make you feel like the only person in the room, in the lake, in the car, who listened harder than anyone I had known, perhaps, until Louis. Then I thought of the mysterious Harriet and the way Elizabeth had looked so fearful at the door that night.

I shook my head. "Not out here, no."

"It makes a difference," Elsie said to me, "to have someone by your side, someone who understands you."

"I suppose so."

She blew cigarette smoke at me. She had such handsome lips. "Sometimes, I feel like I can't go on, but Mairi, who works alongside me in the cellar, is like one of those German tanks. She squashes all opposition."

I thought I would love to have someone talk about me the way Elsie talked about Mairi. I looked over at Louis again. I felt helplessly, hopelessly attracted to him. He raised an eyebrow at me, and I raised my glass back. I thought, *please, please, let him feel the same way about me.*

The soldier was wearing a filthy bandage over his arm but there was something not right about the way it hung. Elsie noticed him before I did.

"Excuse me," she said to me. She strode straight over to him, with me trailing after her, and delicately put a hand on his other shoulder. "You need that checked out."

"They'll hold me back if I do. Need to be with my men." I admired the sentiment, but Elsie wasn't having any of it.

"Don't be a fool. Come and see me, I'll fix it for you."

"Maybe," he said. It was clear he meant no.

"Promise you'll come to see me," Elsie said firmly. "You'll be no use to the men if you're sick..."

He looked about to protest, but then backed down, grinning sheepishly. They shook hands and she walked away. As I rejoined her, I heard him tell his friends, "That's Elsie Knocker, that is."

His mate said, "The one from the cellar house?"

"That's her," he said admiringly. Not long after, more drinks arrived at our table and we waved our thank-yous.

Louis' face was different when he laughed. Looking at him from across the room, I thought, *I want to get closer to this man.* Something that had long been snuffed out was igniting in me. Something I barely recognized. I walked across the room, never more aware of my hips, my legs, the shape I presented to the world. As I swayed over his table, the arguing men fell silent.

"You've been ignoring me all evening," I said thickly, even though it was probably two of one and one of half another.

Louis looked startled, then apologetic. He stood up, took my hand. His hand was big around mine and as cool as mine was hot.

"What would you say if I asked you to dance?"

I grinned, thinking, *finally!* "Are you a *good* dancer, Louis?"

"I'll let you decide," he said.

He twirled me around, capable and confident, so I felt like a spinning top. He was a very good dancer.

Soon, people were looking at us. I heard Ginger call out, "Why are Americans the best dancers? It's not fair!" And Louis called back, "Oi, I'm not American!"

He twisted me around so fast my feet couldn't keep up with him.

"I can't," I puffed.

"You can," he said, twirling me some more. Some of the other patrons were clapping in time with the music. And I turned more and more. It was exhilarating, but exhausting, and after a few minutes of this, I fell back into his arms. I thought he was going to kiss me but, very seriously, he pushed a stray hair out of my eyes, then set me upright again. My legs felt wobbly.

The lively soldier left the piano to take a well-earned break at the bar. There were drinks all lined up in a row for him. Ginger's father, with his droopy, downcast mustache, took his place. His tunes were slower and more sentimental. I didn't recognize the first but the second was "Auld Lang Syne." The lights flickered. Louis' hand was on the small of my back. I closed my eyes; I wanted to be here forever. I wanted to stop time, and for a short while it felt as though we had somehow paused it. I don't know if you could call what we were doing dancing anymore—it was more of a shuffle or a sway. We swayed there in the middle of that room, swaying the world away. I had never felt so safe.

When I next opened my eyes, Elsie and Harold had gone and the bar had emptied out. Tears were dripping from the pianist's eyes. His drooping mustache was soaked at either end. Ginger was learning over him, her pretty face wreathed in concern.

"It's all right, Papa. I'm here."

But nothing could console that old man. He folded his arms and wept into them, over the black and white keys.

I was disappointed to leave. I used to say to the girls, "There will be other tennis matches, there will be other trips," but this time, I thought, *no, there mightn't be.* Some things are just once-in-a-lifetime moments. Tomorrow, La Poupée could be burned to the ground or Louis could be murdered in a field at Passchendaele, or I could be shelled in my tent like poor Elle Harcourt, who never really got to do her bit. *You mustn't drink so much,* I told myself as Louis walked me to the car. *That's why you're so emotional.* But the sight of the old man's heartbreak was locked in my mind.

I fell asleep in the car. Whether it was because I was lulled by the motion, or by the feeling of peace I had from being by Louis' side, I'm not sure.

The lanterns outside the hospital were lit but it looked, blessedly, quiet. My nap had done me good. I felt sober and more like myself again. The world no longer looked so bleak. Louis stopped the engine and turned to me.

"So, what is it you actually do, Major Spears?" I asked, thinking of what Elsie had said. *People are listening to him.*

"Liaison."

"And what exactly is liaison?"

"I encourage people to make the best decisions with the information available." Louis' arms were crossed and he looked thoughtful.

"And how do you do that?"

"Ah well, I do projections and estimate outcomes," he said vaguely.

"Word-soup." I laughed. He shrugged.

But I was curious. "Do you sometimes withhold information or present it in the way you want it to go, to influence the outcome?"

"As if I'd do that!" he said. "I'm not a cheat."

No, I thought. *You're* not.

He leaned over to me slowly and we kissed. It had been a long time since I had someone's lips press onto mine, and it was a shock at first. My lips didn't know what to do. Yet, quickly, I remembered— more than remembered, I learned all over again. I caught the back of Louis' head with my hand, felt his wonderful soft, tufty hair and pulled him closer to me.

But then Louis pulled away. He shook his head, he looked down into his hands, curled into small knots in his lap.

"What is it?"

"May, are you sure?" he asked. I waited but he didn't add anything. I could still taste him in my mouth. Alcohol, cigarettes and Major Louis Spears.

Someone extinguished one of the lanterns ahead. It felt like a punctuation mark.

"How do you mean, Louis? I'm sure. Aren't you?"

Louis sighed deeply.

"Are you not attracted to me?"

In the same solemn voice that he probably used when he was explaining to General Pétain that things were looking bad on the Western Front, he said quietly: "I've never been so attracted to anyone in my entire life."

And I believed him. I could see that whatever was going on inside that beautiful head of his was torture.

"So?"

"You're a married woman."

"Divorcing…"

"And a mother. I would hate to make your life more difficult or complicated, I don't want to confuse things for you."

I looked out at the hospital, *my* hospital, and as my eyes got used to the darkness, I could just make out the silhouetted shapes of the other team. Our ghostly equivalent, tending to the injured men at night.

"Well, then, goodbye."

There was no point waiting around. I opened the door and stepped out the car. This was going nowhere—the last thing I wanted was to get involved with a man who didn't want me. However much I was yearning for him, an unrequited love affair was not for me.

But Louis had got out the car too, and he moved faster than I did. He came around in front of me and caught me. He pressed me up against the passenger door—the handle dug into my back, but I didn't mind—and we kissed some more and some more and even though fraternizing was an offense, and even though I was still a married woman, *that* ship had long since sailed.

We got back in the car.

CHAPTER TWENTY-FIVE

A few days later, Kitty and I walked into town. It was about an hour on the rough tracks and twice we were offered lifts by passing trucks but we turned them down. There wasn't much to do with our free time, so the walk was part of it. Plus, if you ignored the smell, the noise, the dust, the burnt-out houses and the engineers laying down railtracks, there were hedgerows and daisies to enjoy and for a short while, you could pretend that you were on vacation.

In town, the street traders were selling peaches and plums out of old suitcases. The plums were too pale, not quite ripe, but we were too hungry to care.

"We might be dead tomorrow," Kitty said brightly.

We sat eating them on the steps of the city hall. Some small birds darted near us. So bold. My head was aching. Ever since my night out with Louis, I had been filled with terrible tension: I didn't know if he would come to see me again. I didn't know if I *wanted* to see him again. Well, I did, desperately, but I was also frightened. *What does it all mean?* I wanted to ask. What does it mean to fall in love with someone in this place, and what did it mean for my life back home? What would it mean to George?

Kitty was reading *Wuthering Heights* now, all by herself, and she was telling me about it.

"I thought you still had your hour studying with Gordon? Why, when you can read so well?" I interrupted.

"Oh that," she said airily. "That's for medicine."

"Oh?"

She continued with her confident retelling of the classics. "She thinks Heathcliff doesn't love her, so she stops living."

"I didn't know that." I had read *Wuthering Heights* when I was fifteen, about a year before I had run off with George. Perhaps if I had paid more attention, I might not have been such a gullible twerp.

"Well, it's not spelled out, I suppose, it's implied. She dies in childbirth but before that she starved herself and became weaker and weaker, because she loves Heathcliff, but she's stuck with her husband Linton."

"Right-o."

I took another plum from the paper bag. We had said we might save some for the others but on second thought, I had decided, if Matron and Bonnie were *that* desperate for plums, quite honestly they should have come to town themselves. Kitty carried on telling me plot points in *Wuthering Heights* that I had missed. *What would Louis do next?* I wondered. Everything came back to Louis. Was he thinking of me right now? I kept going over that night: his expression, his dark eyes, his hands. We couldn't go back "to normal" after that, could we?

I tried to pay more attention to Kitty.

"I think I could do more," she was saying as she stretched her legs out in front of her. She had a hole in her stocking. The birds chirruped around us.

"How do you mean?"

"In the hospital, I feel I could contribute more . . . if they'd let me."

This made me uncomfortable because if Kitty could do more, then maybe we all could, and right now I was not inclined to do anything except get through the day and daydream about Louis.

"What exactly?"

"I don't know," she said flatly. "Pass me another plum."

*

A medium was visiting some of the hospitals along the Somme and she came to ours one quiet Monday evening in April. Katherine and Lucille's tent was decked out with extra drapes and lanterns. The medium insisted on it for "atmosphere," apparently. The other shift had come away marveling at her insights. Katherine, especially, was elated: love was going to win out after all! Even serious Millicent was all smiles. "She said I'm going to go into politics after the war," she announced proudly.

I told Bonnie I had no interest in seeing a charlatan.

"Don't be such a killjoy," she said as though it was the worst thing a girl could be. "Don't you want to find out if true love is coming your way?"

Naturally, I thought of Louis.

"No," I said haughtily, but Bonnie had already put my name down.

"You don't believe in this tosh?" I asked Kitty, as I waited for her and Bonnie to change.

"Not for a moment." She nudged me. "But it should be fun."

Although I was probably the least keen, I was the first to arrive. As the medium gazed deep into my eyes, she told me her name was Madame Lorenzo. I didn't know what her accent was, but it certainly wasn't French. Her head was wrapped in a curious turban of green and massive gold loops hung down from her earlobes. We had to pay a contribution.

"Entirely voluntary," she said, shaking her tin under my nose.

"Here's Bonnie," I said. I was relieved that she had arrived, less so when she bowed deeply, as though Madame Lorenzo was royalty. "And this is Kitty," I went on. Kitty extended her hand earnestly, then looked over at me and winked.

We sat on cushions around a low table. Someone had brought in a few pillows too and rugs and blankets from Gordon's tent. Doctor Rafferty apparently thought *anything* that helped nursing morale was welcome. Gordon was on leave, and I couldn't help but think he wouldn't be so approving if he knew what we were up to.

Madame Lorenzo talked about how serious this was, and how we all had to believe or it wouldn't work, which reminded me of Tinker Bell in *Peter Pan*. I wanted to point this out to Kitty, but she was too far away. I was stuck next to a fervently nodding Matron, who seemed to be swallowing this hook, line and sinker.

We watched while Madame Lorenzo waited for the spirits to reach her. I thought about making a joke about my husband's love for bottled spirits but there was no one to whisper it to. It was another one for the diary.

"I have something... Is there a Tom?"

I smirked. *Everyone knew a Tom, didn't they?*

We all looked at each other. *Don't let me laugh out loud.*

"My brother was Thomas," Matron whispered.

"He's passed?"

"Yes," Matron said beseechingly. "When he was a boy."

"He's sending you a message."

"And is there a Bonnie here?" Madame Lorenzo asked next.

"How does she know my name?" Bonnie responded wonderingly.

"I told her..." I started, but Bonnie only had ears for Madame Lorenzo.

"Do you know a Laurie?"

"No," said Bonnie apologetically, but she *did* know a Lenny, she went on—could that be him?

"Yes!" Madame Lorenzo's hands were vibrating, her many rings glittered. "That was it."

Bonnie looked at us all incredulously, her mouth wide open. "Lenny lived on my street."

"He's passed."

Bonnie looked pale. Dazzled. "He couldn't fight, he lives at home with his ma."

The medium sighed. "Was it Leonard maybe?"

"*I* know a Leonard," admitted Kitty. "He's my brother's best friend."

"He's passed."

Kitty looked at me. Matron shifted onto her haunches. She leaned right in to Kitty and gripped her hand.

"He loved you," Madame Lorenzo pronounced. She took off her glasses and wiped them on her shawl. Without them, she looked much younger. I suddenly thought how incredible it must be to travel around France, soothing young nurses about the fate of their dead fiancés. She must believe in it, even if I didn't.

"Me?"

"He never told you?" This was no obstacle to Madame Lorenzo. "It happens…"

"He was engaged to my cousin—"

"He loved *you*," she said firmly. "Do you have a teapot? In the kitchen?"

"I do…"

"*Amazing*," I muttered, rolling my eyes. Matron shot me a disapproving look.

"He left a message in the teapot."

"I'll make sure I look next time I'm home and"—I couldn't tell if Kitty was struggling to laugh or cry—"fancy a brew…"

We all sat in silence for a while, then Madame Lorenzo must have caught another spirit, for she suddenly yelped: "George! Is it you? Does anyone know a George?"

Everyone turned to me. Surely they recognized this for the nonsense it was, didn't they?

Matron spoke up, her voice ripe with emotion. "Has he…passed?"

"Chance would be a fine thing!" I laughed. Matron's intake of breath was loud and shaming.

"What's going on?" It was Gordon. Framed by the tent door, he looked furious. "Matron?!"

"I can explain, Doctor…" Matron gathered her skirts. I wanted to snigger behind my hand.

But Gordon was very angry. His eyes glinted in the dark. "I don't want to talk," he barked. He was in quite the flap. "Out, out, out . . . You should be ashamed of yourselves, all of you."

"You shouldn't have said that," Matron said darkly as we scuttled away like naughty schoolgirls.

"Said what?" Although I knew what she meant, I wanted her to spell out my awfulness.

"You shouldn't have wished the father of your children dead."

"It was a joke," I explained weakly. *I* knew I shouldn't have. Not in this company, anyway. Matron hated irreverence. She would have been a great friend to my mother.

"He's your *husband*," said Matron.

"My ex-husband, actually."

"You should be with your girls, you've no place here."

I kept my mouth shut; I couldn't win an argument with her.

"Things are going to get much worse," she hissed. "You'll regret it then, won't you?"

Later, I went to Gordon's tent to apologize. I knew he had thought better of us, of me especially. I found him sitting on the floor, face in his hands, amid all the shawls and cushions. I sank down next to him.

"Gordon? Doctor Collins? It was just a bit of fun, I'm sorry."

But Gordon wasn't distressed about Madame Lorenzo. It was Karim. He had dragged in three wounded soldiers from no-man's-land and taken three bullets to the stomach for his efforts. He was on the hospital train to England. They were sending injured Indian troops to the Royal Pavilion in Brighton. Gordon must have seen the mystification in my face because he added in an ironic tone, "In their infinite wisdom, the powers-that-be think the Indians will feel most at home there."

Awkwardly, I put my arm around Gordon, waiting for him to tell me it was inappropriate, think of our positions, but instead, he turned toward me and sobbed into my apron.

Madame Lorenzo was still waiting for her lift when I went into the canteen an hour later. *Shame the spirits didn't warn her of the delay*, I thought. I backed away because I didn't want to talk to her; I thought of the money she must have raised from us nurses at Field Hospital 19 alone. Other women were shoveling coal, building munitions, growing vegetables and running trains, and what was she doing? Taking our hard-earned wages and giving false hope to the vulnerable—and weren't we all vulnerable now?

She saw me though: "Nurse Turner?"

"Yes?"

"The man you like…with the eyes…"

I caught my breath. *Louis.* She must have been talking about him. Against my better judgment, I urged her on: "What about him?"

"Oh yes," she said vaguely to nothing in particular. "I hear you loud and clear."

She nodded slowly. I could see she was enjoying the power, but I couldn't stop myself from being sucked into the game.

"What do you know about him?" I tried again.

"He's a complex character," she said. I tried to get past her, but she stared right into me. I didn't want her to know that she'd got to me, so I gazed straight back. Her eyes were surprisingly youthful in her wrinkled face.

"You have children?"

"Ye-es…"

I felt this horrible rage boil inside me, rage that my privacy, *their* privacy, had been invaded.

"Daughters of war, is it?"

I stood stock-still.

"You risk losing them."

Charlatan, I thought. She must have overheard me talking with Matron. An ugly anger rippled through me. *I'll rip off that turban, I'll pull off those earrings. How dare she?*

"You need to be strong, Nurse Turner."

"I *am* strong," I said. I heard the scrunch of a car pulling up and she scuttled off, pulling her shawl around her. I thought of *Macbeth* and the three witches with their doom-laden prophecies. They had planted the horrors. I wasn't going to be like Macbeth, *I* wouldn't be swayed by it.

I risk losing my daughters?

She was completely mad.

CHAPTER TWENTY-SIX

Joy had a new passion the Easter of 1916. On the train back from Leamington, she wanted to talk of nothing but art and the new art teacher at school. I wondered if she had a crush—she was twelve after all, nearly a young woman—but she looked astonished when I suggested it. "Mo-other! Professor Deacon is old!" Shyly, and after much prompting from Leona, she showed me some of her drawings. I was so proud. My girl had done these! They were as good as any I'd seen for sale at Montmartre and I told her so. She blushed.

"You're not just saying that?"

"I'm not, sweetheart."

I had five days' leave and by Jove, I needed it. The hospital was expanding. Two more teams brought in and one more tent. A railroad had sprung up only one mile away. George had written that he was away checking piers in Morecambe (I took it that "pier" was a euphemism for "women"). Our Christmas row seemed to have been forgotten, for now at least.

The girls and I were walking down the long corridor at the National Gallery when I saw a sign for a special exhibition in a side room. *Dear God!* I couldn't believe my eyes.

"This way," I said, trying to shepherd my girls away, but Joy, as ever, was not to be shepherded.

"Oh, Mother, can't we go in? Please, Mummy, please! Professor Deacon says Milhouse's paintings encapsulate this moment in our time."

They encapsulate this moment in our time?

It was an entire room devoted to Percy's paintings. And it was *Morning Light in St. Ives,* the one with the red line, that had done it. He had gone from niche London artist to International Superstar. Joy was so swept up with each picture, I think she would have jumped right into them if she could have. Leona was more like me. She read the writing, then gave a cursory glance at the painting. There was an elderly security guard snoring in the corner, but when we came in, he straightened up, re-affixed his hat. Joy pulled me over.

"I love this one..."

"Do you?" I had seen Percy squeeze the oils for this. I had seen him scratch his head in confusion. I had seen the paint run down onto the newspapers on the floor.

"It means that although the war affects all our lives, we go on."

I had never thought about it that way.

Leona had sat herself in the corner with her marbles, but Joy grew more delighted with each painting, which correspondently seemed to mean she grew more delighted with me.

"I can't believe we're here!" She twirled, looking at me. "Daddy would never take us somewhere like this."

"Daddy has never taken us anywhere!" piped up Leona.

"Shall we get some tea?" I said. "And how about a round of I Spy?"

Afterward, I took the girls to Elizabeth's house to visit and this time she was all welcoming smiles. She and her cats were charming hosts. All the windows were wide open as usual, but fortunately, it wasn't too cold. Politely, I inquired about Miss Dobinson and, without her usual smirk, Elizabeth responded, "Harriet has been promoted, it seems she is a most excellent conductress." I was set to ask more, but Elizabeth's expression told me that more was not welcome. Instead, she launched into some hilarious anecdotes. Some of these tales were a little risqué: her mother's opinion on men's new-style bathing trunks, the places sand gets—I thought she might have toned it down a bit in front of the girls—but how glorious it was to hear Joy and Leona giggle again.

*

The next morning, while the girls were at the tennis club, I went to meet Elizabeth at the bathing lake. I was looking forward to getting her on my own. She did her usual ferocious workout as I bobbed around. The water was even bluer than I remembered and one length felt much longer. The sun shone down on us; I was enjoying myself. There were far fewer women than there used to be but they were as welcoming as ever.

When Elizabeth had done, we sat down by the edge, drying off. It didn't take her long to catch her breath but her lips were ever so slightly purple.

"So, how are you really, May?"

She was enquiring about something else, but I wasn't sure what. I realized that although I had said I would, I hadn't written her about Louis. I told myself that was reasonable—there was nothing *firm* yet to say. Although I was entirely smitten with Louis, who now occupied most of my waking thoughts, I wasn't entirely sure where I stood with him. However, that wasn't the main reason I had kept her in the dark. My main reason was that I had a strong instinct that Elizabeth wouldn't be very receptive to this news. She certainly disliked Percy for nothing much at all. And I was beginning to realize, Elizabeth almost certainly had secrets she kept from me.

"How do you mean?"

"I mean, are you happy now?"

Elizabeth rolled onto her front and pulled the petals off a daisy.

"I am much happier," I admitted shamefully because I knew this truth was horrid. "War suits me—" I went to say something else, keen to change the subject, but she interrupted.

"And George?"

"The divorce is going through," I said, although I had no idea how far along in the process we were or indeed how long it usually took. "And how are you feeling about the Big Swim?"

"I can't wait." She seemed cheered again. Then she asked shyly, "You really think you'll be back for it?"

"Is Kaiser Wilhelm an idiot?"

"I'm not sure..."

We laughed again.

I had heard goose fat was the perfect thing for a long-distance swimmer (she would rub it all over her skin to insulate her from the cold) and I had managed to acquire some as a present. After I explained what the odd-looking tin contained, Elizabeth was absolutely delighted. She wrapped her arms around me, cold droplets transferring onto my skin, making me shiver.

"You darling! You really believe I can do it, don't you?"

"Yes!" I said, incredulous that she had to ask.

The whistle blew. Our time was up.

CHAPTER TWENTY-SEVEN

I had just managed to push Major Louis Spears to the back of my mind when he came back, more attractive than ever. As before, he had brought an excuse with him. This time it was not his wrist, but a friend of a friend he was needing to check up on.

I looked at the patient list on the blackboard. "Are you sure he's here?"

"Not really." He was looking at me closely, almost pleadingly. I felt hot just standing near him.

"It's Matron you'll need. She has the general register."

"It's all right," he said vaguely. "Might I have a word outside, May?"

It was sunny. We could have walked over to the rock. Kitty had christened it Little Big Rock and it was where we nurses liked to go to contemplate things after a particularly hard shift, or simply to eat our lunch without the clatter of the canteen, but Louis shook his head. He said he didn't have long.

He had his hands on his hips and was staring at me. I looked down at his great boots and found myself wondering what size his feet were. A 10 or 11 maybe? And I thought my feet were big! Did he have to go to specialist shoemakers for boots that large?

"When can I see you again?" Louis asked fiercely.

I waited. And it's good that I did because the more I waited, the more he gave.

"May," he said, "I *have* to see you, I can think of nothing but you."

"Tomorrow morning?" (So much for playing it cool.)

"What time?"

"Ten?"

"I'll be here."

*

Louis was there at nine. Bonnie heard the car crawl up the road and rushed in to tell me. She was almost as excited as I was. "May is going out with a gentleman!" I heard her tell one of the patients. The poor soul had slipped a disk and couldn't have been less interested.

I kept Louis waiting until gone ten though: this was my deal with myself to prove that I was no pushover. The sun was still shining; it was freakishly good weather. When the sun shone like this it was hard not to be optimistic. I asked where we were going, but he said it was a surprise. The way he said it sent a thrill through me.

"Just tell me, is it in another country this time?"

His mouth twitched. "No, it's only one hour away..."

"Paris?" I suggested hopefully.

"We'll go there together one day," he said, which was music to my ears. I wanted to kiss his face. *Control yourself!* I admonished myself.

"But not today?"

"Not today," he said, staring straight ahead. "Today I have other plans for you."

As we drove away from the front line, the mud tracks turned into roads and the scenery grew more ordinary. By ordinary, I mean it looked less like a mud wasteland and more like French countryside. We put the brown, the gray and the barren behind us and headed toward the green. There was a good population of trees here. At one road, I was surprised to find several bushy trees lined up in a row and, in the breeze, it looked rather as though they were bowing down to us. *Silly*, I thought, because it should have been us bowing down to them.

Louis asked me about my childhood in Chicago. As I was talking, I surprised myself with some of the things that seemed to burst out of me. I really was an exile from not one but two places, an outsider everywhere I went. Louis was nodding to himself. He said, "I know that feeling well."

He had polio as a boy and the hard recovery had left him feeling slow among his peers in some ways, older in other ways. He told me he had adored his mother, but when he was ill, he was sent away to a hospital in Switzerland. His voice cracked as he told me how he had not been allowed to see her. Soon after he was brought home, maybe only one or two months, it was hard to remember, she had died. A brain hemorrhage. The family friends who brought him up were fine people, but they didn't like to speak of her, and he had missed her terribly.

"So that's my sorry tale," he said gruffly. "What's yours?"

I always preferred to talk of my late Grandma Leonora and her achievements, but I also gave Louis a brief summary of my parents and told him about the route out I had mistakenly chosen at sixteen. How I had thought George was my port in a storm, only it transpired the port was run-down and dangerous, and that storms blow over anyway.

When Louis asked me about the hospital, I told him about my work and my friends. I also told him that a medium had come to visit us.

"A medium? What's wrong with a large?"

I groaned and slapped his thigh. *Honestly, Louis!*

"She mentioned you," I added coyly. "She said you're complex."

"Well, I can't imagine you going for a simpleton." I didn't need to look at his face to know he was grinning again.

I should have said, *what makes you think I've gone for you?* but I was too caught up in the moment. Everything felt so right with Louis. I hadn't known things could feel this right; it was a revelation.

The river was surrounded by thick sprays of reeds and brushes. Louis looked up at me, rubbing his cheek cautiously. "You *did* say you loved water... I thought it would remind you of... where was it... Tooting Bathing Lake?"

Did he remember everything I said?

Louis undressed down to his undershirt and long johns. He stacked his clothes in an orderly bundle before, without hesitation, walking toward the water. *Oh, dear God*, I thought, *what was wrong with me?* I felt like my heart was doing cartwheels and somersaults.

"Louis!" I called after him. "I may need some help." I didn't normally need assistance, but I didn't want him to disappear. He apologized, unbuttoned my skirt and helped me off with my blouse. His fingers were cool on my back. My skirt fell to the ground, leaving me in my bloomers, and I struggled out of the blouse so that I was wearing only my soft corset. Louis kept his eyes on the water ahead. The water was sparkling in the sunlight. I waded after him. It was warmer than I had expected.

Louis was as strong a swimmer as he was a dancer. I watched the rise and fall of those beautiful arms over his narrow, yet muscular, shoulders. The way he punctuated the water. Did he have to do *everything* so well? The ripples spread out from where he swam, concentric circles getting bigger and bigger. I thought, maybe Elizabeth would approve of him after all.

I swam out to him, holding my neck high to protect my hair. That was a waste of time since as soon as I was close enough, he splashed me, and I splashed him back. We splashed up a storm. A little voice inside me was saying, *you can relax now*. He caught me by the waist and, for a moment, I thought he was going to twirl me around as he had done at La Poupée, but instead he pulled me closer and closer until there was nowhere to go. His skin was cold and wet, his chest was broad and strong. I put my hands on his shoulders, looking at him admiringly and without shame.

This was here. This was now.

The sun was setting when Louis drove me back to base. It was hard to believe we could have an afternoon as magical as this, during this terrible war, but we had. Perhaps because the war was so ugly, beautiful things seemed all the more magical.

In the car, Louis asked about my girls again. "Do they like cricket?"

"Not really."

"Bridge? Dominos?"

"Not really, no..."

"Soccer?"

"They play tennis."

"Ah well," he said. He took one hand off the steering wheel and put my hand in his. His hand was so big that mine fitted right inside it. "I've always wanted to learn tennis."

I went looking for Kitty to report my safe return but was told that she was with Gordon in the operating tent. Later, I found Gordon washing his hands.

"Is Kitty your assistant now?"

"She's talented. The boy was riddled with shrapnel, she managed to get most of it out."

"I don't know if that's orthodox," I said.

He ignored that. "Do you want to learn to do it too?"

"Not really." I wrinkled up my nose. "I'm happy just being a nurse."

Gordon paused. He dried his hands, then squeezed my shoulder. "No *just* about it. However, it might be a good skill to learn—you might need it in the future."

I frowned. I understood what he was getting at, I just didn't believe it.

There is this idea that nothing changes out here. That we are static, that we are all, quite literally, stuck in the mud. Sometimes, I think it too. That everything is the same, everything is waiting, everything is routine—but then other times, I realize that we are at the heart of an enormous shift, cultural, technological. We are at the forefront of a revolution: our equipment advances, our skills develop, our compassion grows, our morals change, our responsibilities and our passions increase. We are different from how we were yesterday.

CHAPTER TWENTY-EIGHT

Matron had done over one year's service without leave, however, she didn't want a break. She was worried about a decline in morals while she was away. I overheard Gordon speaking to her soothingly.

"Bonnie's fiancé is in England. Kitty is wedded to her work. And May is a respectable mother of young daughters. I can't think of a more reliable team."

She sighed deeply. "We'll see."

I helped her carry out her trunk to the waiting car. I was looking forward to having the tent to myself for a few days. *Take that, invisible line!* I had to conceal my delight at her departure and I was proud of how well I managed it.

"Stay well, Matron," I said earnestly. "We'll be fine."

"You can't wait for me to go, Nurse Turner!" she snapped, slamming the passenger door.

Clearly, I hadn't hidden it as well as I had thought.

Meanwhile, I had received permission for two weeks' leave in July and I couldn't wait. I was going to fetch the girls from school and we would take the train straight to Dorset. I had studied the train timetables and planned our packed lunches with military precision: Scotch egg for Leona, cheese sandwich for Joy. The girls didn't like the same foods (deliberately, I suspected).

Elsie Knocker had written to me with the address of some friends who had a charming cottage on the coast that we could stay in. Five days there: walking on the beach, hunting fossils and eating as much ice cream as we could manage. After that, five days in London. How I looked forward to showing them the sights! We would visit the Tower of London. I had taken the girls there once before, when they were tiny: Joy had wet herself in the Bloody Tower and Leona could remember nothing about it, not even the sparkling Crown Jewels and the suits of armor that had so enthralled her at the time. I had also penciled in the Natural History Museum and was looking forward to seeing the great diplodocus as much as the girls were. The arguments over how to pronounce it had been going on for years. Apparently, my way was wrong and "American." Any gaps in the schedule would be spent at the tennis club—the girls always wanted me to watch them play. And then, the *pièce de résistance*, timed to perfection: Elizabeth's Channel swim. We'd all go to cheer her on! I couldn't wait, this was an event for the record books.

I ticked the days off the calendar in my diary. I dreamt about my girls running down the school steps, past the artificial Greek columns gleaming white in the sunshine, shouting, "Mummy, Mummy!" I dreamt about sniffing their hair.

Throughout May 1916, I was mostly in dressings or convalescence. Field Hospital 19 expanded once again. We opened an isolation unit, a depressing place where young men coughed up blood and stared at the ceiling. Everyone was waiting for something, to get better or to get worse. One time after a twelve-hour shift, I went back to my tent and, I have no idea how it got there, who had been bribed or won over or what, but there on my flat pillow lay a bright daffodil and a note in the most beautiful handwriting:

> *I hereby promise to always make your life more complicated. Yours sincerely, a very complex man.*

I held it to my heart. I didn't want to put it down. I even permitted myself a love-sick sigh. Major Louis Spears. He *was* worth it. I would never let him go, never.

CHAPTER TWENTY-NINE

Early June, Kitty received word from home that her mother had died. She wasn't told much more about it, other than that her mother had gone to bed as usual but didn't wake up. It seemed incredible that someone would just die, peacefully, in their sleep. No shelling, no bombing, no bullets, nothing enormous, just slipping undramatically, quietly, away. We had grown unused to that. It was Kitty's time to go back.

I missed her terribly: I loved having Kitty to bounce ideas off. Bonnie was not sensible enough, Matron was too judgmental, Gordon spent most of his time typing long, coded letters to the Brighton Pavilion…Kitty was the closest thing I had to a special right-hand girl out here. Although our experiences and expectations of life were vastly different, we shared so much.

Louis was doing an inspection of the area and asked if I had an hour or two to spare. Gordon gave permission for me to go; Matron would have certainly said no. She had returned from a wet week in Weston-super-Mare no more invigorated than she ever was. Gordon was still desperately worried about Karim—who was not finding Brighton Pavilion a home from home at all—so he may have indulged Matron less than he usually did. Consequently, those two were brewing up a big storm. I suspected it was also the stress of being without Nurse Kitty, the safest pair of hands on our team.

Louis and I drove toward the front line. The air was even grimier here and the explosions were so much louder. Despite the recent sunshine, the ground was far muddier than near the hospital; I slipped a couple of times and he had to grab my arm. I was too hot in my borrowed helmet and Louis' coat. We walked through the communication trenches and closer to the front line. Men saluted him. He talked to some officers. They had a fabulous dugout with soft chairs, radios and telephones. They'd really made themselves at home. It reminded me of Gordon's tent but this was less exotic, more English somehow.

Further along we went, along these winding passageways. Duckboards with signs for places I had heard of, but never been to.

"You take me to the nicest places," I whispered. Louis pretended he hadn't heard. He knew I didn't care where he took me though. Just being with him was enough for me.

We came upon a massive piece of machinery. Men were gathered around it, polishing it, posing on it as though it were an enormous plaything. Louis went over to one of them and I joined him a little sheepishly. I was out of place here and everyone knew it. I wanted to keep quiet too. I had heard some of the boys going on about Americans this and Americans that. I knew it was just soldiers' talk, but still.

"Ten men?" Louis was saying.

"Ten men ain't enough, sir. We're looking at fourteen at least."

Louis looked shocked and impressed, so I tried to look shocked and impressed too.

It had to be held down otherwise it would shake itself free. It was a monster of a machine with a great snout for a nose, paws at the front. I imagined it breathing fire into the German trenches.

Louis told me it was called a howitzer, which I thought but didn't like to say sounded quite German to me.

Along its long cylindrical trunk, someone—I don't know if it was here or where it was manufactured—had painted the word "Mother."

"Why does it say 'mother'?" I asked Louis.

"Because it can inflict a lot of damage."

I laughed. "Maybe they met *my* mother!"

*

The trucks were bringing in munitions. The men stood in lines unloading boxes and boxes of them and passing them on. And there were tanks too, giant vehicles from the future. I had never seen anything so modern or so chilling.

"They'll be safe in there," said Louis. "It's meant to intimidate"—he gestured—"like the way a goalie spreads out his arms to scare the opposition."

I didn't know that goalies spread out their arms. I looked at him. It was like he was talking a different language and this, 1,000 yards from our base, was a different country. A makeshift terrible country.

"So, we've got plenty of good weaponry," I repeated. I tried to make myself sound intellectual, but I couldn't. My heart was in my boots.

"The best," he said. "To think, when the war started we thought it would be"—he shivered—"knives and shields. And now, it's about planes, tanks, the stuff of H. G. Wells."

Back in the car, when it was just the two of us, Louis swore me to secrecy. I wasn't to tell anyone anything about what we'd seen.

"Cross my heart," I said lightly. I was going to joke about the likelihood of Matron or Gordon being foreign spies, conveying information perhaps to Rasputin or the Tsar, but I noticed he was scowling—I wasn't taking this seriously enough. "The war will be won by engineers," Louis said.

"And the handsome liaison officers." I patted his hand proudly but he went on as though I hadn't spoken. Since November last year, he explained, our men had been burrowing, tunneling beneath us. Like moles, I thought, like in *The Wind in the Willows*. They were going to blow the Germans into the air. Down below, there were mines, and explosions, and glorious work. I glanced down at our boots, at the earth beneath our car: "Under here? Right now?" How could this be?

"Not quite here, May, but not far." He looked anxious. "Hopefully, it'll be a success."

"I'm sure it will." I squinted, trying to work out his feelings on it. "When will it start?"

"Whenever they're ready," he said cryptically. He paused. "Winston thinks it's going to be a disaster."

"Why?"

"He thinks the powers-that-be are obsessed with the Western Front."

"What do you think?"

Louis had a tendency toward fence-sitting. I had no doubt he would be one of the world's best diplomats, but it sometimes meant he could be difficult to disagree with. "On one hand, we need to break the deadlock."

"And on the other?"

He stared right ahead of him. "We might not win."

It wasn't until after my shift, back in the tent that evening with Matron snoring obliviously alongside me, when I had more time to think about it, that I realized exactly how unsettling the day had been. I had seen our weapons of destruction. More ways to kill. Better ways to murder. More effective ways to wipe out the opposition. I needed to talk to Louis again, I decided. I needed to be with him. It felt as though time was running out.

It was a warm June night, but for me, there was a chill in the air. I prayed my girls were safe and I quietly got up to put on a cardigan.

Things I miss in England (apart from the girls)

Baths. Hot, bubbly, wonderful baths.

The sapphire blue of Tooting Bathing Lake.

The way Elizabeth hesitates just for a second before she laughs, loudly.

Her pale eyelashes. Her marmalade hair.

Clean feet. Short toenails.

Cakes. Eccles cake. Fruit cake. Victoria sponge. Elizabeth's macaroons.

Art galleries. The National Gallery. The Portrait Gallery. Even Percy's exhibition!

Shoes. All my beautiful shoes.

Mrs. Crawford's pies.

CHAPTER THIRTY

After Kitty came back from her mother's funeral, she looked different, more determined somehow. She had freckles on her nose and a healthy glow, but it wasn't just that. Her jaw was set, her chin tilted upward and even in her docile white blouse and tie, and her long sweeping skirt, she somehow looked a picture of defiance. As soon as she'd greeted me, she asked, "What's going on out there?"

"How do you mean?"

"The ship, the train, the trucks on the roads—*everywhere* I went, we were packed in like sardines. I've never seen anything like it."

Hundreds of troops were on the move. Marching, chanting. They were Kitchener's Army. All volunteers. There were pals from Battersea, pals from Dartford. When we walked into town, some of them waved and we waved back. I found tears coming to my eyes. I wondered if German wives, mothers and sisters over in Berlin or Düsseldorf were thinking and fearing the same. And there were planes too. German planes, daring as small birds, flying low and watching us intently.

"Perhaps the war will be over soon," Bonnie offered hopefully.

"Something's definitely happening," Kitty murmured. She looked at me questioningly, but I just shrugged. I wasn't concealing anything; I didn't know a great deal more than that. I thought of "Mother"—Mother was going to see to it that everything was all right. Mother and her fourteen children. What could go wrong?

Something else *was* happening now: rain. The clouds gathered overhead, and whereas once at this time of year you'd sensed summer making its presence felt, now you didn't know what it was. Of course it was fun to blame Kitty for bringing it back with her from England. Rain in France. Warm rain. Just running from sleeping tents to hospital tents, from hospital tents to the canteen, you'd be as wet as if you'd gone for a dip in Tooting Bathing Lake.

The ground kept splashing up. Keeping clean was a nightmare, but we managed.

I noticed that our convalescents were being hurried away too quickly, before their time. Even the ones who might have been contagious.

We had no patients, but we needed empty beds?

Another field hospital was built not far from ours. I don't know how they managed it in the rain and the mud, but they did. One minute there was nothing, the next a massive tent had been erected, with a village of small tents around it. It went up so quick, I worried that it wasn't sturdy enough, especially in this rain. I watched wide-eyed new nurses arrive in shiny purpose-built ambulances. Dark-haired and bustling, they were from Portugal. They came to our hospital to see how we were doing. Funny to watch our matron, so stiff, arms folded, talking to their matron with her hands flying and her expressive face. We greeted our dear allies warmly, but we had to get on with our work. Maybe they found us reserved, or unemotional, I don't know.

Louis came by again about a week later. As delighted as I was to see him, I was uncomfortable with this. Matron made it clear she didn't like it, and even Gordon probably thought it was unprofessional. But Louis always did what Louis wanted. He held a large umbrella, but the rain was so torrential, so horizontal, his handsome face was still drenched. He reassured me he only had a minute; he was on the way to a meeting in Amiens. He somehow made it sound as though this was general knowledge.

We got in his car while the rain thrashed at the windshield. We gripped each other's hands as though afraid the other would float away. *If only we could be alone, together, away from all this.*

"When are you getting out of here, sweetheart?" he eventually asked.

"In twelve days." I was sure he already knew this. We had talked about it many times. I could rhapsodize about this trip with my daughters forever.

"How long will you be away for?"

"I have two weeks' leave," I said even though, again, I was sure I'd told him umpteen times. I rabbited on, at first oblivious to his manner. "Gordon's been good about it. Matron had the hump, but I can't wait."

Louis looked over his shoulder as though expecting someone to be there. He slid one of his fingers between each of mine. I had to catch my breath.

"Go now," he said.

I laughed. "Don't be daft, Louis."

Louis' knees were shaking; it wasn't just the cold. He took his hands from mine, clutched the steering wheel. He seemed to be having palpitations; he was struggling to breathe.

"Louis? What is it, Louis?"

"Leave, May, leave now!"

"I can't. You're being absurd."

He could hardly get the words out, his teeth were chattering so: "It's going to be bad."

"That's why we're here," I said soothingly.

"As bad as Verdun. This is the big push, right here..."

I thought of the low-flying planes. "Do you think the Germans haven't noticed all this preparation?"

Louis looked at his hands. I realized this was the wrong thing to say.

"Then this is what's needed," I said, comfortingly. "It may be bloody and terrible, but it has to be done. We have a duty, all of us."

I noticed a small spider on his windshield, perhaps enjoying the view. I thought, *if only they'd start the battle today, they could be done in two weeks and then I could get home, having done my bit.* As it was, I bet I would be away when it was on. *I* didn't want that, even if Louis did—I would hate to let my team down.

"I don't know," he said.

I thought, *but you showed me everything, you said how good it was, how advanced we were! You were cheerful. What's happening now?*

Louis looked at me with pleading eyes. He was still shivering.

"I'll be all right," I told him. "I promise."

"You're sitting ducks out here."

I wished I were back in the lake with him now, the sun beating down on our naked shoulders. That delicious togetherness. The yearning to be alone with him, to be away from here was so powerful it was almost frightening. I had to put it to one side or else I would have been completely overwhelmed by it. "They won't attack the hospitals," I said confidently, although of course I had no idea who or what they might attack. "Come here, darling. Let me hold you."

I made Louis put his quaking arm around me, snuggled into him, his damp uniform and all, and soon he had stopped shivering.

The next day, it felt like some luck arrived. First, the sweetest letter from Elizabeth. Everything was coming together. She had found a new coach and this fellow was a genius—he had trained two men to cross the water before the war. He was taking on the arrangements: her boat, her starting point, her headgear. He didn't think her pace was too fast (always a bone of contention between her and Mr. Albert). He approved of my goose fat! They were even approaching biscuit company Tunnock's for sponsorship. Her enthusiasm bounced off the page. It was all go-go-go! She had encountered some opposition but as always, this delighted rather than deterred her.

No one thinks I can do it, but by Jove, I'm going to cross that sea by sheer will, if necessary. I have also got rather plump but that's all for the best apparently! You won't laugh at me, will you?!

I started a reply wishing her all the best, saying how I couldn't wait to cheer her on. I felt so excited for her that I thought I might venture a light-hearted mention of the mysterious Harriet. *Would I be waving alongside her and would she, on this occasion, be fully dressed?*

Then there was a commotion outside and I abandoned my letter-writing. It sounded like a motorbike. I heard a voice call out: "Where is she then?" and then Elsie Knocker appeared at my tent. It was wonderful to see her. Although I'd known her only a year and a half, and most of our friendship had been conducted by letter, I felt like our relationship was much longer and more familiar.

She had come all this way in the mud slush, in the terrible rain, riding her motorbike with sidecar—and someone in it. I thought it might be Harold but it was a freckly English engineer with strawberry-blond hair. Robin, as he was introduced, seemed fond of Elsie, and she of him (but not as much as he seemed to hope). When I asked how things were in Pervyse, she said, "Beyond terrible," then added brightly, "but I have rum in unspeakable quantities."

"I can't tonight, I'm still on duty."

But the beds were empty except for two boys who had both mysteriously been shot in the feet that afternoon and even more mysteriously failed to remember how such an incident befell them.

Gordon shrugged. "You might as well go, May."

"Really?"

"While we've got the chance."

"What about Matron?"

"I'll see to her."

The *while we've got the chance* rang in my ears as I hurried to get changed out of my apron.

*

At last there was some respite from the rain, but it was still far too boggy to go outside, so Elsie and I spent the evening in the canteen. Her freckly friend went off to the Portuguese hospital—he was doing his bit for "international relations."

"Aye-aye, wink, wink, know what I mean!" He winked so much I wondered if he had an eye condition.

Some of the more chatty orderlies and stretcher-bearers joined our table. Elsie seemed to attract men to her like moths to a flame. We drank and gossiped and I tried to put Louis' last visit to the back of my mind: his panic, his flailing. He was just being extra-cautious. I tried to remember some of the jokes darling Leona used to tell.

"Knock, knock."

"Who's there?"

"Doris."

"Doris who?"

"Doris open, so I thought I'd drop by."

Elsie laughed. "Doris is the name of Harold's horse."

"Harold?" I raised an enquiring eyebrow. "The Man of the Moment?"

"Uh-huh…" Elsie paused. "She's a very nice horse."

At the end of the evening, Elsie and I went outside to say goodbye among the lanterns and the stars. I suddenly felt apprehensive: Elsie being here, Louis' worries, Gordon's words. It was like we were standing on the precipice of something huge.

"Do you have to go back to Pervyse?"

"I do," said Elsie, and the way she said it left no room for doubt.

And I understood this, of course, I did. She had her duty and so did I.

"Good luck, Nurse Turner." Suddenly formal, Elsie seized my hand and shook it so firmly it hurt. I realized that whatever it was I was fearing, she was fearing it too, and that was the reason she had come.

Soldiers' superstitions

Crossed fingers.

Touch wood (Or someone's wooden head!).

Mascots (toys, hankies, blankies).

Favorite underpants! Worn back to front, if necessary!

CHAPTER THIRTY-ONE

I woke up to the most terrible noise: the bang and the boom of bombardments. An influx of dust and grit. Our tents had shaken before, but never like this. You might have thought it was an earthquake. Or a volcano. I imagined this would be the roar that would reach Battersea Common. This would get them chatting in the tennis club. Perhaps Percy, safe in his studio, would wake to it, shut the window, feeling his canvases shake. I imagined he would curse the people who owned bigger apartments.

This was it: it had started. It was 1 July 1916. Two days before I was due to go back to England, to get my daughters from school.

It had to work. The final push had to be done. I was probably more gung-ho than Louis, but I believed the deadlock had to break. The status quo could not go on forever. A push was what was needed so a push is what it was. The bombs would go off, then over our boys would go. Wave after wave after wave of them. We had "Mother" on our side—I had seen it. The Hun would be petrified. We would capture back the land, French land, Belgian land. The Germans would be dead on the other side. That was sad, but this was war, and this was the promise: it would be over soon. I would be back in England soon and I wouldn't need to ever come back to the Somme. Peace would be restored and our lives would return to their normal paths. That was what the leaders said would happen. I still believed them.

I wasn't due on until the evening, but early that morning, someone, I don't know who, started marching up and down the living quarters, blowing a whistle and shouting: "Attention! All hands on deck!" This had never happened before, and I wanted to protest, "But who will work tonight then?" or "We've only been asleep for four hours," but there was no arguing with that racket.

Matron stuttered upright. "I wasn't asleep anyway. Horrendous noise..." We dressed quickly and although I may, in my haste, have tripped across her invisible line, for once she was too busy pulling on her stockings and tying back her hair to care. When she was nervous, Matron talked more, and she did so now.

"Let's hope it's all a kerfuffle over nothing," she said.

"It's probably just a precaution," I said, as though the noise out there wasn't happening at all. She nodded vigorously.

"That's right, just a drill... Nothing out of the ordinary."

No warning telegrams came that day. Not one. Instead, the men just started arriving from all directions. When they started being brought in, it sounds ridiculous but for one foolish moment, I thought they were black men. I actually thought they must be our troops from the West Indies, Jamaica maybe or some faraway African tribe, men from some outpost of the Empire who the British had drafted in to do their business. But soon I realized they were only black because of the soot from the explosives or the mud.

They had the worst injuries I'd ever seen.

Not only that, but there were so many of them. Blind men, men with lost limbs, shell-shocked men with wild eyes. Walking dead, nearly dead. Men wild with grief. I thought, *what about the howitzer? What about the tanks?*

I washed and treated the wounds of the men who had to wait for surgery. They all had to wait, there were so many of them. I tried to comfort them, but the job was so vast, so impossible, that a pat on some unbloodied part of the uniform had to suffice. I wasn't part of the surgeons' contingent, but soon I was called in: "Sterilize, clean, quickly, quickly!"

Men everywhere. Wounded. Dead. I thought of the cheerful troops, whistling and singing. I thought of the boys crossing Battersea Park. Was this them? Might I have brushed past some of them in the street?

Did they look like this the other side? Were our counterparts doing the same as us? The German nurses flurrying around, determined to hide the horror in their hearts?

This was our battle.

We were going to win this.

The rain poured down.

I was told to put up a sign on the surgical tent to turn people away: "No room here." I felt like the innkeeper. If only we had a stable to offer them. I couldn't leave it like that. I added: "Sorry"—I felt criminal.

But we couldn't stop them coming. It was overwhelming. Usually, of course, they came up in ambulances; usually, there were stretchers. Now, I saw the stretcher-bearers were using any old thing to transport the men: planks of wood, bits of old fence, horses, on their backs.

I gave a feeble wave at the Portuguese nurse across the way. She raised her hand uncertainly back at me, and then we shook our heads at each other. We understood each other well in that moment.

A man staggered toward our tent with a heavy rucksack on his back. God knows how far he had carried it.

"Further along, it's only two hundred yards, or if not, try up at the Canadian hospital?" I called to him.

"There's no room there," he gasped.

"One mile away, there's a base..." I didn't know what else to say.

His eyes were desperate. It was only when I looked more closely at him, then, that I saw how badly injured he was himself. And that it wasn't a rucksack he was carrying, it was a man. These were somebody's beloved sons. I stared at him, uncomprehending, and he stared back at me. It was a moment I would never forget. We were quiet in the noise. I just knew that whatever I did would utterly fail him. I had come into nursing for this? I felt someone approach from behind: it was Matron.

"Tent two," she said softly, and together we unfurled the man being carried on his friend's shoulders and dragged him in between us.

It was worse than a nightmare. We had thought we were the best-prepared hospital in the Somme. Were we mad? We *were* well prepared but this, this was...well, you couldn't prepare for this.

Flicking images through my head. Bonnie's trembling lip as she kept mouthing, "He's sixteen." Gordon shouting for bandages, swearing for more. Kitty's wide-eyed terror as yet another truck full of injured men pulled up. Matron keeping us together, keeping us solid. Whisking and allocating men off somewhere, I don't know where. No time for tenderness, no time for painkillers. I thought of my grandma. *A kind word*? We barely had time for that.

Next to the bucket, scrubbing hands, scrubbing arms, alongside Kitty and she was quoting Shakespeare at me and I thought, *we are demented*.

Blood on the sheets. Mud in the eyes. Bullets through the heart.

Bonnie was taking notes from a boy to send to his ma. Was it bad that I sometimes wanted to interrupt? That I wished someone else could have done it because Bonnie's handwriting could sometimes be so spidery? But Bonnie, like me, always jumped to do letters. She said it was a chance to sit down for five minutes.

Bonnie dashing around, wearing her old cap instead of the new veils we wore now, and for once Matron saying nothing. Matron slopping the floor, over and over. Gordon exhausted, arguing with anyone who came near, clutching some poor visiting officer by the collar. "This has got to stop NOW." Talk of court martials flung out like bullets.

Snatching sleep: four hours here, four hours there. Daylight and night-time merging. Kittie and Bonnie in my tent so their tent could be given over to the injured. Katherine, Beryl, Lucille and Millicent sharing a tent too. Dreams of bombs and shells and engineers on day trips, tins of meat, howitzer guns called Mother. I dreamt my mother was in England, looking for me everywhere, and when she found me, I was so coated in mud that she didn't recognize me. Kitty giving me some medicinal spirits to keep me going. The appearance of the mailman, blood running down the side of one cheek. A short note from Elsie like finding treasure on a desert island. *You must be in the thick of it, dear girl, stay strong, be safe.*

Gordon rarely panicked, but he was panicking now: Colonel Hurd was coming in to see his youngest son. His eldest had died in Arras. His second had died in Turkey. Did anyone know where his son, the youngest Hurd, was?

I knew. I'd held the youngest son's hand when he'd arrived in surgery without a hope in hell and after an hour or so, I'd slipped the name-band onto his slender wrist. I went out the back of the hospital where the bodies were, and I wiped every bit of mud I could from the youngest Hurd's beautiful face. I doubted the lad had started shaving yet. I closed his dark eyes and closed his soft mouth. I made him as clean and presentable as possible under the circumstances.

When his father came in, he sobbed and at first, he couldn't look and then he said gruffly, "Did you do this?"

Had I done something wrong? I said nothing, just stood there with my head bowed.

"Did you clean him up?"

I admitted I had.

"Thank you," he said softly and then he fell onto his son. After a few minutes, I put my hand on him and he let himself be guided away. I held him. Yes, I know, you can't hold a colonel... But I did.

"He was my son," he sobbed into my shoulder. "My last son."

It rapidly became apparent that I would not be going anywhere. England would have to wait. The diplodocus would have to wait. My darling daughters would have to wait. The hospital had become our trench and we could not get free. The war had come to the Somme. That was the evening—or was it the next, I can't remember—I woke up the telegraph operator. He was slumped, asleep, over his machine in a tent with all kinds of stains up the wall.

"Two telegrams for England, please."

I couldn't go home. I couldn't leave this place. The medium had warned me, but I had never taken her seriously and I didn't then. What I didn't realize at the time was that, for me, this was the end of everything.

<u>One day in July: Field Hospital 19, Bray-sur-Somme</u>

Private Collins

Private Rawlinson

2nd Lieutenant Rodgers

Sergeant Salt

Private Rodgers

Private Lewinson

Private Fishburn

Private Thorpe

Private Jameson

Driver Bridges

Sapper S. Jones

Sapper Turkington

Rifleman Hart

Temporary Colonel Hawkins

Private Davis

Private Lewis

Sergeant Morrison

Unknown

Unknown

Unknown

Unknown

CHAPTER THIRTY-TWO

Two teenage girls, daughters of a local orderly, arrived. They couldn't have been much older than Leona and Joy. Long and thin, they reminded me of the weasels in *The Wind in the Willows*. Strange thoughts. Gordon and the orderly were talking rapidly as the girls stood trembling next to them. Then Gordon turned to me.

"They'll do dressings. It'll free you and Bonnie to join us in surgery."

The girls were both nearly in tears.

"No," I said. I wasn't thinking of myself, I was thinking of them. They shouldn't have to see what we were seeing. Why weren't they at school?

"Nurse Turner," barked Gordon. "This is not up for debate. Train them up, then you and Bonnie join me."

The girls took our seats and we showed them what to do. Then Bonnie and I went to the worst place in the hospital, where Gordon worked. You weren't allowed to call it an abattoir or mention its resemblance to one in any way. There was a line of men, mostly lying on stretchers, a few lying or sitting on the ground. Most of them were drenched in blood. They were very quiet. I knew Kitty and Gordon's work was terrible, but... Bonnie's hand was shaking next to mine.

"Think you can do it?"

I thought of the card from Elsie a year and a half ago, when she was moving to her little cellar house—the faster the treatment, the better. I nodded, "I can do it, Doctor Collins."

*

The young girls managed well. Between them, they did two hundred dressings a day those weeks, while Bonnie and I learned how to administer a man morphine, pull out shrapnel from his body as he lay on a stretcher and then sew him up. All the while he would be apologizing for being a bother.

As Gordon walked by me one evening, he handed me something. "Better late than never."

"What is it?" I said. I looked and found it was a tiny American flag. It was 6 or 7 July, I think.

I couldn't even find the words to say thank you. I had forgotten how to speak, I didn't know gratitude. I didn't know how to express anything anymore. I would one day sew it onto my coat or my blanket or somewhere. Gordon meant it to be nice, a touch of home, but I had to blink back tears. The little Stars and Stripes said, *"What are you doing in this hellhole? You don't belong here, you don't even have to be here."*

I caught up with him.

"When did you get this?" I asked.

"Before," he said, with his palms up, which told me nothing because I had no recollection of a time before this.

How could the men be living, breathing, walking and dreaming one moment, and then be turned into just a number, a number in a larger number of fatalities, the next? Each and every single one of them was a tragedy.

Louis' car pulled up, some time later. I seemed to have lost count of the days. I had lost count of the nights. Maybe he had been in Paris all this time? Or London? I had lost track of him altogether. I was on a twenty-minute break and was outside, pegging up my aprons. Some were so ruined with blood or mud, they would have to be destroyed. Some I'd do my best to save. I remembered when sixteen aprons had seemed a lot. Now I could have done with double that amount. I was still in a daze. Ever since 1 July, I had felt like an automated thing, a machine, a clockwork ballerina going through the motions. Even Louis' boots sounded healthy as he squelched across the mud toward me.

"My love," he said. As I turned to look at him, he took a deep breath, then with his habitual honesty, said, "Good Lord, you look terrible!"

I had only slept in four-hour snatches for the past month. "Terrible" was probably a compliment; "ravaged" might have been closer to the truth. But I didn't care. I had never cared less about my looks. I fixed my blurry eyes on him. Louis looked the very picture of vitality. *A man who is not physically broken*, I thought. *How rare to see that!* I had been among sick and dying men for so long that Louis seemed to glow. He appeared almost magical. It would not have been a surprise to see him in a halo sprouting golden wings. I thought, *ah, perhaps this is why in the olden days people thought they saw angels*. I nodded at him, then carried on with my work, automatically, unthinkingly.

"Can I have five minutes, May?"

"I'm working," I protested. I accidentally dropped some of my aprons into the mud. Louis bent and helped me pick them up and I went to the outside sink and washed them silently again. He followed me and stood next to me, and I tried to think of something to say to him. I had forgotten how people had normal conversations. It seemed to me that Louis belonged to a different species.

Finally, they were pinned out to dry. Beautiful sight that, white aprons flapping in the wind: a pure and unblemished sight in a world that wasn't. As I stood to admire my handiwork, I had almost forgotten he was there.

"May," he said. "Talk to me."

I stared at my pocket watch.

"I'm working," I repeated.

*

He followed me into the hospital tent. It used to be the convalescence tent but now it was anything goes. The beds were all full, naturally, and there were men on the floor between each of them. This was not as crowded as it had been, but I think for Louis maybe this was the first moment he realized how bad things actually were.

I still couldn't find the words. Small talk seemed impossible. "Are you all right, May?" he asked.

I don't know. I lost myself in the Somme.

I wiped the face of a patient, a dear chap from Cornwall. He had been in surgery last night and had lost his leg.

"He's keeping his arm though," I said to Louis. He flushed, and kind of muttered, "Good to hear."

I nodded. I left the boy, washed up, then walked to the front of the tent. In front of us, stretcher-bearers were coming up. The ambulances were creating their own mud piles.

Louis pulled at my shoulder.

"May, talk to me."

"What's there to say? It's a disaster," I said.

"No, it isn't," he said. I stared at him in amazement. "Listen to me," he said urgently. "It's going well, we're winning."

I don't think I had ever felt fury as I did then. I pulled his arm, and I led him behind the hospital tent. He was protesting as we went, and we both sank into the mud. Then we were there, where the bodies were, where the orderlies tried to give the dead as much dignity as possible. I couldn't speak. Well, in which universe was this *going well*? Louis looked out into the nightmare, then paled. "What are they all doing here?"

"They'll be buried tonight."

"But there's so many," he said.

"I know."

"It's going well," he said as though I hadn't spoken at all. "The commanders are pleased." He seemed desperate to deny what was going on in front of his eyes. "The French are thrilled, it's going better than Verdun."

"Thrilled?"

"Well, we are." He turned away from the view. "The numbers we have in aren't bad at all . . . yet."

"The stories are terrible."

"There will always be terrible stories in wartime."

I couldn't see the bigger picture. I couldn't see what was happening "out there." I could only see two stretcher-men struggling in, and a boy who appeared to have lost one side of his head.

Back in my ward, a patient was whimpering. I knew this one. We had done all we could for him but he still liked to talk. We said usually that hearing was the last to go. Not with this poor chap. I leaned over him to hear what he said. I grabbed the notepad in case it was for a letter to his wife or his mother. You had to tell yourself, *not everyone gets the chance to have their last words heard.* It was a privilege in this strange bastard world.

"The barbed wire was still up. Didn't stand a chance," the soldier said.

Louis sat by his side. I nodded that he could take the man's hand and he did. "Where are you from, sir?"

"I'm a reservist. Lancaster."

"You've been very brave, sir," said Louis.

"The barbed wire was still up . . ." the man repeated incredulously. "We were slaughtered like pigs."

"You did your best," I said. Louis was now gulping air, lost for words.

Gradually, the man's breathing became shallower and even as we watched, his eyes glazed over. I knew what was happening, but I don't think Louis did.

"Do something," he hissed. "May?"

I felt the poor man's forehead and I told him he was loved. I held his fingers while Louis glared at me as though this was my fault. We just stood there. Him and me across the poor dying soldier. There was nothing good, nothing comforting to come out of this. There was only nothingness. Louis swallowed, again and again. His Adam's apple going up and down was the only thing that moved. When it was over, I called for an orderly. He knew: tone of voice, a wry expression did that job.

"I'll write to his mother," I told Louis as I went to the sink.

Louis gripped my arm. "They need to be wearing wire-cutters at all times. It's part of their uniform. Why weren't they?"

He was asking me?

The orderlies took the body. Bonnie took the old sheets and spread the new sheets. An orderly came out with the mop. While Louis was still standing around shaking his head, a new fella, with only one leg, was given the bed. Another patient wanted to be heard. He sat up in bed. I had assisted with the amputation of his arm three days ago. He was recovering nicely but he was so angry, I regret that most of us kept away from him.

"Have you seen the size of the wire?" he said accusingly to Louis. "The cutters wouldn't cut it, we needed bombs to bring that down. They *told* us they'd be down, for feck's sake!"

I was glad Louis didn't shy away but I was also nervous that he went over to this temperamental man. "What happened to you?"

"I was next line, hung back ten seconds then just ran out to get the fella in front...I wasn't going to leave them out there to be riddled with more holes than a colander."

Louis straightened. He looked for a place on the man's arm that wasn't bandaged, gave up and patted his shoulder lightly.

"You've done a great thing for your country."

The man grunted. "What's my country done for me?"

Of course, I knew by then that my Louis was an emotional man, but still, when, in the middle of our great field hospital, he burst into hot, choking tears, it took me by surprise. We hugged. He snorted on my shoulder.

The angry soldier piped up. "Do you need those wire-cutters, sir?"

And suddenly we were shaking and crying with laughter as though it were something hilarious instead of the utter carnage that it was.

Places where mud gets

The beard
The crotch
Between the toes
Behind the ears
The lungs

CHAPTER THIRTY-THREE

The stretcher-bearers had gone out for a soldier stuck in a ditch and had been gone for a while, so the orderly had said he'd go and see what the hold-up was. None of them had returned.

I had some idea where they might have gone so I popped out to look for them. The rain had turned this side of the hospital into a mudslide. And still it rained on. I made out some figures at the end of a once-grassy slope, now entirely churned-up mud. I slid down to them, glad of my outdoor boots. The poor soldier had already gone, submerged in it. The stretcher-bearers were now stuck themselves, trapped and sinking further in. One still had a hand free, but they were both of them up to their chins. The orderly was now up to his waist, he didn't know what to do.

"Leave us here," one of them begged. "Save yourself." I recognized his voice: it was the father of the teenage girls. It was an impossible scene. Each time he moved, he went further and further in. I blew on my whistle, hard as I could. I knew we didn't have time to wait for help though. And probably no one would hear in this torrential rain anyway.

"You're coming out."

The orderly managed to take off his jacket. He threw it to the first stretcher-bearer while I took off my apron and with it, tied myself to a tree. Then we all pulled, an elaborate tug of war. I went further in but my apron held. The second stretcher-bearer was stuck fast, like a cork in a bottle, but we heaved and we hauled. I wasn't scared I would get sucked in myself (that fear would come when I went over it to myself later). Pulling and tugging and crying and cursing my lack of strength. *Do it for the girls*, I told myself. *Do it.*

They are not going to drown, not on my watch, I whispered to myself, over and over again.

Finally, the first stretcher-bearer was freed and in a position to help pull out the other man, who was now swallowing mud. We all of us clambered out the mudbank like prehistoric creatures. The orderly got one of the men onto the stretcher and I took one end, telling the other man lying on the bank, "We'll be back in minutes, hang on."

"Thank you," he kept saying.

"Don't thank me," I told him. "If only I'd got here earlier..."

Gordon met us; he helped the rescued man off the stretcher, glanced over at me.

"You'll be due a medal for that one, May." But I was too weary even to respond. I went back down to the riverbank with two fresh stretcher-bearers, and we dragged the other man to the hospital.

As I dropped into bed that evening, I remembered suddenly that today was the day Elizabeth was swimming across the Channel. I had missed that as well.

Mid-August, correspondence came from George. I would have recognized his scrappy handwriting anywhere. If I had seen that writing before I married him, maybe we wouldn't have got that far. George pressed hard on his pen. Each letter was an act of violence inflicted on the defenseless paper. He was overly disposed to CAPITALS. The page was blighted with ink blobs. I took the envelope enthusiastically though, for through George I would have news of Joy and Leona, and I was ravenous for information.

I sat down next to a man from Bristol who had lost both his legs. (You never did one task at a time, you always tried to do at least three.) He was a commanding officer, but he was like a small boy now, and hated being alone. Some came out as men and left like children.

"I'm so sorry," I said, stroking his arm.

"Don't be," he said. "I'll be away from this horror soon, I got away alive."

Not all patients were this equanimous, by any means. I held his smooth hand, noticing how it was perfectly unblemished. I felt the bones of his fingers; the nails were bitten down to the quick. He wore a handsome, expensive watch. The face had cracked but it showed the right time. Eleven fifteen a.m. Once I heard his breathing change and knew he was asleep, I could concentrate on my letter. Within the first few words, I was smiling with loathing. I had already known for a long time that George was an insufferable old git but this letter would have won prizes for pomposity.

May, he wrote (no dear or darling for me!),

> *I told the church group how you let the girls down this summer. They agreed that you are an abject failure as a mother and wife. A dereliction of duty so grave that were you in the Army, you would be court-martialled…*

I nearly laughed. As if George knew what it was like in the Army!

> *I am devastated that I could have been associated with, let alone married to, someone so selfish as you. Your mother warned me long ago that you were incapable of love, but I would never have expected you to neglect our children.*

Well, what are you going to do about it, George? I thought contemptuously. *I'm still their mother, and you're still a useless father.*

> *To this end, I have been advised to employ a governess for the next school holidays. I can't think why I didn't do it sooner. I will ensure the governess will have excellent qualifications and skills and will be sufficient to supply the girls with everything they need.*

A governess for the holidays, instead of me? Was this some kind of joke?
I felt my blood run cold.

Bonnie was standing over me, wringing her hands. Again.

"May, I've got a patient causing trouble: he's got the shock—"

"Wait a moment, Bonnie," I said impatiently. I had asked her not
to interrupt me several times—why did she always think her patients
were more important than mine?—but she still did this *constantly.*
I was going to have to get firmer about it.

"I'm scared..."

*There is no need for you ever to return from France, May. Stay
there. You belong in the mud.*

Bonnie's patient jumped out of his bed. Gosh, he had a lot of spring
in him—couldn't be that badly hurt! He ran down the ward like he
was competing in the steeplechase. Like he was running for his life.
Bonnie was no slacker; she set off at a sprint after him. I joined them
at the tent entrance. Racing outside, he nearly tripped over the ropes,
righted himself, nearly smacked into the stretcher-bearers carrying
in a new patient. "Steady now. Steady on!" one of them called out in
a broad Lancashire accent.

By the time Bonnie reached him, it was too late. He blew his
brains out just as she was approaching. I was slower and was behind
her, but I still saw the whole thing: the gun he produced from his
jacket pocket, the triangle his arm made, the way he dropped to
the floor like a jug smashing. A bloody jug in bits all over the mud.

You'll never see my daughters again, George had written. *It serves
you right, you're an unfit mother and an American whore.*

Things in Private Simon Lancaster's bag (deceased by injuries associated with shooting)

Photograph of Polly (Polly has golden hair. She is wearing a white blouse, a string of pearls and a self-conscious smile).

An empty Princess Mary box.

Letter to his mother. (I couldn't read it. I couldn't. I would make sure it was returned to her.)

A mascot.

A stamp. First class.

Cookie crumbs.

CHAPTER THIRTY-FOUR

All leave was canceled. As long as battle raged in the Somme, I was going nowhere.

"Wait until things are clearer," Gordon advised over the operating table. "Here and there."

I made a plan that I would go home at October half-term. Eight weeks. I would pick up the girls from school, I would ignore everything George had written—for what did he know about anything? His letter that day was the last I heard from him for some time. I sent letters to him, both long and short. I sent a card with a sweet picture of a toy bear on the front for his stupid forty-eighth birthday. I sent telegrams. I tried various approaches, from the cajoling: "I know you're angry, George, but please give me a chance to explain," to the firm: "The girls need their mother, and I feel confident you always have their best interests at heart."

I sent him kisses, even though I loathed writing them. I even borrowed the last dregs of Bonnie's perfume to spritz on the back of an envelope. I sent him some pressed flowers that I had saved for the girls and said: "These remind me of when the children were young," even though they didn't. The main things I remembered from when they were young were the fug of alcohol, the doors slamming, the dishes on the floor, trying—and failing—to protect them from the drunken ogre who ruled our house.

As summer heat gave way to autumn cool, I remembered the flowers on Battersea Common. I remembered watching the new recruits from Percy's window. I remembered Percy's flustered cleaning. But still the war was unrelenting and the Battle of the Somme continued.

I did get a letter from back home, but it wasn't from George, it was from Mrs. Crawford. I hoped there'd be news of the house: the girls, the new governess, even George's gout, but there was nothing about any of them. She asked if I remembered her son, James. (Of course I did.) James was a good boy, she continued. He wrote regular as clockwork, but she hadn't heard from him for a couple of weeks now. Could I look out for him once again? She had heard he was in the same area as I was.

In the same area? I thought wearily. I hoped he wasn't. Nevertheless, I wrote back with as much confidence as I could muster, for I understood her fears. Also because I saw this as a way to try to get a message to my girls. *PS. Mrs. Crawford, if you see Joy or Leona, please tell them Mummy loves them and will see them soon.*

I wrote my apologies to Elizabeth, but she didn't reply. It wasn't like her not to write; I supposed she was very angry with me. Perhaps I should have been more contrite in my apologies, but this intransigence now made me irritable with her—she had no idea what it was like out here.

When I wasn't writing letters, I lay on my bed and wrote poetry. It was small squirm-inducing stuff at first, but gradually, one midnight, after a fourteen-hour shift trying to mend the broken, I found my writing voice. More and more, I looked forward to being alone with my notebook so I could pour out some of the terrible things I had seen in safety and without hurting anyone.

As October half-term approached, I booked a lodging at Leamington Spa. A room for three. I sent letters every day or so.

One time, I got a postcard back.

Why haven't you written, Mumma? Xxx
PS: we love you, we are sorry if we upset you.

It was only then I realized they hadn't been getting my letters. Someone was blocking them. The school, under George's orders probably. I wept. How could they think I would abandon them? I had to outwit him, I *had* to. Work kept me going, being part of the team; writing poetry kept me going, but when I wasn't occupied, I feared I was losing my mind again. Was the melancholia coming back? It mustn't. What I had didn't feel like darkness though, it felt like rage. It felt like fury.

By hook or by crook, I would see my girls soon.

After fourteen days in a row, I had one afternoon off, and Louis finally took me on that belated date to Paris. He didn't say anything stupid like he was trying to cheer me up; he did say that a change of scene would do me good though.

Only eight days until I would be home.

Louis told me to wait outside a jewelery shop; he wanted to surprise me. I stood obediently in the street, shielding my eyes from the bright sunshine. How I loved being with Louis! He reminded me it was good to be alive. He came out smiling, with three beautiful brooches. One each, "For you and your girls." As he pinned mine onto my collar, his eyes were filled with compassion. "You'll be by their sides soon, May, I promise."

Somehow this moved me more than anything else he had done. I knew that he was the little boy who had endured an enforced separation from his mother. I knew he, more than anyone else, was capable of putting himself in my girls' shoes.

I had such a sense of dark foreboding about the trip to England though. I thought of the medium and her prophecy and I hated her too. I couldn't bear the prospect of fighting with George, but I knew, if there was going to be a fight, I would have to see it through. I would have to. This was more than my life, this was my daughters.

CHAPTER THIRTY-FIVE

The morning I was due to take the ship back I woke up feeling distinctly odd. Not odd in the melancholic way I used to feel in London, but in a new paralyzed kind of way. Aches and pains. Hot and cold. Shivers. No matter, I told myself, I was on my way to my daughters.

About ten, I heard Kitty's voice outside my tent—I still hadn't been able to get up. She was calling, "May, the car is here," and then, in her gentle, authoritative tone, "Please come and say goodbye before you go."

I called back that I was on my way. What an effort that took.

Anyway, I wasn't.

I looked at my watch, but I couldn't read it any more: I had lost the ability to tell the time. No matter, I told myself again, I just have to get dressed. That's all.

Sweating profusely, delirious, I tried to dress. I had put my shirt on the wrong way round. Taking it off, I tried to start again. The effort of buttons exhausted me. This simple task was beyond me.

This was worse than wading through mud with the stretcher-bearers. This must be what swimming the Channel feels like, I told myself. I thought of Elizabeth and felt hot again. It had been so long since I had written to her. Perhaps I should write now. But I had forgotten how to write. How does one know which way round these things go on? And why had it never troubled me before? I put on one skirt, tried to pull on a second. This wasn't going to work.

*

Matron found me collapsed on the floor. She was probably furious that I had crossed the invisible line.

I knew someone was talking to me, but I didn't know who. Kitty, was it? I was doing my best to reply but I couldn't get a word out. She was explaining to me that I must have caught an illness. Jaundice, exhaustion, pneumonia, flu, a catatonic tiredness at the worst possible time? It must have been Kitty because Kitty never did anything without explaining it first. It was a tic she had; Bonnie and I had often laughed about it. Now, I was grateful to her, as she laid me down: "I'm putting you on your bed now, May," and "What a beautiful brooch, May, I'm unpinning it. I'm just putting it here, now, on your table here... Oh, you have two more, May! They are so beautiful, they must be for the..."

Knock, knock.
   Who's there?
   Boo.
   Boo who?
   Don't cry!
I spy Leona lying in bed reading aloud, sucking her thumb. *Mummy, why didn't you come?*

I spy Joy: *You never come, do you, Mummy? Daddy says you're useless. That's not true,* I said loudly. *I am doing my best.*

Leona holding a buttercup to my chin. *You really like butter, Mummy. Do you not like me?*

Joy in her tennis whites. *Mummy, I'll teach you how to serve. I know how to serve, darling.*

I heard voices—"Wake up!"—trying to reach me but not quite. The silver birch in front of the door at home. Hang on to that.

Images of boys drowning in mud, images of mud, waves of it, seas of it. Young men calling out for their mothers. Joy calling out for me.

Elizabeth diving into the lake but she remains upside down. It is her feet talking. "May, you should have stuck to cats. Girlfriends first, Louis last. Drowning in between."

Her cats, staring at me, wandering off.

I imagined the telegram man being woken up again. I saw in my mind's eye Louis walking into the tent, telling him to send a message to England: *May Turner is dead. Long live George.*

I felt my arm raised, Gordon's voice, clear as mud: "Out of danger."

Are we ever out of danger?

All I want is my girls. I saw the Channel red between us. I saw the sea, the sea, and everything was red.

Favorite memories of my girls

Coming down the stairs at school and flinging themselves onto me.

The way Joy shyly puts her hand in mine when no one is looking or says, "Mummy, I'm not really angry with you, it's just I get so annoyed sometimes."

Brushing Leona's lovely frizz, looking into the mirror, seeing our faces next to each other.

Reading or chatting together in bed, a warm and cuddly daughter on each side.

CHAPTER THIRTY-SIX

When I woke, Louis was dozing in a chair next to me, an open book stretched across his chest. I was in my bed, in my tent, but I didn't recognize that chair. A bunch of wilting flowers were in an unfamiliar vase on the old bedside table. I vaguely remembered being frightened by the petals in the middle of the night. But they were just silly petals. I tried to speak, but his name didn't come out as Louis, but as "Ooh."

"Thank God, you're all right!"

Jumping down from his chair, Louis knelt by my side. He held me tight; he was sobbing.

I'm not all right, I thought. *I have ice in my heart. The girls... The girls...*

"How long have I been sick?"

He rubbed his bloodshot eyes. "Nine, no, ten days."

"What day is it today?"

"It is..." He paused as though he too had lost count of the days. "November second."

I sobbed.

I hadn't realized Matron was there. Louis spoke, and she responded in soft tones that she'd never used with me before.

"Has she had a drink?"

"Not yet..."

Matron poured water into my tin cup, the very one I had brought with me from Battersea, and they both watched me drink it with satisfaction.

"Nurse Louis," I said tenderly. Even Matron gave a whisker of a smile.

"He's barely left your side, May. You're a lucky woman."

"I know that," I said. But as I thought of my darling girls—*what must they think of me now?*—I didn't feel lucky.

CHAPTER THIRTY-SEVEN

I didn't ask him to, but Louis told Winston about my troubles with George. Winston was no longer First Lord of the Admiralty—"Long story," Louis said wryly—but he was still a man of influence. Winston immediately said he'd get the Home Office to put in a word. I liked that about Winston: it was never "that's not my department" with him; he always went out of his way to listen to a problem and then try to do something to fix it.

A few days later, a note came from George. I ripped it open eagerly. It was just a few scrawny lines long.

I have never said you can't see the girls, he said. (He lied.) *On the contrary, if you are back in London at Christmas, you are welcome to spend the holidays with them.*

I couldn't believe it. I hadn't lost my daughters, of course I hadn't. *Winston*, I thought, *you're a bloody genius.*

Louis visited me whenever he could and he would take me for short walks. I wasn't well enough to go very far. Sometimes he came with his new driver, a fella who was sweet on Kitty. We talked of a double date, but nothing ever came of it.

"Why not, Kitty?" I asked, remembering her not believing in love.

"Does everyone have to be lined up in twos like the animals in Noah's ark?" she said with uncharacteristic vehemence.

"No, I don't suppose they do," I said, surprised. "And I'm not sure how the ark worked anyway…"

Kitty gave me her slow smile. I was forgiven. "Can you imagine the noise?"

"Can you imagine the honk?"

"Can you imagine the excrement?" joined in Bonnie.

I thought to myself, *not unlike a field hospital in the Somme*, but I didn't say it.

Louis was my constant. One time, while we were taking one of our short walks, my notebook fell out my bag.

"Anything important?" he said, looking at it.

"My lists," I said shyly. "And some silly stuff…"

"Some of it reads like poetry," he said, eyeing me closely, so I admitted it was. I told him about my love for Walt Whitman's poems, and how, during the worst days of the battle, to sit at that blank unsullied page, to work out my thoughts there, was just marvelous relief.

Louis listened carefully as usual. Then he said:

"There are many who write incredibly about the war: Owen, Sassoon, Brooke, important, profound stuff, but…"

"But there aren't any women?" I finished for him.

"Exactly," he said with his magnificent smile.

"Who'd want to hear my point of view though?" I asked nervously, but my heart was pumping fast.

"I would," he said. "Many people would."

"I love you," I said, and it was as though the words had escaped from my mouth without my consent. I slapped my hand over my lips. "Sorry."

Louis pulled my hand away from my mouth, kissed me and said it, the first time of many: "May, I love you too."

*

While I was recovering from my illness and growing stronger, Gordon was suffering. A telegram had come from the Brighton Pavilion. Karim had now contracted pneumonia. Things were touch and go.

"He's young and strong," I reminded Gordon. "And handsome..." It was gratifying to see that my feeble humor made him smile. "He's in the best place, with the best doctors—apart from you, of course."

I was sitting with Gordon in the canteen, contemplating our miserable potato soup, when the second telegram came, not six hours later. Gordon rose, his expression tight.

He read it, then shook his head at me.

"He didn't make it." Gordon stalked off to his tent and I didn't see him for the next day. When I passed him a while later in theater, he looked all right—he was as cleanly shaven and as tidy as ever—but if you looked closely, and if you knew him before, you would see that the light in his eyes had gone out.

It wasn't for a little while after my illness that I realized that Matron and I had stopped bickering. In fact, we occasionally shared anecdotes or gentle looks. One night, she was so tired, I offered to brush her hair and to my surprise she agreed. Her hair was long, gray and very beautiful and I told her so. She smiled and said her mother used to tell her it was her best feature.

"What's your mother like, Matron?" I asked.

"She died when I was very young," she said abruptly. "I was brought up by my grandfather and he was very distant."

"That must have been hard."

Matron looked lost for words. Finally, she found them: "It was what it was."

I probably shouldn't have, but I couldn't help but think, *that explains a lot.*

CHAPTER THIRTY-EIGHT

I was back at work: they put me in post-operative with Bonnie. There were a lot of men, but we did our best to keep everyone's spirits up. Bonnie told me that she had a sweetheart, Billy. He'd been with us for a fever that no one had ever quite got to the bottom of and got himself sent home on sick leave.

I felt a bit ashamed that I had no idea about this. It was like the pregnancy all over again. You wouldn't think Bonnie was that secretive. She shrugged complacently. "But you were ill, May. How *would* you know?"

It had started with the autograph book. Billy had written little poems to her, and then one time he wrote, "Would you be my girl?" How could Bonnie resist? He regularly sent packages, the contents of which both impressed and amused us.

"Billy bought Bonnie bully-beef?" asked Gordon, one eyebrow raised. "Does he also sell seashells on the seashore?"

Bonnie ignored him. "Me and Billy want to marry soon."

Kitty froze. I think it was the first she'd heard of it. "Why?" she asked, her voice unsteady.

"You know...so we can...you know."

"That didn't stop you last time," Kitty said.

Apparently, Billy already had a sweetheart in England, but Bonnie assured us he was going to break up with her.

"It's not like they're *properly* engaged," she said brightly. "At least, she doesn't have his ring. He can work on the machines with my pa, he's keen to take on an apprentice."

Bonnie made life seem so simple, so straightforward. Did I over-complicate everything? Whatever it was, I admired Bonnie and her ability to choose happiness. I knew I could learn a lot from her, but I also knew that, as Mrs. Crawford would have put it, she was a very different fish from me.

On our next afternoon off, one misty November morning, Bonnie stayed back at camp to clean her clothes and write to her Billy, so it was just me and Kitty wandering into town. I preferred it that way. When Bonnie wasn't talking about Billy, she talked about baby Freddie and although I knew how desperately painful it was for her to be away from her baby, I kept thinking to myself, *you only saw him a few weeks ago, and you'll see him shortly. I haven't seen my girls for months now!* And then I hated myself for thinking like that because it wasn't Bonnie's fault and anyway, our situations were not alike.

As we stomped along in our winter boots, Kitty was in contempla-tive mood; we talked about life before the war and life after the war.

"I can't go back to Bethnal Green," she said firmly.

I was surprised. I had heard Bonnie and Kitty reminisce so many times about the games they played, the vegetables they grew and the boys who chased them that I had assumed they would both return as soon as possible.

"What will you do instead?"

"I don't know."

It was early in the morning and I was in the canteen when I saw Louis and a man walking toward me. However, Louis was lagging behind as though he didn't quite want to arrive. The man he was with was wearing a long black cloak like a cape, which somehow matched his long and drooping mustache. He looked entirely unlike the military men I was used to seeing, and very different from my own, dear Louis.

My first impression was that either the man was in fancy dress, or he was a runaway from a circus. I couldn't imagine what on earth Louis was doing with him, or why he was bringing him over to me.

"I believe you two know each other?" said Louis curtly.

"I c-c-can't believe I found you, May Turner," the cloaked man said. He shook my hand up and down like he was trying to extract water from a well. "How the devil *are* you?"

"Good God!" I uttered when I had finally worked out who it was. "I don't believe it! Percy!"

It seemed that the War Office had caught up with Percy, even insulated and isolated as he was, in his studio apartment overlooking the common at Battersea, and he was told he had to do something. Percy was open about it: "I didn't want to fight, but I wanted to do what I could, without dying that is, and I knew I could d-draw soldiers. Thought I would glorify it a bit. Paul Nash got me in. You've heard of him, no? May, you *still* haven't heard of anyone! The first day, the fellow I was next to went pooooooofff, flew up ten feet in the air, dead as a d-d-odo. I couldn't draw for two weeks for the shaking. Then they drugged me up, shipped me back and here I am."

Louis edged away, muttering something about meetings he had to go to.

Percy looked relieved. "He's not the friendliest..."

He took something out of his Princess Mary box and inhaled it. Snifffff! His face was suddenly suffused with peace.

"I'm feeling much better now."

I had still hardly said a word. Percy hadn't noticed though.

"Doing a series on stretcher-bearers, orderlies, doctors and nurses. Unsung heroes. The British public will love it." He surveyed me. "Thought, I know the v-v-very girl."

"I would have thought you'd want to draw Elsie," I said as soon as I could get a word in edgeways.

"In her b-b-bloody cellar house? No, thank you. Blimey, it was hit-and-miss enough coming out here!" He eyed me disappointedly. "Why aren't you in uniform?"

"I'm not on until later," I protested. "And anyway, I don't want to be drawn, Percy—I was just having some tea."

Luckily for me, Bonnie walked in just then, and she was wearing her uniform! And very lovely she looked in it too.

"Do her instead," I said. I called out, "Bonnie, over here a minute!"

"I wanted you, May," Percy muttered awkwardly. I pretended not to hear him.

When Bonnie came over, I explained. "Mr. Percy Milhouse here wondered if he might sketch you? He's, um, a very highly regarded artist."

Bonnie's face lit up, as I'd expected it might.

"Have you heard of me?" asked Percy.

"Who hasn't?" said Bonnie vaguely.

Percy remained unenthusiastic. However, he dutifully picked up his sketch pad and his pencil and began. He looked at Bonnie with the same diligence as he did his triangles and squares. He sketched. I went to make them some coffee and, from a distance, watched Percy's elbows and hands move in that strange rhythm as I had done hundreds of times before, back in London. Within minutes, Bonnie looked bored. She kept smoothing down her skirt, which I knew would irritate him.

About ten minutes later, he unclipped the picture from his board and turned it toward her.

"It's wonderful," said Bonnie, looking anxiously from it to me. She really was a terrible liar. "Can I go now?"

As I walked her out, she whispered, "I preferred the one from Montmartre."

"I owe you," I whispered.

I went back to Percy, who was laboriously packing his things away.

"So, whatever happened to Georgie Porgy?" he asked abruptly.

"Oh, we drifted apart. Percy..." I knew I had to say something about him being in the divorce, but he wasn't making it easy.

"Kissed the girls and made them cry, did he?"

"Something like that..."

Percy moved over to me, then suddenly he got to the floor. His knees were in the dirt and his hands were on my knees. It was excruciating. Katherine, Millicent and the other team were coming in and I saw them gazing over at us in amazement.

"Percy, please get up," I hissed.

"I heard about the divorce."

"I'm sorry..."

"I always thought if you ever left George, you and I would make a go of it." He made a grab for my hands.

I spluttered.

"Did you?"

"Of course! I was working up to asking you..."

I shook my head from side to side. Could I have been any clearer?

"Please don't, Percy, there's no need for this...show."

Percy finally did rise. He pulled out the seat next to me. I could see Katherine's excitement. I knew exactly what she would be thinking: *I thought Nurse Turner was with the Major! Who the devil is this strange-looking guy?*

"But you d-d-disappeared," Percy continued.

"I did *tell* you I was coming out here," I said, thinking back to our last meeting. The kiss that he had planted on my hand. The *you are very precious to me.*

"I didn't think you actually would," Percy said, as though that decided everything. "I thought it was a bluff. I thought you wanted me to propose...I've regretted it ever since."

I shook my head helplessly. Surely he knew he was blatantly rewriting history, and if he could do it, he who was employed to document it, what hope did any of us have?

After a bit, Percy's hands got shaky again and he went to take whatever it was in his Princess Mary box and I told him I really had to get ready for work.

Twenty days to go until Christmas leave. I no longer believed the war would end in time for Christmas 1916. I no longer believed the war would *ever* end. We decorated the wards with holly, ivy and a small twig of mistletoe. Someone brought in a tree. It wasn't *exactly* a Christmas tree, but it would have to do. We decided we would buy each of the men a secret something from Santa and put them under the not exactly a Christmas tree. Everyone wants something to open on Christmas morning. The men who could sit upright made paper chains out of newspapers. My girls and I had done this once...

Farmer Norest's chickens were as temperamental as ever, but a huge campaign in England meant thousands of eggs were being shipped out to French hospitals daily. The Germans were bombing our ships, but those eggs kept on getting through. A nearly fresh egg from a farm in Kent or Sussex could almost put a smile on an injured soldier's face.

"Egg-citing," we went around saying. "Egg-straordinary."

I couldn't wait to tell Leona the puns; I knew she would adore them.

A few nights after Percy's visit, after my shift Louis and I sat in the canteen, drinking black tea from tin mugs. We both knew it would be the last time we would see each other for a while. The next time would be in 1917.

"A better year for everybody, I hope," Louis said grimly.

"It couldn't be much worse, could it?"

The picture of Bonnie was laid out in front of us—it was quite charming, really. Percy had said to give it to her but Bonnie was adamant she didn't want it—*Why did he have to draw my nose like that? It's not that big, is it?* She refused even to send it to her Billy, so I had been landed with it and couldn't bring myself to throw it away. Outside, the moon was full and heavy; it was the sort of night the Gotha pilots liked. Louis' cigarette dangled from the side of his mouth.

"You had a thing with that artist fella then?" Louis asked shortly. His hands remained in his pockets like he was trying to stop himself from doing something. His disappointment was palpable.

"He may have had a thing for me," I admitted awkwardly, "but it wasn't reciprocated."

"Oh," said Louis. He finally removed the cigarette from between his lips.

"You're not jealous, are you?" I couldn't help teasing.

"On a scale of one to ten?" Louis grinned.

"Ye-es."

"I'd say a nine."

We both grinned.

Louis stubbed out his cigarette then lit another. "I trusted you to have better taste."

"Oh, that's not fair! Percy's actually a very nice man."

"I'm sure he is." Finally, Louis looped his fingers around mine. That smile, those eyes... nothing could hold my attention like Louis could. "But I'm a better match for you."

I dressed smartly to travel back to London and when I went to say my goodbyes to the patients, I got a few wolf whistles, which made me laugh.

"You're a tonic," announced one cheeky chappie and another said, "Just what the doctor ordered."

I thought guiltily of Elizabeth, who I had once said the same thing about. I would make it up to her soon.

It was 21 December. In two days, I would have my girls.

Five great things about Christmas with my girls

Reading "The Night Before Christmas" in bed on Christmas Eve. (Clever Joy knows the names of all the reindeers.)

Their faces when they wake up and see that St. Nicholas has visited!

Crossing the common after church.

Watching Leona clear her plate and ask for more Brussels sprouts.

Christmas pudding.

Mistletoe.

CHAPTER THIRTY-NINE

I walked fast from Clapham Junction train station. It was cold and damp. *Far too much weather*, I thought. *Gray skies no delight.* Apparently, there had been snow at the beginning of December, a wonderful four inches of snow, but there was no sign of it now. I'd missed it all. Once again, it felt strange to be among the civilians. So many children and old people. These were the ones I had missed in France. My rucksack was full of presents. Nothing could ever compensate for my absence, but I would damn well try: sewing equipment from a stall in Amiens, little chocolate coins from a street hawker at Dover. Pens and second-hand books and black-and-white postcards bought from the banks of the Seine, complete with little squiggled promises, "I will take you here one day." And Louis' thoughtful gift: two pretty brooches to match mine.

I couldn't get back quick enough. Each step was bringing me closer to my girls. I marched where the recruits had once marched. I marched where we had returned from church. I marched away from Louis, Kitty, Bonnie and the Somme. I marched toward my daughters.

I stood outside my house, surveying it for a moment. That this was once my home seemed incredible to me. I remembered the first time I saw this house: standing outside it, George telling me we had bought it, it was all ours. There was a bicycle chained to the railings outside. Was it Joy's, or perhaps Leona's? The sight of it, the possibility that it was theirs, made me smile to myself. But where was the silver birch? He couldn't have pulled it down, could he? Surely even George wouldn't...No, there it was, to the side of the house. Proud and strong. In my imagination, I had put it in the wrong place. I laughed to myself.

I really had been away a long time.

George appeared at the door, mercifully quickly. I was relieved it wasn't the angry replacement housekeeper again. He was sporting a different mustache. It was strange seeing him again after so long, and for a moment, I felt a weird kind of affection for his homely face. I could have put my arms around him. He was familiar. He stood for the pre-Somme, old times—actually, yes, a less topsy-turvy universe. That is, until he spoke.

"I don't know why you came, May."

I shifted my weight from one leg to the other. The key was to remain calm. My lips were dry.

"I came for the girls."

"You're not taking them."

"You said I could." I had never thought George would renege on this promise. Never.

"I've changed my mind."

George was loving the power. He stood on the doorstep of our house, glaring at me, like Rasputin. The house that *my* grandmother's money had paid for. People in the street were staring at us, intuiting that here was a domestic drama. The owner of the bike came over, tipped his cap at us and hastily wheeled it away.

But I had George's letter, his promise. I had read it and reread it a thousand times. I had not got it wrong.

"Can I...can I at least see them here?"

"No."

"You *said* I would see them at Christmas, you promised."

"Well, you can't."

The people in the street, the women sauntering, the men strolling, all listening.

"Let's discuss this inside, please, George."

"No."

"But...but George, I have it here. In writing." Unfolding, then fluttering the note at him, I moved closer and closer to the doorway.

"Meaningless," he said, blocking me. A chill ran through me. This couldn't be happening. "Go away, May. We don't want you here, you're nothing to me now."

"They're my children too," I said. I was nearly sobbing but I wouldn't give him the satisfaction of seeing me cry.

He hissed at me in a lower voice, "And if you ever try to get the bloody Home Office involved in my private affairs again, I will destroy you. Do you hear me, May?"

"I hear you," I hissed back. I would push him down and run past him. I would get in that house by hook or by crook. I would have my girls back.

"I want to see the girls."

"You couldn't be bothered before."

"Of course I could."

"You gave up your chance."

"I was ill and— for goodness' sake, George, I was at the Battle of the Somme!" I snapped, losing my cool. I don't know where it came from, the words just blurted out my mouth. Even now, I couldn't quite believe that I had been in the eye of the storm, at the Somme. Even if I said it aloud, every day, for the rest of my life, I don't think I would ever really believe it. Even if I said it in the mirror, heard the words coming out my own mouth, it was hard to believe I had witnessed hell. What does one do with that?

"It was terrible. I couldn't leave. I knew the children would be safe here in England. Safe with you."

"I know about the Somme, I saw the film," George said tartly. I stared at him, startled. *The film?* "It was on at the cinema, it was rather entertaining."

I couldn't think of a single thing I could say to that.

"I don't think it was that bad."

"How..." I stammered. "How do you mean?"

"They only showed the worst bits, you know... Not the good bits."

"What good bits?"

"Where they captured all the Germans. They didn't show *any* of that. They wanted us to think it was *really* bad. Propaganda."

I thought of something Elsie had once said to me: everyone's an expert *before* they've gone to war.

"It was horrendous. I couldn't... I had to be there."

George folded his arms. He looked portly and pleased with himself.

"Don't you start using it, May."

"Using it?"

"*Oh, poor Mummy-kins was working so hard...*" He sneered at me. "You know *exactly* what I mean."

How? How had I *ever* been taken in by this vile man?

"And what have you been doing all this time?" I snapped back at him. I would have stuck a white feather up his fleshy nostril right then, if only one had been to hand.

"Essential war work," he said smugly.

"What exactly?"

He tapped his finger on the side of his noise. "Mind your own beeswax, May."

My fury grew. I was consumed with an unstoppable rage toward him and a hunger to see my children. He wasn't going to get away with this. I pushed past him and ran into the hall of my old home, my old prison cell. I cried out, "Joy? Leona?," but there was no answer. My voice echoed around the walls and then his voice joined mine, shouting at me to get out.

"Where are they then?"

"Gone."

"Where?"

"As if I'd tell you where." He laughed like a maniac. "Somewhere safe, where you can't get to them."

I had waited and waited for this for so long. The thought of this Christmas had sustained me these last weeks. And now all hopes were dashed. I felt a despair I had not felt before, even on the worst days of the Somme. I had lost my family. My loves. Hot tears stung my eyes, I could hardly see.

"You can't do this to me, George."

"Oh yes, I can," he roared as he shoved me down the front steps. "Get out and never come back!"

CHAPTER FORTY

I sent a telegram to the Pilkington family. I tried not to reveal that I had somehow lost track of my own daughters but there was no avoiding it.

The reply came mercifully quickly.

> No, the girls are not with us these holidays although we saw Leona in the school carol concert. She sang wonderfully. Merry Christmas.

I felt a mad compulsion to go to the ice rink. It's not that I thought they were there, more that I felt I might be able to connect with them if I went there. This was where Joy had let me hold her hand. This was where Leona had made a joke about bears. It wasn't very funny, but her little face: those teeth, those cheeks. Next to me, there was a man in a wheelchair and a woman holding onto the handles. She looked tired and worried. Her hair stood out at odd angles. They too seemed full of nostalgia.

"Skate for me," he said. The woman was clearly reluctant and I could hardly blame her. She bristled and curved her body away from the rink, but he was quite insistent.

"Skate for both of us, like we used to."

She was slow and hesitant at first—she was nervous—but when she let go of the bar, she was really very good. She glided around, she was a thing of grace, she did figures of eight, then spun in the middle of the rink. I turned, smiling. I thought he must have been very proud. When I next looked at him, I couldn't see his face: it was hidden by his handkerchief. Then I realized that his shoulders were shaking with grief and I couldn't stand to see him anymore. This was a stupid idea.

The lawyer was tall, potbellied and gray. *Messrs Tom Madison Fletcher and Collinson* was engraved on a brass sign next to the shiny door. I had heard from somewhere that Mr. Fletcher was American and I thought we might have something in common. He was not, and we did not.

He sat behind a great mahogany desk and I felt horribly sure the chair where I was sitting was deliberately smaller than his. I thought, *where is Madison or Collinson?* Fletcher had a privileged face; I imagined he was prone to gout. His watch rested on his large protuberant stomach, making a feature of it. As we talked, the feeling that he had no idea what I was talking about grew larger and larger until that was all that I could see in front of me. The tummy became insignificant compared to his great obliviousness.

"I need to see my girls, Mr. Fletcher."

"How are you going to pay?" he asked. He was doodling ever-decreasing circles in his notepad. I didn't know what this said about a person, but I didn't like it.

"Well, what can we do first?"

"One letter is twenty pounds."

"Is that it? A letter?"

He raised his bushy eyebrows at me. "I like to call it a shot across the bows."

He said "bows" like "bowels." I wondered if that was what he meant.

I remembered George's antipathy to "scraps of paper." How was a letter from Messrs Collinson et al. going to affect him?

"I can't imagine he'll do much about a letter," I said.

"Two letters then?"

"I want to see my children."

"Three letters for fifty-five pounds," he replied, "that's my best offer."

On the step outside, I rolled myself a Woodbine. If my mother could have seen me now, she would have been disgusted. Sitting on a concrete doorstep would give you piles, at the very least; worse than that, it would make you lower-class. How low I had sunk! I inhaled my cigarette gratefully. The smoke curled free, both upward and down, and warm into my throat. The sun was setting red over the city. All the hopes I'd had before today were now dashed.

What would George do with letters from a lawyer? Crumple them up and put them in the fire, no doubt. He'd probably throw on some whisky and watch them burn with his smug, satisfied look. *I'm winning, look how May bleeds.* I might as well just whistle into the wind for all the good a letter would do.

I had paid for six.

Pulling my overcoat around me, I discovered some of the buttons were missing. Matron used to offer to sew them back on, but she hadn't lately. Despite our rapprochement, she still disapproved of me. George hated me. My mother loathed me. And I couldn't reach my children. So many enemies, so little time.

The wind was up. A street full of law firms and banks and accountants. Conspirators. I felt like putting a brick through the windows of the lot of them. If only George had fallen dead at the bottom of those church steps all that time ago. If only I had walked on by.

What a mess I had made of it all.

I tried the house one more time. I hammered on the door desperately but George didn't answer. I knew it wasn't helping, but I was full of impotent rage. How dare he? I had been sitting there furiously for some time, deciding on my next move, when I saw Mrs. Crawford hurrying past. She seemed to have aged years in the twelve months since we had last met. I was so relieved to see her but at the same time I felt quite crazed. I leapt up and pursued her.

"I don't know where my girls are," I said frantically. "Do you know where they are? Please, Mrs. Crawford."

"All I know is George has employed a governess," she said nervously. "That's all."

"I heard that, but where are they?"

She didn't know. She had seen the girls in the August holidays and again this past October, but Mr. Turner hadn't needed her for Christmas. He'd said he had "plans." I didn't think it was possible to feel even more heart-broken than I already was, but I did. Observing my despair, Mrs. Crawford added quickly that the girls were as happy and as tennis-crazy as ever. I felt sick with jealousy that *she* had seen them and *I* hadn't. *It's not her fault*, I reminded myself. *Be fair.*

"Are they furious with me?"

"Never!" she said and her tone was reassuringly certain. "You know the girls—they love you."

I won't sob, I told myself.

"How is your James?" I asked, remembering the sweet young man with a cloth cap who would sometimes mow our lawn or run errands for us.

"Dead," she said.

The telegram came on her birthday. She had thought it was him sending birthday wishes. I couldn't imagine how horrendous that must have been.

"He always remembered my birthday," she said mechanically, and it was like she had said this so many times before that it had lost meaning. "Always a little something."

"I am so sorry, Mrs. Crawford."

She squeezed my fingers. ""At least the girls are safe. *Your* children are alive, Mrs. Turner."

I nodded. There was nothing I could add to that.

I was afraid Elizabeth wouldn't answer the door, but she did. She stood, her face serious, hair swept back, that beautiful white brow. The pale lips, pale teeth, pale eyes all somehow framed by the doorframe, and all looking angrily at me.

"You said you'd come to Dover," was the first thing she said.

"I know, I'm so sorry."

"I needed you there."

"I'm sorry."

"I *waited* for you."

"So, what happened?" I asked cautiously. This was going far worse than I had imagined. "Are you the first lady to swim the Channel?"

She looked at me incredulously, then, shaking her head from side to side, said: "I thought you were coming, I thought you were doing a big surprise reveal—ta-da, here I am! You were always so reliable."

"I should have sent a telegram, Elizabeth. I am so sorry. Just... What happened?"

"They wouldn't even let me get to the beach."

"No! Who wouldn't? Why?"

"Everything was arranged. The conditions were perfect. The tides. The weather. My fitness. They said the Channel was riddled with U-boats, it wasn't safe."

"I'm so sorry, Elizabeth."

"Well, you can't borrow my car. I'm afraid I need it."

"I don't want the car. Oh, Elizabeth!" I said. I had never seen her so furious or so miserable. "I did write though. Did you not get my letters?"

She shook her head. "Delia has a habit of destroying the post."

"Please."

Finally, she let me in to that cool elegant room in my favorite pale elegant house. As she went to fetch tea, I joked that I would do anything for a macaroon, but she raised an eyebrow humorlessly: "Don't you know there's a war on?"

I could think of plenty of retorts, but I didn't rise to it.

Usually, all the windows would be open, but I was slightly relieved to note that only about half were. I sat down in my usual armchair and listened as Elizabeth's footsteps faded away. I still felt shaky: George. The lawyer. Mrs. Crawford. I could hardly breathe.

The chess set was on the table to my left and I gazed at the figures. I wondered who Elizabeth had been playing. Was Harriet Dobinson a chess player? White had the advantage: I estimated it was only four moves from victory.

There was a newspaper cutting on the table to my right. I read it greedily. WOMAN'S CHANNEL BID FAILS.

Poor Elizabeth, I thought. It was a nasty little piece: *This self-admitted suffragette didn't even get started. While our boys suffer in France, Miss Martin bemoans the lack of training facilities for girls. While our boys fight for their country, Miss Martin poses in her skimpy swimming costume. Back to the kitchen for you, Miss Martin.*

Her skimpy swimming costume? I felt furious. What was she supposed to wear?

But I had let her down too. I was part of the problem. I must have fallen asleep some time after that. I woke up at about 3 a.m. I was under a blanket; the lamp had been extinguished, the curtains drawn and everywhere I looked seemed black and hopeless.

In the morning, Elizabeth came in with coffee for me and drew back the curtains with a flourish. The cats slipped around the door and jumped up onto my lap. It was comforting to see them. Elizabeth seemed in different spirits today: she asked me about the girls and George and France and I told her everything, weeping a little as I did so. She was kind and comforting in her uniquely bracing way and I assumed all the tension of the night before had been forgotten. While we ate porridge for breakfast she told me funny stories about her mother and her mother's friends and we laughed a lot.

But later that afternoon, we went walking on the common and when we saw troops on their exercises, Elizabeth wouldn't stop staring. Eventually, she turned her face to me, and I saw she looked utterly distraught again.

"I suppose you also think I'm a do-nothing. A silly shirker with her silly dreams and her silly cats."

"I'd never think that of you." I was going to add, "or the cats," but Elizabeth clearly wasn't in the mood. I was startled by this change of tone. I had never known her to talk so negatively about herself.

"Everyone is contributing to the war effort. And what about me?"

This *really* wasn't like Elizabeth.

"*I* certainly don't think that."

"Everyone else does. And now I've failed."

"But you can still do the swim this year, can't you?"

"It's not *actually* going to happen though, is it? No one is prepared to support me like they support the men. Some man will come along, and they will run around for him. Not me though. I can hardly find a place to swim to practice, never mind anyone who would train me. It's just a self-indulgent pipe dream. And women must not be self-indulgent. Or dream. I know it, and you know it too."

I didn't know what to say. I wanted Elizabeth to be happy. She had helped me to find my path, I owed it to help her back to hers.

"But you still have your meetings and your teaching…"

Elizabeth lowered her gaze.

"I was thrown out."

"What?"

"The refugee center, they made me leave. I was teaching the students about the suffragettes and, well, apparently there was a complaint."

The image of some stuffy school manager overhearing Elizabeth's radical lectures made me laugh. A snort escaped me.

"It's not funny, May!" said Elizabeth irritably.

"I know," I said.

"And I'm plump," she went on.

"You're not," I said, for she looked healthier than ever, broad and strong.

Elizabeth tossed her hair. "Oh! I even bore myself sometimes. The problem is, I haven't swum for six weeks now and it always makes me feel quite cuckoo."

I took her arm in mine, laughing. "Cuckoo? You? Never!"

"Anyway, we'll get you to see your girls, May," she said, suddenly restored to her old self-confident self. "We will find a way."

And I believed her. I always did.

Things I adore about Louis

His diplomacy/tact!

The way he kisses me.

His blue eyes and those eyelashes.

His mouth.

His jowls! He doesn't like them, but I do!

His shoulders. Broad.

His long legs.

His impeccable manners.

His calm temperament.

His kindness. I have never known kindness like it.

His constancy. He is trust-worthy. He always wants the best for me.

CHAPTER FORTY-ONE

Back, back, back to France. Back to the frozen mud plains, back to hell. My mood was lower than ever. Perhaps this was the place where I fitted best. Perhaps this was the *only* place I belonged now. Where I had once felt full of purpose, I now felt crushed by limitations. How I missed my girls. I had left the presents outside the house—who knew if they'd get them? It was the first Christmas I had not spent with them. I wrote to them every day. Nothing came from them.

We had more terrible news: Matron's husband was killed. It was Kitty who told me. "May, something sad has happened."

Matron was writing a letter when I ran into our tent. I knew she wouldn't look to me for comfort, but we were roommates after all. Who else was there? We mightn't always see eye to eye, but this, this, I felt I could help her with.

"I'm so sorry, Matron."

She ignored me. The only way I knew she had heard was because she hesitated just for one moment before she lowered her pen into the ink.

"Matron, I'm sorry. Do you want to go back home?"

"I *am* home," she said with such finality that I didn't dare cross the invisible line to her. I stood stock-still.

"Very well. If there's anything I can do..."

Early February, Louis and I traveled south to the Dordogne for one night to stay with his oldest friends. He had hinted that their place was grand, but he hadn't explained it was a chateau. When we arrived, I could only call out "Oh!" in astonishment and delight. It looked like something out of a picture book. The empty swimming pool in the garden gave the scene a slight air of abandonment but this only added to the atmosphere of faded beauty. We were staying in one of the chateau's towers, where a circular stairway led to a circular room, a room for a princess to let down her hair. I have been fortunate in my life to see some splendid places, but I had never been anywhere so lovely as this. To be here with Louis was like some fabulous dream.

Our hosts were Pierre and Mathilde. He was short, stout and jolly; Mathilde was a slim, aristocratic beauty. I only rarely suffered from jealousy, but I nearly did when I saw her. Everyone who met her must have fallen under her spell. She greeted us warmly. My French might have been better than her English, but she was determined to speak English. It was incredible to be in a place untouched by war, it felt like we were in a bubble here. "Money insulates," Louis always said. But I soon found out they had been blighted too.

"My little brother," Mathilde told me impassively. "In the Somme."

I wondered where he had died: on the fields, in the dressing station, with us—or had he made it to the hospital? So many stages, so many parts to the chain. Not that it made much difference to those picking up the pieces at home.

"Thank you for trying," she said. Her hair fell like curtains over her face, so I couldn't see her expression. "Louis told me you were there. The nurses are formidable."

I told her that *everyone* involved in the war effort was formidable.

I learned that Mathilde was a volunteer in a bandage center in the village. The volunteers went out in the countryside, collected moss and wrapped it at the local school to turn into bandages. She mimed the raveling with her hands. I knew Elizabeth had done this in England too; I had heard it was back-breaking work. Mathilde wasn't just a wealthy (and beautiful) face and I was sorry I had dismissed her as such. I, of all people, should have known better about judging a book by its cover!

It was a happy and carefree evening, eating venison with grilled vegetables, and I was delighted to discover Louis loved a moldy cheese as much as I did! We even managed to talk about things other than the war, although not much. The war crept in everywhere. At midnight, Mathilde and Pierre looked at each other, then rose from the table as one.

"Don't hurry up in the morning," Pierre said kindly. "What is the English phrase? Lovebirds?"

Louis laughed loudly while I could only blush.

What a joy it was to be alone with my Louis. "Such impropriety!" as Matron would say. We took our hosts at their word and were still in bed at eleven o'clock on the Sunday morning, smiling at each other, deliriously.

"We should go down for breakfast," Louis said eventually.

"We're too late, lunch maybe?"

"But I'm hungry..."

"I'll take your mind off it, darling."

"Again?!"

As we went down the spiral staircase to the kitchen Mathilde came in from her vegetable garden, where she had been watering tomatoes. Even in her gardening clothes, she looked immaculate. She smiled knowingly at us: "Quite the romance." She tore baguettes and put them in a basket. She collected butter from the windowsill: "Eat," she ordered, "you need your strength."

Pierre took Louis to admire his tractor. When we were alone, I wanted to ask Mathilde if Louis had brought anyone here before, but I couldn't bring myself to. She would think Americans were mad. She might have been right—I *was* crazy when it came to him.

The coffee Mathilde made was better than any I had drunk in a long time. While we were chatting, Mathilde mentioned children. I realized she had assumed—naturally, I suppose—that I didn't have any.

"Oh, I have two," I said quickly, "two daughters. In England."

"Of course." It's hard to shock the aristocratic French. "I didn't think you were old enough."

"I'm thirty," I told her.

"Still young," she said, as I confess I had hoped she might.

She asked about them and I told her fragments: Joy and her art. Leona and her sports. One hobby each was manageable. It was too beautiful a day for the sad story of my separation, and I didn't want to be pitied. She seemed to appreciate my role as a volunteer nurse and I feared she might lose respect for me if she knew what the real me was like.

Mathilde complimented me on the brooch Louis had given me. She was so captivated by it that I took it off so she could examine it more closely. After she turned it over and over in the palm of her hand, she eyed me closely and said:

"I have never seen Louis as besotted as he is with you."

I liked the sentiment, but I didn't like the word "besotted"—with its undercurrent of transience—and I hoped it was just that something had been lost in translation.

CHAPTER FORTY-TWO

Sometimes, in the morning, the sun was so bright it was almost as if the rays were dropping on us like rain. Our tents were drenched in heat and brightness. You couldn't usually sleep through it and if you did, you'd wake up dry-mouthed and with an aching head. And that's how it was, that morning, I woke stupidly early, bathed in white light. I would usually lie there with my eyes closed, thinking of my daughters, thinking of Louis, thinking of all my mistakes, but I didn't that morning because there was a quiet. Impossible to describe exactly, but it was that suspicious kind of quiet, like when a dog stops barking and you know he's got something he shouldn't have.

Matron was too quiet. I sprang from my bed over to hers. Panic was a frequent bedfellow in those days, but I had learned to swallow it, to de-tremble it, to calm it, to plow through it. Now, though, I was overcome with it. I shook her. Then I hauled her up. She looked terrible: her skin tone, the shape of her mouth, everything was wrong.

My head didn't know what it was, but my instincts kicked in fast.

"What did you take?" I scrambled around on my hands and knees. Under the bed. Unlike my side, with its abandoned socks, snake-like stockings, half-written poems and letters, hers was normally spotless. But not now. That morning, a whisky bottle lay beached on its side. Boxes of pills from the hospital tent. She was delirious, dozy, she wanted to sleep. No.

Please Kitty or Bonnie, someone help me.

I tried to make her sit upright, but she wouldn't, she couldn't. Her body was repulsively soft and bouncy in her nightshirt, fleshy where I had only known her rigid and starched.

"Matron," I kept whispering. I was torn between wanting to screech and wanting to preserve her dignity. I slapped her face—I didn't know what else to do. The slap did nothing. I had to make her sick. I stuck my fingers in her mouth, like I was trying to disarm a dog. She whimpered, she fought against them.

She forced my fingers out but she had understood: she replaced them with her own. She jammed her fist in, down her throat, choking, at last, vomit coming up. I held the bucket for her. The noises made me feel ill.

Thank heavens, Gordon ran in. Later, he told me, he had suspected something. A tiny feeling, an intuition of doom, the kind that can so often be wrong. Then, just as he was getting up, he heard the distinctive sound of a struggle.

"Allow me," Gordon said. He took the bucket and gratefully, I backed off.

I was so angry with her, I was almost shaking in my fury. When I'd slapped her, it was half to rouse her, half from that fury. *People dying when they are not wanting to and here you are, bloody killing yourself. You don't deserve this precious thing, this precarious life.*

Lunchtime in the canteen, Kitty and Gordon came to sit with me. Kitty spoke so softly, I had to strain to hear. "It must have been horrendous, May."

I didn't want to talk about that, though. I wanted to understand. *How? How could she be so stupid?*

Kitty and Gordon looked at each other.

"She doesn't know how to look after her parents and her husband's parents anymore."

My fury wouldn't dissipate. "What do you mean?"

"She has to provide for them all."

"But the pension," I asked uncertainly, "*his* pension will keep them, surely?"

Kitty shook her head.

They looked at each other again. Then Kitty whispered the truth. It turned out Matron's husband, her Willy, had been a deserter: he had been caught fighting in the crew. He complained to the doctor his head hurt. It's on record. He told him, "I'm going out of my mind here. Do something." But what could the doctor do? Wasn't *everyone* going out of their minds? Certainly, all the sane ones were. So, Willy ran away. They don't know how exactly. One moment he was there, the next he was gone, slipped away, disappeared. He was caught trying to board a boat at Boulogne; there were a few of them apparently. Traitors. He was shot in the back of the head against a wall outside the city hall in Poperinghe.

"Matron, this is not your fault," I said, but she wasn't listening to me. She stared straight ahead, her haughty chin hardened. "We will find a way through."

She closed her eyes.

I loathed myself. I felt like everything George had ever said about me was right. How could I not have spotted this? I considered myself a good nurse, I saw myself as a loyal friend, yet last night, I had lain down next to Matron, called out "Goodnight" and then extinguished the lantern, without a care in the world.

I tried to go back over the last few days to see what I had missed. We had cycled to the bakery, exchanged words about Farmer Norest— the chickens were laying.

Matron had written letters; we had eaten apples. We had picked wildflowers. I pressed them for my girls and she had done the same— for her parents, I had assumed. We read newspapers. Matron told me again that a cousin of hers had been on the *Titanic* and survived. All fairly mundane. We had been getting on better than ever.

How had I been so angry with her? I, who knew what despair felt like? I was appalled and ashamed that I had judged her. If someone who had felt despair could not be sympathetic, what chance did we all have? I asked Gordon if there wasn't a way Matron could have a pay rise. Hadn't she been a most loyal and hard-working nurse? Hadn't she endured the very worst of humanity? He sighed. It was a nice thought, but there were scales, lengths of service; how would it look?

That evening, I told her I had money for her. It would be my present. She was horrified by this; she was shaking her head so much that I feared a relapse. I changed my wording: it became a loan arranged over several years at low interest. Finally, she acquiesced. She pumped my hand: "I will pay you back, May, I promise, if it's the last thing I do."

"Don't thank me, thank my grandmother, Leonora," I said, and she nodded, tears in her eyes. She gripped my fingers so tightly, I had to ask her to loosen her grip. Apologizing, she did. I laughed, "At least your strength is coming back."

Gordon and I sat out on Little Big Rock, sharing a cigarette. It was always easy with him, we didn't have to talk. The crimson sky reminded me of Percy's paintings. I knew now they were more prescient than I had realized and better than I had given him credit for. I remembered the spikes, the jagged edges.

I thought of the man who shot Matron's husband, Willy. The one who cocked the pistol, fired at his own men. Surely he knew Willy was no enemy? Did he go back to his quarters, did he sit back and drink his tea, write a letter to his wife or his ma? But then, what choice did he have either? We were all just cogs in this great big terrible machine.

For several weeks after that, I dreamt about firing squads. Wondered how it felt to be him, to line up there, waiting for the final blow. Whether it was a relief or not. Matron wouldn't talk about it. The shame. *The shame.* Those poor men facing their end, waiting for the moment of oblivion. Thinking of their mothers, or their wives or their girlfriends. Did they long for another chance, or did they just wish it was over?

CHAPTER FORTY-THREE

Louis was supposed to pick me up at two for my half-day off, but his car didn't roll up. We had planned to go for a picnic. I didn't hear anything from him all afternoon. I spent my break in my tent with my stomach in a frightful knot. I couldn't bring myself to speak to the others about it. I felt myself swinging between anger and fear: one moment Louis was dead in a field in Lens, his uniform soaked in blood, the next he was in Poperinghe, flirting with Ginger or slow dancing with nurses less complicated than me.

I couldn't stand it. I washed and cleaned. I wrote letters. At four, although I was not due on, I reported to Matron and she let me back to convalescence, where injured soldiers told me their life stories and I could lug out pails of old bandages until midnight.

The other nurses were already feeling sorry for me, and I couldn't have that; I made my expression extra jolly. Hearty-faced May. Inside, my heart was breaking. The longer I didn't hear from him, the more it was decided: he was dead, he was dead, he must be dead. I just had to wait for confirmation from the telegram.

He came the next day at two. I had just left the dressings tent for my break when I saw the car pull up. I was thrilled to see him, determined to playfully scold. "A whole day late!" But once I saw his expression, I knew something wasn't right. He was unsmiling and rigid, far from his normal soft self. Something had happened. I wanted to crawl inside his coat and nest there. Instead, I grabbed his hands and found they were lead weights in mine.

"What is it? Is it Winston? Pierre? Mathilde?"

No, it was none of them. He told me to sit down on our favorite rock, yet he did not sit but stood, his hands clasped behind his back, like he was talking to General Pétain.

He said he wasn't going to see me anymore.

"What? Why?" A part of me wondered if this was another of his bad jokes.

He cleared his throat. "No particular reason."

I tried to make sense of it. I tried to see what he was saying but I couldn't. Nothing made sense. I felt hot and humiliated, my cheeks burned, but at the same time, I felt sure it was a misunderstanding.

"I need an explanation, Louis," I said, as coolly as I could muster. He wouldn't get away with this with General Pétain and he wasn't going to get away with it with me. "What has changed?"

He just stared at the ground. I couldn't read his expression. The sparrows that usually reflected back our happy chatter now seemed mocking. What had I done wrong? We had been happy in the Dordogne, I was sure of it. We had been happy *all* our time together. We were lovebirds, weren't we? I suddenly remembered Percy's visit and Louis' concerned face. The way he'd kept his hands buried in his pockets in the canteen.

"Is it...it isn't something to do with Percy Milhouse?"

"Who?"

"The artist who came? Is it—you thought he and I were... together?" I was shaking with disbelief. This was horrible, *horrible*.

Something changed. His eyes were unreadable, guarded. He shook his head barely imperceptibly but at the same time, he said, "Yes, that's what it is."

"But I told you it was nothing. You have to believe me, Louis."

"May, accept it. I don't want to see you again." He didn't say anything else. After all we'd shared, he just turned away and strode back to his car.

The sparrows continued to sing. I sat on Little Big Rock unable to take it in: he wasn't dead; he just didn't want me.

When I relayed the conversation to Kitty, it made even less sense. She was as confounded as I was; in a way that was a comfort because it suggested I hadn't missed something obvious, he really had presented to me and the world that he was in love. But it was also infuriating: Kitty kept saying, "That doesn't sound like Louis" or "I never thought Louis would do something like this..." and it reminded me how fooled I had been.

I remembered him saying, "Don't you trust me?" I had said yes. I'd had no reason to suspect that was the wrong answer. I had been completely blindsided. I couldn't trust my own instincts anymore. I clutched the brooch he had bought me, I remembered the feeling on my skin where he had touched me.

I would have done anything to have my Grandma Leonora hold me then. To whisper, "There, there. It's a terrible shock," into my ear. I had never felt so let down.

Work was the only thing that stopped me from falling to pieces. Nursing was my tonic. The war was my distraction. Just as swimming and Elizabeth and Percy had filled the whacking great holes in my life in London, so did each trembling patient and each repetitive task here. I had to get up, I had to keep going, I had to perform my duty every day. I couldn't let down the men or my team.

I can't lose you all, I thought. *Not the girls AND Louis, that was just too much.* I had to concentrate on getting my girls back for now. As for Louis, my fathomless grief at losing him would just have to wait.

<u>List of things I love by Leona</u>
<u>(age ten years and two months)</u>

Winning tennis matches.

Singing, but not choir.

Dancing. Always.

Buckets and spades at the seaside.

Mummy's laugh.

CHAPTER FORTY-FOUR

In March 1917 I went back to England for a weekend. I went straight to Elizabeth's house, and we drove up to Leamington in her car. This was Elizabeth's plan. Once we were outside the school, Elizabeth changed her shoes. She put on a bonnet and glasses. I didn't think the disguise was necessary, and she looked more rather than less peculiar to me, but she insisted. She made me redo my hair too and told me that I should let my slip show. Smirking, she said, "All the young ladies do nowadays."

We went to the front gate and fortunately it was not the headmistress, who knew me, who answered.

"My daughter and I are here to look around," croaked Elizabeth, in a voice that explained why she had never been involved in amateur dramatics.

"Have you made an appointment?" asked the gatekeeper.

Elizabeth and I looked nervously at each other.

"Yes," I said just as Elizabeth responded, "No."

"No," I said, the very moment Elizabeth changed her answer to: "Yes...I think so."

Anyway, we were in. No, we didn't want a guide, thank you. We would walk around and then come to the headmistress's study with any questions we had. Yes, thank you.

I couldn't believe we had done it. *Elizabeth* had done it. We'd got in. We giggled down the corridors. Now we just had to find my girls among the schoolgirls who were all dressed the same. Not an easy task. But then, a godsend, a timetable stuck on a wall, showed that class 5W—Joy's class—was playing hockey. We strode out to the sports fields. Elizabeth dropped her elderly-lady stoop and I pulled up my slip. And there, out there, I picked out my lovely Joy at once. It was the menace in her movements that gave her away. She wielded her hockey stick like a scythe, cutting down the opposition. My heart leapt to see her.

When the final whistle blew, I waved. I saw confusion on her face, followed by pleasure. She ran over to me, her hockey stick held high in the air as if in salute.

"Mummy?"

"Darling, sshhh!" I said, as per the plan. "I shouldn't be here, don't say anything."

Joy nodded. She was always quick on the uptake.

"I know. Daddy said you're banned."

I paused.

"Can you come down to the playing field at the far end? The door in the fence there? About five o'clock tonight. Bring Leona."

"Of course, Mummy. I can't wait."

"Nor can I."

It was agony to let her go. She looked at me longingly, but I could see her teacher was getting tetchy.

"Leona will be happy," she told me with an odd expression. "She cries at bedtime now."

How slowly five o'clock came around. We avoided the headmistress's office, and crept back to the car, where I willed the minutes to move faster. After what felt like a lifetime, we made our way to the meeting point.

But not only was the door heavily padlocked now but the wire fence either side of it was at least six feet tall.

Elizabeth and I gazed at it in dismay.

"That's one problem I didn't anticipate," admitted Elizabeth. She was furious with herself. "How in God's name are we going to get in—or out?"

I rummaged in my bag and with a flourish produced something heavy and iron and sharp.

"Wire-cutters?" asked Elizabeth incredulously.

"Keep them on you at all times—" I choked. *Must not think of Louis.*

My sweet girls were waiting on the other side by the time I cut through the wire. They stared at me like they couldn't believe I was real. And then I had made a gap, large enough for Elizabeth and me to pull ourselves through. We hugged and kissed while Elizabeth stood in the background, then I pulled her forward and we all hugged and kissed and squealed some more. Then we remembered where we were and what we were doing and shushed each other. We sat quietly on the grass, near the fence, under the protection of an old oak tree.

"Do you want to come away with me?" I asked urgently.

"And leave school?"

I had known this would be their reaction. "We could go and live somewhere." At this they looked even more horrified, if possible. "That's a 'no' then, girls? Are you absolutely certain?"

They were. In that case, I estimated, we had three hours together. Elizabeth, far more conservative, thought we should send the girls back inside after one and a half. We didn't want to get them in trouble. The girls talked quickly, tripping over their stories, competing with their tales. They told me about the procession of evil governesses that George had employed. One of whom had the audacity to cook rice. I relaxed. "Well, that doesn't sound *too* bad."

"You haven't eaten it," said Joy flatly.

We made plans for the next school break: tennis club, of course, Ice-skating. Museums. Art galleries. And we talked about things we had done together in the past. Such a relief that they had sweet memories.

"You are so beautiful!" I couldn't contain myself. "Both of you. And I love you so much. Will you remember that, whatever happens?"

"Fine," said Joy casually, stretching out her legs in the evening sunshine.

I looked over to where Leona was now giggling and playing elastic with Elizabeth. She pulled her curls behind her ears. The normalcy of it killed me.

"I've got you both in my locket here," I added. "Next to my heart." I showed Joy the photo I carried of her. A reluctant smile crept over her face. "I always knew you did, Mummy," she murmured. She let me hold her hand.

The girls and I hugged and clutched each other one last time and then they ran off toward school, beaming and waving, and we made our way back to the car. The moment they left me I felt bereft, but I told myself: *Be strong, they are well and happy. We can do this.* We were only a few miles from London when Elizabeth said she had something to tell me. I felt myself tense—I wasn't in the mood for revelations. It was taking all my effort not to burst into tears or to beg Elizabeth to drive me straight back to Leamington.

"So…" she began. But she was smiling, so it wasn't going to be unpleasant. I relaxed slightly.

"So?" I said.

"I want to become a VAD, a nurse, like you, May."

I remembered her nearly running over a man in the car, her revulsion at a woman in the lake with a verruca—as a nurse she would see a whole lot worse than that. I couldn't imagine Elizabeth doing dressings or bedpans. My best friend had so many wonderful qualities: resourcefulness, courage and passion—but empathy was not one of them. And Elizabeth was such a water baby too: she *needed* the lake. What would she do without her regular life-affirming swims?

"Don't you think I would be a good nurse, May?"

Then I remembered Elsie's kind words to me in Percy's studio. How fearful I was once, yet how naturally it had come in the hospital: that urge to do my best, the desire to not let down my team.

"Yes," I said as sincerely as I could. "Why not?"

It had started very lightly to rain. We both gazed out the windshield as the wipers slowly and noisily flicked the drops away. My girls would be indoors now, changing into their soft flannel nightgowns. Leona would be holding on to her bear Cardinal Wolsey; Joy would be finishing her drawings, getting ready for bed.

"I could come out to be with you," Elizabeth added softly. "You and me, together at your field hospital in France."

My heart dropped further still. "Yes," I said, cautiously, "I imagine you could."

It did me good, as always, to swim in the lake the following day, to feel light and weightless again. But the elation didn't last long. Who knew when I would see my girls again? Was it feasible to keep breaking into the school like common thieves to see them? Were they really as robust as they pretended? Did they secretly despise me? My mood remained dark and even the magnificence of the outdoor bathing couldn't help me. When the whistle blew for session's end, I jolted with fear, and when Elizabeth, in the next cubicle, dusted herself down with talcum powder, it reminded me of the dust clouds after explosions and I could feel myself shiver. *Don't go down that road*, I told myself.

We sat on a bench on the common, our picnic in the space between us. Elizabeth cuddled her knees close to her chest, her long red plait curling up at the end.

I would have liked to have skipped the buttered roll entirely and gone straight to the macaroons, but I felt this would be uncivilized. So I was tucking into the sandwiches, when Elizabeth, who was never a fool, asked quietly: "May, what's wrong? Is it about me coming out to France?"

Why did I feel so peculiar about that? I had always suspected that I was an unpleasant person. My mother had always said it. George said it. Now, I realized I was a monster. But France was *my* place. The team were my team. These were my friends and experiences... I had grown strong and indispensable there. I had found myself and I was a different person than the May in England. And what if they grew to love Elizabeth more than they did me? I chewed and chewed and made my friend wait. I couldn't imagine her at our hospital though, really, I couldn't: she would be a fish out of water. Finally, I swallowed.

"What would Harriet say?" I said quietly, "Your friend, Harriet Dobinson?"

Elizabeth stroked her hair. "It has nothing to do with her, does it?"

"And it's dangerous," I said weakly. "How would your mother cope if something happened to you?" I mentioned Elle Harcourt, hating myself as I did.

Elizabeth nodded slowly. Her face was even paler than usual. Then I thought: *they're always looking for volunteers for the hospital trains—no, for the boats!* I sat up, suddenly excited at my own idea. This was it! I said, "I bet you'd enjoy being a nurse on a ship more, it's the next best thing to being in the water. Really, I can picture you doing that—floating around the Mediterranean..."

She nodded again, still silent, and I realized what I was doing. I tried to backtrack quickly: "I could always ask my matron, though, if there might be..."

Elizabeth packed up the remainder of our lunch. She had not touched her sausage roll. Usually, she was famished after a swim. "No, May. I understand. I will look into that other idea, thank you."

But the air between us had rapidly cooled. We went our separate ways as we had planned, but try as I might, our goodbyes were far less effusive than usual. Elizabeth's face was stony. As I walked back to the station, I couldn't understand why I had been so mean. It dawned on me that I had let Elizabeth down, again and again, when she had only ever gone out of her way to be kind to me. I was a horrible person.

List of things I hate by Joy Turner (age thirteen)

Rice. Especially overcooked and soggy. (Rice pudding is okay.)

Sharpening a pencil to perfection—and then it breaks. Grrrr!

Leaving the Pilkingtons' house.

Dissecting mice in biology.

And pigs' hearts.

The basement toilets at school.

Mummy being miles and miles away in France.

People saying: "I bet you want to be a nurse like your mother..." I don't. I want to be a great artist.

CHAPTER FORTY-FIVE

Louis was in the newspapers in France again. He was quoted as saying: "Mon Général, if by your action the British Army is annihilated, England will never pardon France, and France will not be able to afford to pardon you."

Gordon was impressed. "That is one clever man," he said, tapping the front page in his tent. He looked at me pointedly. Classical music was playing in the background as ever. "Why don't you write to him? You know you want to."

"He has to come to me."

The truth was, reading the newspaper articles only made me more confused. How could I forget him if he was always there in black and white? And seeing Louis held up as a hero in his public life when I felt he had been such an untrustworthy coward in his private life: well, wasn't that just the eternal story? I pretended I was indifferent to his heroics, but I was still a long, long way from that. I missed him so much.

I wondered, had Mathilde been right? Was Louis only ever *besotted* with me? Yet that didn't ring quite true. Other times, I wondered if perhaps Louis had discovered the real monstrous me, the one who turned on her best friend, and had become revolted by me? But I couldn't believe that was the full story either. All I knew for certain was that I had never loved a man as much as I loved him, and I would never love in the same unconscious, free and trusting way again. He had seen to it that all that was finished.

I dreamt he came back to me and had been shot in the heart. I dreamt blood was spurting ferociously from his chest. "Save me, save me!" he'd cry and I would turn him away: no, I would dig my hands deep into the cavity: "Here it is, Louis, I've found your heart."

And then Winston appeared in the convalescence tent one morning. Once I'd established there was nothing wrong with him—he had come to pick up someone he knew—I dared ask:

"How's Louis?"

"Moping," he said, which I confess was music to my ears. It told me that Louis was alive. And more importantly, it told me that he too was miserable. Louis *should* be moping. Ideally for the rest of his days.

"How have you been anyway?"

"Brilliant," Winston said cheerfully. "Nothing in life is so exhilarating as to be shot at without result. And how have you been, May? Writing lots of poems, I hope."

"I have been and they're not bad, if I say so myself," I said, smiling.

"If they're anything like you, May, they'll be pretty wonderful."

Here was someone who had the gift of the gab. And what a gift it was.

"You've sent them out to the magazines?"

"Wha-at? No, I haven't done anything with them."

"Send them off."

"I don't think—"

"That's an order."

"You're not *my* commanding officer." I laughed. Winston was so shocked at being answered back that he tripped over a rope—he *never* looked where he was going.

"I insist, as a friend."

"Why would anyone want to publish me?" I asked. I didn't really think that, but fishing for compliments with Winston was easy. He always came up with a great big trout.

"Why not you? You're lyrical, you're thoughtful. Rise up, young woman!"

I laughed. Winston could be very silly at times.

He continued, "If you don't bloody send them off, May Turner, I will creep into your tent, go through that notebook of yours and send them myself!"

"Have you never met my roommate, Matron? She'd give you what-for if you tried that!"

Winston shook his head. He was not joking. He looked suddenly downcast.

"Good God, May! What am I going to do with you and Louis? I should knock your heads together!"

Kitty was still grieving for her mother. After our shifts, we talked about her. Kitty explained that her mother had made her feel loved, respected, admired even.

"But how?" I asked.

"I don't know," she said, wiping away the tears. "She wasn't a clever woman, she wasn't an educated woman, but she just did."

My mother had carried, fed, educated and clothed me, but I had never felt more than a fly in her ointment, a spider in her soup. "Take her out." "Get her upstairs." "What does she want now?"

No wonder I found it painful to speak to her. No wonder I was a sitting duck for a man like George.

Not long after I had gone back to France, a letter came from Elizabeth. The envelope had a black footprint on it and I opened it apprehensively, afraid she was still hurt or angry at my selfishness. She had every right to be. I had not been a good friend. Elizabeth began with her usual updates on her cats, but then she cut to the chase:

Anyway, May Turner, here is the news! I have work! I am going to be a nurse but I am NOT going to a hospital overseas, nor a hospital in England. Can you guess where I am going?

I stood stock-still.

I am going on a ship! It was such a brilliant idea of yours, I can't believe I didn't act on it sooner!

I imagined her grinning delightedly as she wrote that. She was going in one week, she said, which meant—I checked the date at the top—she was already there! She would be helping to transport patients from France to England.

Isn't it marvelous how so many of the ships are called "castle" these days? And mine has the best name of all: Glenart Castle. Remember that, darling. And make sure you look out for me. We might even dock near you!

I'm nowhere near the sea, I thought, but this was so Elizabeth. Why let a silly thing like geography get in your way?

I plan to jump over the side and swim like a fish every morning, so I haven't given up on my Channel crossing dreams just yet. The goose fat is in my suitcase. The record may still one day be mine!

I started laughing to myself.

I can hardly believe how well it all worked out. Thank you, thank you, sweet May! I'm sorry if it seemed like I was agitated by your comments on your last visit. Forgive me. I understand now that

you were exactly right, as always, your loving and plump friend,
Elizabeth.

Elizabeth was incorrigible. Of course she would still be crossing the Channel; of course she would! And she didn't hate me at all. Things had worked out just perfectly. I ran to my tent and wrote her a long and grateful reply.

CHAPTER FORTY-SIX

Louis was in the canteen talking enthusiastically with Gordon. I couldn't believe it. How dare he just appear like this?! It wasn't kind to come back into my life with no warning.

My stomach knotted as I watched Bonnie walk over and greet him warmly. Both she and Gordon were traitors, I decided. Then Kitty arrived and, although slightly more reticent, she still shook hands with Louis and laughed at something he said. I was boiling with rage. In their excitement, no one noticed me draw nearer.

"How's young Freddie?" I heard Louis say. *Ever the liaison man*, I thought scornfully, *always trying to win over a crowd.*

"He's two now!" Bonnie beamed, predictably thrilled that her bonny boy had been remembered. "I just got back from leave with him. He babbles and everything."

"I'm so pleased." *Everyone* looked pleased.

I couldn't wait any longer. I called hello. Louis spun around, and his smile told me that I was the reason he was here.

"May!"

I felt all my old feelings for him flood back, but then that had never changed, not really. It was him who had changed, not me: he had rejected me. I cautioned myself to remember that.

"What are you doing here?"

Bonnie and Kitty excused themselves and scuttled away. Gordon made his exasperated face and went after them. I knew it would have suited them all if I was kind to Louis. Well, I wasn't here to make life more pleasant for them.

"I didn't mean to cause you upset," Louis said hesitantly. His bottom lip turned pale under his teeth. I think he was disappointed with my tone (he had no right to be).

"I'm not upset," I said coldly. *Don't flatter yourself.* "I asked, what are you doing here?"

He wrung his hands—the hands I used to clutch and kiss. "It's a little strange, but I've, we've, been invited to a wedding…"

I laughed, then realized that he was being serious.

"A wedding? What? Whose?"

He gave his dry, uncertain cough. "Elsie Knocker's."

"Elsie? What on earth? Who is she marrying?"

Elsie had never mentioned anything to me about marriage. With some women it was always on their mind. If it had been on hers, it had been obscured by thousands of other more pressing things. Louis licked his lips uneasily. "Baron T'serclaes."

"Who? Is that Harold?" *Her Man of the Moment?*

"Yes…" Louis gestured to the canteen chairs. "Shall we?"

I shook my head. I thought, *why are you always trying to get me to sit down?* We weren't going to get comfortable together ever again.

"Really? Elsie Knocker is getting married to a baron?"

"Yes!"

He chuckled nervously, and I couldn't help but grin—until I reminded myself again, *this man is not your friend.*

"Is it in Exeter?" I asked, vaguely remembering Elsie mentioning that she was from there.

"Um, no," he said even more nervously. "It's… it's in a little church, near the Western Front…"

Who on earth gets married along the Western Front?
Elsie Knocker does, of course.

"I'd be delighted if you'd agree to accompany me."

I tried to look non-committal, but my mind was racing ahead. Elsie and Harold were getting married and I was invited. Louis and

I would go together. This was a chance for me to show him what a terrible mistake he had made, to show him that I was a desirable and lovable woman and he was a fool.

What to wear though? There was no way George would release my clothes. And there was no way I would even ask. He would be delighted to know he had more leverage over me. That's if he hadn't dumped them on a bonfire yet.

I would have to order something gorgeous from Liberty's. The type of thing people wore before the war. I would somehow style my hair into the latest look—whatever it was now—and I would be irresistible, and Louis would tell everyone that he rued the day he'd left me. If I wrote to Liberty's now, this very evening, they could get something to me within the next month. Or perhaps, if Kitty or Bonnie were going back to England in the next few weeks, they could pick out something and then Bonnie could make sure it fitted. She was a whizz at making a dress look unintentionally tight.

"I'm not sure." Suddenly, I felt less interested in the wedding and more interested in making Louis squirm. I knew the hurt I could inflict on him would be just a drop in the ocean compared to what he had done to me, but it felt very important to me then. *Which would upset him most,* I evaluated coolly: *refusing to go with him, or going but snubbing him all day long?*

"Elsie very much wants you there," he added. He laid his cap on the table and it seemed to me he was intentionally making himself more vulnerable. Why did he have to have that handsome face, those blue eyes? I remembered Madame Lorenzo's warning that he was complex and again, I thought she wasn't *completely* wrong.

"When is it then?"

Louis looked more uncomfortable than ever. He twisted his hands. "It's tomorrow!"

*

Louis insisted he hadn't had any more notice than that himself. He had come right away, as soon as he had heard. But still, it was ridiculous, wasn't it? Only one day's warning? *How could I get ready*? I would look shabbier than the scarecrow in Farmer Norest's fields. But then I thought, actually, Kitty had several fine hats—her uncle was a milliner—and Bonnie had just received a delivery of boot polish that I could surely use in exchange for some rouge, if necessary. She had also come back from her last leave home with a very pretty jacket "borrowed" from an unsuspecting sister. That might work. So, I accepted, and it was arranged that Louis would pick me up the following day.

"I look forward to it," he said as he left. I didn't bother to reply, and his words hung unanswered like the cobwebs in the air.

Gordon was the first to return. "So, May, what's going on?"

I was still dazed. Elsie was marrying on the Western Front and I was going to her wedding with Louis. It was so surreal that for a moment it felt like I had stepped into one of Percy's paintings.

"It's no big deal, Gordon. I just have to go somewhere with Louis tomorrow."

"You *have* to go?" he echoed, laughing. "You don't *want* to go?" This made me furious. Gordon thought he was right about everything, but he really wasn't.

"Louis and I are over," I snapped. "What would make me most happy would be if I never had to see that pathetic man again."

There was a noise at the entrance. Both Gordon and I swung around.

"Er, hmm…" Louis was standing in the gap. Sunlight shafted around him. "I think I forgot my cap…"

CHAPTER FORTY-SEVEN

The next morning, Gordon, Kitty, Bonnie and Matron gathered to see me off. I felt silly at the fuss, but grateful too. Bonnie had made my boots gleam and her sister's stylish jacket did indeed fit a treat. Kitty's hats did nothing for me, but Millicent had lent me a beautiful cream colored bonnet. I felt quite the glamorpuss!

"You should have seen the clothes I brought out here," Millicent said, shamefaced. "I was such a ninny."

I confided in her about my abandoned bathing suits and my long-gone weekend shoes and she laughed. "Glad I wasn't the only one."

Louis didn't say anything until we had started the drive. Then, staring straight ahead, he said I looked elegant. I shrugged as if to say, *your opinions aren't important to me anymore.*

He asked how the girls were and I told him fine. I didn't want to talk. We were not lovers anymore and we had never been friends; I had no need to elaborate. He had made his decision, he had chosen not to be with me. I would not reward him by being nice. Perhaps if he groveled, perhaps if he begged for my hand, I might. I eyed him nervously. He did not look like he was about to grovel or beg.

Today is about Elsie and Harold, I reminded myself. *That's all. Not us. Let's get this done with.*

As we drove, I remembered my own wedding. Drunken George rubbing his clammy hands together, making insinuations about our wedding night. Drooling through the endless speeches. The worst mistake of my life. My mother's face like thunder—but then she had never been pleased with me. My grandmother had once let slip that I was supposed to be a boy and it seems she never got over the disappointment. Funny how she had been dismayed that I had married George, yet doubly dismayed when I left him—how clearly I could see it all now.

It was a magnificent church. Elsie had found a diamond in the ruins, one of those freak survivors of a storm. If you were superstitious, you might say it had been saved by God expressly for this reason. Exquisite stained glass of fishermen and farmers completed the interior. Gorgeous blue and yellow shades everywhere you looked. *Think of all the work that had gone into this!* I thought, *think of all the love.*

Louis and I were seated in a middle row, at the far side, but I still had a good view of the aisle Elsie would walk up. I could see no sign of Harold and it fleetingly crossed my mind that something, anything, could still go wrong. How awful that would be. The place was crowded, mostly with men and women in uniform, but there were a few in civilian clothes too. There were a couple of babies with their mothers furiously rocking them to keep them quiet. A few small children looking around for things to do. An elderly Belgian man who kept talking loudly, others who kept saying "sshhh!"

It was ridiculous but when Elsie finally arrived at the church door with the sunlight behind her, it was almost like we were in the presence of something holy. She was wearing a veil, so of course you couldn't see her expression, but you could absolutely tell that underneath she was calm and content and that everything was in place, everything was exactly as it ought to be.

Harold stood up, *ah there he was, of course, he had been waiting in the front pew,* and could a fellow possibly have smiled more? His face was bursting with pride. As Elsie moved toward him, she looked as though she were floating, so smooth and graceful were her movements.

Usually, I can't abide a slow service, but this was excellently paced. The priest alternated between Flemish and English, but he had an expressive, clear voice and he virtually skipped through the introductions. I found I couldn't take my eyes off them all. I was hardly aware of Louis next to me until he coughed. No one declared any reason the couple shouldn't wed. A ripple of relieved laugher ran through the crowd at that point. Their vows were exchanged in low, serious voices. When the priest said Elsie's full name, Elizabeth Blackall Shapter, I raised my eyebrows at Louis for one moment—*I did not know that was Elsie's real name!*—but when he smiled back, I hastily looked away from him:

He is not my friend.

Harold lifted Elsie's veil. They stared at each other with such longing and intent, I could hardly breathe.

At the same time, it occurred to me that there was something so unlikely about all this: Elsie had never shown any interest in marriage, in monogamy, in the old institutions, yet here we were. Harold must have pulled her back to the traditional ways. It must be love.

Louis wiped his cheek. He looked at me and for the first time in a long while, I let down my guard. I forgot the pain he had caused me, and it seemed natural to place my hand on his. Almost like a reflex he closed his beautiful eyes.

I had to close my eyes too and hold my breath. Our legs brushed together briefly. I don't think I had ever wanted him more.

Outside, the English threw rice while the Belgians looked appalled, muttering about the waste. Elsie and Harold stood in the midst of it all, in the center but aloof somehow, elevated and hardly there. There was the usual faffing around outside the church door. And then there were the photographs, always with the photograph! Elsie wasn't known as the most photographed woman on the Western Front for nothing. The photographers took over, the occasion was theirs for now. They organized Elsie: they took shots of her on her own, and she looked as cool and self-possessed as she ever did; then they took shots of her with Harold and I couldn't help but smile to see her so girlish.

An old man swept the rice into a neat pile. When he thought no one was looking, he knelt on the ground, knees in the dirt, and with wizened fingers pushed all those tiny grains of rice into a paper bag and then strolled off nonchalantly, bag under his arm.

The reception was held at La Poupée, of course: it was Elsie's favorite place. Nowhere else would make sense. We drove the thirty minutes in silence. And darling Ginger was there, greeting everyone, matching names to faces, taking coats, making drinks appear from thin air, making sure the pianist was playing the songs everyone wanted to hear. Her father looked redder and more tired than ever, but he too dashed around the tables, magicking up whisky and gin.

Elsie transformed from blushing bride into perfect host, rotating around, checking we all had a drink and had been fed. And there were too many people to talk to; Louis and I were never left alone together, thank goodness. When it was my turn, Elsie hugged me, told me that I was a vision—she loved this jacket—it has to be from Harrods, no?—and she was thrilled I had come. She hugged me, held me by the shoulders so she could look at me properly, then hugged me again.

"I hear you have medals from the Somme."

"Oh…" I flushed. I hated talking about it. Hated, hated it. Wished those horrendous months, like the medals, could be locked away in a hidden box. "You know how it is."

Elsie nodded. "And you drive, now?"

"Drive, ride motorbikes…still afraid of horses though," I admitted.

"Two out of three isn't bad."

She looked around, and I wondered if she was losing interest in me. But instead she leaned forward, whispering, "We war nurses have a special bond." I agreed, but later, I wondered if we did. I wondered if there was something that you could tell about us that distinguished us from other people, other nurses, other veterans. If there was a special bond now, in two years, ten, fifteen years, would it fade, and would we be unremarkable, invisible women again?

"And how is it with Louis?"

Elsie didn't know? Louis hadn't told her?

Goosepimples on my arm. "There is no 'it.' We no longer..." I couldn't think of the word. What did we no longer do? "Communicate," I said weakly.

"But..." She gaped at me. "Why? I was certain you adored each other!"

"You'll have to ask him." I shrugged. Then a Frenchman in a uniform covered with medals came along and possessively put an arm around Elsie. "Hurry! The queen of Belgium is here."

But Elsie just shrugged.

"You must come and speak to her," he insisted.

"But I am talking with my old friend..."

"Go, go!" I said, laughing, and apologetically, Elsie allowed herself to be pulled away from me.

At any gathering now, there were men with no legs or men with no arms, so sometimes you didn't even look twice. Even Elsie's Harold hadn't escaped unscathed: he had a limp. The atmosphere was buoyant. I didn't get to see the queen but I mingled with fine ladies and hospital matrons and there were Australian, New Zealander and Canadian servicemen in addition to the usual Belgians, French and British. The sun was just setting behind the old clock tower when Harold picked Elsie up in his arms. She tried batting him away half-heartedly, but was laughing too much to put up much of a fight.

Harold staggered away with her in his arms out to their car. It was surprising they made it that far. I suppose they went somewhere to be alone. A hotel perhaps. I had no doubt her wedding night would be better than mine had been. Better than my life ever had been— except when I was with Louis. I looked over at him, remembering our previous visit here and after, after in the car. I was smiling and cheering along with everyone, but I wanted to cry.

I thought, *to be loved, to be accepted, isn't that what we all want?*

I drained my glass of champagne and took another from Ginger's father. My emotions were churning. I wondered, was it possible Louis and I could try again? I *knew* there was something still between us. I had felt it in the car *and* in the church. I wasn't wrong about it, surely? Mightn't it be that Louis had finally realized his mistake—and would beg for me to be his once again? Sure enough, just as I was wondering this, Louis strode over to me purposefully. I gave him my first genuine smile of the day.

"Oh Louis, the bubbles are going to my head," I said with the tinkly little laugh I hadn't bothered with for so long. "Are you enjoying yourself? They say the queen of Belgium is here!"

"It's a wonderful party," he agreed. He was drumming his leg, which I knew meant he had something on his mind.

"Louis, I want to say, I don't think you're pathetic," I talked quickly before he could stop me. "But you must understand, I was very hurt and...taken aback by your rejection."

Behind him, I noticed a young French soldier with pockmarked skin watching me uncertainly. Too late, I realized he was waiting for Louis.

"I regret hurting you, May," Louis replied shortly. His skin was a furious flush. He gestured to the young soldier to come forward. "Sergeant Forzay will drive you back whenever you are ready."

Sergeant Forzay's hand was plump and damp.

"My pleasure, Nurse Turner."

I couldn't think of what to say. I didn't want Louis to go yet; I felt like I'd played everything badly.

But there was nothing I could do.

Louis gave me a nod. His eyes, so gentle, so intelligent, were shaded. This was it.

"Goodbye, May."

CHAPTER FORTY-EIGHT

Since Elizabeth was now somewhere on the English Channel, I was very grateful that Kitty agreed to come with me to Leamington. It was kind of her to give up a precious day of leave. On the train, I felt excited and optimistic. We were the only people in the compartment and we ate Bath buns and read aloud the more interesting articles in the newspaper to each other. Kitty read beautifully now.

We were met at the school gate, and we tried the same ploy as last time: I was the unlikely daughter, while Kitty, in a black shawl and glasses, was my mother—we wanted to look around. The woman who we met seemed to accept this. The war perhaps hadn't aged me as much as I feared, I thought; however, most unexpectedly, she insisted that I stay behind in an empty room to fill out a detailed application form.

"I would prefer to look around," I said desperately, "with my... mother."

"It's our policy," she said, looking down her pince-nez at me. *Since when? I wanted to argue. It wasn't before!*

"Bring it to me when you're done. I'll leave you to it."

So, Kitty went off with two girls acting as her guides, leaving me anxious in an airtight room with a sheaf of papers and a blunt pencil.

Twenty minutes later, Kitty came back. It was evident before she spoke that it was bad news.

"I couldn't find them, May. I'm sorry. How are you doing with the form?"

"Nearly done. Keep looking," I urged. We had come all this way and I was not ready to fail.

"It's not easy."

"Ask one of the girls where they are."

"I have," said Kitty. "It's just…" She paused. "No one knows anything."

"Go back out," I urged. It wasn't fair but I couldn't help but feel this wouldn't have happened to Elizabeth. She would have bulldozed her way through. Why did Kitty have to be so reticent about everything?

"I really am trying, May," she said softly.

The application form was endless, ridiculous. I was incredibly tense and angry, I suppose. All I wanted was to see my children: was that so complicated?

Kitty came back about ten minutes later. I knew from her expression it hadn't happened. The blood had drained from her face.

She whispered, "May, apparently, they're not here anymore."

"What? They must be."

"It seems they're at a different school. George must have moved them."

Pince-nez lady walked in and asked if I had finished my form. I couldn't be bothered with the pretense any more. I shoved the papers over to her, stood up and announced that we were leaving. I stormed out the school, leaving Kitty to smooth over the goodbyes.

George had taken them when they'd been nothing but happy here? And where, where in God's name, had he put my babies now?

"Any addresses? Anything?" I hissed at Kitty as she joined me by the gate.

"Nothing. I'm sorry."

We didn't talk much on the train back to London. If only I could work out where they were. *There must be a clue somewhere.* I kept thinking of the game my Grandma Leonora and I would play, the one with the tray of objects. Something would no longer be there: *Darling, try to see what is missing.*

How could George have done this? Was it just to spite me? It must be, because they loved their school.

I knew mothers who had lost their sons. I had written to them, tried to send morsels of comfort. My situation was very different: I had not lost my daughters. It was a tragedy for me, but my tragedy was not half as bad as many people's, for my children lived on. In these terrible topsy-turvy times, I was one of the lucky ones. I think this was the first time though that I understood deep down how much George hated me.

I would continue to search for them, I would continue to write, I would reach them eventually. In the meantime, I had to get on with my life; but I was a mother without her children and the guilt and the shame was overwhelming.

Favorite Christmas hymns

"Silent Night" (mine)
"God Rest Ye Merry Gentlemen" (Joy's number one)
"O Come All Ye Faithful" (Joy's tie for first place)
"O Little Town of Bethlehem" (Leona's choice)

CHAPTER FORTY-NINE

Gordon rejigged the shifts so that we could be together for Christmas 1917: me, Bonnie, Kitty, Matron and him, the old gang. The few heroic British soldiers who had managed to keep going since the very beginning of the war called themselves the "Old Contemptibles." Gordon was trying to get us to call ourselves the "Old Despicables." Fortunately, it hadn't caught on.

I wasn't going back to England for Christmas that year. For one, I had run out of leave, but even if I hadn't, what would have been the point? I had nowhere to go. No one to see.

A few days before the 25th, I read a notice in the canteen: *Patients and Nurses Variety Show*

This had Katherine's fingerprints all over it. My hands trembled when I saw someone had written my name (irritatingly misspelled "Mai") on the list of performers.

"You haven't gone and signed me up?" I asked Gordon, furiously.

"No, I didn't!" he said in an offended voice before laughing and admitting, "Bonnie did."

"There's *no way* I'm doing this!"

Gordon chuckled some more. "Everyone's in the same boat, May. You'll think of something you're good at."

"Bedpans?" I said.

When I arrived in the canteen the night of the show, one patient was already playing the spoons. It was surprising how musical it sounded. I wasn't the only one impressed; the crowd of patients and staff gave him a big roar when he finished. I grew more apprehensive—I hadn't expected standards to be quite this high.

Doctor Rafferty, the evening's compère, walked to the front of the tent, clapping loudly. "Well, that was a very well-rounded performance, and they were very well-rounded spoons."

We groaned. Doctor Rafferty always fancied himself as a comedian. I thought, *his jokes are worse than Louis',* then I scolded myself—*stop thinking about that man, for goodness' sake.*

Of course Gordon had a skill. How could I have imagined otherwise? He sang a new song, "Danny Boy," and he had quite a wonderful voice. Doctor Rafferty, pretending to be looking for something, called out: "Oh, Danny boy, where are you? It's safe to come out now!"

As Gordon took his seat next to me, I nudged him. "Well, who knew you could sing?"

"Don't have much occasion to out here." He looked sad. "Karim sang beautifully."

I squeezed his hand.

Two patients played "Goodbye" on ukuleles and while the players were both talented, their ukuleles had seen much better days: one was missing strings and the other had lost its entire headstock.

Then Bonnie took to the floor and did a robust can-can. Many patients would later say it was the highlight of the evening. Although it was less sexy than the one at the Moulin Rouge (or so I had heard), Matron's head shook violently throughout, and she kept her arms crossed.

"Far too salacious!" she snapped when Bonnie returned, flushed. "See me tomorrow morning."

I shot Bonnie a sympathetic look. I still had doubts about what I had decided to do; following a crowd-pleaser like hers was going to be very hard indeed. Dancing was out of the question, singing was even worse.

Our compère came on, laughing. "If you've still got two hands— you lucky things!—put them together now for the indomitable Nurse Turner."

I stood at the front of the room, cringing. *Indomitable? Really?* It felt like there were eyes everywhere, boring into me.

I opened my notebook and, apologetically, read out the poem that I had scrawled on the back page.

This is the song of the mud,
The pale-yellow glistening mud that covers the hills like satin;
The gray gleaming silvery mud that is spread like enamel over the valleys;
The frothing, squirting, spurting,
liquid mud that gurgles along the road beds;
The thick elastic mud that is kneaded and pounded and squeezed
under the hooves of the horses;
The invincible, inexhaustible mud of the war zone.

The room remained hushed for a moment. And then there was applause, tremendous applause. Doctor Rafferty thumped me so hard on the back that I almost tipped forward. In the surgical tent he was measured and meticulous but outside it, he was a clumsy man who drank to forget.

"I've never heard that one, Nurse Turner! Who was it? I know, I know, let's ask the audience to guess."

The crowd shouted out suggestions: "Owen? Sassoon? Keats?" I could see my team smirking at each other. "Shakespeare?" Even Matron had uncrossed her arms and was nodding approvingly.

I said "no" to all their guesses. Finally, Doctor Rafferty pushed me to answer: "Who wrote it then, Nurse Turner?"

"Me," I admitted. And everyone clapped and whooped some more.

Afterward, we went to Gordon's tent, to listen to music and to eat mince pies baked with love in Bournemouth by Lucy, Gordon's sister. We drank, we chatted and I was proud because I didn't mention Louis once. I was so tired, though, I fell asleep with my head on Matron's shoulder and I don't remember how I got back to bed.

CHAPTER FIFTY

They brought Little Stan in first, and the stretcher-men were laughing with the orderlies: they'd thought it was a small boy, so what a relief it was to find it was only a silly dummy, a mere toy. But soon after, Stanley himself was carted in with a nasty injury. He'd popped his head out of a trench when he shouldn't have—and the Bosch was always ready to take advantage of a mistake. Matron sat with him all night. When I went over with a cigarette, she said he was improving. He had even told her a naughty limerick. But later, the moment she left his bedside, he stopped breathing and there was nothing we could do. Matron was terribly shocked.

There was some debate about what to do with Little Stan—was there anyone in England we could send him to?—but in the end, we decided the best thing to do would be to bury him alongside Stanley.

Of course, you could never predict which death would hit the hardest: some, strange to say, you could sail through almost unmoved; others, even unlikely ones, would break your heart into tiny pieces. Of all the deaths, Stanley's got to Matron the most. And not long after, she announced with regret, she was going back to England. *Her parents*, she babbled, *her late husband's parents*.

"Do you think you will nurse again?" I asked her privately.

"Never," she said with complete and utter conviction, and I understood.

So, we went on through 1918. And whereas the tragedies were never as concentrated as they had been during the Battle of the Somme, there was individual heartache every single day.

Kitty spent more time with Gordon, Doctor Rafferty and the other surgeons than she did with us. They were refining medical techniques by the hour. Often, she came out of theater, shaking her head: "Genius! I can't believe how we did it." She was interested in transplants, said that one day we would transplant livers, kidneys, hearts, perhaps even faces! Bonnie and I mostly ignored her far-fetched schemes. We passed our rare afternoons off with Manuela, a Portuguese nurse with better English grammar than us. Occasionally, we got to spend time with Katherine and Millicent, if the shifts worked out that way or if it was quiet.

I still wrote long letters to my girls, of course I did, hoping that even if ten letters didn't find their way to them, the eleventh might. I didn't know where to send them, so I dispersed them widely: the Pilkingtons, George, Mrs. Crawford, Elizabeth's mother, the Leamington school. Occasionally, a pressed flower would appear from Leona, and once a drawing of a fox came from Joy, but there was no address for return, no information at all. It seemed like they had lost belief in me too.

I didn't get many letters from Elizabeth—I imagine it was harder from a ship—but occasionally, she wrote that she hoped I was well, that the work was not too dire. She said she worked mostly with the men with the influenza, a horrible disease; she had got it, but had recovered quickly. (Of course she did!) She said before she left England, she had gone to a professional photography studio in Earl's Court and had a lovely little photo taken of her in uniform. And what had her mother said when she saw it? She said, "Oh yes! We need more cat litter." They had proceeded to have a massive row about Elizabeth leaving the country and abandoning Tiggy, Winkle and Delia. (A row that Elizabeth had won, obviously.) She remarked on the camaraderie of the men: how they got up in the night to light each other's cigarettes or to hold the hands of the distressed. She wrote *If I hadn't seen it with my own eyes, I would never have believed it. I have seen the best of human nature. What a privilege, May—To think I never knew all this!*

One time, I heard nothing from her for about three months and then came a wonderful drawing of her three cats: she wrote,

I miss them. And you, I miss you too, my darling, my little American friend. I'm glad it worked out like this and I know we'll be together again, splashing our way across Tooting Bathing Lake soon. Look out for my feet…

First thing in the morning, I couldn't help it, I wished I was with Louis. I wished I was in his arms, wished he was holding me, kissing me, laughing with me. Sometimes I was petrified he was dead, but in my heart I knew he wasn't pushing up daisies—not Major Louis Spears—he just didn't want me. It wasn't complicated. Or maybe he did want me, but the crux of it was, he didn't want me *enough*. And that wasn't even his fault, it was just one of those things. It was a tragedy, although in comparison with the terrible tragedies around me, I knew I was getting off lightly. But as the sun rose, at 4 a.m., it didn't always feel like that.

Throughout the spring, troops were on the move. There were big, horrendous pushes all over Europe. Not so much forward or backward now, more sideways. Still action, still terrible deaths, but after the horrible Battle of Amiens, rumors flew that this time we really were on the up and a ceasefire was on the cards. Patients whispered that they had heard this, that and the other, and who knew better than them? But after so many false dawns, most of us were reluctant to even dare hope that the war was coming to an end.

Some hot April morning, 1918, when the heat had made the post yellow and curl up at the ends, Kitty took a knife to the seal of an envelope, burst into tears and threw herself on the lunch table. Bonnie was toying with the "monkey meat" on the plate (even Bonnie couldn't stomach French canned beef); she put down her fork and so did I.

I wondered who had been lost now as I waited patiently with Bonnie by Kitty's side. In my head, I was going through the members of Kitty's family: There was sweet Andrew, who died last year in Gallipoli. Her father, who had disappeared when she was only little. Hard-working Paul was wounded and lived back home with his dear wife. Her mother had only recently died. It could only be her half-brother Henry, the clever engineer fighting in Egypt.

But it wasn't that. Waving her paper like a white flag, Kitty said slowly, "I don't believe this. I've been accepted into medical college. In America. Once the war's over, of course."

"That's brilliant, Kitty!" Bonnie, then I, hugged her.

"I can't go, how can I possibly go? It's impossible."

Bonnie and I looked at each other.

"Why is it so impossible?"

"The money, everything...it's crazy."

"Kitty," I said slowly. "I might be able to help."

I sent a thank-you up to Grandma Leonora. She'd done it again.

Bonnie and I quietly did the dressing for a poor apologetic fellow who was covered in burns from Amiens. The vehicle he was driving had turned into a firebomb. We said he was lucky to have been pulled out alive, but privately, I wondered if he was. He fell asleep the moment we were done, still clutching Bonnie's hand.

I offered her the same amount of money I was lending Kitty—it was only fair.

"No." Bonnie was adamant. "That's not for me, I don't do borrowing."

"But Kitty—"

"Kitty will earn it back and pay it to you thrice over. I would never be able to. Honestly, May, it's the way I was brought up: in my family, we make money ourselves or not at all."

Bonnie stayed put with the burned man and I went to find who we would see to next.

CHAPTER FIFTY-ONE

It fell to me to collect the new matron from the station. As I drove, I remembered my arrival three years earlier—there hadn't been a station near here, or even a proper road—and I thought about Matron and her invisible line and that made me chuckle to myself.

New Matron was a tiny neat woman with tidy white hair. She had many years of nursing experience in England. I didn't know what had prompted her to come out to France just now. It was something I planned to ask her on the way back. I still could never see a newspaper without reading it, so when she placed the previous day's *New York Times* on her lap in the passenger seat, I asked, "Could I just? You wouldn't mind?"

And she said, "This? Oh, yes, go ahead. There's nothing much in it."

HOSPITAL SHIP SUNK BY A U-BOAT IN THE BRISTOL CHANNEL, it said.

I was relieved to read there had been no patients on board. The ship was on its way to France to collect the wounded. Good. And wasn't it just a mark of desperation that the Hun were doing abhorrent things like this? Targeting innocent doctors and nurses? They *must* know their time was nearly up.

Then I saw that it was the *Glenart Castle*. *The* Glenart Castle? I felt suddenly breathless.

My eyes raced across the words. I realized with horror how I knew the name, *the very best name of all,* but in the next instant, I had no doubt that Elizabeth, my superb swimming friend, would have escaped. She just had that way about her. Elizabeth was far too alive to die, it was impossible.

Survivors were landed by an American destroyer.

That would be my Elizabeth.

Eight boats are still adrift.

Or maybe that.

I'm not sure how much time had elapsed before New Matron cleared her throat and asked, "Nurse Turner? Are you going to drive?"

"Wait!" I snapped.

164 persons are missing.

Not my Elizabeth though, I decided with utter conviction. People like her didn't, *couldn't*, just disappear. I remembered her flexing her muscles, doing cartwheels, the time she smacked into the bookshelves.

Elizabeth lived for the water. She, more than anyone, understood its potency. Twenty-foot waves? If anyone could survive that, she could. In a way, it made sense: all those handstands, all those laps, all that training had been to save her from this. A purpose unforeseen! I smiled to myself. *Not my Elizabeth.* Had these reporters never seen her slice through Tooting Bathing Lake, fifty, sixty times? The size of her shoulders!

We drove back to the field hospital in silence. New Matron clutched her newspaper against her and eyed me nervously, but I wasn't distressed anymore; I was certain: Elizabeth would be fine.

It wasn't until the next day, when I read the newspaper with her name in it, that I saw how stupid I had been. Ninth down, in a sea of names, it read: *Elizabeth Kay Martin. London. Born 1890. Missing presumed dead.*

Even after that, even after seeing it in that cold, cold print, I still occasionally dreamt that Elizabeth wasn't drifting somewhere in the sea but had determinedly picked up some passing boat and was telling them about her record-breaking plans there.

Elizabeth.

It didn't take long for me to see what I had been missing: I had done this. I should have let her come here with me. This was where she had wanted to be. I could have looked after her. Instead, I had forbidden her to join me here; I had sent her out there instead. *I can picture you doing that!* And for what? Just so that I could feel like special May here? I might as well have killed her.

Into the darkness I went, wave after wave after wave, drowning in grief, Elizabeth's ghostly feet now lost in the sea.

My darling friend was dead, her Channel record attempt undone. There was nothing I could do. Doctor Grange was right about reading the newspapers—I wouldn't have known if I hadn't read it. Bed. Pillow. Silence. Nothing but the ticking of the clock. Cups of tea were left by the bed. Cookies on a plate. A sandwich. Could I not be tempted by a rock-cake? I felt as though I was dying of sorrow.

Gordon was sitting by my bed, in the place where Louis once sat. *Louis.*

"Where's the new matron? I'm so sorry."

"It's fine. I told her you've got"—he winced guiltily—"a migraine."

Not even Gordon would tell the truth about illnesses of the mind.

He had a nervy smile on his face, though, and was flapping a magazine.

"I know you're not meant to read, but I thought I'd let you have a quick peek at this anyway."

He placed his magazine on the end of my bed.

"You're a published poet, Nurse Turner."

"What?" I said flatly. "It isn't me."

"It is."

"It *can't* be me, Gordon. They would have contacted me first."

But it *was* me, or rather, it was my poems, there in beautiful typed print, and there was a sweet introduction by a Professor Edward Morgate from New York University. I raced through his piece and saw he liked them. Even better than that, he understood them, he really did.

And then there were my words, my ideas, suddenly made serious by this amazing black typed font. I had sent it in my handwritten scrawl, dark pen on Morley's unlined paper, and here it had been transformed into something so respectable and professional that it was hard to recognize it as the verses I had labored over late at night in my tent. I touched the white space on the page that surrounded my poem. My poem was an island and the rest of the page was the sea. My words had been held and nourished. It looked exactly how I would have wanted it to look (if I had ever dared to dream of this.) What would my girls say if they saw this?

Why did I get to achieve my dreams, and Elizabeth didn't? Why was it all so unfair?

The next time I woke, Bonnie and Kitty were in the room, playing gin rummy. I could hear them talking earnestly, but I couldn't make out the exact words.

"Is the war over?" I pulled myself up onto my elbows.

"May!" cried out Kitty, happily.

"Not yet," said Gordon. I hadn't noticed him; he was sitting at New Matron's desk, sketching a barn owl.

"But...soon?"

"Hope so."

Elizabeth never was still; she never hung around doing nothing. She never wasted time; she understood how precious this existence was. She was determined to make her mark. And she had; she had made her mark on me, so much so that she had turned my life around. "I'm just a normal twentieth-century girl," she used to say, but, oh, she was so much more than that. She was my darling friend. A thousand thoughts criss-crossing through me. A thousand tasks to fulfill. I was still here, I was still alive, and so were my girls. I had to grab hold of whatever life was left in me, whether it was just the next ten minutes or the next forty years. I would grab hold of it and squeeze the pips out of it.

The magazine was where Gordon had left it, on the end of my bed. I wondered if Louis would one day see it. I hoped so. And that poem, I promised myself, that poem would be the first of many. I wasn't going to stop fighting.

"Do you mind getting out of my tent, Gordon?"

Gordon could not have looked more apologetic. He jumped up, grabbed his notebook and his pencils.

"So sorry, May. Forgive my intrusion."

"It's not a problem," I said. "It's just...I need to get dressed if I'm going back to work."

CHAPTER FIFTY-TWO

We were making plans for the autumn and winter ahead. We would have football, book recitals—and perhaps we could do another variety show.

"And you could do the can-can again," I suggested to Bonnie.

"It won't be half so much fun without the look of horror on Matron's face," Kitty added.

Although New Matron had been with us for over six months now, she would always be New Matron to me. She was easier to share a tent with, never talked about my failings and was always kind and calm, but I missed our Old Matron. I hadn't expected to, but I had grown to love that cold, obstinate woman very much.

I was struggling with a poem I was writing. I couldn't seem to *feel* anything, it felt like I had a blank where all my feelings should be. I had seen this in wearier soldiers: an indifference to life or death; but it wasn't a great attribute in a poet. But I plowed on, forcing out words, because I knew the difference between a finished poem and an unfinished poem was perseverance. Ostensibly this poem was about churned-up clay, but I suppose it was a meditation on how life doesn't always go according to plan, and if we can grow after we have been destroyed.

Kitty appeared at the tent opening. Her expression was so serious that I had already got up before she said a word. And then she took my arm.

"It's Louis..."

It was as though my whole body was turned to icy liquid.

"How bad?"

Kitty squeezed me, and I knew it was very bad.

"We'll do our best."

I started to pull off my nightgown. "I'm coming now."

"No." Kitty was as careful with her words as ever. "We can't have you there, May. I promise, though, as soon as I know anything, I'll get you."

Of course I couldn't sleep. At first I paced, then I read and after that I tried to write a poem. Matron came in. She'd heard "someone important" to me was in but not what the prognosis was. I knew she needed her sleep, so I pulled on my coat and crept out to my favorite rock so I didn't disturb her.

The stars held memories out there. I thought about driving a car through the night to Leamington to see my daughters, I thought of Elizabeth in the freezing sea, waiting for her lift. I tried not to think of Louis, I tried not to think of our short time together, but I couldn't help it. It had been magical, it had been blessed, even if its ending had been so abrupt and ugly. I had given him my heart. I thought about what Elsie once said to me: *If you get too attached, they die*. Why hadn't I listened to her?

It wasn't until about 3 a.m.—a full five hours later—that Kitty crept up in the darkness, whispering my name.

"Kitty!" I called. "Over here."

She stood tall in front of me. In the dark I could just make out the blood spots all over her apron. She had come out immediately, as promised. Kitty was always a woman of her word and I knew whatever she said next would be the un-sugar-coated truth.

"He made it, May."

I sank into her arms.

"Oh, thank God, thank *you*, Kitty and...Gordon and everyone."

The relief on her face told me that it had been a very close thing.

"He's still got some way to go—but I think, *we* think, he'll recover well."

I knew it wasn't my place to care. I knew Louis didn't love me anymore—if he ever had—but I couldn't stop myself from caring. The world without Louis in it, even if he were not by my side, was unthinkable.

I saw him the next morning. He was propped, pale-faced, against his pillow, a bandage around his abdomen where he had taken the shots. I wanted to run over, but I took my time and saw to my other patients first. When I finally made my way over to him, it seemed to me that he had to force a smile onto his wan face. I wanted to look closely at him but instead, I merely asked if he wanted a shave. Louis refused. His teacup bobbled in his hand.

"May," he said quietly. I nodded. I wasn't sure I could bring myself to speak. "I can ask to be transferred somewhere else."

"Why would you do that?"

He looked at me steadily. "Then you wouldn't have to see this pathetic man ever again."

His hands weren't as steady as his gaze and he spilled tea all over himself. I marched off to get a cloth. When I came back, New Matron was already dabbing him down and trying to maneuver him away from the wet patch. She said firmly, "*I'll* see to him, thank you, Nurse Turner. You've had a long night, we're quiet, why not take the rest of the morning off?"

I walked out of the ward with my head held high. I went to my tent, unfastened my veil, took off my apron, lay on my bed, and it was only once I was there that I let the tears come.

*

Early evening, Matron said I could go to his ward again, but I was not to "show favoritism." I scowled at her, but I knew Old Matron wouldn't have let me anywhere near him.

He was sitting upright with his cup safely on his bedside table. I took in the thin cheeks, the protruding cheekbones, the shadows under his lowered eyes. When he saw me, though, his expression seemed to become some strange combination of hopeful and hopeless.

"How are your daughters?" he asked. I didn't reply.

"I saw your poems," he continued. I remembered how I had really wanted him to see them, but now that he had, I thought, it didn't matter. What was the point? And I wondered how he had seen them. Gordon? Winston, maybe? But I didn't want to ask. "They were unmistakably yours."

"They're just small pebbles in a big ocean," I said. I didn't want him to know how proud I was of myself. He would probably find it amusing. *May thinks she's a poet but actually, she's just a silly, useless girl.*

"Small pebbles create big ripples," he replied. "It's a nice legacy."

I nodded. Louis was not George after all. And Louis understood my self-indulgent desire to leave something tangible behind.

This is going to be all right, I told myself. I would treat him like any other patient. Louis *was* any other patient. In the canteen, Kitty was gazing at me so anxiously, she almost put me off my plate of Maconochie stew. Between mouthfuls, I recited: *I am fine. It is fine. It will be fine.*

After dressings were changed, water distributed, bedpans emptied, beards shaved, letters written, I went and checked on Louis again.

"You didn't ask to be transferred then?"

"I *did* ask," he responded with lowered eyes. "They're too busy now."

It felt like another kick in the teeth.

I asked if he was ready to try some more tea, and he flushed, then I flushed, because it sounded like I was making a dig. He must have been hating this. Nevertheless, he nodded. I got him his tea and he held on to it. Patrick requested a wash, and I was about to go over to him when Louis called out to me.

"You didn't tell me, May, how *are* your girls? Has Leona won Wimbledon yet?"

I searched his face to see if he was joking. Patients sometimes got silly, with the fever or the medicines, but this wasn't silly, it was cruel. Was he trying to get me back for my dig about the tea?

"Does Joy still love art?" he continued.

I frowned at him, but he wouldn't stop.

"Or is she more of a poet," he asked shyly, "like her talented mother?"

"You don't know?"

"What?"

I set down the towels I was holding. I hoped he couldn't see how much I was trembling.

"Louis, I haven't been able to see the girls…"

"What?"

"I tried, and I tried, and I managed, very briefly, last summer… But George won't let me anywhere near them. He won't even let me know where they are."

"That can't be." Louis blanched. I stood by his side, my arms crossed, my eyes filling with those damned tears again. He started coughing, a hacking, horrible sound that alerted Matron. She strode over furiously. "How many times have I TOLD you not to upset him, Nurse Turner? Out!"

Louis raised his hand. The coughing subsided. "Please, Matron, it's all right. Nurse Turner and I need to talk."

Squinting at him, New Matron relented. "Just for a moment, mind." She tapped my arm. "But if you upset him again…"

Louis reached for my hand, but I wouldn't let him take it. I didn't know why he felt we needed to talk: the time for talking was long past.

"May, I had no idea."

I shrugged. "Why *would* you know, Louis?"

He cleared his throat. "I-I-Because... George promised me you would see the girls."

My legs buckled under me. I dropped onto the end of the bed, then scrambled up again as I saw Matron gesturing angrily at me.

"What do you mean, 'promised you'?"

"He wrote to me when we got back from the Dordogne. He said, if I gave you up, if I split up from you, you would be reunited with your girls. He said he wouldn't stand in your way ever again."

George had destroyed everything I ever had. I had hated him for a long time, but even so, I hadn't realized how duplicitous he was. He had crawled into every sphere of my life and sought to blacken it.

Louis was staring at me, his craggy face wreathed in sympathy.

"So, you... you wrote back to him?"

"Not exactly." He looked at me again, his face reddening as he admitted, "I went to meet him, May. He assured me it was a deal. As long as we were not lovers or partners or... he would accept you seeing the girls. We shook hands on it." Louis stared up at the tent ceiling. The cloth billowed low over his bed. "I thought I was doing the right thing," he continued. "For you and the girls."

"But why didn't you tell me?" I asked, uncomprehending.

"Because then you wouldn't have to choose."

It was about then I became angry at Louis as well. *Furious* at Louis. If last night I had been missing the emotions for a poem, I had found them all now.

I remembered him explaining what he did at work.

"But... but I was not some *project*, Louis. I was supposed to be your... your sweetheart."

"I chose what was best for you all."

"But you shouldn't have chosen on my behalf. You shouldn't have taken that away from me. And I could have told you, *anyone* could have told you, George would never keep to that promise."

"It seems I was wrong," he said reluctantly. "*Very* wrong." His voice quavered. He was as close to tears as I was. "I . . . I genuinely thought we had a gentleman's agreement."

"George is not a gentleman," I yelped. For a moment, I wanted to shake him, I wanted to slap him around the face. That was the last straw for Matron. She stalked over, put a hand on each of my shoulders and pushed me away.

I walked into town the next afternoon. Bonnie was supposed to come but we were expecting in two young men poorly with trench fever and Matron asked if she would stay back. I had a quiet time. In Chez Tartine the waitress must have sensed my mood for she didn't ask me for the latest news as she usually did, but only brought me over a croissant without asking. "Sshhh!" she whispered, "for our regulars." My eyes swam with tears at her kindness. My rage at Louis was subsiding but I wasn't yet sure what it had been replaced with. I seemed to vacillate between pity—for him and for myself—and sorrow, but then all those emotions were overtaken by my fury at George, then my fury with the whole goddamn world.

As I was walking back I heard a sudden crashing noise ahead of me, then around the bend in the road came two horses. I saw there was a man with them, desperately holding on to one of them, but it seemed the other had worked its way free. It bolted, pulling ahead of the man and the other horse. It went the other direction from me, thankfully. As I grew closer, I could see what was wrong. They must have been hit, maybe by a vehicle. In front of my eyes, the remaining horse, dark, with a smooth cared-for coat, sank on wobbly legs to the ground.

The man shouted at me: "Stay with her, I'm going after him!" He disappeared down the road.

Trembling, I squatted down next to the great big beast in the dust. She was on one side, stretched out and making a horrible whinnying noise. Now I saw that there was blood on her lower body. It looked like she was wearing little red boots, and her undercarriage was all torn up too. I changed my mind about a traffic accident; it had to be shrapnel, I think, but I didn't know where from. I didn't know what to do. Her hooves were still and therefore harmless, I supposed. I looked at her great big teeth and they didn't frighten me like horses' teeth usually did, even though there were bubbles coming out of her mouth. Tentatively, I laid a hand on top of her head.

"I've got you..." I said to that horse. I soothed it and whispered kind words. "You poor thing." I looked down the road helplessly. Wouldn't the man please come back? He was still nowhere to be seen. "I'm here, you're not alone." I called on my Grandma Leonora then, and she came to me, as helpful as ever:

"It's a shock," I told her. "It's a terrible shock."

The horse's black eyes were locked into mine. I knew she was terrified. I tried to convey to her with my eyes, with my voice, with my everything, not to be frightened, to be calm and to let be.

"You are a lovely horse," I said. I meant it too. I maneuvered her so her head was in my lap, poor dear beast, and I could stroke her quivering body with both hands.

Eventually, the man returned with the other horse, now safely on a rope. He moved purposefully and quickly. He tied the other horse to a tree trunk.

"Thank you," he said brusquely as he came over to me.

Out the corner of my eye, I saw he had something square and black in his hand. A pistol.

"Hold her tight..."

I was too stunned to do anything.

"No!" I exclaimed as he placed the gun between her eyes and pulled the trigger.

The horse convulsed again and again, and then nothing.

CHAPTER FIFTY-THREE

There were more rumors flying around than there were mosquitos. Rumors of agreements and ceasefire. Every day we all held our breath and waited, but it was always not yet, not yet. Then, on 11 November 1918, there was a sudden nothing. A silence so unfamiliar it was almost frightening. The roar of guns, the ugly unrelenting clatter and crunch of explosions, all the backdrop of our lives out here was suddenly muted. Or had I gone deaf, maybe? When I had dreamt about this moment, I had pictured unadulterated jubilation, but when it actually happened, it was bewildering. I was comforting a poor young boy pre-surgery and he was in such a morphine fug the heavy silence seemed only to make him worse.

"I'm a swimmer," he murmured as he writhed on the stretcher. I told him I was too. I thought of Elizabeth then, of course. "Will I keep my legs?"

No one had told him yet that they were gone. Doctor Rafferty came over for him. It only took the slightest nod from him to bring tears to my eyes.

I hadn't been in the convalescence tent for two weeks. New Matron had given me tasks away from Louis, and I was grateful to have been kept busy. It had been too painful to attend to him. It was not that I was actively avoiding him—although I imagine he might have thought I was—I just needed to gather my thoughts. Of course, I could have chosen to go in there on my breaks, but I did not.

Kitty popped her head around the tent side, her eyes bright and wet.

"We're celebrating near Little Big Rock when you're done here."

I *was* done, but I didn't go outside; I went to find Matron then went to the convalescence tent instead. There too the routine was going on much as usual. Some patients were playing cards, some were sleeping, although Bonnie was wandering around between beds looking more wide-eyed and baffled than usual.

"I can't believe it, May!" she said as soon as she saw me, and we clutched each other tight. She smelled of elderflower.

"I'll take over here," I told her.

"But Matron..."

"It's fine," I said as Bonnie skipped away. She didn't need to be told twice.

One patient, Patrick, was scouring the newspaper. He was a printer before the war. He was always telling me how he couldn't wait to get back to the press—he called the machines his babies. "Is it true then? I'm not dreaming?"

"It's true," I said. "Want me to pinch you?"

His eyes filled. Awkwardly, we clasped each other's hands.

"It's been a long time coming," he whispered.

Louis was lying in the same place as before but now with a damp cloth over his eyes. I approached apprehensively. When I softly said his name, he removed the flannel straight away and pulled himself upright.

"Join the celebrations, May," he said throatily. "We can manage."

"It's all right, Louis."

"You shouldn't miss the fun. We're all right here, go outside."

"Stop telling me what to do," I said, anger bubbling to the surface.

He paused, then set down his cloth. "I'm sorry."

"I *want* to be here," I told him.

I couldn't look at his sad face. I went to find us some whisky. There was only one cup left in the cupboard; we would have to share. As

I poured, out of nowhere visions of the dying horse kept intruding. Horses were something I had always feared, yet I had done my best. I remembered the fear in the poor creature's eyes. I had to let it go.

I returned to Louis' bedside. Next to us, a new patient, Horace, sighed in his sleep while Patrick rhythmically turned the pages of his newspaper. I remembered waking from the darkness last year, and Louis being there and, what was it Matron had said? *He's barely left your side, May. You're a lucky woman.*

"I should have told you about George."

"You should have."

It was really going off outside. Not the panicky thudding of boots or the screeching of ambulances, it was singing. People were singing "Pack Up Your Troubles." There was loud laughter, then shouts for Doctor Collins to sing "Danny Boy." The war really was over. I imagined Gordon clambering up onto Little Big Rock, his stethoscope round his neck, tears rolling down his cheeks. He was never afraid of a bit of emotion.

I could hear it now. "Oh, Danny boy..."

I guessed the news would reach England soon, or maybe it already had. I imagined Joy and Leona at school, listening to the bells ringing out the same peace all over Europe. I hoped they were celebrating.

Louis drank a little whisky, then spluttered, "I'm not used to it!" Then he set down his cup and gazed at me. "I didn't say anything because I knew who you would choose..."

I knew exactly what he meant.

"You know me very well."

"*Alors*..." He smiled at me, that smile I would never tire of seeing. "And that's why I love you."

I shivered with pleasure. Gordon's voice was reaching a crescendo outside and the crowd was joining in. The patients in the corner were disagreeing with each other over whether aces were high or low,

Patrick was still reading his newspaper and Major Louis Spears, *my* Louis, had just told me he loved me.

"So, you *do* love me?"

"Yes," he said. "May Turner, you always have been and you always will be the love of my life."

CHAPTER FIFTY-FOUR

The ring had belonged to Louis' mother. It was gold with an emerald and I wore it on my necklace, next to my locket. We'd have to wait for a wedding—I wasn't prepared to marry without my daughters being present, but Louis understood and agreed. We might have to wait a very long time, but I knew about waiting: I was a war nurse after all.

Over the next few days, the German troops slowly evacuated, and our forces poured into no-man's-land and beyond. Barbed wire ripped down, wire fences pulled out, mortar collected, loaded high onto trucks. There were great bonfires of God-knows-what, a never-ending procession of trains, some coming in with equipment, some leaving with soldiers desperate to get home. The Portuguese hospital was dismantled. We said tearful farewells to Manuela and the other friends who were leaving. We, the Old Despicables, were staying put for a while. What a change in atmosphere there was, though. Perhaps it wasn't until the constant threat and stress had gone that you realized how all-consuming the fear had been. Everything sounded different now, everything *was* different. We smiled at each other in the morning, we were still smiling in the evening. We doled out the whisky willy-nilly. Word came that Farmer Norest's hens were miraculously laying again.

A few days later, a familiar car pulled up. Winston sprang out of it with far more bounce than you'd expect for a man of his size. He was here to take Louis back to London.

"He's not ready," I told him, "he's still weak."

He eyed me suspiciously.

"Honestly, Winston," I responded, exasperated. "Do you think I'd lie just to keep him here?"

He shrugged. "Love makes people behave strangely."

"Not *that* strangely."

We both laughed.

"It's good to see you, Nurse Turner."

"Likewise," I said. Arm in arm, we went to find Louis.

Later that evening, Louis, Winston, Gordon, Bonnie, Kitty and I sat drinking whisky around Louis' bed. New Matron kindly pretended not to see us.

Winston was pontificating as usual. I kept thinking Louis had dropped off, but occasionally, he would squeeze my fingers, or raise my hand to his lips for a kiss.

"Americans are so sheltered," Winston was saying, sighing. "They think they are the saviors of the world."

I couldn't help but take it personally.

"We don't, Winston."

"Oh, not you, sweetheart, the negotiators—"

"Yes, but you *said* Americans—"

"Don't interrupt me while I'm interrupting."

The next morning, Winston decided to drive Horace and Patrick to the hospital boat. As we loaded them up, he tried one last time to persuade Louis to go with him.

"I'm not going to London anyway," Louis said.

Winston stood with his hands on his hips, his stocky legs wide apart.

"Where are you going then?"

"We haven't decided yet." Louis grabbed my hand.

"*We?*" Winston laughed. "'*We*,' is it now?"

Louis laughed. I bit my lip, embarrassed.

"I hope so," Louis said, smiling at me. "We've wasted enough time as it is."

They shook hands, the tall one and the shorter one. Or, the love of my life and his best friend.

The celebrations were short-lived, of course. Poor souls were still being brought into our hospital: there were horrendous accidents, building injuries, car crashes and sickness. Many areas had been booby-trapped: pick up a branch and find you've detonated a bomb. How I pitied those families who lost their boys now. Such injustice! And we were seeing more and more cases of fever. Everyone knew that the real work was about to begin: rebuilding Europe together.

Sitting up in bed, reading newspapers and reports that were being sent in, Louis was even less optimistic than I was.

"The French are furious at the Germans. They just want to destroy them…"

"Don't let them. It won't be good for the future."

Louis' expression said, as it often did, *Honey, I know that.*

"What do you think will happen?"

"I fear they will go too punitive: the German economy will gradually collapse. Once there are food and fuel shortages, the people will look for a scapegoat; they may blame the foreigners, and it will be very ugly indeed."

I shivered.

"What's the British stance?"

"Depends who you're speaking to." He sighed. "Some of them just want to wash their hands of Europe. Some of them think closer ties are the answer." He readjusted himself in his chair. "I can't wait to get back to work."

"What do *you* think, Louis?"

"I'm half-British, half-French, I was cured in Switzerland, schooled in Germany. And I'm in love with an American woman. What do you think I think?"

Things I am today

Mother

Girlfriend

Ex-wife

Daughter

Granddaughter

Artist muse

Poet

Knitter

Lover

Friend

War nurse

CHAPTER FIFTY-FIVE

We chose Paris. I wanted to start again—I needed a clean slate. I was still afflicted by the melancholy sometimes, but I did my best to get up, to get out. Louis was a great help.

What a place Paris was in those crazy months after the war ended. It was reopening, reawakening, a city resuscitated, back from the brink. The artist Rodin returned to great fanfare, bountifully holding parties in his wonderful house and gardens. Louis and I wandered the grounds, hand in hand. It was beautiful in whichever light there was. Sculptors and artists who had been hidden away during the war now opened their doors wide. Others who had been doing service, or ambulance driving, or truck driving, came back full of fire for their next projects, for peace. Picasso. Montparnasse. There were plenty of my co-patriots around to complain about the weather too: Man Ray, other photographers, writers. It was thrilling to have a social circle, to be part of a team in peacetime as in war. I thrived in company and Louis did too. And when people asked him about his wartime experiences, overlooking me, he would push me forward: "Oh, didn't you know? May also served." And if anyone asked what he was working on, he would say, "Oh, May has published poems." He was so proud of me. What a truly novel sensation that was!

My profile was low, compared to those of the soldier poets, and always would be, but this was the world we lived in. I knew that. We women had boxed our way out to become war nurses, tram drivers, factory workers and surgeons. And although I feared there would be attempts to return us to our boxes (I was not deluded about power struggles), I hoped for the best. Things were changing and perhaps, for my daughters, there would be more opportunities.

I missed Joy and Leona so desperately that I had to not think about them else I would have returned to the dark road, the melancholy. I didn't want to go back to that place, especially now there was no Elizabeth to pull me out.

I missed Elizabeth too.

Another sad thing: there were insane people everywhere. I had never seen streets quite like these. Mild ones, harmless ones, ones you didn't want to go near, ones you wanted to wrap up and put somewhere safe. And then there were the homeless people, unemployed people, mediums and ventriloquists, con artists and thieves. Or, as Louis said, "Just people just trying to do their best."

If I kept myself whirling, if I kept myself socializing, nursing, writing and madly romancing, then I could just about manage to survive on the occasional censored letter from my daughters, who were goodness knows where. There was succor in those notes but little pleasure: it was as though they were telegrams, payment by the word. I guessed that the girls wrote them but that they didn't believe I would receive them or welcome them. How long can you write to a specter?

I wrote to them, of course I wrote to them. I wrote three, four times a week, but I never knew if they would receive my letters or not. It shouldn't have, but it did color my stories, it affected my tone—how could it not? I went back to London but the house had been sold and a new family with a new housekeeper lived there. Mrs. Crawford was very poorly and had moved north. I learned the Pilkingtons' golden boy, the son at Cambridge, was missing in Verdun. Not even a grave to visit. I waited outside the tennis club and caught up with the Framptons' oldest boy. Once again, we had a long and warm conversation, and it wasn't until he walked off, his racquet swinging behind him, that I realized that he had returned from Gallipoli with a missing arm.

No one knew where my girls were. People were too busy or in too much grief for me to press them for more information. How could I keep on at them about mine when they had properly lost their own? Even Winston admitted his hands were tied. A divorced woman, I had no rights to my children, not *legal* rights anyway. The headmistress at Leamington had retired and the new one declared she had no notes. I began telephoning all the boarding schools in the country, but several put the phone down on me. When Louis did it, they were slightly politer, but still no leads. The same with the tennis clubs. "No, sorry. We can't give out names." I insisted they took my details, just in case, but I imagine they crumpled the paper into an abandoned drawer; that's if they even wrote down anything at all.

I knew men in similar positions to me—did they call it estrangement?—but it was easier for fathers. Not so *strange* as it was for mothers. Society did not look down on them like I knew it looked down on me. I had lost my girls and didn't know where to find them. "*Leave them alone and they will come home dragging their tails behind them.*" Joy used to love that rhyme when she was a little girl. It was about the only thing that would calm her at night. I wasn't going to leave them alone, but I guess to the outside world it looked as though I had.

Maybe even to you, it looks as though I gave up.

Louis told me Mr. Bertram was the best picture-framer in all of France. "He'll know if they're real or not."

"Of course they're bloody real, Louis..."

I had a short temper these days; I had no patience. I wished I didn't, but frustration would pop out of me when you'd least expect it. You'd think, once the war was over, those of us who were there, those of us who'd survived—the Contemptibles, the Despicables, whatever—would spend our remaining days in unmitigated relief and gratitude. But it didn't work like that: fear, horror, guilt and grief stay with you and sometimes they come out quite unpleasantly.

At parties, I overheard people complaining about such-and-such: "What a grumbler he was these days!" Or so-and-so: "Did you ever know such a moaner?" They seemed genuinely puzzled that so-and-so who had been a prisoner of war, or such-and-such who had been a sniper in the French Army, was no longer the life and soul of the party. I thought, *don't expect this of us*: don't expect that those of us who have suffered will become *better* because of our suffering. If anything, we'll become worse.

"I know, I'm sorry, I meant, Mr. Bertram will have an idea…"

Louis was the only one who could pour balm on my troubled waters. He was a wonderfully patient man and very good with me.

It was a tiny shop on the Left Bank, set behind the second-hand book stalls, and it had bullet holes in the door. Louis hadn't warned me that Mr. Bertram looked like an English garden gnome, though. He was beardy and tiny. When I told him I had pictures to show him, he sighed heavily and then clambered off the stool he was standing on. I realized he was even smaller than I had first thought.

I unrolled the twin papers as he scowled, muttering under his breath. I gathered that a lot of people had come back from the war with doodles, expecting the moon. I wished Louis had perhaps directed me to the second- or even third-best framer in the whole of France; anywhere in fact where the service might have been more welcoming. Grumpily, Mr. Bertram flattened the papers, studied them and then took his magnifying glass to them. The one of Bonnie looking extraordinary in her nurse's outfit and the one of me, Percy's surprising Christmas gift, were upside down and suddenly unfamiliar to me.

"Percy Milhouse?" Mr. Bertram was so surprised that he dropped his glass onto the papers. He scooped it up quickly. "I didn't know he did portraiture."

"He doesn't normally."

Mr. Bertram was quite transformed. He stroked his beard thoughtfully. "Well, this is not what I expected at all..."

"Any good?" I asked nervously.

"*Fantastique!*" At last he smiled. "This is very, very valuable."

I would send a telegram to Bonnie that evening. I hoped it would bring an even bigger smile to her face than her smile in the picture.

Elizabeth's mother—who in all these years I had never met—asked me to visit her. It was an invitation, but it felt like a summons. I had a lump in my throat as I approached that lovely pale townhouse that no longer contained my lovely pale friend. I was frightened Elizabeth's mother would blame me for her daughter's going away, but if she did, she didn't say.

"The one good thing is we'll never go to war again," Elizabeth's mother—call-me-Helena—said grimly. "Humankind couldn't be that stupid, could they, Winkle?" Winkle blinked at her with his knowing eyes.

The macaroons didn't taste as good as I'd anticipated, and I puzzled over whether I'd remembered them wrong. Or perhaps nothing would ever taste as lovely without Elizabeth there.

After a while, in the same straightforward way that her daughter had used to, Helena set down her cup and saucer, and said:

"I met Harriet last week. A lovely young woman. Broken-hearted she was."

I nodded, not sure what would be a good thing to say. I didn't know what she knew—I didn't know what *I* knew.

"Tell me everything you remember about my daughter."

I told her how Elizabeth had saved me from the blues: the story of my grabbing her kicking white feet made Helena smile ever so slightly. I said that every time I visited, she showered me with such kindness; that she taught me how to drive and lent me her car, and

I talked about how I had always admired her ambition to swim the Channel very much, and how—my voice faltered—I had loved her very much. I could not continue for sobbing.

Helena, unlike me, was not a crier. When I next looked up, she was staring out that beautiful bay window to the back garden, where an elderly man was raking the lawn. She stood up and made some incomprehensible sign to him. I stroked Winkle, feeling useless. I didn't know what else to say, so I asked after Delia. Tiggy was sleeping elegantly on the sofa arm, so I knew she was fine, but Delia was nowhere to be seen. I braced myself for more bad news.

"Ah," said Helena as though she had been waiting for this. "Since you ask..."

Helena explained she could just about manage Tiggy and Winkle but Delia was just too much. She looked at me beseechingly, and reeled me in.

"I'll take her!" I offered brightly.

"Oh, you can't, but really? You would do that?" Helena responded and that was when I guessed I had been set up.

"Elizabeth would be so pleased," Helena added. I thought, I don't know if Elizabeth would be pleased *as such*, but she would certainly find it amusing.

A fun journey back to Paris that was, with the furry little lady scrabbling around in a cardboard box. I wrote FRAGILE on the top flaps but AGGRESSIVE or UNPREDICTABLE might have been a truer warning. I had made air holes in the box with hairgrips, but Delia wouldn't rest until the sides were open.

Lots of people on the ship wanted to have a look at her. Servicemen and nurses, Scottish crew members and French ladies. Some were charmed. Some tried to stroke her, and she scratched at their wrists. She had an excellent aim. She drew blood on one gentle soldier and he jumped back. "Who taught her that? The Hun?"

Louis took one look at my surprise souvenir from England and laughed his head off. "Dear God, May, what *have* you done now? Must you rescue everything?"

Late autumn, President Woodrow Wilson, *my* president, came over to France. He addressed the crowds from the Hôtel de Ville. There was an incredible turnout, and as Louis and I moved among the cheering crowds, I felt as though I might burst with pride. It was not just pride at being American, being European and being a war nurse, but of this being our victory. Our hard-earned victory and our hard-earned peace. In my pocket, I had the tiny Stars and Stripes that dear Gordon had given me. I rolled it between my fingers. I had become superstitious in my dotage; this was a good-luck token.

There was talk of naming one of the avenues or boulevards after Wilson, and I was agitating for that to everyone I met. It couldn't come soon enough. For I had noticed how quickly people were forgetting the war had been a world war. How quickly they dismissed the contributions of their American, Canadian, Indian and Chinese allies. And I had noticed too how hardly anyone remembered what we nurses had done. Well, I would be here to remind them for as long as I lived.

The crowds were still cheering, we were still cheering, although our throats grew hoarse. You couldn't hear much. I tried to tell Louis something, but he couldn't catch it. I did occasionally suggest to him that he was growing deaf—so many soldiers suffered with hearing loss—but he merely shrugged and said, "How would I look with an ear trumpet?"

Absolutely gorgeous, probably.

In the end, I had to shout at the top of my voice.

"We'd better get back. For the cat. She's not used to it."

"Damn cat!" Louis shouted back amiably.

*

Louis was climbing up the greasy pole at work. He was promoted to major general. And that made me proud too. He was a remarkable man and he so often said that I was a remarkable woman—albeit with a poor taste in pets—that I began to believe it too. At parties, people commented that we were made for each other. Louis was a good man, I was repeatedly reminded, he was the most loyal man of them all.

I would never take it for granted that we were together, but gradually I was learning to relax. Louis was mine and I was his. We were in this for the long haul.

"When's the wedding?" Winston wrote. "I need an excuse for an expensive cigar."

"Like he needs an excuse," snorted Louis.

Louis' friends from the Dordogne came to visit. Mathilde looked around our apartment and at the pretty cafés and shops in the street beneath and claimed to be green with envy. I think she would have loved to live in the city again. Watching your husband drive tractors in the countryside is not for everyone. She liked Delia, who, recognizing someone almost as elegant as herself, rolled onto her back and begged for tickles whenever Mathilde was in the room. In fact, Delia acted almost like a normal domesticated cat for the entire three days they stayed with us.

"You've done well, Louis," Pierre said, patting him on the back. "The perfect life."

It was. If you didn't know what was missing.

One morning, over warm croissants and hot coffee—how different hot coffee tasted from the tepid stuff I had grown used to in the hospital—Louis told me he had heard that the new cinema on St. Michel's Boulevard—only fifteen minutes' walk away—was showing *The Battle of the Somme*. We had talked about it before and I had said that one day in the future, I wouldn't mind finding out what

the film was about. Without any pressure, he asked would I like
to go that evening. I couldn't answer at first, I didn't know if I was
ready. When I had said "future," I had meant in ten or twenty years.
No time at all had passed since that terrible time. Not really. Two
years was nothing. I remembered it like it was yesterday. What could
be worse? To see our experiences turned into entertainment. *Really
entertaining*, as George said.

Still, we went. I dressed up for it, because one did still dress for
the cinema in Paris back then, in a crisp blouse that reminded me
of one of Bonnie's. I had started wearing trousers too. Not the old
baggy work ones, but ones that a tailor made for me: slick, black
and stylish. Louis was handsome as ever in his uniform—he didn't
need adornment.

The room was packed. A man in black tie was also pushing his
way forward and everyone scowled at him. "I'm the pianist," he
pleaded, "let me through."

That room was so loud, I wondered: if they did manage to capture
the horrendous sound of the Somme, would we even hear it over the
din here? The man next to Louis, in seat 2C, had not dressed up.
He took off his shoes and socks and proceeded to pick at his toes.
Louis whispered to me, and I wasn't quite sure what he said because
of the cacophony, but I think it was: "Remind me never to come to
the cinema in Paris again."

But when the projector started up its crackling and whirring,
and the hall was pitched into darkness except for plumes of cigarette smoke, silence finally fell in that room. Even our toe-picking
neighbor let his foot fall to the floor.

It was so jolly at the beginning. Full of victorious plans and high
hopes and everyone working together. English boys spiritedly waving
their caps at the camera as they marched. French peasants throwing
turnips at each other. But it went on. As I watched the screen, my
defenses came down. My tears flowed. The camera had not flinched.
And I didn't know if this was a good thing or not.

Agony it was to watch the suffering. Agony to watch men waiting for their turn to suffer or die. It showed the injuries. It showed the dying. It showed the dead. In the middle of one sequence, the pianist stopped playing. I think for a moment he forgot where he was and what he was supposed to do. A silhouetted arm reached out and pressed him on the shoulder and he started up again.

Louis gripped my hand. His palm grew clammy and he removed his hand to wipe it on his trouser leg. I couldn't wait until he returned his hand to me. I gripped onto him for dear life. I had not expected this. It should not have been like I was there all over again, because it didn't have that smell, the taste in your mouth, the fear in your stomach, but it was. I was as there all over again as I ever would be.

The audience were in shock. One woman a few rows along from us fainted. The man next to her called out for smelling salts, "*s'il vous plaît*," and someone, surprisingly, had some and the bottle was passed from person to person along the line, as though they had been anticipating this all along. The barefoot man clasped one of his shoes to his heart.

At one particularly harrowing bit, a woman shouted from somewhere toward the back of the room, "*Il n'est pas mort?*" He isn't dead, is he? And somebody nearby shushed her and impatiently said, "*Si, si, ils sont tous mort.*" They are all dead.

And someone else called out, "My boy! My boy! My boy!" Three times, just like that.

Never again. Please.

CHAPTER FIFTY-SIX

I was preparing for our first Christmas in Paris when Elsie Knocker came. I had decorated the apartment with abandon. Fresh branches, berries, leaves, paper chains, everything. A house of red and green. I knew, and Louis knew, that I was driven by a kind of desperation: I was covering up all the holes where the people I loved should have been, but that didn't stop me.

We had employed a housekeeper, Jeanne, a small mouse-like woman from the south of France. She was a young widow like so many, and she also supported her two brothers, who didn't work; I wasn't sure why, but I presumed war injuries. She helped me string up mistletoe from all the light fittings and I found her a box to take the remainder home in. At the time I imagined that I was a kind benefactor making a difference in her unhappy life, but afterward, I wondered if she would have seen it as patronizing. I fretted at my self-indulgence. This was one way the years at war hadn't changed me at all.

The Christmas tree was so large, the top foot or so had to bend to fit in—and our ceilings were by no means low. To Jeanne's consternation, I clambered onto chairs, placing bows and drapes on the higher branches and a golden star and ribbons on the top. I took a long time over it—I wanted everything to be right. It wasn't just for Louis and me; we were entertaining a lot. We had dinner parties where we discussed punishing Germany or not punishing Germany; and which was better, London or Paris. The Christmas cards I set along the fireplace. The absence of a card from my mother, which used to hurt me, meant nothing to me this year. The lack of cards from my own children certainly did.

But I had a card and long letters from Kitty, who was having the time of her life at medical school in New York. And a comedy card from Gordon. He was now in a teaching hospital in Delhi, near where his beloved Karim had once lived. It helped him feel close to him, he said. He told me he was doing what he did best: cutting people open, taking out the bullets and sewing them back up. "People will always need trauma surgeons," he wrote, "so that's nice."

Elsie looked stunning as usual, even here in Paris where, to my eye, most everyone was stunning (even if, as Bonnie said, they were a little on the short side). The dress she was wearing, although dark gray, reminded me of the green dress I had first seen her in, back in Percy's apartment, surveying his artwork with her knowing eye. She always was a woman who knew what suited her.

Jeanne didn't live in—my choice. Louis didn't quite understand it but accepted my need for privacy. I liked to wake and for it to be just the two of us in the apartment for a while. I was getting to know my way around the kitchen, and besides we ate out most nights. The day Elsie came was Jeanne's day off, so we sat in the kitchen together. If Elsie felt it was inappropriate, she didn't say.

We ate the *pains aux raisins* she had bought from the boulangerie at the end of the street. She picked out the dried fruit from hers and left most of the pastry too.

"Waste not, want not," I said pertly.

"Eat less bread," she parroted back, laughing. She could make a joke about anything. "Victory is in the kitchen."

She petted Delia affectionately, then asked me about my life in Paris and life with Louis. I could tell from the fond way she said his name that she approved of him, far more than she had of Percy—or perhaps she just thought we were a better match. It needn't have, but it meant a lot.

I talked and talked. I was a long way into telling her about the hospital and the injuries we saw there and the people we met before

I realized that I hadn't asked her much about herself. So, I tried, but she batted questions away.

She was vague about Harold, she was vague about her plans as "a newly-wed," she seemed shy even of the phrase. It occurred to me now how vague she had always been about everything. I thought of a game the girls and I used to play called "Pin the Tail on the Donkey." You could pin *nothing* on Elsie, you wouldn't be anywhere near the bottom.

She had friends to meet elsewhere, she said. Montparnasse later. Saint-Germain-en-Laye early tomorrow and then the ship home. I realized that she always left earlier than you'd think. I told her that.

"I never like to outstay my welcome," she responded cryptically.

"You could never do that with me."

She smiled. "Always so kind, May."

It struck me then that she was someone always on the run, always on the move. *What*, I wondered, *was Elsie Knocker running from?*

She asked about Leona and Joy and it gave me a warm flush that she remembered their names. I didn't want to talk about my battle to see them though; it was a thing of extraordinary shame. It was the thing I woke up to, and the thing I went to sleep to. It was the thing I wore all day, like a hair shirt, under my clothes. Oh, I knew what people thought: a mother who can't see her children—what has she done wrong? They thought, *there is no smoke without fire*. They thought, *she must, deep down, be a nasty lady*. I suppose this is what *I* would think were it happening to someone else.

I grunted that it was difficult and then I tried to make a fuss of Delia, but she swept away from me and gave me her disdainful look.

Elsie pushed on. "How long has it been since you saw them?"

I wanted to lie—it really was a terribly long time—but I didn't lie. I don't know why. I didn't usually feel the need to confide in people—I had Louis for that—but I did then.

"Fifteen months…"

Elsie put her hand on mine and we sat there in silence, drinking in the pain. I was telling myself, *don't cry, not now, don't.*

Finally, she spoke. "Did you know I have a son, May?"

I didn't. I stared at her; I don't know why this came as a shock, but it did.

"His name is Kenneth. He is ten now."

"I had no idea."

"No," she said. "Not many people do."

I wanted to know the story behind it. Were they estranged? How, what…? But she just repeated, "Not many people know about him," and I realized she was sharing this with me to make me feel better and I should just try to accept that gift for what it was.

Elsie said it was time to make a move. At the door, I had a feeling that we might not see each other for a long time. It was silly and I knew better than to trust it. People were talking about intuition a lot recently. Where had my intuition been when it came to Elizabeth? Death comes like a bolt out of the blue, it doesn't announce itself with calling cards.

"I'll see you again." I felt as though if I said it, it had to happen: an oath to fate.

Elsie tipped her beret at me, then firmly put it back in place as she walked out backward onto the street. A cyclist nearly rode into her. Wobbling, he almost lost his balance, but he hung on gamely. Once straight, he shouted at her, a screech lost in the wind, but Elsie being Elsie shouted merrily back, "*Fou!*" with a hand gesture for good measure. Then she waved at me again, quite delighted with herself.

Now Louis wanted a dog. He was partial to Alsatians. He said, "Being around Delia has reminded me that, actually, I'm a dog person."

At night we would lie in bed wrapped up in each other and argue which were better: cats or dogs. Cats for their beauty, their elegance, their nonchalance. Dogs for their warmth, their fidelity. I was glad Louis was a dog person though. Sometimes he slung his leg over mine, and I had never felt so loved.

Christmas dinner
(enough for four adults, one child)

Turkey—Stuffing—Gravy.

Potatoes—cook French style, *bien sûr*!

Pudding—speak with Jeanne for more ideas?

Apples—is it time to try new French apples?

CHAPTER FIFTY-SEVEN

Little Freddie's favorite game was hide-and-seek. Unusually, I think, he liked being the seeker best. Louis was crouched, cramped, under the desk—if he developed neckache later, here was the reason why. I slid behind the sofa. Bonnie, giggling, was by the window, only half covered by the drapes. Freddie didn't have a clue. He kept looking behind the Christmas tree as though he couldn't believe none of us had used such a prime hiding spot.

When I watched Louis play like this, I felt such an ache in my heart. If only *he* were the one who'd fallen down the steps of the church that fall morning of 1902. If only *he* were the father of my girls. How simple my life would have been then! George was intent on destroying me. I would never admit it to anyone but Louis, but he had half-succeeded.

In 1914, I was a shell of myself. Now, four years later, this shell was strong and unbreakable. But it was still a shell. My lawyer's letters—all twelve of them—had been nothing but scraps of paper to George. Nothing could fix it. I knew the saying that time was a great healer, but what does that mean? Go to bed, get up, go to bed, get up and one day you find it doesn't hurt so much?

"I see you!" Freddie screeched, pulling at Louis. Louis hauled himself out, threw Freddie up in the air. "You rascal, how did you know I was there?"

The presents under the tree were mostly things for Freddie that Louis had enjoyed choosing in the flea markets. There were a couple for me. I think, or rather I hoped, they would be jewelery. Louis had intimated that I needed some good pieces. We were mixing with some fine company and sometimes you were blinded by the gems on their fingers. I had been enticed by shopfronts where necklaces and pretty rings were coming out of the safes, back on display after having been hidden for years. Sometimes I felt guilty for my magpie attraction to shiny things, but Louis said, "Why should we take up like monks? Could you blame anyone for wanting parties and jewels after what we've been through?"

Louis took Freddie for another walk along the road. The plan was to tire the boy out (and Louis too!) and to allow me and Bonnie to catch up without interruption. Louis also liked to show off Freddie to the restaurant and shop workers who were his friends.

"Any news from your girls?" Bonnie asked.

"Nothing. It seems I must wait. Four more years."

"Why four?"

"They'll be of age then and they will be able to come and find me, whether George approves or not. That is . . . if they want to."

"They will want to, May," Bonnie said kindly.

I doubted it.

"What time are we expecting Matron?" Bonnie asked for what felt like the umpteenth time.

"Not sure."

I explained that I'd offered to meet her train, but she had stubbornly insisted on walking.

"Typical Matron! Always has to do everything the hard way."

"She'll never change," I said fondly. It had been over a year since we'd seen Matron, and, like Bonnie, I was impatient for us to be together again. Matron had been such a huge part of my life over the last few years.

Bonnie told me about Billy. He didn't go to work on the machines with Bonnie's pa. He had chosen to stay in the Army and was now somewhere near Turkey, she said vaguely. Bonnie was never good at geography.

"So, you're alone in London?" I asked her.

She nodded. "Makes no difference really."

She took it in her stride like she did everything. Uncomplicated.

"And now that I've got the money from Percy Milhouse's drawing," she said with a smile, "thanks to you, May, the world is my oyster."

Louis was agitated. I supposed he wanted to go and get on with his work as usual. He kept looking at his watch and out the window or over at Bonnie. It was a dark night; the moon was high. The Eiffel Tower was a dark silhouette at the corner of one window. I liked it—it had something of a protective mascot or talisman about it.

Louis drummed his fingers on the card table. Laughing, I told him he was worse than Freddie.

"I just hope she didn't miss her train," he said, pacing around the room again.

"I didn't think you'd mind."

Louis had never been Matron's greatest fan. I had a sudden memory of us jumping over her invisible line in the tent, snorting with laughter.

"What *are* you so excited about anyway?" I nudged him in the ribs playfully.

"Supper," he said promptly.

Games I used to play at Christmas with my Grandma Leonora

I Spy

Spinacles

What's the Time, Mr. Wolf?

The Memory Game or "What is missing?"

CHAPTER FIFTY-EIGHT

It was pitch-black outside by the time the doorbell chimed. I had drawn the curtains, a job I enjoyed all the more for having been without them for so long. After a long day of food preparation, Jeanne had gone home to her brothers in Pigalle. Freddie was having his story; Bonnie was reading Kitty's old copy of *Peter Pan* to him. It made me smile to see the little notes Kitty had diligently written in the margin:

> *The moment you doubt whether you can fly, you cease forever to be able to do it.*

Freddie had refused to go up until he received promises of more hide-and-seek tomorrow. Louis was a pushover and submitted easily. Bonnie and I made jokes about Freddie's superior negotiating skills.

Our doorbell was loud and jolly. (I remembered the gloom that used to come over me when the doorbell went in my and George's house in London.) I ran downstairs, smiling. I couldn't wait to open the door. And there she was: Matron. The woman who'd been both the bane and the savior of my life. My old enemy, my old friend. And she was grinning impishly at me. I had certainly never seen an expression like this in all our time in France. Her hair was grayer, her eyes were lit up with excitement and she was wrapped in a long winter coat. It took maybe three, four seconds before I realized that she wasn't alone. Behind her in the darkness there were two shadowy figures. My first reaction was irritation: *What a cheek! Why hadn't she told us she was bringing people?*

"Who's here?" I tried to be polite but it came out quite abruptly. Suddenly the figures ran at me. "Mummy, Mummy!" It was my girls, *my daughters*. Leona and Joy. *Joy and Leona were here.* I gripped them tightly, almost afraid I was dreaming. *My girls.* We must have stood like that for some time, on the porch, in the porch-light. I heard Louis, next to me, warmly greet Matron. I heard Bonnie dashing down the stairs. I heard excitement and squeals. *My daughters.* I wouldn't let go of them. I kissed their damp heads and then led them in, up to the living room. This gave me time to catch my breath and to relearn how to speak.

"How on earth...?"

I had tried *everything*, hadn't I? Lawyers' letters, Winston's intervention, appealing to George's "better" nature, pleading... How could Matron have succeeded where all other efforts had failed?

"Don't ask," said Matron with her stern expression, before breaking into a massive smile. She was barely recognizable to me as my tent-sharing nemesis.

"Did George...?" I began, confused. "Did George actually *agree* to this?"

Matron gave Louis a knowing look. "Not exactly, May..."

Leona had put her soft hand in mine. *My girl.* Joy, more cautious, more critical, was wandering around, looking at our bookshelves, Gordon's typewriter on the desk, the tree. She suddenly squealed: "Mummy, you can see the Eiffel Tower from here!" Her eyes were shiny with pleasure.

"Then how?" I insisted, gazing at Matron.

"We war nurses have secret powers," she said.

"No, really." Matron wouldn't fob me off with this fairy-tale nonsense, I *needed* to know. "How did you do this?"

"George trusts his governess..." She shrugged happily at me. Her face said, *voilà!*

"No! How? When?!"

"Only since November," Matron explained. Happiness was written all over her face. "The last one got fed up with him." She lowered her voice. "'Too frisky' apparently." (No surprises there!) "There was a vacancy, I went for the interview and I got the job. No fear that he'll get frisky with me!"

Matron hoiked up her bosom in the way I'd seen her do more than a few times in the tent we shared in the Somme.

"I picked the girls up from school and we came straight out here. Joy was a bit wobbly on the boat, but we got our sea-legs soon enough."

I couldn't believe it. *Matron* was the new governess?

"How long have we got?"

"Until term starts. Seventh of January, although I understand George might condescend to meet them for supper on the sixth."

Three weeks. Three whole weeks with my girls! This was unimaginably wonderful. They squeezed in close to me and I inhaled them. My darling Joy was my height now, and little Leona was up to my chest, and clutching me tight as though she too wasn't quite sure this was really happening. My daughters were home.

I could no longer hold back the tears. Tears that had been waiting for years to break through now had their way.

"You wait until you hear what we've got planned for Easter break!" Matron smiled tenderly at me as I covered my snotty face with my sleeve. "Girls, girls...I think Mummy needs a handkerchief."

We pulled away from each other, smiling. I ruffled Leona's hair and gazed at Joy's pretty face. How had she got so grown-up? Where did those womanly features come from?

I grabbed Matron again and hugged her, tears pouring down my face.

"Thank you, thank you so much."

"No," she said. "Thank *you*. Eternally..."

I stared at the face I had hated and loved and felt the emotions churn inside me.

"You crossed the line this time, Matron."

"Oh, I did, I did," she said, and we embraced once more.

I didn't want to overwhelm the girls with my crying and since it seemed I couldn't stop, I excused myself for just a few moments to escape to the privacy of the bathroom. The dam holding back the tears had well and truly burst. I wept and wept with my whole body. I blew my nose, then wept some more.

I had suppressed it, I had suppressed so much of myself. I had consoled myself, *at least they are not dead*, at least they live on while so many others do not. They might not be by my side, hand in hand, but at least they exist. But even that was agony; it had been torture, and only now that it was over could I finally admit that to myself.

It had been a wound so deep that I had dared not to look at it—I had pretended it was nothing, I had minimized my own pain, just plowed on. Now I could look at it. I had missed my daughters, but I had them back.

Louis evacuated to his study so the three of us could cuddle up in our bed. I dropped him in some blankets and a pillow, but he was already working at his desk and planning to stay there at least until midnight. He was on mission "Rein in the French," or as I called it, "Mission Impossible." He had started wearing spectacles recently—I thought he looked more handsome than ever. He took them off now and rubbed his eyes. Then he went back to his file. He put his hand over mine, patted it absently.

"Happy, my darling?"

I nodded but this was not mere happiness, no simple flash of light, this was the warm glow of contentment. I felt like the universe had finally righted itself, as though everything was in alignment. I was who I wanted to be—nurse and poet May Turner; I was where

I wanted to be—Paris; and I was with who I wanted to be—my two darling daughters and the love of my life, Louis Spears (not forgetting my very dear friends). In a few moments, I would go to my room and find Delia prowling across the covers and the girls insisting she must be allowed to stay. And of course I would relent! We would spend the night telling each other stories, planning and plotting. We would whisper, cuddle, tickle and laugh until dawn broke in the Paris sky and only then would we let ourselves sleep.

AUTHOR'S NOTE

My first book, *The War Nurses*, was based loosely on the story of Elsie Knocker and Mairi Chisholm and followed their time in the cellar house in Pervyse, Belgium.

This book was inspired by Mary Borden, but as anyone who knows about her life will know, I have diverged considerably from Mary's story.

In fact, Mary achieved far, far more than I wrote about here. Mary was no shrinking violet; she was a formidable nurse, ground-breaking novelist and an extraordinary poet. She wrote numerous excellent works, including the classic *The Forbidden Zone*, which explored her time in the Somme. Not only did she finance and open a hospital in France during the Great War, but she also made a massive contribution in the Second World War too. Later, she became involved in politics. She was fascinating!

Mary was my springboard, my starting point, a doorway to a different world. You could say *Daughters of War* is about the conflict of the war, and also the inner conflict many women have with the constraints of motherhood. For women, balancing their own desires against their parental duties is a story that is both contemporary and as old as the hills.

I'm aware that my May—fictional May—might be seen by our modern standards as a "neglectful mother." I don't think she was, but I hope the story provides a platform or space for that discussion. We women can do incredible things. Let's raise each other up!

I have also taken quite the liberty with Winston Churchill(!) but I endeavored to capture the spirit of the man. Always a great orator, in 1946, in Zurich, Churchill spoke these words, which I believe are as relevant today as they were then:

"Is there any need for further floods of agony? Is the only lesson of history to be that mankind is unteachable? Let there be justice, mercy and freedom. The people have only to will it, and all will achieve their hearts' desire."

I'd also like to give a very honorable mention to Gertrude Ederle. On her second attempt, in 1926, this nineteen-year-old American was the first woman to swim across the English Channel. She started from Cap Gris-Nez in France and reached Dover after fourteen hours and thirty-one minutes in the water (bettering the previous record by two hours). Atta girl!

ACKNOWLEDGMENTS

Book bloggers made such a difference to my experience of being published. I chewed all my fingernails waiting to hear what they thought. I really appreciated how carefully and patiently they read and reviewed my work.

Here are some bloggers and reviewers who made the petrifying experience of releasing a book slightly less petrifying:

Mrs. Bloggs The Average Reader, Katie's Book Cave, Chells and Books, Ginger Book Geek, Bookish Jottings, Waggy Tales Dog Blog, Short Book and Scribes, Em the Bookworm, The Writing Garnet, Frankie's Reviews, Lucy London, Booking Good Read, Blooming Fiction, Whispering Stories, and Bad Mum Book Club…

Thank you for your encouraging words and I do hope you read me again. (Massive apologies if I've missed anyone out!)

Thank you so much to everyone at Bookouture who have carried me through the scary process of book two. We have the best publicity department in Kim Nash and Noelle Holton—so reassuring to be in their safe hands. It's also lovely (and a privilege) to be among the supportive and uplifting Bookouture authors in the Bookouture Lounge.

Special thanks must, of course, go to my brilliant editor at Bookouture, Kathryn Taussig, for her great ideas, her trust in me and her guidance. When I see the word "sense?" in the margins I know I need to pull my writing socks up. A smiley face in the margins means the world to me! And thanks also to Bookouture's Maisie Lawrence for her astute editing and generous encouragement.

Thanks to my lovely agent, Thérèse Coen at Hardman and Swainson, who is always unfailingly enthusiastic and energetic. A big smiley face in the margin for her.

And thank you to Marian Hussey and all those involved in the fabulous audiobooks. I love them.

Thank you to all my lovely friends, old and new, who have been so generous in their support of me and my writing. I'm lucky to have you.

Special thanks to Beth and Alistair for giving me work with the fantastic Blade Education and for encouraging me to wear a polyester War Nurses outfit. Thanks, guys!

Huge thanks again to darling husband Steve and Reuben, Ernie and Miranda. They are all very patient with me.

Big thanks go to my sister, Debs. After all, she does actually read my books ☺.

Cheerleader, confidante, comedienne...where would I be without my Debs?

READING GROUP GUIDE

DISCUSSION QUESTIONS

1. The novel starts with May's melancholy, which would probably now be diagnosed as depression. In May's case, it was a rather natural response to the predicament she found herself in: an intelligent, feisty young woman trapped by conventions of the time. Could you identify with May's state of mind in the earlier part of the book? Have you ever felt like that and what did you do that helped?

2. "I had made my bed and now I had to lie in it." This was the phrase May's mother used to tell her. What sort of things were you told when you were younger that have been unhelpful to you? By contrast, Elsie reminds May, "You're your own woman." Have you ever been given any advice that gave you the kick start you needed to make a change?

3. The First World War was a time of massive social change and upheaval, especially for the English class system and the way women were regarded in society. Change was happening already, but it's generally agreed that those four long years at war accelerated it. Can you think of events in your lifetime that have similarly caused a cataclysmic shift in thinking or behaviors?

4. In France, May finds the thing she was looking for: purpose. But it came at a terrible price. Do you believe May did the right thing in leaving her family to volunteer in the Somme? Why?

5. Elizabeth is one of my favorite characters. I loved her determination and brusque manner. Who is your favorite character and why?

6. Elizabeth's philosophy of life can be summed up as: "Cats first, marriage last, swimming in between." If you had to sum up your philosophy of life in less than eight words(!), what would it be? I think mine might be "Children first, housework last, books in between." (Don't tell my husband.)

7. May's attraction to Major Louis Spears is powerful and instant. People might find that contrived, but it does happen, especially in the heightened times of war. Have you ever been hit by a romantic thunderbolt like May? How did it work out for you? Do you think their relationship will last?

8. Elsie asks May if she has a "right-hand girl." Female friendships feature strongly in this book. Are they important to you? What is so special about them? Matron goes from being May's enemy number one to the person who saves her. Was that plausible? Have you ever had a big change of opinion like that?

9. "The one good thing is we'll never go to war again," says Elizabeth's mother, Helena. This was the prevailing feeling at the time—the Great War was supposed to be the war to end all wars. As we know now, it turned out differently, and just over twenty years later the Second World War began. Can you think of a political or social issue you got completely wrong and why?

AN INSIDE LOOK AT THE MAKING OF *DAUGHTERS OF WAR*

by Lizzie Page

Who Is the Real May Turner?

When I started *Daughters of War*, I knew I wanted to shine a light on a remarkable woman from history.

Lucky for me, there were a lot to choose from in this time period. The more I researched, the more I thought: How come I haven't heard of her? She sounds so brilliant. So many women's stories have been lost in time, but I knew I wanted to write about someone who really captured me, someone whose dilemmas seemed relevant to me, someone with whom I had a personal connection.

Mary Borden was the answer. She was an amazing nurse—she made a massive voluntary contribution to nursing in both world wars—and she was a poet and a novelist. As usual, it was a few hints about her private life that really piqued my interest: her divorce, her wartime love affair, and her estrangement from her children.

Now, on the surface, Mary Borden and I have absolutely nothing in common: I'm not American, nor am I a socialite or the heiress of a millionaire family (I wish!). I've never served as a nurse, in a war or otherwise. I'm not gutsy, beautiful, and brave, and although

I am divorced, it wasn't that bad. As for poetry, let's not go there. But something about Mary really chimed with me.

The more I dug, the more I was inspired by Mary Borden as a woman torn between doing something for herself—"something with purpose"—and the demands of her husband and young family. I think these issues still resonate today. I have three children and although my husband is nothing like George, I still sometimes feel that conflict too. These are timeless women's concerns. And even though she was born in 1886, I hoped Mary Borden's story would really click with modern readers too.

So she became the inspiration behind the conflicted character of May Turner.

The Great War

Before I started researching and writing *Daughters of War*, I had lots of misconceptions about the First World War. I was very much a "Second World War woman." I have strong family connections with the Second World War, yet I can't trace the family back to the First World War. I have watched countless films, read countless books about the Second World War from when I was a young girl. I didn't know much about the First World War, and I'm really glad I've had the opportunity to relearn history.

I thought World War I was all about men. It is true that men suffered incredibly: millions were killed and injured in the most terrible circumstances. But the men's story is not the only truth. Ninety thousand women worked as nurses during the war. It was a time of radical change. As men poured into the armed services, women poured into the workforce—running the trains, the trams, the factories, and serving as clerks. As a result, resisting giving women the vote was more difficult than ever. Even when men returned to their peacetime jobs, the spark of women's liberation was well and truly lit.

I thought World War I was mostly a war about white men. Battlefields were filled with European, Canadian, Australian, and New Zealander soldiers, that's true. But again, it's only one truth. Thousands of Chinese laborers, Commonwealth soldiers from the Caribbean, and Indians fought and lost their lives. The shift in the European power balances brought about by World War I would eventually lead to the collapse of empires and the Balfour Declaration, world issues that are all still relevant today.

I thought World War I didn't affect the English home front. Now I know that even my (insignificant!) hometown, Southend-on-Sea, was bombed. A junior school in London was tragically bombed. Over 1,000 people were killed on the British mainland. It's true that people at home didn't/couldn't understand the experience of men in the trenches, but they *were* affected by severe rationing, malnutrition, fuel shortages (nothing compared to mainland Europe, of course, because we weren't occupied, and again, the repercussions of that can be seen today).

I thought World War I was a static, stuck-in-the-mud kind of war, which in many ways it was. It was a war about inches being won, stalemates and no-man's-land, but it was also a time of massive innovation, mind-blowing steps forward in technology, weaponry, tanks, airplanes, engineering, and medicine, including growing interest in mental health and shell shock.

I thought World War I lacked a good vs. evil narrative. As a writer or a filmmaker, good vs. evil is a gift: you've got ready-made drama. In the Second World War, there are evil Nazis vs. the good guys. It's hard to see the First World War in that way, and although there have been some attempts to frame it as the evil commanders and the good troops, I don't think it's simple as that. I still don't think there is a good vs. evil narrative, but I no longer think that's a bad thing. I like writing in the gray, the complex, the un-simple. Not everything is black and white, and that can be fascinating too.

What I knew about World War I before, and what I still know, is that it was a tragic, tragic waste, particularly of young men. That fact hasn't changed throughout my research, but it remains why it's so important we understand what happened and see how it has shaped us today.

What's Real and What Isn't?

I tried to keep to Mary Borden's history as much as I could, but there was one thing I changed deliberately, and that was the age of her children. When Mary left London, her children were very young; her third was born in 1914. In *Daughters of War*, May's children, Leona and Joy, are much older and are both happy at boarding school. I could well imagine leaving two older daughters at boarding school to go off to war, but three tiny children would be a much harder thing to write. I chose to reimagine that, and I still think it was the right decision.

The bar La Poupée ("The Doll"), where May sees Elsie again, is still in Belgium with a different name. It was a hugely popular place one hundred years ago, where soldiers and medics went to "let off steam." Nowadays, there's a statue to the indomitable Ginger nearby. There are also statues in Ypres to war nurse Elsie Knocker, who was very real. And so was Percy Milhouse, the artist.

The Somme is perhaps one of the most famous of all the battles of the First World War, one all English schoolchildren know about. Three million men fought in it and a devastating one million men were wounded or killed there. There is also a documentary film called *The Battle of the Somme* (released in August 1916), which you can see at the Imperial War Museum, London.

The lovely Elizabeth was made up, but she was partly inspired by the feats of an incredible young American swimmer named Gertrude Ederle, who was the first woman to swim across the Channel in 1926. Huge kudos to all open-water swimmers. One (sunny!) day I will join you.

I have (more) bad news for the romantics. Major Louis Spears, the great love of May's life, was real, and their relationship by all accounts was passionate and dramatic. The bad news is in real life, he had lots of affairs too, even after he was married to Mary, but I chose not to include that aspect in the book.

The Louis in my book is faithful to his May, always.

Research and Resources

I did a lot of my research in Ypres in Belgium, one of the most fought-over areas of the war, exploring the trenches and the various war museums there. I also visited several museums back home here in England. The Science Museum had a timely exhibition on World War I nursing, and the Imperial War Museum has a brilliant permanent exhibition devoted to the First World War. Stow Maries airfield is a small but perfectly formed World War I center near my home. Mostly, research for me means reading a lot of books and documents or surfing the internet and making notes so I don't forget all the fabulous information. (And it helps if you don't lose the notes too!)

If you are interested in finding out more about the First World War, a book I always recommend is the memoir *Testament of Youth* by Vera Brittain. As a study of a generation devastated by war and an account of grief, it really is unparalleled. For historical fiction, I love *Birdsong* by Sebastian Faulks.

The First World War was a war documented in poetry. Do have a look at some of the wonderful poems by Siegfried Sassoon, Wilfred Owen, or Rupert Brooke. I recommend *The Penguin Book of First World War Poetry*, edited by George Walter, but there are many excellent poetry anthologies to choose from. Mary Borden's *Poems of Love and War*, edited by Paul O'Prey, is fabulously illuminating, as is her memoir *The Forbidden Zone*. There is also a biography, *Mary Borden: A Woman of Two Wars* by Jane Conway, about Mary Borden's life and writing.

If you've not had too much World War I after that, may I recommend my own novels *The War Nurses*, which is Elsie Knocker's story, or *When I Was Yours*, which explores the war efforts of artist Olive Mudie-Cooke and songwriter Lena Guilbert Brown Ford as well as other volunteer nurses and ambulance drivers.

When I wrote the most harrowing hospital scenes in *Daughters of War*, I listened to Radiohead's "Harry Patch (In Memory Of)," which uses the words of Harry Patch, the last surviving combat soldier of World War I. It is exquisite.

Journey's End by R. C. Sherriff and *The Wipers Times* by Ian Hislop and Nick Newman are two plays that brilliantly depict life in the trenches in very different ways.

Peter Jackson's *They Shall Not Grow Old* is a powerful documentary that manages the complex job of colorizing old footage. It is incredible how color brings the stories to life and makes the era more accessible.

That's something I strive to do with all my fiction: bring about a new way of looking at old stories. It's been an absolute pleasure. Thank you for reading. For more info on news and events, you can follow me on Twitter @LizziePageWrite.

ABOUT THE AUTHOR

USA Today bestselling author Lizzie Page lives in a seaside town in Essex, England, where she grew up. After studying politics at university, she worked as an English teacher, first in Paris and then in Tokyo, for five years. Back in England, she tried and failed at various jobs before enjoying studying a master's in creative writing at Goldsmiths College. Lizzie loves reading historical and modern fiction, watching films, and traveling. Her husband, Steve, three lovely children, and Lenny the cockapoo all conspire to stop her writing!

You can learn more at:
Twitter @LizziePageWrite